IMPACTS: A Novel

IMPACTS: A Novel

David Radmore

 **VANTAGE**Press
New York

This is a work of fiction. Any similarity between the names and characters in this book and any real persons, living or dead, is purely coincidental.

Vantage Press and the Vantage Press colophon
are registered trademarks of Vantage Press, Inc.

FIRST EDITION

Copyright © 2010 by David Radmore

Published by Vantage Press, Inc.
419 Park Ave. South, New York, NY 10016

Manufactured in the United States of America
ISBN: 978-0-533-16372-4

Library of Congress Catalog Card No:2010904918

0 9 8 7 6 5 4 3 2

Contents

Acknowledgments

It is with genuine gratitude that I acknowledge the enormous help, so freely given by dear friends in the United States and other countries. Without their support and assistance, this novel might not have been completed.

J. Hans deRijke, of the Netherlands, now residing in England, had read some of my early works, and for years has asked when I was going to finish them, and combine them into a novel. He has devoted untold hours of thought and reading, and has given valuable suggestions for this, and other works.

During my three stays with Drs. Grigory and Ludmila Levine in Nizhny Novgorod, Russia, they created an environment that encouraged my creative writing. It was there that a chapter was written which later became part of *Quest,* the sequel to *Impacts.* Since that time, Ludmila has contributed to my writing through proofreading and her insightful responses to my stories. Currently, she is the head of the American School, at the Linguistics University in Nizhny Novgorod.

Bonnie Partch, now deceased, had been a teacher of creative writing in Stockton, California, and had been active in an organization that read, analyzed, and evaluated novels. After learning that I was writing a book, she volunteered to be of help, and became a continuing source of enthusiasm and support through the first four novels in this series. Her background made her questions and comments of great value. At the outset, she advised, "Even though you haven't written the pages yet, please put your thoughts down on paper, so that your stories won't be lost. Remember, any good secretary can correct spelling and grammar. They can't write the story." Bonnie often phoned several times a week, eagerly saying that she was ready for the next chapter. Frequently she would add, "This sounds so *Real.* Did it actually happen to you?" My answer was always the same: "This is a book of fiction, with portions based on actual experiences and people. It is what you imagine it to be."

Professor Claudine deFaye is a former instructor of Shakespearean literature at the University of Poitier, France. She volunteered to read and evaluate *Impacts,* and has given important and perceptive suggestions about writing, which have influenced not only this novel, but also the sequels that will follow.

O'Mosunlola Williams Johnston Smith has been an educator, administrator, deputy director of education for Lagos State, Nigeria, and is a published author. While my wife, Audrey, and I were serving as teachers with Peace Corps in Nigeria, Mosun was our principal, and became a close personal friend. During several of her visits to Stockton, she spent much of her holiday time reading and critiquing my books. Her keen observations and comparisons of their content with traditional Nigerian life have benefited both my writing and my understanding of the customs of Nigeria.

Clariece Wise Frederick, an extremely bright and capable classmate from high school days, was uniquely helpful and encouraging during periods of writing and rewriting this book. Her judgment and expertise are valued and trusted.

Throughout my writing, I have expressed my appreciation to my wife, Ruth Audrey Turnbull Radmore, for giving priority to my requests for proofreading and reflections on my work. Without her encouragement and enthusiasm, this book might still be in my computer. While being a teacher, business owner, and accomplished creative artist, she devoted much of our married life to supporting my wishes to pursue personal interests, hobbies, and goals. Our independent travels together, and the trips we have made as individuals, have provided me with the details and background information that has been incorporated in *Impacts* and its sequels.

I must give special thanks to the many unnamed individuals who have influenced my life and my underlying philosophy of how to live it. My public school and university friends, teachers, and professors encouraged and interacted with me, and have enriched my life, making it an enjoyable and open-ended adventure.

One unique member of my family was not only a major influence during my childhood, but also became an essential part of this novel. I am indebted to my grandmother Annie Louise Watts Radmore, who was the real Gran in my life, and who became the fictionalized Gran for Danny, in this novel. She had a dominant influence on my youth, and I have tried to present her true character, personality, and wisdom as a major impact on Danny's entire life. She gave so much love, care, and guidance to her grandson, as well as the occasional secret piece of hard candy, along with her cockney accented admonition, *"Not ha word. Not ha word."*

To all, I express my sincere and lasting gratitude.

David Radmore

Introduction

Impacts is the first novel of a series, and involves the life of Danny, from age four to twenty. It begins in the depression years of the 1930s, and portrays his life with his immigrant father, Cockney grandmother, and midwestern mother who guide his values and interests. International influences expand when his family moves next door to a Japanese couple who have a son, Danny's age. Their new neighbors share their home with the former owner, an elderly German. Close, almost constant contact within this expanded family formed bonds of interest, and relationships that grow rapidly and in astonishing directions.

Danny's curiosity and his love of learning and adventures lead him and his loved ones into an enterprising business venture, guided by the German's metalworking training.

The boy's search for positive answers and solutions help him as he copes with and gains understanding about the realities of childhood, increased responsibilities, puberty, deaths of loved ones, and his military service near the end of World War II.

With only a few exceptions, there is little or no violence, anger, or hate that intrudes on his eventful life. Instead, it is rich with understanding, devotion, and relationships that have positive impacts on the man he becomes.

The author's sensitivity and philosophy contribute to Danny's character and how he relates to family, friends, work, and to his diverse activities and encounters.

For women readers, this book may provide an insightful view of a young boy's world as he develops to young adulthood. It provides details that men may hesitate to reveal or even acknowledge. Danny is the kind of youngster and man whom many people could wish to have had as a close and lifelong friend.

IMPACTS: A Novel

1

Danny and Beverly Jean

"Go stand in the closet with the light off! Think about what you told me you've done." This was the most severe punishment Mary could devise for her four-year-old son, Danny. Her entire body was trembling, and she wanted to lash out and slap him. "Not another word from you until I tell you to come out!" The intensity of her physical reaction was contrary to her usual tranquil nature.

Danny was at the age when his vocabulary was expanding rapidly and many words were no longer under family control. Mary had barely been able to deal with the chagrin of hearing her son say naughty or curse words such as *damn it, piss,* or *hell.* She had been dreading the time ... even denying the possibility that he would ever come across the worst of them all, but it had happened ... and he was only four years old.

Mary had been ironing bedsheets and Danny was helping. He already pressed handkerchiefs by himself, and she was proud of his eagerness to join in on the household chores. He was pulling some wrinkles from a large expanse of a sheet when she asked, "What did you do this morning before I called you?"

Mary was aghast when he casually and conversationally replied, "I fucked Beverly Jean." He calmly continued smoothing wrinkles from the sheet. He might as well have told her they had made mud pies, picked buttercups, or he had pushed Beverly Jean on a swing. To him, he had simply been playing with a friend. One activity was no more important to him than the other. An explosion of suppressed laughter had come from the living room where Danny's father was reading the paper, but the boy's mother was in a state of shock! She nearly dropped the iron. "Where on earth did you learn that scandalously naughty word?"

1

"What word?" the boy asked innocently.

"That word! The word that you said you did to Beverly Jean!" Mary's upbringing would not allow her to say it, and she didn't know how to describe it to him. "You know what you said."

"Oh, I said I fucked Beverly Jean and..."

"Don't you dare use that naughty and wicked word again or I'll wash your mouth out with soap. Besides, I doubt if you actually did that, or understand what it means."

"I do so understand," he declared adamantly. "I put my pisser in her pisser. It tickled us so much, we had to stop and rub ourselves. But we didn't hurt anyone." The boy had never seen his mother so upset, and he wasn't certain what was wrong. Tears welled up in his eyes. He wondered why she was so angry with him.

Mary asked the question that horrified her, "How far did you put it in?"

"About that far." He indicated a finger and thumb gap of about half an inch.

"We were playing doctor and nurse and I was the doctor. Beverly Jean was the nurse. Girls don't have anything on the outside..." His voice trailed off into silence as he became more aware of his mother's increasing disapproval and state of shock. That was when Danny was ordered to stand in the closet.

In the past, he and Beverly Jean had looked, touched, and tasted each other. She had envied his prick, which was right out there and easy to use. He didn't have to pull down his underpants and squat and splatter, or worry about getting a skirt wet. He could just unbutton, whip it out, and let it fly. He had the pleasure of directing the stream where he wanted it to go. He could wash an ant off a blade of grass, or make them scramble from the entrance to their nest. He could have contests with other boys to see who could squirt the farthest. No doubt about it, boys had superior equipment that was the source of great pleasure.

Local kids looked into each other's mouths and counted teeth. Boys and girls looked the same. One girl had places in her mouth where teeth had come out, but others were growing in. Down below, girls didn't have anything, but maybe it had fallen off just like her teeth. Would she grow another one before long?

2

Would his drop off just like teeth did? He was going to ask his mother about those and other questions, but now he was happy he hadn't. He was uncertain of himself. Had those things been naughty and scandalously bad, too? In the closet he could hear his mother talking to herself. "It seems that Beverly Jean is not a very nice girl, and Danny shouldn't play with her anymore!"

The boy didn't understand why Beverly Jean wasn't a nice girl, but if she weren't, maybe he wasn't a nice boy? Reasoning powers were not highly developed among children Danny's age, but he knew he had learned another "bad word" to go along with *damn, liar, shit,* and *piss.* He didn't really understand why they were bad words, but he knew they should not be used in front of his parents, or other old people. It troubled Danny that he wasn't really sure whether what he and Beverly Jean had done was bad, or if the word he had used was naughty.

Danny's mother was unable to cope with the revelation, but John, Danny's father, did not take the incident seriously ... he even laughed about it. Mary couldn't understand that, because her religious convictions lead her to believe that her young son's actions had placed his immortal soul in jeopardy. She was still crying when she asked Gran, Danny's paternal grandmother, to call Danny out of the closet and talk with him. Mary had tried to bury the shocking secret of the incident deeply within her subconscious in hopes that it would become completely inaccessible. Her composure was still shattered when she left for church and a meeting with her women's group. She silently prayed that the minister would be available to help her through the trauma of the situation. This was the worst moral crisis she had ever faced involving her son.

Danny's father sensed no crisis. That evening, his all-male quartet met at his house. John had a fine baritone voice, and was a valued member of the group. They were to sing a special anthem at church the coming Sunday. John recounted the incident regarding Danny and Mary's reaction, and the men howled with laughter for ten minutes. Each time they started to sing, one man or another would begin to chuckle. They could be partway through the song when one of them would explode. Men understand boys, and their curiosities.

"Well, we didn't get much singing done," Bob, the bass, com-

3

mented, "but we had a grand time. What are we going to do this Sunday if one of us gets a crazy grin on his face?" Then he added, "Danny's had an early lesson, to be careful about what he tells a woman about his past experiences. I confessed a premarital affair to my wife years after we were married. I was locked out of our bedroom and my breakfast consisted of cold coffee and burned toast for a month. She's been giving me the third degree about other possible affairs ever since."

Asking Gran to talk with Danny was absolutely the best thing Mary could have done. They were able to chat freely about almost everything that came into the boy's mind. Gran opened the closet door and enfolded him in her arms, and his anguish was partly relieved by sobbing and subsequent huge gasps for air. She wanted to be sure he didn't become fearful of dark and enclosed places, so they remained there. Her hugs were comforting and reassuring. Then she asked, "What seems to be the problem, me fine young lad?"

"I told mother that I fucked Beverly Jean, and she said I had used a scandalously naughty word, and I heard her say that I shouldn't play with Beverly Jean, because she isn't a nice girl, so maybe I'm not nice ... and everything. Did we do something wrong, or what? Am I bad? And where do naughty words come from, if we aren't supposed to say them?" Gran gulped a time or two as she gathered herself to deal with Danny's questions. "Well now, laddie," she began in her Cockney accent, "the word *fucked* is a proper word in other countries and other languages. In this country we use the words *breed, copulate,* or terms like *make love* and *sleep together.*"

"Oh? But what makes it a bad word?"

"People do ... yes, I reckon it's people who make it a bad word. It's best if ye don't use that word or talk about such things."

"Is it like talking about picking noses when people can hear you?"

"Not quite, but near enough for now."

"But how am I going to know a word is bad when I first hear it?"

"If ye have a question, ask me before saying it elsewhere."

"Okay," the boy replied. Gran was always his ultimate source of wisdom and good sense. He accepted whatever she sug-

4

gested. He continued, "Why was mother upset when I told her I put my pisser in Beverly Jean's?"

"That's something that is done mostly by grownups."

"Why do they do it? It tickles too much."

"When a person gets older, it doesn't tickle and they express their love for each other in that manner ... and that is the way they start making babies."

"Did Beverly Jean and I start a baby?"

Gran chuckled and replied, "No, laddie. Ye be much too young for that."

"Oh." Danny thought about that for a minute and concluded, "That's good. It's not much fun playing with babies."

He found paper and pencil, and made a printed letter *A*. Next to it he made the same letter in Arabic script with a straight line going down and hooking to the left at the bottom. He followed the *A* with the entire alphabet for both languages. This indicated to Gran that he was over most of the earlier trauma and was ready to begin one of their learning games. "That's it, laddie. Well done."

Earlier in the year, Gran had started teaching Danny the alphabet in English and Arabic. She had learned to do this many years before, back in England. Each day she and the boy practiced and then combined letters to make words in each language. It was easier to do in English, because they used words that Danny saw daily. The first word he learned to spell was *stop,* because it was on the sign that was at an intersection near his house. Dozens of other words were written in both English and Arabic, and they learned ten new words each day.

Later, Danny's thoughts returned to Beverly Jean. They had participated in the early-childhood game of Doctor, a common children's game. Seeing led to partial understanding. Smelling, touching, and tasting added reference knowledge. Listening to her inner workings by putting an ear to her tummy and chest provided information, but much remained an unfathomable mystery. Still, enough had been discovered to satisfy their initial curiosity.

"Gran, is my prick going to drop off pretty soon?"

"Lord no, laddie boy. Whatever put such a notion in your head?"

5

"Beverly Jean doesn't have one and she's older than I am, and one of her teeth dropped out of her mouth this morning. I was just wondering if...?"

"Put your mind at ease. Ye will not lose that equipment ... it's there for life. When you're young, teeth fall out and new ones replace them, but not the other."

"Then what happened to hers?"

"That's one difference between boys and girls. Girls never get one."

Danny felt a momentary sadness, realizing that Beverly Jean had never had a gift like his. Then he remained perplexed by his mother's earlier question. Where had he learned that scandalously naughty word? He recalled that Beverly Jean had been talking with an older neighborhood girl and then they tried it. He knew that if the word had been Arabic, he would have learned it from Gran. But then Mother would not have known it. He did learn the word *scandalously* that day from his mother. He had a good idea of what it meant by the way she used it.

Danny gave Gran a huge hug and said with satisfaction and security, "I know I won't learn naughty words from you." That was true, but she would teach him so much more, and all of it would be good.

2

John's Thoughts and Reminiscences

It was the 1930s, and the years ahead had never looked brighter. John let his mind wander, "My future is on this bus. *Two Johns and Two Bobs,* we sing under that name. The Two Johns are the lead soloists in our male quartet. The first John is our high tenor. Not only is he 'high,' he is always on pitch. His voice is thrilling and his volume can fill a huge concert hall, and yet be as delicate and light as a summer evening's breeze. I'm the second John. Critics described my voice as, 'being as rich and full as dark brown gravy and yet can probe one's emotional depths.' Bob One, our second tenor, is always 'right there' with unusual, but exactly correct harmony chords that totally support the lead soloists, the Two Johns. But the chords are often unexpected, and add a scintillating quality that keeps the audience alert and applauding at the end of every number. The second Bob finally joined us. He is the basso profundo who doesn't want to solo, but can he ever provide depth to the bottom end of a song! He hits that almost unattainable G below the staff. He not only hits it with precision, he can make it sound as if it came from a great pipe organ, anywhere from a whisper to a cathedral-filling and thrilling experience. Below that, his control remains impeccable but his volume begins to diminish."

Local radio appearances had led to an electrical transcription. Before long, this found its way to a Portland station. The quartet had performed their first radio broadcast from the largest network station in Portland. A contract had been signed that specified live thirty-minute programs every Sunday for a year. The pay was adequate, and this network blanketed the entire nation. The inconvenience of having to bus to and from Portland every Sunday was a minor thing compared with the opportunity and the potential for the future. Even before the end of the broadcast, a San Francisco station had inquired about the quartet. Booking agents were also making inquiries. It was instant success. Excitement and floods of adrenaline inundated the four men with dreams of the future. They talked together as they sang together ... all at the same time with similar intensity, but with each taking a turn as soloist. Bob, the bass, supplied support for the others' dreams. In time, the hypnotic effect of tires swishing on the wet roadway, the wind, and bus noises lulled each man into his own fantasy world.

The mind of Danny's father functioned in spurts of incomplete sentences as memories flooded the emptiness of the rainy miles ahead. "Now" was suppressed by memories, anticipation, and frequently, grim reality. Sort it out. Parts of the past were, indeed, disturbingly unpleasant. Think through the past one more time; appreciate it for what it was, and then move on. The ride home will take another two hours, maybe more. Plenty of time to think back, yes, back ... back ... back.

"Childhood London, England. I was only seven years old and these were hungry, cold, bitter times. Dad left us when I was five. Mother did the best she could. She served dinners, and washed up after rich people's parties. Table scraps and scrapings from the pots and pans, and the leftover bones were special perks that went with the job. We had to eat. Regular work was almost impossible to find. Too many people were in the same situation.

"My tin pail ... get what I could find in the garbage can behind the eatery. Never much thrown out there. Sometimes a crust or two of bread, potato peelings, or bones, but someone would have gnawed off all the meat and fat."

"Jack, don't forget the lettuce, beets, carrots—get everything—we've nothing hin the 'ouse," she called in her Cockney accent.

"Lily, off to the railway with ye. Smile pretty and wave like ye were taught. Maybe the fireman will throw ye a few lovely lumps of coal as he goes by. Ye be nine years of age now and ye shouldn't need telling. What do ye be crying about now, Jackie, lad?" He wondered why his mother called him Jack when she had named him John.

"'That big bully Jimmy Stone punched me in the stomach

8

and took all our food.' When Jimmy jumped me again the next day, and had me down, Lily kicked him in the mouth and said, 'It'll be the two of us ye will have to deal with from now on.' He wasn't a bad lad. His family was plagued with the lack of everything that many people in London experienced. However, a few things were in large supply, including gut-wrenching, debilitating hunger, disease, and hopelessness. Jimmy was trying to deal with his family hunger problems in the same manner as John. Competition was fierce and often, it was a genuine battle for survival. After the licking, Jimmy had three less teeth available to eat whatever he could scrounge."

As John continued his reverie, he thought, "It's funny, Lily and I must have been talking Cockney English, but she and I have gotten completely away from that, and I don't even think of us as ever having that accent."

John's reminiscence continued, "I came to America when I was fourteen. Here they called me John instead of Jack. I was one of literally tens of thousands ... some suggest millions ... of children who were virtually sold into a status of slavery by various English churches, governmental departments, members of the aristocracy, and men of higher birth."

This form of slavery was still taking place even sixty-plus years after black slavery was officially abolished in the USA. Most youngsters were sold to people in the "Colonial Empire, on which the sun never set."

The wealthy, church officials, and political authorities exported some of their poverty problems, and were paid handsomely by a market in need of cheap labor. The child became, in effect, an indentured servant who was to pay off transportation costs by working for an unspecified number of years. In many cases, the physical status of the child actually improved.

"Huge numbers of us lost all contact with home and family, and it wasn't until the end of the twentieth century, when their children or grandchildren started doing research to find relatives in Britain, that some of these records came to light. Girls had the worst of it. If they were placed in a private home, they assisted with all chores demanded of them, worked in sweatshops, and often became sexual toys to be exploited by the male members of the household. If they dared complain, they were not believed. Frequently they were beaten, further abused, shunned, and branded as young vixens, and perhaps harlots. In such cases, they were deprived of future opportunities."

John's mind raced ahead on machine-gun-like bursts of incomplete sentences that did not need to be complete, because they were his own thoughts. "Lucky me, I worked hard, and there was plenty of food, and I learned the carpentry trade. Then I joined the army. This was World War I, 'the War to end all Wars!' I was sent to France, and was assigned to an engineering battalion. We rebuilt things that had been blown apart or torn down. The stench of death was all around us. Army cooks tried to cover up the bad food that had the smell of rotting flesh, by smothering it with cinnamon. Never could stand cinnamon after that. We were often cold, and wet. We had 'know-nothing' superiors who took credit for all the plans I drew. Even though the officers said everything I did was first-rate, they said I'd never make corporal, because I wasn't a Mason, and they were right.

"When the war ended I came home with my US citizenship. All foreigners got that for being in the US military. Later, I met Mary and we married. The birth of a baby girl, an incredible dream come true, followed ten days later by the nightmare of the infant's death. We moved to a larger city where there was plenty of work for a good carpenter. We built our own home. A couple of years later the birth of our son, Daniel, provided another highlight, and he survived. Mother emigrated from England and she became known as Gran. Then came the Great Depression. Conditions had to get better almost anytime. The country couldn't carry on as it was. Then came a glimmer of hope that blossomed into a garden full of flowers. Yes, we are together here on the bus, Two Johns and Two Bobs, that is our name and we have arrived, and the bus has also arrived.

"Three weeks later that 'dream reality' truly ended. The diagnosis was cancer for John One, the high tenor, at the age of thirty-five. He had seen his father die a slow and terrible death from the same disease. One shot from a .22 special rifle dissolved the male quartet. How do you replace such a voice? Two months later, Bob One, the second tenor, used the same rifle to end his life. We never learned why."

Dreams were shattered. John had lost more than his singing group; he had lost two of his best friends. He understood why John One had killed himself, but why Bob One did the same was a mystery. Bob Two, who was not married, went to Portland and became the foundation bass for a quartet that was nationally broadcast each Sunday afternoon for fifteen years. In addition, they were in great demand for live performances. John's musical options were to keep on singing in church choirs, and with the male chorus known as the Mighty Twenty. Both were good musical groups, but John dreamed and hoped for a professional career in music. For the near future, that anticipation had to be abandoned.

3

Gran

Gran was John's mother and Daniel's grandmother. She was born in 1862. Her given name was Annie Louise and it wasn't until the birth of a grandchild that she happily assumed the title of Gran. Mary was John's wife, and welcomed Gran into the household with pleasure, love, and appreciation for her cultural background.

Early and untimely deaths were not strangers to Annie Louise. She was one of seventeen children and five of them had died before she was ushered out of the family home at age thirteen. She was, "old enough to shift for herself, and needed to make room for them what was coming." The deaths of her brothers and sisters were attributed to the pestilence, malnutrition, and some of the other diseases common to the poverty-stricken London of her day. Hunger and cold played a prominent part in determining who would die. How could this happen in a city that the British proclaimed was the finest and the most modern city in the world? The answer was simple. That was the way things were ... always had been and always would be.

Five older brothers deemed it an honor to be members of the British Royal Artillery and "to fight and die for the greater glory of the British Empire." The benefits derived from such service rarely, and then only accidentally, filtered down to commoners. And fight they did and die some of them did.

Annie Louise benefited from her occasional association with two of her older brothers. They were serving in His and/or Her Majesty's forces in Egypt and the Sudan. While on duty, they had become functionally literate in Arabic. When they returned to their parental home on leave, they would slip into speaking Arabic to discuss private topics. The keen ear and quick mind of ten-year-old Annie Louise picked up the sounds of hundreds of words and duplicated them almost immediately. It seemed only natural for the brothers to teach their little sister what they knew of this language, as well as the history, geography, and character of the lands and people. For the youngster, learning was a game and her greatest pleasure in life. It took only one telling for her brothers' words, stories, and information to be indelibly etched in her mind.

Brother 'Arry (Harry), her favorite, bought an Arabic–English dictionary, which included a section on how to read and write the language. He gave it to Annie Louise. It was the first book she owned and was her most prized childhood possession. It remained with her all her life.

Although she had very limited formal education, Annie Louise had been a brilliant student during the four years the London authorities of the 1870s were willing to bestow on her and others of her socioeconomic class. She learned quickly and thoroughly. Perhaps the most devastating lessons were those two imperatives that remain the basis of the British aristocracy: "Those of lower birth should not try to rise above their station in life." And, "Your betters will tell you what's best for you."

Annie Louise's teachers pleaded with higher authorities to allow her to continue her schooling. They were reminded with stern admonishments that such matters were properly left for their "enlightened betters" to decide. Besides, they should know that it would be a waste of time and resources. Nothing of worth could be expected from those of such lowly birth.

Centuries of emphasizing these "truths" had indoctrinated and conditioned most commoners to accept "the divine rights of kings" and other members of the nobility. This was also extended to the remainder of the privileged class. The subservient position of the masses needed to be assured. Even today the aristocracy "Presumes and Imposes." Annie Louise knew when the boundaries of her own domain had been broached and she did not hesitate to "slip into 'em and give 'em the sharp edge of me tongue."

A lifelong characteristic of Annie Louise could be observed when she shrugged her shoulders, stubbornly set her jaw, and uttered the inevitable, "No use grumblin' about it, just get on with the job." Added to that was a second well-chosen phrase by which she declared her independent nature, "We'll not be lookin' to others for help as long as we 'ave our two good 'ands and a strong back."

Annie Louise married in 1891 and subsequently gave birth to three children, who were bright, attentive, and quick to learn. Free British education for the commoners had been extended by an additional four years. This made a total of eight years that authorities were willing to "waste on the likes of that class." Actually, this was one of the most advanced standards of education in the world at that time. Perhaps it was the disparity between the public and private educational opportunities and attitudes based on a class structure that opened the system for such harsh criticism. Certainly, it was far more advanced than opportunities available to most youngsters in the United States and unquestionably so for people of color.

The "commoners" in Britain took pride in the history, monuments, great public parks, and the cultural heritage of the nobility. To leave the magnificent London Zoo, the huge buildings of business and government, as well as private mansions and great cathedrals of Britain and to immigrate to a small western town in the USA must have challenged Annie's sense of proportion. Historical monuments in her new community amounted to a Civil War-era muzzle-loading cannon, which sat on a small plot of land in front of the county courthouse. This building was somewhat functional, but its architectural heritage was questionable. Gran did not complain or demean the people or amenities, or lack thereof, to be found in her new homeland.

Within her new community, Gran was easily recognized by her charming Cockney accent. She was best known as a hardworking immigrant woman who was not one to grumble or complain. Annie Louise (Gran) was ready to give "a hand with 'ousecleaning, caring for an infant or the elderly, or any other domestic chores that needed attention."

Gran had spent her life without the burden of extra money beyond the absolute essentials, and all too often, minus many of those. She was also known to be scrupulously honest and accounted for every penny when she did the shopping for elderly people who were shut in.

A penny's worth of candy to share with Danny would be

accompanied by the admonition, "Not ha word, not ha word to hanyone else." This was her way of making her grandson aware that this tiny touch of luxury signaled momentary prosperity she wanted to share exclusively with him.

As mentioned before, Annie Louise became "Gran" when the first of her grandchildren was born. Danny was not the first, but Gran lived most of her life with her son, John, and family. The values Gran cherished in life were shared with her grandson, young Danny. Most important of these were love, attention, devotion, and respect. Her Arabic–English dictionary and its contents were a source of so much satisfaction to Gran that she and Danny devoted hours studying it daily.

But this dictionary was not the only written treasure Gran and Danny enjoyed together. During those preschool years, the fairy tales Danny learned came mostly from Sir Richard F. Burton's English translation of *Alf Laylah, Wahad Laylah* (Thousand Nights and One Nights: The Arabian Night Tales) and Gran's volumes of these same tales in Arabic, which she "came about while clearing out the rubbish" of a retired university professor's estate in town. The sixteen-volume set and the six supplemental volumes were a treasure beyond her imagination. Companion volumes in the original Arabic were given to Gran as well, and these proved to be extraordinarily valuable. There were also four volumes of history written in Arabic. When the estate administrator found her reading the Arabic books, he gave her the lot if she would "simply cart them off." These were the first books Danny remembered.

It had been a major undertaking to carry the books eight blocks to the bus stop and load them onto the bus. The walk to her home from the closest bus stop was an additional five blocks. Gran made her newly acquired library into several heavy bundles and carried each, in turn, to the departure bus stop, left them with the woman of the house close by, and walked back to collect each succeeding bundle. In her fashion, Gran "got on with the job." She enriched her life and that of Danny through the bonds of affection and developing mutual interests.

When speaking about Danny, Gran would say, "He's smart enough, that lad, but he'll not abide the aristocratic rights of the nobility to rule. He's a product of this country right enough."

She and Danny played spoken and written word games long before he started school. Gran found it much easier to speak the words of affection and love in Arabic than in English. During her childhood and young adult years, she had heard very few such words spoken in English. In her dream world, her words were almost always formed in Arabic.

Gran started relating adventure stories about magic carpets that flew, winged horses, a lamp that produced powerful kinds of witches, or djinn, and all sorts of accounts that intrigued Danny. These were always told in the language she called Arabic. From the time of his first memories, the Arabic language was associated with magic, adventure, thrilling experiences, romance, and secrets. Gran could weave a tale of love and romance that appealed to the boy. In turn, he was encouraged to create stories from his own imagination.

Despite the difficulties of her life, Gran was living the most luxurious existence she had known. Her dream world was reality. She was not struggling daily for food and shelter for herself nor for her children. Although not regularly employed, she was bringing in enough money to be sure she was "earning her keep." Perhaps the most important thing to her was that she had time to be with Danny and enjoy teaching the lad, as well as learning with him.

Youngsters learn from their parents, elders, peers, and the environment. From early on, Gran shared the joy of her knowledge and games involving history and language with Danny. Together, they developed some understanding of the remarkable intricacies of traditional Arab culture, as presented in Burton's scholarly and interesting books. Their evenings were spent without radio or other distractions, as they explored these books and the others, which were written in Arabic. In this manner, lifelong patterns of reading, studying, discussing, imagining, and learning were established. These were pursuits of pleasure, not work. They were part of the challenge and pleasure to be found in life.

"Come on, lad, we 'ave our words to learn." This was a nightly routine that persisted from the earliest of Danny's memories through his high school years. It was so ingrained that they agreed on the words they would learn each week even if they

16

were not going to be at home Learning the words included spelling, reading, writing, and their singular and plural usages.

Frequently Gran related stories about uncles Harry and Alfred, and their adventures and military battles in Egypt and the Sudan. These accounts would be related in English and Arabic depending on the characters she was representing. But there was always a place in her tales in which a boy Danny's age played an important, if not improbable role. These were stories Gran had not had time enough to share with her own children. During their childhood, they had been beset with the necessities of obtaining food, clothing, and heat to survive another day. By telling the stories about her brothers, Gran was keeping them alive in her own memory and transplanting them into Danny's. One of the sad things in Gran's early life was the reality of poverty. There was simply not enough money to afford the luxury of paying for overseas postage. When a person emigrated, that was the end of the family connection.

Strange languages were not totally unique in their community. A family in the next block had come from Norway. To Danny's four-year-old mind, this was a strange country even more remote than England. Their language was a complete mystery to him. They spoke English with a musical singsong accent that was entertaining and pleasing.

The other foreigner in that part of the community was Grandma Skelen who came from London. She was easy to understand because she sounded so much like Gran. They both retained their Cockney accents.

Danny's breakfast plate was made of aluminum and it had the ABC's embossed around the edge as well as the numbers 0 through 9. It seemed as if he always knew those letters and numbers. His father, John, even encouraged him to learn them backward. This was a fun game for a day or two. Having learned to recognize the letters, and the sounds associated with them, reading seemed to be the next logical step. Guesswork was involved in the process, because words didn't always look as they sounded or sound the way they looked.

From a realistic point of view, three and four years of age seemed to be young to associate the abstract letters of an alphabet with words. But these words were imprinting, forming, and organizing in the boy's young mind. As time passed, they blossomed into understanding.

Gran made a collar to fit around Danny's ABC plate. The Arabic alphabet was inscribed on it. As far as possible, letters in English and Arabic, which had similar sound, were next to each other. The results were predictable, but not easy. Of course, difficulties arose when one of the languages had a letter and sound not found in the other. For example, there is no letter *P* in Arabic and no equivalent sound. There were too few opportunities to write in Arabic, and it took Danny much longer to write reasonably well in that language than in English. Learning the English language involved daily vocal, visual, and physical contact. Other than when he was with Gran, there were no opportunities for seeing, hearing, and speaking Arabic.

Arabic calligraphy is an art form in itself. Gran, with her penchant for fancy crocheting, found an additional outlet for her creative nature in the decorative, aesthetic media of Arabic script. Although Danny was able to read and write well enough within his own vocabulary limitations, he never approached Gran's artistic flair.

It was while writing that Gran discovered that Danny was truly ambidextrous. He wrote English words from left to right with his right hand. Arabic was written from right to left and he wrote it with his left hand. It was easier for him that way because his hand was not in the way of his writing, but he could do it with either hand.

Danny caught and threw balls equally well with each hand. When he would thread a needle for Gran,—"Ye have the young eyes to see the task better"—it made no difference whether he held the thread in the right or left hand.

Children of Danny's age loved to establish a form of privacy from parents and other adults by communicating in a "secret language" such as "Pig Latin." A wink from Gran and the two were off in their own private world of conversation and fantasy that others could not enter. Although they were two generations apart in actual age, they engaged in this routine so frequently that they thought nothing of it. As a matter of fact, they were likely to be speaking more Arabic than English when just the two were together. Danny's parents enthusiastically supported the close and loving relationship between the boy and his grandmother. It pleased them to see how rapidly they developed extensive interests and anticipated what was the next thing to be learned.

Both acquired an increasing command of the Arabic language as well as other aspects of related information. Gran had been functionally literate with Arabic in speech, reading, and writing before acquiring Burton's books and the others. It would have been a mistake to suggest that she really "knew the language" because it is extremely rich with words. Arabic was estimated to have nearly three times as many words as English. Many English-speaking people go throughout their life with a working vocabulary of less than twenty-five hundred words.

The hours Gran and Danny spent reading, studying, and enjoying their library improved their knowledge and understanding. They were learning words and communicative skills in a manner that pleased them.

A question in their minds was whether or not Arabic-speaking people would understand them. Gran's familiarity with the sound came from her two brothers. They, in turn, had learned what they knew in the Sudan and Egypt. Gran's Cockney accent persisted after years in the USA. "Hit's part hove 'o hi ham, hif hi start trying to talk like ye, hit would sound funny." But they understood each other, enjoyed the Arabic game, and were not too concerned. Danny grew up hearing the language and it was second nature for Gran and Danny to converse in it.

Gran left a legacy of values that became part of the foundation of Danny's character. "Honest pay for honest work." "Make a game out of even the most difficult tasks ye undertake so ye can find fun in it." "No use grumbling, just get on with the job." "Learning is one of the ultimate pleasures ... it's a game of choice." "Give respect and ye may receive it." "Work for what ye want, then ye will know the value of it." "Don't look to others to do what ye can do for yourself." "Make your own happiness and share it with others." "Build the life ye want and never stop the discovery process." "Perhaps the greatest luxury in life is time."

Danny was aware, in a child-like type of innocence, how really lucky he was to have such an interesting, concerned, loving, and fun grandmother. Other kids he knew had grandparents living in the same house, but they were not much fun. The special relationship Gran and Danny shared was truly unique.

4

Preschool Memories

"Mother, come look at the funny cars. They bumped into each other. One man acts like he had twisted up too much on a swing. The other man is all yucky."

Knowing her four-year-old son's creative imagination, she asked, "When and where is this supposed to have happened?"

"You can see it from the porch. The yucky one is like the cat that was run over."

"Land o' Goshen!" she exclaimed. "Do you need help?" she called to the man who was sitting on the curb. He held his head in his hands, and he was groaning.

"Maybe the other driver ... and the police." He replied without looking up.

"You need a doctor ... you have a nasty bump on your forehead." She did not say he was bleeding. "You needn't worry about the other driver." She did not report that the other man's head had gone through the windshield of his car or that it had been severed. "Our neighbor has a phone. I'll be right back."

While his mother was talking with the police, Danny ran to the neighbor's house and interrupted her, saying, "That man is shivering and shaking, and then he fell forward into the street. I'd think he was asleep if he didn't shake so much."

Danny could hear the policeman at the end of the phone line say, "I'm calling the ambulance and a doctor, but you raise his head with a pillow, and put blankets under and over him if you can. I'm on my way."

Mother and Buna, the neighbor woman, took pillows and blankets and followed the police officer's instructions. A bump formed on the injured man's forehead, and it continued to bleed. The ambulance, police, and a doctor arrived simultaneously. The officials spent almost no time with the driver from the other car.

21

Danny heard them say the word, "Dead." He knew the word. Before this wreck, dead was something that happened to cats that were run over by cars. Mice were killed in traps and were called dead. Leaves, grass, and trees died and were called dead. Danny heard talk about people being killed or dying, but now dead was real, graphic, and awful.

The fragile nature of human life was obvious. Instead of a little trickle of blood, such as comes from a cut finger, there was a large puddle of blood on the pavement. The bright red blood gradually darkened and thickened. The black hair on the dead man's head was partially soaked in blood. It became matted and "dead" had an ugly meaning to Danny ... this was dead from car violence. The part of the body that had remained in the car was taken away. The head was taken away. The car was taken away. But the blood remained and turned that section of the street where kids used to play into a nightmare place for Danny.

"Did anyone witness this wreck?" the policeman asked.

"I saw it happen." Danny replied.

"I really was wondering if any adults among you saw it." No one answered. "Well then, Danny, tell me what you saw."

"The green car was coming toward me really fast, and it went right in front of the black car. Then they crashed."

"Did the green car stop at that sign? Do you know what that sign means?"

"Yes, I know all the signs and that one has STOP written on it. Anyway, the green car didn't stop."

"How do you know what that sign says?"

"S-T-O-P spells 'stop' and the shape of the sign and the red color mean stop."

"How old are you, Danny?"

"Mother says I will be five years old in April."

"And you can read at your age?"

"Not everything, but some things. Gran and I play fun word games every day."

"The green car came through the stop sign and went in front of the black one. Correct?"

"No. It came by the stop sign, but it didn't come through it. If it had, the sign would have been knocked down. Anyway, the green car didn't stop until the crash."

While the police officer was talking with Danny, the doctor was examining the injured man. The doctor entered the ambulance with the victim. He instructed the driver to go fast to the hospital. Just before they left he said to Buna, "Phone the hospital and request that their staff prepare for emergency cranial surgery. We should arrive within twelve minutes."

Mother and Buna looked at their pillows and blankets. They were bloodstained and dirty, because they had been on the road. Both agreed that strong laundry soap and cold water could help remove the blood from the pillows. They would have to do the same for the blankets, because they were woolen and would shrink if put in hot water.

Three weeks later a tall and distinguished man arrived at Danny's house. "Is your mother at home?" he asked the boy.

"My Gran is." Moments later she came to the door, with Danny next to her.

"How may I help ye, sir?" Gran asked.

"I was involved in a car wreck at your corner nearly three weeks ago. The prompt action and assistance on the part of this boy, the lady of the house, and a neighbor helped me survive until I could receive emergency surgery. That is a clumsy way of saying they helped save my life. The two women provided blankets and pillows that must have been a terrible mess. These two boxes contain replacement pillows and blankets for this household and your neighbor. I have tried the other house, but no one answered the door. I will return in a day or two to express my sincere gratitude, personally. In the meantime, would it be possible for you to deliver the other set to your neighbor?"

His card identified him as Dr. Wayne, dean of the school of law at the university.

Perhaps that car wreck was one of Danny's earliest time-oriented memories. Other childhood incidences were identified as having occurred either before or after "the wreck." Starting grade school provided an additional, but later time reference.

Long after his family had moved away, Danny visited his childhood area. Years of rain, sun, and traffic had eroded all traces of the thickening puddle of blood, but it was indelibly fixed in Danny's memory.

"Gran, why do you and father use the same word, but they sound different? Are you right or is Father right?" Danny asked.

"We both be right. I speak as we did in Hengland where ye father was born. Before he came to Hamerica we both spoke the same. He learned to speak the way that is common 'ere. I'm the one who is out of step 'ere. So ye should be learning as yer mother and father speak."

Although Danny was not really aware of it, he imitated the speech patterns of the people with whom he was talking. Monk and Ole were from Norway and they spoke their singsong type of English. Danny soon learned to do the same when he was with them. It made it easier for them to understand him.

Danny was five years old when John asked, "Son, would you like to stay up a little later tonight? The sky is almost moonless and the stars should be brilliant. Also, we are supposed to have a glorious meteor shower."

"What's that?"

"You'll discover that for yourself, after it's dark."

What a special treat! Any chance to stay up late was a great adventure. Danny's father wanted to share some of his discoveries of life with his son. These were things his own father had not done with him back in England, because his dad had abandoned the family when his children were young. Danny's father was rich in motivation, but had lacked a role model. Still, he was creative and overflowing with heartfelt care and love for his boy.

Hand-in-hand the boy and his father went to a neighboring field away from houses and lights, but he avoided crossing the street where the puddle of blood had formed from the car wreck. "The earth is a planet that circles around the sun," he explained. "There are other planets that do the same. Planets have no light of their own. They reflect the light from the sun, just as a mirror would. The moon is a satellite that goes around the earth."

Danny didn't understand everything his father told him about the differences among planets, constellations, meteors, and stars, but he was interested and that was a good beginning. With a flashlight in hand, John held his chart which showed many of the constellations and named them. As the two of them studied it, John asked, "Can you look at the sky and find any of those shapes?" It was "discovery time." Shortly thereafter, Danny excitedly blurted out, "There's one! What's its name?"

"It's commonly called the Big Dipper, because it looks similar to a giant ladle or spoon. The Little Dipper isn't easy to find, because the stars are crowded together and not very brilliant. The shape also is less distinct." Danny looked, but didn't immediately see it. Then he said, "There's another one that's on your chart!"

"Its name is Orion and often is called the Mighty Hunter," John replied.

Visual images were bombarding Danny's eyes. "There's a streak of light and now it's gone. Did you see it? There's another one, and more, and more!" A new universe was beginning to reveal itself to Danny, because of the gentle guidance from his father.

"Those are part of the meteor shower. If you like, we can come out several nights this week, while the meteors are still easy to see, but now, it's time for me to go to bed. I have to work tomorrow and I need my sleep." The warmth and urgency of Danny's hugs and his handclasps reassured John that this was a night to remember, for both father and son.

Mary had already gone to bed, but Gran was patiently awaiting the return of her grandson. He was bubbling with excitement and was eager to share his discoveries with Gran. Her receptive and calming influence prepared Danny for a good night's sleep.

The following morning, Danny greeted his parents and Gran with his usual affection and enthusiasm. Perhaps it was John's imagination, but he sensed a feeling of adoration on Danny's part that had not been there before.

As usual, Mary prepared a delicious, but simple breakfast. The family talked about their plans for the day.

Mary volunteered, "I have organ lessons to give to three students from the Northwest Christian College. That means walking to church. Then, I'll rehearse the special music I'll play at Sunday's church service. This afternoon, Mrs. Bracket's funeral service will be held, and I'll play for that. Gran, I should be home in time to prepare dinner, but I'm planning on potato, onion, and celery stew with bits of chicken in it."

The pay for Mary's professional music service was a meager

pittance. The effect of "the Great Economic Depression" was still severe. The total compensation might be as much as one dollar, including the funeral. Whatever the amount, she shared it equally with her church.

John's work as a master carpenter and cabinetmaker was sporadic at best. He was employed in a mill cabinet shop, when work was available. Pay for that work was around a dollar a day, and he felt lucky to get it. As he was leaving, John asked Danny, "Will you have time enough to look at the stars with me tonight?"

The young lad's reaction caused an implosive rush of air that made his reply nearly inaudible. "Oh! Yes, please!"

John took Gran aside and asked, "Would you and Danny have time to go over the star charts that are in my astronomy book? He seems so keen to learn."

"He is that, but it is your time and companionship that he be treasuring."

"Will you be coming with us to view the stars this evening?"

"I'll not be intruding on the two of ye just yet. I've time aplenty to be with the lad. We talk over almost everything. Opportunities to be with you, including sky gazing, are too precious. They don't come often enough for our laddie."

Gran and Danny studied the star charts and played word games. Since he knew the alphabet in both languages, they started working on spelling, as well.

After dinner that evening, father and son crossed the street to the open field. Danny pointed out the Big Dipper and asked, "Is that the Little Dipper? Why does the chart give their names as Ursa Major and Ursa Minor? Gran explained to me that *major* meant 'great' or 'big,' and *minor* was a way of saying 'little' or 'small.' But what does *ursa* mean?"

Danny amazed John by making long statements, asking compound and complex questions, and then relating these before receiving answers.

"*Ursa* is a word that means 'bear,' so *Ursa Major* and *Ursa Minor* Mean 'great and little bear,' but most people refer to them as the Big and Little Dipper."

"What is a bear?" the boy asked.

26

"A bear is a big animal. I'll show you one this coming Sunday."

"Who owns it?"

"Well, Danny, it is actually owned by everyone in the city."

"Oh. When is it our turn to have it come to live with us?"

"It is much too big and dangerous for that. You see that hill right over there?" His father asked as he pointed north and east.

"That's the one we called 'the Butte,' isn't it?"

"You're right. Two bears live there in big cages. That area is a public park where anyone can go to swim, eat, and hike. There are even swings and rides for kids. Some people just like to lie in the grass."

Danny was distracted by the meteor shower that put on a display a child might compare to a current-day Fourth of July fireworks show. "There goes one! Oooh! Aaaah!" Such comments marked the passage of matter into the earth's atmosphere as it was incinerated. His father explained more about the concept of deep space and the distances of stars and planets. The boy's understanding of distance was limited to the mile-and-a-half walk to church, but he was vaguely aware of his father's sense of wonder about the space–time–distance relationships.

When they returned home, Danny's father said, "Mother, would you and Gran like to go to the Butte this Sunday? I promised Danny that I'd show him the bears."

"If I pack a picnic lunch, we could go right after church. But do you think he is old enough to walk all that distance?"

"When he doesn't want to walk, he can ride in the little red wagon, you know, the one that belongs to Ronnie. His dad said we could borrow it. Our picnic basket can go in it, too, but he needs to have a wagon of his own. It would be convenient on many occasions and he'd have fun with it."

Trips to the Butte became the favorite family outing ... one that was shared by many families. The park had the usual playground equipment that was common during those times, but the caged black bears were the central attraction of the park. Danny called them Ursa Major and Ursa Minor. Feeding time was posted and it amazed the young children to observe how delicately the bears nibbled individual grapes from their stems. They loved fruit and vegetables and devoured a dozen apples, beets, carrots, and three loaves of bread. Finally they were given some meat. It was frightening to see them crush bones with their mighty jaws.

"Where do bears come from?" Danny asked.

"They have lived wild in this country for thousands of years. They like to stay away from people, so they live where there are no houses, and where people seldom go."

"Do they eat people?"

"They eat grass, berries, fruit, nuts, and other animals, but since I've lived in America, I've never heard of them eating a person. Still, they certainly could eat one."

Danny watched the animals for some time and then commented, "They don't look happy. I'll bet they would like to be back in the woods."

"You're probably right." Danny's father changed the subject. "Would you like to go to the river to wade and skip rocks? Until you learn to swim, you must be careful about how far you go into the water. You could drown."

"What does *drown* mean?" the boy asked.

"Drowning in water is one way of dying, but never mind, just wade in the water no deeper than up to your knees and you will be okay. Before long, I'll give you swimming lessons. But for now, we can skip rocks."

"After the wreck" memories included the deep terror the boy experienced when he understood that death was permanent. One time his father started swimming across the river and was swept downstream by the current. He appeared smaller and smaller and nearly disappeared. When he reached the far bank and waved, everything was fine until Danny realized his father had to swim back. When his father was next to him again, a flood of relief swept through the boy, and his father assumed a near God-like status of invulnerability.

Danny's mother, father, and Gran taught him that love provided a life force far beyond the sum of their individual strength. They demonstrated the tenderness of being hugged, and loved, and the excitement of being thrown high in the air only to be caught and secure at the last second. The physical thrill was real, but total trust was established, and grew through all his relationships with his family. When they promised to do something, they did it. On the rare occasion when they failed, they

28

took full responsibility, and explained the reason. All three tried to help Danny understand. It could take a week, a month, or a year to fulfill their commitment, but in time, and in some way, they made good on their promises.

Danny's family did not steal, lie, or cheat. If a store clerk gave them too much money in change, it was always returned. The family shared a sense of pride and respect for each other and for those in their community.

When Danny was five, Mrs. Bracket's family gave a tricycle and a wagon to Danny in appreciation for the funeral service where Mary had played. They had belonged to Mrs. Bracket's grandson, who had outgrown them. These became Danny's pride and joy. Cycling became one of his adventures and lifelong passions. It extended his range of travel. He even rode it to the Butte, and hauled the family's picnic lunch in his wagon.

Danny's mother expressed her concern. "I think it will be too much for him."

"Do not sell that 'un short," Gran replied. "He's a might stronger and more determined than ye may imagine."

John resolved the problem by building a wooden rack to fit the wagon. "If the need arises, that can carry Danny and his trike, and I can tow the wagon. But I'm betting he will manage the trip as well as we do."

Under her breath, Mary commented, "Better than I will." She cheered up and commented, "With that wagon, I don't have to carry extra wraps and the picnic basket. The more I load it, the more determined that little rascal becomes to tow it behind his trike."

That was the summer of frequent trips to the Butte. At almost any time, Gran was ready to take Danny there. Mary found the walk there and back home far too strenuous for weekly trips.

Danny's mother gave piano lessons to a girl who was about thirteen years old. The agreement was that the girl would do two hours of housework for every hour of lessons she was given. One evening, John asked Mary how the work for piano lessons exchange arrangement was progressing. "I do declare, that girl has the lightest touch imaginable. She can wipe woodwork and walls without disturbing the dust!"

During a Saturday-morning piano lesson Danny asked his mother, "May I go for a long tricycle ride?"

She was busy and didn't really listen to his request or understand his intent. To her, a long ride meant going around the block. "Yes, but remember that lunch will be very late today."

Danny set off on an adventure. He knew the way to church and had often wondered what lay beyond it. So off he rode on his tricycle in his discovery quest. He reached the university area, where he found many buildings that were larger and more interesting than any he had ever seen.

As he looked, he heard a friendly voice. "You're you a long way from home. Do you know your way back?" It was Dr. Wayne, the man who had been hurt in the car wreck a year or so earlier.

"Sure I know! Does your head still hurt where you bumped it?"

"Not anymore. Are your parents with you?"

"I came by myself to see what was beyond our church."

"Does your mother know where you are?"

"Yes. I wanted to go for a long ride on my tricycle, and she said I could."

"But so far! Would you like to ride home in my car? I had to buy a new one after that wreck. I can put your trike in the back and we can drive to your home."

"Oh, yes, please! I like riding in cars. The only time we do that is when the preacher takes us."

"I think I remember how to get to your home, but would you tell me how to get there, in case I make a mistake?"

And Danny did. "Turn here ... go straight ... now turn ... no, the other way." In a few minutes they were there. "That was fun riding in your car. I'm glad you saw me. Thanks a lot. When you came to our house last year, my mother wasn't home. She should be now. You may come in, if you want to."

"Thank you Danny, I'd like that."

When she heard where Danny had been, Mary was frantic. She expressed her gratitude to Dr. Wayne, and suggested that father and son would have a serious talk when he arrived home from work. Danny went off to wash, and his mother and Dr. Wayne visited for a short time. He left shortly after Danny returned to the living room.

John helped his son understand that going so far away from home made Mother and Gran extremely worried. He needed to be considerate of their feelings. There was no scolding—after all, Danny had asked permission to go for a long ride—but he should have explained where he wanted to ride. Positive reinforcement for the nature of his adventure was tempered by his obligations to those who loved him. They should talk about such adventures ahead of time, and Danny should leave it to his parents to agree on the limits he would be allowed to explore.

John and Gran were "good walkers," although Danny's mother was not. Gran would usually go with him almost any-place he wanted to walk or ride his trike. It was following this incident that Danny was taught to give his home address, as well as his name, when someone asked who he was.

Grandma Skelen lived two houses east from Danny's home. During one visit she told the boy, "I've not any family in this country. Yer Gran is me dearest friend." They had both come from the same part of London, and enjoyed talking in Cockney about the way things were in the olden days. Grandma Skelen had celebrated her ninetieth birthday and fifty of those years had been in her current, little home. "I'll die 'er if I 'ave me choice," she told the boy.

John had constructed a picket fence between the sidewalk and Grandma Skelen's flower garden. This delighted all the kids in the neighborhood. They would run along the sidewalk adjacent to her fence and hold a stick of wood so that it would rap against the pickets. The *rrrrrrrrrr, rrrrrrrrap, rrraaaap* sound was music to the kids' ears and was a torment to Grandma Skelen. "Off with ye, ye young rascals. I'll 'ave ye fathers tan the 'ide off yer backsides," she would call. But there was a note of merriment in her voice that carried the message that she was helping them feel the thrill of being "given the dickens" without their really being bad.

Grandma S, as she was called, grew violets, pinks, pansies, lavender, and a few other flowers that Danny didn't know. She enjoyed sharing her flowers with a few women in the neighborhood. "Danny, me laddie, pick a few flowers for your Gran. Every woman likes to receive a few flowers now and again. The same can be done for your lovely mother."

31

On two occasions, Danny was left in the care of Grandma S. She was to provide dinner and a bed for the youngster. He felt a strange sense of excitement and adventure. When a person is five years of age, a ten-year-old boy is not exactly old; maybe *big* is a better word. Numbers going up into the twenties and thirties were beyond realistic understanding. Gran said Grandma S was ninety, and that age was beyond his comprehension.

She and her house smelled as fresh as the flowers she grew, and Danny was happy to stay with her. Dinner was served and Grandma S ate in the same fashion as Father and Gran. The left hand held the fork with the tines down. The right hand held the knife. There was no switching of the fork from one hand to the other. But Grandma S followed one practice that was not allowed in Danny's home. Both her knife and fork went into her mouth. She would cut butter with the knife that had come from her mouth. She would lick her knife and then dip it into the jam jar or the honey container. Ugh! That nearly turned Danny's stomach, although he still enjoyed and respected the elderly woman.

Almost all youngsters of Danny's age dreamed of finding a fortune ... and a penny was a wonderful treasure. There was an age when almost all boys watched where they walked, particularly if they were far from home. They felt certain that if they looked hard and willed it strongly enough, the money would materialize. On one occasion, Danny's dream came true. He skipped all the way home chanting "found a nickel, found a nickel." To him, that five-cent piece represented the potential to buy about anything he could want.

Buna, the neighbor woman, had come to visit Mary. She arrived with her older daughter and her two-month-old infant. While there, Buna undid a flap on her dress and the wonderful fullness of her milk-engorged breast was in full view for a few moments. The greedy lips of the infant surrounded the proud nipple and life-sustaining milk, and early bonds of family were forged. Little milk bubbles formed around the baby's mouth, and sounds of affection and contentment came from both mother and child.

"Danny, please go outside and play," his mother insisted. Something in her Puritanical upbringing deemed such intimate sights as being unsuitable for a young boy. Unfortunately, one of the beautiful bonding relationships found in nature was somehow sullied and degraded for reasons he didn't understand.

Many children find that playing with matches is compulsively fascinating. Danny was no exception. Creating fire was thrilling. A large box of matches was kept in the basement by the furnace. He would strike the match, watch it burn and then go out. On two different occasions he was caught. The first offense resulted in a stern and very logical lecture given by John. The second resulted in a similar lecture with a razor strap liberally applied to his bare bottom for emphasis. Even this did not deter Danny. It only made him craftier to avoid detection.

Eventually, Danny's dedication to playing with fire, ended even though he was doing so with permission. It was Halloween time when someone gave Danny a collection of club pins, medals, and a small American flag made of rayon. He attached the pins and medals to the flag and then secured the flag to his shirt. He felt so proud. He had carved his own jack-o'-lantern and had a candle in it. When he leaned over the lighted candle, the flag flared into flame, as only rayon can, and his shirt was instantly on fire! All the heat and flame seemed to sweep up into his face. He ran without direction or purpose, other than to escape the heat and pain. He literally tripped over a tub of water, which the neighbors kept full for their chickens. He scooped water from the tub and put out his burning shirt.

Danny ran home to Mother sobbing and out of control. He was more terrified than hurt. A warm bath and being put to bed offered a sense of security and comfort. A cup of hot peppermint milk was a special treat that helped "make everything better."

Valuable lessons had been learned. Fire could be extremely painful and you didn't have to be bad or misbehave for it to burn you. John taught Danny to roll over and over as one way of putting out flames. He also demonstrated how a blanket or coat could help smother flames.

Neighborhood sidewalks were made of concrete and were ideal for tricycles, skates, scooters, pedal cars, hopscotch, rope skipping, playing kick the can, and for scraping knees and elbows. Most girls were better coordinated for skill activities than the boys. Boys scorned jacks, hopscotch, and rope skipping as girl things and sissy stuff. In reality, the boys didn't like being beaten by girls in games.

The neighbor boy, Ronnie, was Danny's age, and he had a big wooden trunk absolutely packed full with toys. He had a Buck Rogers Zap Zap Gun, and a cowboy cap gun that fired a full roll of caps as fast as he could pull the trigger, but you had to buy the caps. For his age, Danny could run faster than any of the kids in the neighborhood. Ronnie had a squirt gun, a bow and arrows, and an Indian headband complete with feathers. He even had cowboy chaps! But Danny could outrun Ronnie. Ronnie had an erector set, log cabin toys, "pick-up-sticks," and playing cards for many different types of games. He had a pedal car fire engine and Danny only had a tricycle, but Danny could go faster and farther on his trike than Ronnie on his pedal car. When they switched vehicles, Danny could still beat Ronnie.

Danny received a broomstick horse for Christmas with a horse's head fashioned from a truck inner tube. This delighted Danny beyond belief. A week later Ronnie received a similar one, with a head far more elaborately fashioned, but Danny could "gallop" his faster.

Gran helped Danny become aware that money could buy so many things that wore out, but what he could do with his own body could only be inherited, learned, and trained. Danny could kick the ball higher, farther, and more accurately than many boys, even ones who were much older than he. The same could be said for throwing, running, jumping, and so many other "boy type" activities. Gran used to say to Danny, "The other lads 'ave toys. Ye 'ave your body. Their toys wear out, and this body of yours will last a wonderful lifetime, if ye care for it. Ye have the advantage, and ye also have the brains to go with it."

Danny understood the words and the ideas. He and the neighborhood boys continued to play together. They understood that Danny was better at almost everything. More important to all of them, was that they were good friends and had fun together.

5

First Grade

Danny was eager to start school. He loved learning and he was told that trained teachers would be there to enrich the children's minds. He envisioned five or six hours a day of magical learning with his friends and others who would soon be his friends. He could hardly wait. No kindergarten was available during the Great Depression, so he would start school in the first grader when he was six years old.

School began on the playground: running, chasing, and swinging on the monkey bars with youngsters he knew. When they heard the first bell, it was their signal to make that essential final stop before ... first grade began. He joined the other boys in their rush to the door with their identity painted in large bold letters: BOYS. Danny had been in lots of restrooms, starting with those marked LADIES, and later to the MEN. He knew this one would be special, and indeed it was.

The urinal at the old Lincoln School had started life as a water tank about six feet long and a foot and a half in diameter. A longitudinal section had been cut out, part of the metal flattened, and the tank made a long trough that hung horizontally along one wall. Four or five fellows could line up along the side for simultaneous use. A common game was to try to "cut the other fellow's stream" with your own, as if they were dueling. The challenge of seeing who could piss the farthest or the highest led to mishaps in the restroom among the first-grade boys.

The favorite positions were at each end. Arch high, piss far, and aim straight! These were the ultimate challenges of control and prowess. To squirt higher than everyone's head and to have the stream drop at the far end of the trough ... well, when you could accomplish that, you had arrived at the pinnacle of pissdom!

Misdirection of the stream was a common failure among the first-grade group of boys. One such incident prompted Junior to go running to the teacher, Miss Choke, and weepingly protest that, "Danny peed all over my breast." And he had. Boys and men can understand how that can happen. Sometimes the opening in the end is a little different and the stream can go off cockeyed.

"You must be mistaken, I don't see how that could happen," said Miss Choke, and she didn't believe him, because she could not see how it could happen. She had no such association with little boys ... or big ones.

"It did so happen! Just look, I'm wet there and you can take a smell of it if you don't believe me."

Miss Choke declined the invitation and probably relegated the incident to being one more of the dirty and disgusting things those nasty little boys did. Who could understand them anyway? But why bother? They were atrocious little monsters, and how could he dare suggest that she smell the soggy front of his shirt?

But misdirection of the stream is an accident of nature that is not confined to children. Many a woman becomes really frustrated when it is time to clean the toilet in her home, only to find spatter and even puddles of urine on the floor. She knows for certain that she and her daughter didn't make the mess. Why, she wonders, can't men be civilized and sit down to keep the mess in the bowl where it can be flushed neatly away?

From the viewpoint of her young boy-students, Miss Choke represented a puzzle. Danny realized that Gran was a teacher. Miss Choke only had the training and the title. She was a gray, frizzy-haired, old woman. Her cheeks and jowls wobbled about and bounced when she walked. She was as lumpy as a burlap sack full of potatoes and her bare upper arms had soggy-looking balloons of fat dangling and flopping around whenever she wrote on the chalkboard. Her slip straps were always hanging off her shoulders across those fat upper arms. Unkind, nasty little boys started calling her "crabapple face," once they had been in her class for a month; not because she was old, but because of her sour outlook on life. Of course, she was not called that to her face.

Most students had grandmothers who were similar in appearance to Miss Choke, and were delighted with them, because they were kind, cheerful, and fun. Miss Choke smelled old, or that was the association that was indelibly imprinted on her student's senses. Danny's neighbor, Grandma S, was ninety years old, but she always smelled of fresh or dried flowers. Gran was old, but she didn't smell old. Danny didn't know how old Miss Choke was, but she smelled stale, and what he thought of as "being old." Years later, he found this resulted from neglecting personal hygiene. Gran referred to Danny's teacher as being "moldy."

One of Miss Choke's first lessons was to ask every child to recite the alphabet by memory. Girls went first, and that was the way it was with about everything. And if there wasn't time enough for the boys to have a turn that was just too bad for them.

Most of the students knew the alphabet but some were too embarrassed to speak out in front of the class and they stumbled. The boys who didn't know it were given withering looks of contempt. When it was Danny's turn, he decided to do it backward, "Z, Y, X, W, V . . ."

"That is *not* correct! Obviously you don't even know your ABCs!"

"I do so know them, backward and forward, and I know them in Arabic, too."

"I'll not be corrected by such an ignorant and insolent little boy! Sit down and be quiet." All were devastated by her outburst and the remaining boys stumbled and became tongue-tied. "Just what I expected from boys . . . slow to learn and ill-mannered."

The boys were convinced that Miss Choke had one uncompromising mission: Every boy in her class was going to wet his pants before the school year was over, and she nearly succeeded. To obtain permission to go to the toilet, a student should extend one arm high above his head, and indicate with his fingers the nature of his emergency. One finger meant pee, and two fingers meant poop. For some perverse reason, teachers insisted on knowing the exact nature of the emergency.

Danny was a rebellious little kid regarding things that seemed unreasonable or unfair, and disliked being told what to do and what not to do by some strange woman. The nature of his personal necessity seemed to be none of her business. At this age, he already knew that everyone had to go to the toilet, including teachers and preachers.

For all their wisdom, good intentions, fine training, and loving nature, most women seem not to understand how totally and uncontrollably susceptible the male member of the species is to the power of suggestion when it comes to taking a leak. Every guy who has slept in a sleeping porch, or a similar dorm situation, is well aware of the "piss call." In the wee hours (or should it be the "wee-wee" hours of the morning?) he has been awakened by a prankster uttering the inevitable phrase, "Wake up? You've got to take a leak." And sure enough, he did. There was no use staying in bed and trying to forget about it.

Sidewalk pissoires are found in many major European cities. They are constant reminders of a demanding urgency. Fortunately, city planners during the eighteenth and nineteenth centuries were mostly men who understood that passing by one reinforced the necessity to have one available within the ensuing block or two. It remains a mystery for men that women can escape the compelling urgency, which, among men, is initiated by the mere power of suggestion.

Miss Choke was not a woman of good intentions and loving nature when it came to boys. A little girl who needed to go held up her hand with one or two fingers extended. Miss Choke smiled sweetly and nodded ... the response of a kindly and caring woman.

When a little boy gave the same signal, it seemed as if Miss Choke was sure that he had some nasty and evil mission in mind. She would frown, scowl, shake her head, and the flab of her cheeks and jowls would jostle and bounce. Other times, a malicious and malevolent smile would form and her face became a particularly grotesque mask. She would then announce to the entire class that it was only a few minutes until recess, lunch, or whatever, and everyone could easily wait that long. Usually she was right, but the power of suggestion had all the boys squirming in their seats, and school was out for them as far as any learning was concerned.

There were fourteen boys in class, and ten of them had wet their pants at least once in Miss Choke's classroom during the first three months of school. Danny was pretty proud of himself for having avoided being included among the "soggy society." "Pride reigneth before the fall." In times past, he had escaped the dishonorable discharge group by sneaking out the swinging door at the back of the classroom when Miss Choke's head was down over a textbook or perhaps the roll book. This had been easy to manage, because his seat was closest to the door and farthest from Miss Choke's desk. The difficulty was returning to the room when she was not looking, because he couldn't see her from the hallway. She had the girls assigned to seats clustered around her desk. By the very nature of their being, unworthy boys were more remotely seated.

Danny never knew if someone told her, or if she discovered his avenue of escape for herself. In any case she said nothing about it. She simply moved his seat to one that was next to the windows and far from the door. Sooner or later he would be doomed and that time came on Arbor Day, the day when all American schools were supposed to plant a tree. Danny's school was observing this special day by planting a tree in a side yard of the grounds. The hole had been dug, the tree and a bottle of water were placed adjacent to the hole. Everything was ready and waiting for the time when all students assembled outside.

The class was "first-grade excited." The great event was about to happen. Danny raised his hand, and felt that under the pressure of his circumstances, he'd better indicate his need by extending one finger. Miss Choke looked directly at him and did not see him, would not see him, refused to see him. When she looked in another direction, Betty had her hand up with a finger extended. The usual smile and nod that was reserved for girls followed, and Betty left the room. The class rule was "only one student at a time."

When Betty returned, Danny's hand sprung upward with a degree of urgency, and it was ignored. Dorothy's hand signal was greeted with a smile and a nod of permission. The boy's status was acutely uncomfortable. Dorothy's return prompted Danny to leap from his seat and wave in a fashion intended to transmit the desperate nature of his situation.

"Oh, do sit down! You must learn to be civilized about these things. Yes, Shirley, you may leave the room!"

Danny was at the point of rupturing a water main when Shirley returned.

"There have been far too many of you leaving the room to go to the toilet. You simply must learn to take care of these needs when class is not in session. It will be only thirty minutes until the tree planting ceremony and everyone will be able to go to the toilet on the way outside. In the meantime we will learn about the occasion.

"All of you know Doris, who was voted queen of her fourth-grade class, and also of the school. She has the honor of placing the small hawthorn tree in the hole that has been dug for it. Then each of you children will help fill the hole by picking up a handful of earth, and dropping it into the hole to cover the roots. Thereby, each of you will be participating in the tree planting. When all the earth had been put in place, Ruth will take the bottle of water and pour it slowly around the tree and say, 'I christen thee little hawthorn.'"

Danny's fate was sealed. The image of water pouring from a bottle was far too graphic for the agonizing necessity of his circumstances. To his last day he would remember the unsophisticated and errant logic of a six-year-old boy who thought that if only a trickle were let out, it would relieve the pressure. Just a teaspoonful should do. All too late he learned the unmistakable truth that once the floodgate had been breached, there was no way to stem the flood until the reservoir was empty.

The Arbor Day planting went on as scheduled and when Doris pronounced the final words, "I christen thee little hawthorn," one of his fellow students commented none too quietly, "Danny christened his pants."

Danny learned five unforgettable lessons in school that year. 1. When it comes to taking a leak, it is all or nothing at all. 2. Wet woolen short trousers are really scratchy and irritating. 3. Urine-soaked wool has a totally unpleasant odor. 4. The word *christen* had a special and personal meaning. 5. That he truly was capable of anger, no, rather say unabashed rage.

In fact, Danny was in that state of rage when he marched up to Miss Sue, the school's principal, and a woman for whom Gran cleaned house on occasion.

He announced to her the circumstances of the day's events,

40

and that ten boys had wet their pants in class before he did, and that he was number eleven. Only three remained without the yellow stain of disgrace etched in their minds.

Miss Sue questioned the custodian about how frequently boys had wet their pants in Miss Choke's class, and he said it had been going on regularly for many years!

"I'm terribly sorry, Danny. This will not happen again in my school." It didn't. Miss Choke maintained her sweet and understanding ways with girls, but scowled, glared, and looked daggers of hatred at the boys on the rare occasion when a hand went up to leave the room. The flab of her jowls bounced, her complexion went from bread dough, pasty white to a livid red-purple almost unknown in nature, except when observed in the wattle or gobble of an excited turkey, or the posterior of a baboon. But she did not deny boys permission to go. In retrospect, Miss Choke probably wondered why little boys couldn't be nice, polite, tidy, dainty, and genteel creatures, similar to little girls. But, of course, they couldn't be what they were not. All boys in school who had Miss Choke for their first-grade teacher received sour looks and lower grades than girls. Three grading levels were awarded. "S" indicated satisfactory. Only girls received that grade. "W" indicated weak. Most boys received that as their grade. "U" indicated unsatisfactory. No girls received any of the lowest grades and most boys were awarded several such marks. Even fourth-grade boys, who met her in the hall, continued to be rejected by Miss Choke. Indications were that they held an extreme dislike for her as well.

Kids who had the other first grade teacher maintained a cordial and friendly relationship. Such a teacher remembered names long after her students had passed on to higher classes.

The following year, Danny's second-grade teacher did much to mitigate the sense of antagonism and aversion that so many of the boys felt toward teachers.

Danny was relieved when his family moved to another town. The change of schools midway through the second grade meant that Miss Choke and Danny didn't have to look at each other. Most likely she had dismissed him as a nonentity, just as she apparently had done with most of the other boys who had been

41

in her classes over the years. All were unworthy of her time and consciousness.

But the boys who had been forced to join the soggy britches brigade and yellow stain society while in Miss Choke's class remembered her with aversion, at best, but more likely with subliminal hatred for everything she represented to them.

And perhaps, years later, a "final pass-by in review" on the part of all the little boys who had been forced to wet their pants in Miss Choke's class could soothe their humiliated souls. In their imaginations, the little boy who was locked up in each man would stop in groups of three along one side of her grave. Two more would assume the positions of honor at each end, and all would arch high, aim straight, and empty full and bitter bladders of hatred. Perhaps that would purge their individual souls.

6

The Move

Danny's parents could not afford to have a telephone, and in rare emergency situations, a call would be placed to Buna, the neighbor woman. She would give a message to Danny's parents. The second call that day was from Mary for Gran.

"I'm at the hospital and John has a broken back. I'll be here for hours. Can you make dinner for yourself and Danny ... Oh, Gran, what are we going to do?"

"Not to worry, Mary, we'll manage and not for just today. The storm is always darkest before..."

"Oh, do be quiet, Gran. I'm worried sick ... I'm sorry. It's just that so many things have gone wrong recently!"

"Quite right. Times have been difficult with the Great Depression and all, but we will get by. We always have and we will. So now, tell me what happened?"

"You know John and another man were re-roofing a two-story house. John was carrying two bundles of shingles up the ladder when that grinning fool on the roof took the top of the ladder and said, 'Hey John! What would happen if I shake the ladder like this?' He found out. One foot of the ladder lost its grip on the ground and it whipped around. This pitched John from the ladder and he landed sitting down. The thing that probably saved his life was the cushioning effect of the shingles that had been removed from the roof. He landed on them. His back was broken, and the doctors say he will be in the hospital for three weeks, and in a cast for at least six weeks after that."

John was devastated! The Great Depression had virtually shut down the construction industry. Even so, he had been able to find short-term employment, because some types of home and commercial repair could be delayed for only a short period of time. It would be more accurate to say that the "work found him." His reputation as a master carpenter, hard worker, and honest person guaranteed at least occasional employment.

He had adjusted to the loss of regular employment. The occasional jobs had allowed him to feed and clothe his family, but there was no money left over to pay the property taxes for his home. Temporarily, the city and county had agreed to be lax about tax collections until the country got back on its feet. This arrangement was extended to most taxpayers. But the time came when governmental agencies had to pay their bills, and the only way to do that was by way of foreclosure sales.

Fate had delivered three crushing blows within a single year during the Great Depression. Tragedy number one had been the dissolution of the quartet, Two Johns and Two Bobs. John had continued singing, but that dream was shattered. The second blow was his broken back. Before he was out of the hospital, the county informed him that it could no longer carry the accounts of those whose taxes were delinquent. In effect, the notice said, "Pay up or your property will be sold for the taxes due." This included the plot of land for which he had paid cash, and the house he had built. He owed no money on anything except the property taxes. That loss was the third and final blow. He felt himself to be a failure, and the family had to move.

Fortunately, by the time the move took place, the vertebrae in John's back had healed, and he had started a physical routine to toughen his muscles. This increased his physical endurance, so he could do a full day's work. His back hurt, as the doctors said it would, but they didn't tell him that "agony" would better describe his pain.

A church friend used his Model T Ford truck to help the family move their household belongings. Four trips were required. The move was to a small town across the river. Mary's upright piano was the largest and heaviest item to be transported, and was among the first things to be moved. The men off-loaded and placed furniture in various rooms.

While the truck went back for the second load, Gran, Mother, and Danny remained at the new home to distribute boxes to their appropriate rooms and start unpacking. Almost immediately, a small woman about Mary's age came to the front door. She was very different in appearance. Her skin was almost ivory-colored and her hair was blacker than any Danny had seen before. It was the shape and slant of her eyes and her fragile delicacy that confounded and attracted Danny the most. He thought she was lovely.

"I am Mrs. Watanabe, your neighbor just to the east. My husband, Sugio, and I are from Japan, but we are now Americans. We have a son, Ito, who is in the second grade." She went on to say, "Mr. Schmidt, from whom we purchased our home, lives with us. He came from Germany in 1920." She stopped suddenly, realizing that she was the only one talking, and she had come to deliver something for her new neighbors. "You will be hungry soon, and I have brought you a few sandwiches and a quart of applesauce. We canned the apples last summer. These will make it easier for you to continue unpacking. At six-thirty this evening, we will be having chicken dinner. We would be honored if you will come to our home and table. Our son will be home this afternoon and he will come here to help your son with the things he needs to do." With a quick nodding type bow of her head and shoulders, she departed. Mary, Gran, and Danny had been surprised and pleased, but were speechless. They had merely smiled and nodded in response.

Shortly after noon, the truck was back with their final load of the household belongings. The family ate Mrs. Watanabe's sandwiches and applesauce, as well as some cookies Mary had made the previous day. It was obvious that Mother and Gran had been in the house and working hard. Everything was clean and ready for the final distribution of furniture and boxes. Mary's beloved piano occupied the place of honor in the living room. It was the first thing to be seen when the front door was opened.

The house was larger than the one they had left, but it was in terrible condition. The paint was flaking off, both inside and out. There were leaks in the roof, the floors sagged, creaked, protested, and seemingly threatened to collapse under every footstep. Most rooms had walls that were partially covered with wallpaper, which sagged and was peeling in many places. A single electrical light cord hung from the center of each room. It was switched on and off by a pull cord adjacent to where the lightbulb was supposed to be.

At six-thirty that evening, eight people were seated around

45

the Watanabe dinner table. Everyone enjoyed the delicious and different flavors of Japanese-American cooking. Initial impressions were confirmed about how kind, thoughtful, interesting, and generous the Watanabe-Schmidt household was. Each family enjoyed the comfortable and congenial relationship.

John, Mary, Gran, and Danny would have enjoyed visiting and helping with clearing the table and doing dishes, but they were ushered out politely, with the understanding that the Watanabe family knew there was much to do before bedtime.

This was the first real contact with the Watanabe-Schmidt household. Gran and Mr. Schmidt were about the same age, and they found many similar experiences and memories to share and develop. Mary and Mrs. Watanabe had similar interests that ranged from home canning to church activities. This was a revelation to Mary, who had limited contact with people outside her white, Protestant, and farm community background. John and Sugio Watanabe found real comradeship in their hopes for the future, and the realities of their lives as immigrants.

"Goodness, gracious!" Mary commented, using her second most explicit phrase, "Land a Goshen" being the most serious. "They are just like real people!" It was a revelation for her.

John responded, in the words of the Sunday school song so many little children learn:

Red and Yellow, Black or White
All are precious in His sight,
Jesus loves the little children of the world."

Mary was embarrassed when she realized what her statement had implied. She had struggled through the childhood turmoil involving the adamant conviction of a mother who avowed that the three "evils of the world were alcohol, tobacco, and Indians." This attitude was quietly contested. Her father associated with Indians economically, religiously, and socially, to the extent the Indians would allow it. Within Mary's generous nature was a dedication to doing "what was right."

Shortly after they met, Ito and Danny became what might best be described as "a compound functional unit." They did not need to establish dominant and submissive roles in their relationship. The strengths of one complemented the weaknesses of the other. Their mutual abilities bound them together to strengthen such areas. Genuine appreciation expanded as they spent more time together. They seemed to know from the outset that they were uniquely matched and needed to prove nothing to each other.

The new house faced north and had porches on all four sides, but they were not connected. The front porch went all along the front and continued around to the side facing the Watanabe residence. The front door entered directly into the living room. John and Mary's bedroom was off the living room. Behind that was the dining room and the next door back led to the stairway to the only upstairs room, which was Danny's. Beyond the stairs were Gran's bedroom and the kitchen. The kitchen had a sink complete with cold running water, anytime the handle was pumped. There was also a dining nook and an area adjacent to the stove where a washtub was placed for taking baths. The door at the back of the kitchen opened onto a little hallway in the enclosed porch. To one side was a huge fruit room complete with shelves for storing several hundred fruit jars. Across the hall was the woodshed. The rear exit from that porch gave access to the path to the outhouse.

There was a chimney in the living room, but no stove. A chimney connection was available, although the heating unit was missing. Gran purchased a sheet-metal stove from a friend for fifty cents, but a roaring fire in it made the sheet metal red-hot. The threat that it might burn through and set the house on fire, prompted John to keep a pair of five-gallon buckets of water near it. He also made sure that two heavy blankets were kept on a chair in the same room. He instructed the family to soak the blankets in water and use them to smother the flames, if needed. The stove's only function was to heat the house.

John never went to bed at night until that stove had cooled enough so that none of the metal looked red when the light was off. Of course, the kitchen stove also helped heat the house. It was a good "kitchen range" with a fine oven for baking. The firebox was made of heavy cast iron. It had come with the family from their previous house, and Mary was an accomplished cook using that stove.

The room universally used by all was not a room at all. It was a small wooden building located fifty steps to the rear of the back porch door. This outhouse was a luxury accommodation. It provided seating for two people, where they could "while away an hour." In addition, it had been constructed with a large square hole for the men to use when there was no need for them to drop their trousers. The outhouse was a major change from the complete indoor bathroom that John had built in their previous home.

During the summer months, this little house was frequently the domain of yellow jackets, occasionally hornets, and always swarms of houseflies. To suggest that it had its own distinctive odor would be an understatement, but the stench was never so bad as when someone from outside the family used it and left a stink. The outdoor facility was affectionately referred to as a privy, backhouse, outhouse, et cetera. Members of Danny's household, except for Mary, called it "the bughouse."

Danny's bedroom was at the top of the stairs. On moving day, his mother handed him an empty gallon pot complete with lid. "Take this with you when you go to your room," she requested. "And don't forget to use the lid."

"What's it for?" Danny asked.

"In the middle of the night you may need to do a 'little job.' You probably won't want to walk down the stairs and all the way to the privy."

The boy's mother was circumspect in her choice of words. Commonly used words to mean "urinate" were truly absent from her vocabulary. *Pee, wee wee, piddle, take a leak, tinkle, piss,* or *number one* were never used around her nor by her. A "little job" covered that natural necessity. A "big job" was the term she substituted for the more solid excrement. "You are responsible for keeping that pot empty and clean. That means you are to empty it and wash it out with soap and hot water daily. There will be no exceptions. Be certain you put the lid on your pot when you finish using it, and when you take it from your room. We will not abide any spills." Danny had seldom heard his mother speak so sternly. This was not merely a request: It was an admonishment!

The morning parade to the bughouse was humiliating. Carrying the pot that needed to be emptied made it worse. Danny hated it. He resolved to get up and go outside when necessary.

A few days later, John told Danny, "The stairway creaks and wakes us up when you make your midnight trips. You'd better find a different way of handling your problem." He had not said that Danny had to use a pot, so there was an opening for improvising.

One totally useless item brought from the city residence was a water hose. Since there were no faucets, the only water available in the new home was hand-pumped. Danny's midnight need could easily be met by using the hose. He ran it out the upstairs window, across the porch roof, and down to the ground. He dug a pit, covered it with lumber, and ran one end of the hose through a hole into the chamber below. This was covered with earth. To make sure there was no spillage, Danny found a large-capacity funnel to put in one end of the hose, which was upstairs. He also found a large cork and fitted it in the top of the hose. The boy felt he had devised a brilliant solution to his waste problem. There would be no spillage, no odor, and no steps up and down the stairs at night. Even the top end of the hose could be anchored outside. The only time it needed to be inside the house was when it was being used. It was the ideal solution to an inconvenient problem.

"Rejected," with absolutely no appeal permitted. It was one of the few totally illogical things his mother demanded. He secretly wondered if she didn't envy the convenient anatomical addition that men had. He tried to emphasize that this was a solution for solutions. That it was not even remotely considered for solids had no impact. "REJECTED!"

The best way Danny found to resolve the problem was to restrict the consumption of liquids after dinner every evening. In that manner, he seldom had a need for pressure relief. Chamber pots were in common use during those days. Many older hotels were equipped with them. Their purpose was to meet the nightly needs without requiring the long journey down the hall to the toilet. However, it was not considered a daytime convenience. Emptying and cleaning the pot was a standard part of the housekeeper's job, along with making the bed, cleaning the washbowl, filling the water pitcher, sweeping the floor, and dusting.

Boys really did have toilet advantages. At night it was so easy to walk partway to the bughouse, whip it out, and let it fly. Boys didn't have the potential emotional trauma of bare-bottom discovery, disclosure, and humiliation, that plagued girls, if they paused along the way.

Frequent rain, even during the summer, dictated that the most pressing job to be done on the new residence was to repair the leaky roof. John went up on the roof and from the attic Danny spotted daylight coming in. A long piece of baling wire with a small scrap of white cloth tied to it "flagged" successive holes. John closed these with shingles. It took all of Saturday to do the job, but it stopped the leaks.

So much still needed to be done on Sunday. However, Mary was determined that her family would maintain the proper priorities. At ten fifteen everyone joined the Watanabe family, to go to church. The women had made that arrangement the previous evening. Most people walked to church, because only a few owned cars during the Great Depression.

Church members greeted newcomers with enthusiasm and friendship. This encouraged people to return. Ito and Danny were invited to attend the 9:30 A.M. Sunday school sessions, which were held specifically for the younger set. At the regular service, both families, all eight of them, sat together as a single-family group. When it came time to sing the hymns, John did not hold back. Heads turned and Miss Kelly, the choir director, who was a beautiful raven-haired woman, stood in awe of the voice she was hearing. Two choir members knew John. They had sung together in the Mighty Twenty, the male chorus of twenty voices.

Mary played piano more than competently, and was invited to play for services. A fine pipe organ had been a memorial gift to the church many years previously. The organist, who had played it, was developing debilitating arthritis, and Mary was asked to assume that responsibility whenever the regular organist couldn't. Mary had developed a fine level of professionalism, and soon played at all the services, and for special occasions such as weddings and funerals. She was given a key to the church and to the organ, which allowed her to practice at her convenience. The pay she received for performing at special services was divided, as always. She kept half and donated the other half to the church.

John joined the church choir, to the delight of virtually everyone. From time to time, the beautiful Miss Kelly came to his house to rehearse a duet that she and John would sing. Mary would accompany them on her piano. Danny sat in awe that a woman could be so beautiful. He was sure he was in love ... whatever that meant.

John maintained his membership in the Mighty Twenty, even though transportation presented problems from time to time. He often rode with a member who had a car, and who lived in the community. Sometimes he rode his bicycle the seven miles each way, which wasn't too bad during good weather.

Home improvement tasks remained paramount on the list. When John inspected what existed, he insisted that the owner do something about the electrical hazards. Hard words were exchanged. The gist of the discussion was, "What do you expect for five dollars a month rent?" At that time, five dollars was between three and five days' wages for a master carpenter, if he could get work.

The other side of the verbal battle centered on a single word, "Safety!"

A compromise was struck. The property owner would supply the material and John would do the work. Danny worked with his father and learned some of the fundamentals of electrical wiring. A third party also participated, Ito. The two boys were in each other's company most of their waking hours, with the exception of classroom time at school. Although both were in the second grade, the school was large enough to have two classes for that level. The electrical work started at the meter and they put in a completely new service. It was not as elaborate as John would have liked, but economy of time and material limited what could be done. At the least, the electrical system was safe.

The next job was to install a large portion of the foundation that had never been built. Floors in some areas of the house were nearing collapse, but the property owner refused to pay even for the repair materials. Danny and Ito were a great help, because they were able to wiggle through places under the

51

house that were too restricted for adults. Over a period of several weeks, John had the time and money to buy the materials and install the concrete piers, posts, bell jacks, and timbers. The house would creak and groan as the frame was tortured back to its original alignment. This work required sound judgment and experience. A correction that was too great at one place could initiate a collapse in another.

At first, Ito found the work under the house uncomfortably confining and hard on his nerves. It was no problem for Danny. By working together, it didn't take Ito long to adjust.

As with every piece of real estate, there were always needed repairs. Urgent jobs were completed first, and gradually, a reasonably comfortable and safer house evolved.

Danny and Ito were only eight years of age, but they learned many things about house construction and electrical installations. Most important, they developed an even greater appreciation for Danny's father, and his knowledge and skills.

The same could be said for Mr. Watanabe. He frequently would appear just at the time John needed a helping hand with a particularly difficult task. The two worked together in complete harmony. John commented, "Sugio Watanabe is the best guy to work with that I've ever known. What he doesn't know about carpenter work, he learns the first time he is shown. He's always at 'the right end of the stick.' I've been at this trade most of my life, and he often teaches me a thing or two."

They completed various projects on both homes. Mr. Watanabe commented, "John and I don't count hours, we just get the job done. Time goes by fast, we enjoy our projects. We don't consider it work."

John and Danny had shared some of the wonders of astronomy in years earlier. Now Ito joined them. The hill behind their houses provided a magnificent view of the stars. It was far removed from local street and house lights. Later, Mr. and Mrs. Watanabe accompanied them. Occasionally, they camped overnight on that hill. Mary found the journey too difficult, but Gran was always eager to go with them. The other person missing was Mr. Schmidt. He had a heart condition that precluded strenuous exercise. These occasions contributed to a sense of "an extended family" and pleasure that continued to grow.

Mary surprised John by commenting, "I miss the conveniences of hot and cold running water, and a flush toilet, but it seems to me that we are better off here than in our former home, and our neighbors are so charming, polite, enjoyable, and good Christians."

7

New School Second Grade

An emergency closure of the school had coincided with the move of Danny's family, so it had been possible for the boy and Ito to help with the home repairs.

When school resumed, Danny, his mother, and Ito left home early Monday morning to register Danny. There were two separate second-grade classes, and to his great disappointment, Danny was assigned to Mrs. Rogers, and not to Ito's teacher.

A new kid in school always represents a challenge of some kind, and Danny was no exception. For the teacher, there were questions to be answered. Would he behave himself? Did he have any special needs? Could he keep up with the class? And there is every teacher's hope, almost a prayer, "Let him be a nice boy, not a troublemaker."

Mrs. Rogers followed her routine of introducing Danny to the class, assigning a seat, and asking a girl and a boy to be his special friends for a few days, until he got to know the kids in class and in the school.

Mrs. Rogers was a thoughtful teacher, who avoided putting the new boy under extra pressure in front of students he didn't know. When students were reciting, she kept an eye on him to observe if he appeared familiar with the material, and his willingness to participate. Danny was somewhat shy and was happy to "just be there," without having to talk out in class. Allowing time to become acquainted would help him fit in.

The bell rang for recess and the students swarmed for the door. Mrs. Rogers beckoned for Danny to come to her desk. "Will you please read in this book a few minutes, and then I'll ask you some questions? I want to know if you have any particular reading problems with which I may be able to help you."

"Yes, Mrs. Rogers. How far do you want me to read?"

"Just that first story." Danny read it while Mrs. Rogers worked on her roll book. After a few moments she glanced up. "Daniel, aren't you going to read the story?"

"Yes, Mrs. Rogers, I have."

"Really? Would you like to tell me about it? Did you like it?"

So he told her about the story and how he felt about it.

"Had you read this story before? How is it that you seem to know it so well?"

"I just read it, so I should know it, shouldn't I?" Danny replied.

"Mmmmmm ... Yes ... Yes, I suppose you should. There are a few minutes left for recess. You may want to go to the toilet, and then run around the school yard, but be sure to come back to class when you hear the next bell."

Mrs. Rogers had hit a raw nerve. He remained sensitive to the idea of any woman telling him when to go to the toilet and when not to. He figured he was old enough to hold his own pecker, and he could direct the stream where he wanted it to go, without interference. But she was right. It was a relief to find the boy's toilet. Then Danny went outside and joined in a race around the play shed. All too soon, the bell rang and the children returned to class.

Arithmetic was the subject just after recess. Addition and subtraction problems were presented and taught. Gran had taught Danny this subject before he started school, so he had no problems. Besides, Mrs. Rogers was a good teacher and made things easy to understand.

It was during geography class that Mrs. Rogers absolutely enchanted everyone. She had a personal love affair with Holland. She explained that the name of the nation really was "the Netherlands." Holland was one of several states within the nation, but she asked students for permission to call it Holland, even when she really meant the entire nation. Color photography was in its infancy, but she did have some color prints of tulip fields. She even brought some real tulips to class. Mrs. Rogers read to the class and talked about wooden shoes, canals, cobblestone streets, and clean houses. Her students could almost see little blond boys and girls, and even the storks nesting in chimneys. Magically, bread and cheese for breakfast sounded delicious. But so many of her students were hungry when they came to school, she quickly passed by that topic. They could imagine the dikes, windmills, and on, and on. The class saw the reds, yellows, blues, and greens of fields and even the black-and-white cattle. She created vivid images through the eloquence of her verbal picture painting.

Mrs. Rogers had never been to Holland, and it was unlikely that she would be able to go. But she shared her love for that country with her class. Together, they took glorious vacations through the use of books, stories, and imagination.

Every time a new kid showed up at school, there were challenges to be met. The first order of business was to find out just where he or she belonged in the "pecking order" in the classroom, in the grade, and the entire school. No second grader was going to be much of a challenge to bigger kids in the third or fourth grade, but Danny still had to be taught the proper respect and deference he owed "his elders."

Ito was with Danny. Together, they weathered the swaggering, bumping, posturing, tough words, and displays of the older kids. The challenges came from kids in their own grade.

The principal of the school, Mr. Hill, was also one of the fourth-grade teachers. He was tall, slim, and assigned himself school yard supervision before school, during recess, lunch, and after school. He possessed an acute awareness regarding play yard power struggles. For the most part, he did not interfere. He relied on experience, wisdom, and a sixth sense, to alert him when conflicts were getting out of hand.

The order of things was immediately upset when Danny beat Bobby in a footrace around the play shed. The semi-volatile situation was somewhat defused when Danny told Bobby, "Gosh, I don't know how you can run so fast when you are wearing those heavy boots. I have tennis shoes on, and I barely beat you." This was not said to be tactful, after all, what does a second grader know about tact?

The fact was that each boy was wearing the only shoes he owned. The tension did ease off, but only for a short time. Cecil was ready to assert himself. "Just because you can run fast, don't think you can run away from me."

"Why should I want to run away from you?" Danny asked with not quite the innocence he was pretending.

"Because I'm the guy who can beat you up, and who will tell you how many marbles you have to give me to keep yourself safe. Now, I'm going to hit you in the stomach just to let you know who is your boss."

Danny had been one of the stronger kids at his other school. He would never pick a fight, but he would fight back. This time, he didn't wait. Danny hit Cecil hard right on the Adam's apple. Everyone could see the pain, surprise, and fear well up in Cecil's eyes. His mouth gaped open, as he tried to protest being hit, but he couldn't speak.

Mr. Hill had witnessed some of what had happened, but he didn't hear the conversation prior to Danny throwing the punch. "This is your first day here in school, and already you have had a fight! What do you have to say for yourself?" Mr. Hill asked.

"It wasn't really a fight. Cecil said I had to give him marbles to keep him from beating me up. Then he said he was going to hit me in the stomach just to let me know he meant business. All I did was to hit him first. But we didn't fight."

"Do you plan on having a fight with Cecil later on?"

"No! I don't want to fight anyone, but I won't just stand there and let someone hit me, unless you tell me I have to," Danny replied.

"No, I'd never tell you to do that. I hope you are going to make friends, and like it here at our school. I'll talk with Cecil about what you said, and that you don't want to fight anyone. We'll see how he reacts."

This was Danny's first encounter with Mr. Hill. The boy wondered what it would be like to have him as a teacher, when he got to the fourth grade. He also wondered if Mr. Hill would remember that fight on his first day at that school.

"You'd better be careful," Ito said to Danny. "Cecil has big brothers."

"I didn't want to fight Cecil, and I don't want to fight his brothers, but I'm not going to just stand there and let some kid punch me in the stomach, without doing something about it," Danny replied.

The next morning, Cecil's older twin brothers were waiting

for Danny and Ito at school. They were in the fourth grade and were a lot bigger than most of the rest of the kids because they had failed two classes. They should have been in the sixth grade. "How come you punched Cecil in the neck when he wasn't looking?"

It was Bobby, the runner with the heavy boots, who said, "That isn't the way it happened. Cecil told Danny that he would beat up on him if he didn't bring marbles to school to give to him. He said he was going to punch him in the stomach just to think about. So Danny just punched him first."

"We didn't ask you, Bobby. What have you got to say, Danny?"

"Bobby is right. Cecil did say he was going to hit me, and I believed him. I just hit him before he could hit me. But I don't want to fight Cecil, or you guys, or anyone else."

"Yeah, that sounds like something Cecil would do. You won't have any problem with us. Just don't go around beating up on him, he's still our brother. If he gets crazy and figures he can take you, go ahead and whip him good. Then maybe he'll leave the other kids alone."

"Yeah!" said the other twin. "I'm goin' to tell him that if he picks on you again, just tell us when he's goin' to do it 'cause we want to be there to see him get his butt kicked."

"Thanks."

On the way home that afternoon, Ito said, "Maybe my father will start teaching us *A Way*. It is a self-defense discipline he has talked to me about for at least the last two years. He figured to start lessons any time now. I'll ask him if you can join in, if you want to, and if your dad will let you."

"Gosh, yes! It might be a good idea the way things are here at school."

The next day, Mrs. Rogers's class could hardly wait for the geography lesson, in hopes that she would continue taking them on her dream trip through Holland. She had a wonderful surprise for them. A set of ten books about Holland was on her desk, and that meant that there was one book for every three students. The desks were screwed to the floor so they couldn't be moved together, but students were invited to sit together the best way they could. To make things even better, this was during reading lessons.

"If each of you takes a turn at reading, the other two in your group can make a list of any words you don't know, and words that look hard to spell."

This was a whole new way of teaching and Danny liked it. Kids in Mrs. Rogers's class were accustomed to it, and already had their favorite groups. Three were "left over." Little Teddie had already been pointed out to Danny on the playground as not being any good at anything. The third in Danny's group was an extremely shy little girl, named Ruthie.

It turned out that Ruthie was only afraid to speak out in front of the class, but with just two others, she was a real whiz. Teddie was a paper-and-pencil guy, and he kept the group's records in a systematic manner that most kids would never consider. He was a good reader and liked to do it, but he preferred to keep records. He kept books for each of his team members, and for his group as a whole. Words they didn't know went in one column. A separate spelling list was made for them. He did the same when it was just a problem for one of them. He was an expert at organizing information and figures.

"Slow down, Danny," Teddie said. "You're reading so fast that we can't understand you. Use the same speed you use when you are talking."

Ruthie was a good group member. She was sensitive and caring about the problems, and the people represented in the book. She had her own, unique way of looking at things, and the two boys liked to hear her ideas. She became accustomed to speaking out in their group, and being appreciated.

Then came "terror time." Each group had to make a report to the class about what they had read, their ideas, and words that were difficult to spell or read. Everyone had to participate. Mrs. Rogers picked the trio of Ruthie, Teddie, and Danny to go first. Danny was asked to represent his group as the general spokesperson. This was perfect! Ruthie had less time to be frightened.

"Teddie kept a good list for us, so he should give that report first."

Teddie wrote the list on the board for all to see and announced, "These are our problem words, but we've looked them up in the dictionary. We know them now and we can spell them, too." He sat down and Ruthie and Danny were proud of him. He had shown everyone how really good he was at some things.

Danny gave a general account of what they had read, and then introduced Ruthie. "Teddie and I would have missed lots of the feelings and special ideas in the story, if Ruthie hadn't helped us, so maybe Ruthie will tell you what she told us."

There stood poor little Ruthie in front of all thirty kids. She was in agony. Teddie moved down in front of her and wiggled his finger at Danny to join him. With pleading eyes she looked at the two boys, and started speaking in a weak little voice that could hardly be heard. She was encouraged by the boy's attentive interest. Her voice grew a little stronger. Her attention focused on them, and her ideas tumbled out. When she saw the entire class, her voice would tighten up again, her breathing became similar to that of a panting dog. As a cue, Teddie opened his mouth, blew out all of his air and took a deep breath. Ruthie did the same and her voice came back stronger.

"You have to blow out all the used air, so you'll have room for fresh air," Teddie reminded her. She learned to do that, and it helped her control her feelings of panic.

When she was finished, Teddie went up to her, took her hand, and sat her down between the two boys. They leaned against her and wiggled appreciation. She squirmed, shivered, and smiled her pleading smile. In their own way, they thought of themselves as being the ones on the outside, the leftover three of the class, and perhaps they were. But they had done a good job, and were rightfully proud of themselves.

Mrs. Rogers maximized the potential of this lesson. Geography, reading, spelling, speech, and arithmetic classes were all based on this one program. It took three days to do every group's report and presentation.

For arithmetic, Mrs. Rogers used the number of spelling errors, had students count the number of words per page, add them up, subtract them, and made up all sorts of problems to be added and subtracted. Although division was not a topic for second graders at that time, she did explain how it could be used to find other types of information. She helped her students understand that arithmetic was a useful tool. In her classroom, working

60

with numbers was fun. They were not totally abstract, made-up problems intended to confuse them and keep them busy. Teddie immediately grasped the concept. He was good with numbers.

Mrs. Rogers followed a formula of basing most of a day's or even a week's lessons on a single topic involving the many disciplines she was teaching. A simple, short story of fiction could become a geography lesson when students tried to find the location on a map. They also looked for other sites where it might have happened. When the place was located, it could become a math problem to find out how far it was from their town.

Ruthie, Little Teddie, and Danny continued as working and studying partners throughout the year, and for several years to come. Each improved and learned. Ruthie remained shy and retiring, but could be assertive and take over when necessary. Teddie and Danny appreciated her sensitive nature and learned from her to be more retrospective.

Teddie remained "Little Teddie," the inept kid on the play field, but a force to reckon with when it came to his favorite topic, mathematics. And his organizational skills were much admired. He wasn't good at everything he did, but he was respected in the classroom.

One evening, the beginning of a new form of education was introduced. Danny later realized it was based more on mental, than physical, activity. Mr. Watanabe called it *A Way*. As he said, "There are many directions in life a person may go. Stress and conflict are a part of everyone's life. What we will learn is just *A Way*, but not the only way, of dealing with such stress and conflict. With this discipline, we attempt to find solutions to problems. There are times when combat will occur. This mental and physical discipline will help you achieve your main objective. You will find it is the most gentle, kind, and least injurious method you can use to defend yourself. You should always try to convey respect to an opponent, even though this may be the most difficult task you face.

"*A Way* is a lifetime study involving, among other things, self-evaluation. The ultimate goal is to redirect negative energy, your own or an opponent's, in a manner that will be most constructive. If that is not possible, your actions should be the least destructive alternative. The mental discipline is more difficult to learn than the physical," Father Watanabe concluded.

So, Ito and Danny studied and practiced *A Way*, not just the thirty-minute sessions with Father Watanabe. It truly was a foundation of *A Way of Life*.

The trouble with Cecil remained fresh in Danny's mind, and he wanted to be sure of being able to beat him up, if Cecil tried picking another fight. That was an attitude that represented what Father Watanabe called *A Different Way,* a way that should be avoided. Attention should be focused on preventing further problems.

One major benefit of *A Way* was the awareness that there are often many satisfactory ways to preclude conflict. Being able to convey regard for the other person was one of the most powerful forces in conflict resolution. Confidence in one's own skills in combat, if all else fails, was another. But these were abstract concepts for boys, who were only eight years old. The *A Way* program was not a quick fix for problems of the moment.

For the remainder of their lives, Ito and Danny practiced the discipline of Father Watanabe's *A Way*. They did not always succeed, but it was their guiding philosophy and motivation.

8

Mr. Schmidt's Background

Hannes Schmidt was born in 1869, the youngest of four boys and three girls. His father, Willie Schmidt, was a farrier, who was highly respected in his community in Hamburg, Germany. His success with shoeing horses was partly due to his uncanny ability to watch an animal walk, trot, and gallop, and then diagnose what he could do to help the animal move more efficiently. He did this by adapting shoes to a special design and custom fit. Horses from other farriers sometimes were brought to him with hooves that had been trimmed and shod incorrectly. Subsequently, they had gone lame. If the condition could be reversed, he would correct it.

He was sought out by owners of racehorses and by military personnel, because their horses always ran faster after he had diagnosed, treated, and shod them. In addition to being a farrier, he was expected to be a good animal doctor, pharmacist, and general-purpose blacksmith. Willie Schmidt was expert at his father's disciplines. He counted among his clientele many of the most politically important and financially influential people in Hamburg.

It was common in the nineteenth century for a man to instruct his sons in the methods and techniques of his trade or profession. Such was the case with Willie Schmidt and his four sons. Each became an expert farrier in his own right. The "right of the firstborn" was established law in Germany, and this meant that only the eldest son would inherit the property and business of his father. The other three sons had to leave the premises and establish their own businesses, well away from where they would compete with their father and elder brother. Alternatively, the younger ones had to forgo independence, and work for the older brother.

Hamburg was a large commercial city, seaport, and transportation hub for northern Germany. Thousands of horses were in daily use. The surrounding agricultural area depended on horses. Use of tractors to replace horses was a generation or two away. There were adequate opportunities for the four sons to establish their own businesses in the areas surrounding the city. Their father had been so successful, he was able to provide money to help each of his sons launch his own blacksmith shop and also provide an attractive dowry for his daughters.

Many people thought young Hannes Schmidt had inherited his mother's inquisitive nature. His interests went beyond the family tradition of being the best farriers in the area. He developed metallurgical skills beyond those needed as a farrier. He journeyed to Solingen to learn about making knives, swords, and table cutlery. From there he returned to the great blast furnaces and steel-making centers in the Ruhr Valley. His greatest interest was to develop a blade that would sharpen easily and hold an edge, even during prolonged and abusive conditions.

He was called "Young Hannes" to distinguish him from his father. He might have remained in either Solingen or the Ruhr Valley except for his preoccupation and love for a young lady in Hamburg. It was time to return home, marry, and get on with his life. At the relatively advanced age of twenty-five, Young Hannes married Helga. They celebrated their marriage during the following eight years by producing four greatly loved and cherished children.

The roads in and out of Hamburg were frequently surfaced with *katzkopf* Cobblestones. These were domed stones, similar in shape to a cat's skull, hence their name, cat's heads. Normal, malleable horseshoes would rapidly wear out when subjected to such surfaces. Young Hannes started experimenting with a totally unique technique of "hard facing" critical areas of wear on the shoes, and they lasted three to four times longer than normal. The shoes still needed to be removed so hooves could be trimmed but "downtime" for the horses was greatly reduced and the cost was also less over a period of time. As a result, important political, military, and police officials became clients of Hannes Schmidt, and by 1913, the German military officially became aware of the Schmidt innovations. His presence was requested by the Kaiser and refusal was unthinkable. Hannes's family remained in their home in Hamburg. During the subsequent months of demonstrating his skills and lecturing, Hannes was kept so busy there was seldom time for him to join his family, even for a weekend.

Two events shattered the life of Herr Hannes Schmidt. The first was the assassination of Archduke Ferdinand, which plunged Germany into World War I. This was followed by a cholera epidemic that swept through the section of Hamburg where Hannes's family lived. His entire family died. His grief was so great that he simply lost interest in life.

He was well beyond the normal age for military service, but Hannes was inducted into the German army to continue the work he had done as a civilian. He cared for the welfare of the horses ridden by headquarters personnel. A quirk of fate placed him well away from headquarters, and he was captured in a surprise raid by British troops. His special skills in dealing with horses were soon recognized, and he was transported to Britain as a prisoner of war. He spent the remainder of "the Great War" caring for the horses in the Royal Stables in London. Hannes became known as Mr. Schmidt and was well established in his field when the war ended. His extensive English vocabulary was spoken with a Hamburg, Germany, accent.

Hannes had become highly respected and totally accepted at the Royal Stables, but he was German, and many returning British farriers were ready to assume the position he held. He was relieved of his post and faced repatriation to Germany, but his native land held too many memories of anguish and loss. Instead, he joined the flood of Europeans who entered the United States passing by the great lady of freedom at the entrance of the New York harbor. In addition to his professional tools, he brought his knowledge, skills, accent, and some books, which were written in German, that he purchased in used-book stores in London.

Wherever he worked, Hannes did a superb job and was recognized for his skills, high standards, and hard work. Curiosity and willy-nilly traveling led him to the West Coast of the United States. In Oregon, he purchased fifteen acres of land complete with a large house, barn, blacksmith workshop, and several other outbuildings where he practiced his skills and trade. He foresaw the demise of his occupation as a farrier with the advent of the wheel tractors, some of which were already on rubber tires. The development of the Holt Tractor in Stockton, California, which became the Caterpillar Tractor, would replace horses in the logging industry throughout the nation. Still, he had more than an adequate income to meet his modest requirements and to maintain a viable lifestyle. His financial status seemed sound. He owed no money and had a substantial cash reserve in the local bank ... plus a portfolio in stocks and bonds.

Fate had dealt Mr. Schmidt many devastating blows including the 1915–1918 war and the cholera epidemic. But bitter fate was not through with him yet. The stock market crash of 1929 wiped him out financially. He was still able to farm his own land and care for the horses, cattle, and other animals in the community. He made a living, which was about what most people were trying to do. The additional hammer blow fell in the latter part of 1931. He developed a severe case of scarlet fever! Most frequently a childhood disease, it was not readily diagnosed. This delay may have been a factor in leaving him with badly damaged heart valves. Now he was virtually incapable of participating in the rigorous pursuits of his trade, and barely able to farm part of his own land in order to raise his food.

Mr. Schmidt found himself in the dilemma shared by others of his age and circumstances. They had property they could neither work nor maintain. Their cash investment reserves had been taken from them by the vagaries of an uncontrolled economy. They owned property, for which there was virtually no market, because almost no one had any money. Property taxes had to be paid, and the owners were thought of as being "land poor."

He was better off than most men. He had no family for whom he was responsible. He did have a place to live. He could collect the eggs from the chickens, harvest the honey he ate from the bounty the bees provided, and he could milk three cows. A bonus was a cow that had just one horn. Somehow that cow associated the up and down movement of the pump handle with water. She took over the chore of keeping herself and his other two cows well supplied.

Days and weeks of being physically unable to do anything

beyond the absolute essentials, prompted Hannes to place a FOR SALE sign in front of home near the road. There it remained becoming semi-obscured by Canadian thistles. It was unattended and unheeded. The thistles grew, bloomed, spread seeds on the wind with little white parachutes, and then died, just as Mr. Schmidt's hopes for the sign fulfilling any purpose had died.

The winter of 1932 had been bleak for many people throughout the world. People were hungry everywhere, and yet farmers produced huge surplus quantities of food they could not sell. The systems of banking and distribution had broken down.

Mr. Schmidt considered himself lucky. He had survived the winter by closing off most of his house. His large kitchen had been converted to serve as his bedroom and living area. The heat that cooked his meals also provided the warmth he needed when the weather outside dipped to near-freezing levels. In this manner he had conserved his wood supply and it looked as if he would be able to last another year as well. A new vegetable crop would be essential, but for the moment he was okay.

Although his heart condition would not improve appreciably, Mr. Schmidt learned to compensate for his weakness by being more efficient in the use of his energy. He planted a little corn, some potatoes, onions, and other vegetables for his own use. His fruit orchard had to get along without the usual pruning and other care. Farmers were anxious to use his skills at diagnosing animal ills. They could not pay him cash, but a sack of wheat or oats and hay would be exchanged for his services. Several households depended on him to supply their need for milk, butter, and eggs, and yet, his future appeared bleak to him. He did not think of applying for assistance from the very people he was helping.

9

Watanabe Family Background

Mr. and Mrs. Watanabe had been born, reared, educated, and married in Japan. Their parents had worked in the household of an American missionary couple. Both at school and at home they had learned American English. From early childhood, their exposure to English and Japanese was so evenly balanced, they were equally familiar with each language. Only a touch of a Japanese accent could be heard in their American variant of the English language. In Japan, their respective homes were over a mile apart, but they, and about a dozen other children, made up the school's first group of students.

They were not typically Japanese in their attitudes and spirit of adventure, nor were they Americans. They were a part of the unique group of world citizens who became known as Japanese Americans. As such, they were renounced by the Japanese and rejected by Americans.

From early childhood, Mr. Watanabe's father had instructed him in a system of self-defense, and also offense, that was totally passive in the former state, and equally deadly when used offensively. He referred to it as *A Way*. Both systems demanded complete self-control and elimination of emotional involvement.

In light of their similar background and the occupation of their parents, it was recognized that, in time, the two youngsters would be married. Time passed and they assumed adult responsibilities in the church community, and assisted their parents and the missionaries with their projects.

For undefined reasons, members of the community rioted and attacked the missionary school. One missionary was killed, as well as both parents of the future Mrs. Watanabe. Following the teachings of his combat training, young Watanabe assumed an offensive role in combat, and efficiently dispatched three of the attackers. His father had to restrain him from further pursuit of his deadly retaliation.

The mission school remained, the American personnel were replaced, and it was deemed advisable, even imperative, for young Mr. Watanabe and his wife-to-be to leave the community, and better still, to leave Japan.

Mrs. Watanabe had been trained in a different and unique discipline, which she called *A Different Way*. The primary function of her studies was to access many dozens of nerve centers to produce a variety of sensations. Most were comforting, relaxing, and even erotic. But special direction and intensity of application with the fingers could produce agonizing and even temporary paralyzing effects.

In 1924, Mr. and Mrs. Watanabe were married and immigrated to the United States. They worked in a variety of jobs, primarily as servants for wealthy Americans. They worked hard, lived frugally, and saved all the money they could. In 1927, Ito, their son and only child, was born. Their employers held the Watanabe family in high esteem and when the 1929 stock market crash occurred, they remained employed until 1932. Then, due to the deepening of the Depression, they had to be let go.

Most people in the United States had placed their savings and investment money in banks and in the stock market. With the stock market crash and the subsequent rapid bank failures, money was something most people didn't have. The Watanabe family was an exception. They had a modest amount of cash in their own "bank." Their bank consisted of many one-pound coffee cans filled with silver dollars. Following the stock market crash and bank failures, their reserve of silver dollars became a significantly large resource.

The Watanabe family had originally come from a farming background, even though their parents also had worked at the mission school in Japan. They knew how to live off the land. Then one day while walking through the community, Mr. Watanabe observed the old FOR SALE sign that Mr. Schmidt had placed there the previous fall.

Mr. Schmidt, whose German background and upbringing left him talking with a distinct German accent, was astounded when a Japanese man approached him speaking almost flawless

American English with a West Coast accent. He was delighted when he saw Mr. Watanabe was carrying the homemade FOR SALE sign. The two foreign-born men negotiated a price that pleased each of them. Mr. Schmidt had in his hands 101 brightly shining silver dollars when Mr. Watanabe left, and the promise that the balance would be placed in his hands that same afternoon. It was.

The two men took an immediate liking to each other, most likely because they treated each other with genuine respect and appreciation. The house had five bedrooms, but Mr. Schmidt had lived there alone for many years. He had been a good housekeeper in former times, and the kitchen-bedroom arrangement he currently lived in was immaculately clean and tidy. The remainder of the house was closed. When it was opened, the usual accumulation of dust and spiderwebs offered evidence of disuse.

Mrs. Watanabe, as was the case with her husband, felt instant esteem for Mr. Schmidt. Their son, Ito, discovered an additional source of wisdom in Mr. Schmidt, who represented a different point of view and culture.

It seemed completely natural that Mr. Schmidt would remain in his home, even though he had sold it. He resumed taking care of the flowers and trees as best he could. Mr. Watanabe assumed the heavier work, and Mr. Schmidt enjoyed caring for his beehives. His way of tending his bees was so slow and gentle that there was no need to wear protective clothing. He simply did not get stung, even when he was removing frames of honey.

For once, fate had dealt Mr. Schmidt a winning hand. From years of emotional darkness, he bloomed in a family environment of affection and regard.

No one in the community seemed to know about the arrangements Mr. Schmidt had about paying for living with the Watanabe family, and it was a point of speculation among the "busybody" people of the area. The only thing they knew was that Mr. Schmidt had what was considered a huge pile of the silver dollars he had been paid for the house and property. Strangely enough, he still lived in the house and didn't buy food for himself.

Mr. Schmidt milked the cow, and Ito would accompany him to the barn and collect the eggs. It wasn't long before Ito was helping with the milking. He was a little young to do the final "stripping," which was the last part and was supposed to be the richest milk, because it had the most butterfat. But time, experience, and increasing strength quickly took care of that.

Mr. Schmidt enjoyed doing as many chores around the home as possible, and gratefully accepted his position as a family member. According to the community, it was a strange household, but harmless. The fifteen-acre plot, with the house set just forward of the center, was semi-isolated, particularly in view of the fact that the two-acre lot and house to the west had been vacant for several years. This was the land and house that John rented, and later purchased. The ten acres and house to the west of John's home was frequently vacant until the late 1930s.

For Mr. Schmidt, life ceased to be a daily struggle to survive. One of the most impressive things every visitor to the Watanabe-Schmidt household observed was that consideration and love dominated every interchange of ideas and activity. Danny and Ito were surrounded by these positive influences.

Following the move of John and family next door to the Schmidt-Watanabe household, Ito and Danny shared so much time together they were almost always at one house or the other.

Mr. Schmidt was a gold mine of information about forging and tempering iron and steel, and making various metal items. He enjoyed being asked about the techniques of his trade. Ito and Danny appreciated being in Mr. Schmidt's workshop, and also found the barn delightful. Loose hay provided a cushion in which they could jump from platforms and do some gymnastic activities. They could practice *A Way* throws and falls without being concerned about hard impact with floors or the ground.

Mr. Schmidt's forge and foundry occupied an isolated section of that barn, and was a place where fascinating metal things could be made. On his better days, he might go to his workshop and make wind toys. The boys were delighted to observe his techniques of making things from iron and steel. During his working years, knife making was something that he had always intended to do but never had time to undertake. Now he had the time, but not the physical stamina for long periods of activity.

With Ito and Danny there to do the heavy work, he could pursue his interest even though he was not well enough to do some types of the physical labor. In addition to his own knowledge, he had his extensive library to consult. Even more, he shared the boys' interest in experimenting with proven techniques. As the boys were nearing the end of their second year in school, he started teaching them how to use blacksmith tools.

A few weeks later Ito's father was given a doe rabbit as partial payment for a repair job he had done. Another man let him borrow a buck for a few hours. Raising rabbits was no problem, although it did take time and work. The boys collected the buck and put the two rabbits together in the same pen. The pair sniffed and circled. In about a minute he mounted her. He humped and pumped madly and hung on for dear life, but he didn't seem to be accomplishing anything. Then it was her turn. She flattened her back, raised her hind end and the buck went wild. When she squealed, the buck went rigid and fell off sideways.

"Gosh, Danny, do you think he's dead or something?" Ito asked.

Before he could answer, the buck got up, started circling around as if he were dizzy, or dazed, or something. Then they sniffed a couple times, and they were at it again.

"Wow, how many times do you think that's supposed to happen?"

After four or five times the buck went off by himself to investigate the food supply. The doe had a good pee and they didn't pay much attention to each other. "It looks as if they are done."

Hay and grass was available along the roadside and from what the cows ate so no additional expense was incurred. Thus another supply of meat was available to both families because they shared the fruits of their combined labor.

72

10

Mrs. Bass, Third Grade

For Danny, school still offered an underlying dread. As he progressed to the third grade, on that first day, would he walk into the class and find another "Miss Choke"? But fate was kind and his new teacher was Mrs. Bass, who shared some of Gran's remarkable qualities of caring and understanding. One of her lessons came as a complete surprise, because it dealt with chickens. It involved arithmetic, biology, cooking, vocabulary, spelling, and how to raise some of the food that was lacking in many households. This food lesson required sensitivity and compassion, because nearly half of her students came to school hungry.

"How many of you raise chickens at your house?" Mrs. Bass asked as she pointed to the blackboard where the word *chicken* was written. Three hands, including Danny's, went up.

"And what are chickens good for?"

"Eating!" That enthusiastic response was unanimous. Mrs. Bass wrote on the board, each word that she thought might be a source of spelling difficulty or new to the students' vocabularies.

"Are they good for anything else?"

"Eggs to eat," Joy offered.

"People make feather pillows." Both words were written on the board.

"Poop to mess up the place," Donald offered, and everyone laughed, including the teacher.

The word *poop* was put on the board. "Do you know a nicer word for poop?"

"Number two," Chuck offered. He held up his hand with two fingers extended.

Shy little Inez said, "There is that word that starts with an *s*, but I don't think it is a very nice word. My father says it and my mom gives him the devil for saying it in front of us kids."

73

Mrs. Bass wrote several terms or words on the blackboard: *number two, s-word, feces, manure,* and *stool.* "I think we all know that 's-word' and will agree with Inez's mother that most people do not use it in polite company. Now, back to the chickens, and our list of words."

"Making more chicks, or chickens, but you need a hen and a rooster," Danny replied.

Mrs. Bass added the words *chicks, rooster,* and *hen* to the list.

"Why do you need a chicken and a rooster?" Julie asked in all innocence. Stifled snickers erupted. Most kids wondered how *that* question would be answered.

"To dust off the hen." Danny said. "Just like people, you need a mommy and a daddy." Danny started to tell the class about their big red rooster.

"Our Big Red Rooster has spurs that are two inches long and he rules the chicken yard. When we throw special treats to the chickens, he's the first one there. He will call the hens, stand in the middle of the treat, and spread it out. He takes credit for it. 'Dusting off' a hen or two is his reward. Other roosters are in the chicken yard, but they have been defeated in cockfights so often they just wait around the fringe of things. They get beaten up in almost daily battles. So they became hit-and-run experts. One will claim a hen, dust her off, and run like crazy when the big rooster comes after him. Then another rooster will have his chance while they are playing tag, only they weren't playing. I've seen that big rooster hurt one so much that we had to 'put him in the pot.' But that—"

"What do you mean when you said you 'put him in the pot'?" Lois asked.

"What do you suppose he means, dummy?" Jimmy asked. "Chop his head off, pull out all the feathers, gut him out, and cook him."

A gasp went out from most of the kids in class. Not because of the graphic description of what had happened to the rooster. They knew about that, but showing any classmate disrespect, by calling her "dummy," simply was not the way to behave in this class. Jimmy immediately left his seat and apologized. He wasn't told to do so. It was how things were done, because of the influence of Mrs. Bass. If she felt she had been harsh in her treatment of a student, she immediately went to that youngster to make things right. She led by example. "There are occasions when I let things slip out of my mouth, some of which are not well thought out. Other words sound harsh, and are not what I really wanted to say. There are many excuses for making mistakes, and we all make them. However, we should correct our errors before there is time for resentment, anger, or hurt to build up." She set the example that many students followed throughout their lives.

Pauline asked, "What did you mean when you said, 'the rooster dusted off a hen'?"

"That means he screwed them," Eleanor quickly replied. Suddenly she felt embarrassed by her impulsive remark. Nervous laughter radiated around the room.

Mrs. Bass dealt with "naughty words" in a manner that made them less sensational. "We all need a large vocabulary to be able to communicate with everyone. This means we will know words that are not normally used in public. But you should still know them. An important part of being well educated involves having a large and picturesque vocabulary. Equally important is selecting the words that are appropriate for the situation.

"How many chickens do you have, Danny?"

"That depends. Usually we have thirty. That Big Red Rooster is daddy to most of the younger ones. We keep about twelve hens for eggs, and some of the hens grow up to replace the older ones. The others ... well, we have chicken or rabbit dinner most Sundays, with mashed potatoes, peas, beans, and gravy."

"Yum," escaped the lips from most of the class.

"How many eggs do most hens lay each day?"

Elmer replied, "Usually one egg from each hen during good weather. When winter comes, they don't lay as often ... sometimes only one egg a week, but my folks sell some eggs to help pay our grocery bill."

The most poignant question came from Danny's little partner, Ruthie, who was always hungry. "Danny, what do you do with all your extra eggs?"

"My mother gives them to some of the elderly people at our

church, who don't have enough to eat. She'll give away a chicken, when we get too many of them."

"Little kids get hungry, too," Ruthie said almost inaudibly. Her father had died when she was in the first grade, and her mother had a difficult time providing a home and food to eat.

When Danny's mother heard about little Ruthie, she added an extra hard-boiled egg and a big sandwich to his lunch bag for her.

Danny's mother had asked about the wheat kernels she found in his pants pocket one washday. "Well, Ruthie doesn't have any breakfast, so I take some wheat to school with me. She soaks the kernels in her mouth. Before long she can chew it, and that fills her up a little. She saves the egg and sandwich until lunchtime so everyone can see that she has food, too."

"Gracious! We are blessed!" From then on, Mary made up extra oatmeal mush and put it in small bucket with a tightly fitting, clamp-down lid. She added a generous supply of sugar or honey, and lots of milk with thick cream. Danny took this to school and Mrs. Bass, who always understood such circumstances, allowed Danny to leave it in her room before school. When Ruthie arrived, she ate her breakfast without other kids knowing. If they had found out, Ruthie would have been embarrassed.

When Danny's father, John, heard what was happening, Mary was a little fearful that he might object, and she pleaded, "We always wanted a daughter, and then the Depression came, and your back was broken, we lost our house, and things were tough ... still are, but we can manage this little bit for Ruthie, can't we?" His understanding smile said all that was needed.

"Danny," his father called, "how are we doing with rabbits and chickens? Count how many we have and let me know."

That Saturday afternoon John killed an extra chicken, climbed on his bicycle, and delivered it to Ruthie's home. When he returned, he said to Mary, "They have been living on boiled potatoes, carrots, and cabbage as their evening meal, and not much else. Ruthie's mother cried when I gave her the chicken. It will go in the pot with the vegetables and should last all week. Tsugio suggested I should take a rabbit next week. We can do that for them. Danny, will you and Ito keep us ahead of the game, as far as rabbit and chicken breeding is concerned?"

76

"The problem is nationwide," Gran said. "There are so many in the same situation. We can't help them all, but we must do our bit."

Danny's entire family felt united strength when Mary commented, with a good deal of satisfaction, "We can help this one family ... especially Ruthie." John's attention seemed to wander as if searching the past. His thoughts drifted back to his childhood days, when he made his daily patrol of the restaurant's garbage cans for any scraps that could be used to help make a meal. He looked at Gran, and under his breath he said, "We know what it's like to be hungry."

John found his mother's eyes riveted on his, and she nodded. "That we do, Jackie, me lad, that we do." Apparently Gran was reliving those desperate days in London as well. She had not called him Jack or Jackie for ... how many years had it been?

"Which was worse," Gran wondered, "the hunger or the humiliation?"

The following day, Mrs. Bass continued the lesson about chickens, dealing with questions involving simple addition and subtraction and some multiplication. "If twelve chickens lay one egg each, how many eggs will they lay in a week?" "Four people eat one egg a day. How many eggs will they eat in a week?" "Twelve eggs a day for twelve days equal how many eggs?" "If you eat a chicken each Sunday, how many chickens will you eat in a year?" Little Teddie always had the answer first, but he gave everyone else a chance to answer. Then Mrs. Bass would ask, "Is that the correct answer, Teddie?" He was admired for his quick and accurate answers.

Mrs. Bass knew the impact the talk about food would have on hungry kids. The school lunchroom was all the way to the other end of the building, but hungry kids thought they smelled chicken cooking. The power of suggestion was overwhelming.

"How many chickens would be needed to serve a class of this size, if each chicken were cut into ten pieces?" Mrs. Bass asked.

Immediately, kids were counting noses. "Twenty-nine people," Bruce shouted.

"No, there are thirty of us, you forgot Mrs. Bass, or yourself," Bobby corrected.

77

A chorus of students affirmed, "Yes, thirty. We would need three chickens."

Mrs. Bass asked, "If each person eats two pieces of chicken, then how many?"

The class answered in unison, "Six chickens."

"Now suppose potatoes weigh four ounces each, and every student wanted a potato. How many pounds of potatoes would we need for everyone?"

The math questions continued in rapid succession, and answers were accompanied by hunger.

The time was eleven o'clock. "Shall we go to the lunchroom and find out what's cooking?" Mrs. Bass asked. This was beyond the kids' comprehension. They shifted in their seats and stared with wide eyes at Mrs. Bass, then at each other. It wasn't until she left her seat and started for the door that a buzz of excitement and activity took place in the room. No one had to tell the kids to be quiet in the hall. They knew they should not disturb other classes, particularly this day.

The menu was as described in the math problems, except green peas and corn were added. Three extra chickens had been cooked and four extra pounds of potatoes as well.

By the time everyone had just about eaten their fill, one youngster's dad, who had come to help prepare the meal, announced, "There are nine necks and pope's noses left for anyone who can eat them." There wasn't a scramble to get them, but each child who wanted more could have it. Even Big James figured he'd eaten enough ... and so did little Ruthie.

"How many want oatmeal and raisin cookies? There are three each." A cheer of enthusiasm erupted. Everyone was full, but kids always had room for cookies. That class party happened only that one time in the history of the school. Perhaps it didn't need to happen again. Miracles are seldom repeated, but it did happen that one time in Mrs. Bass's third-grade class, when kids were so hungry.

Before summer vacation, Ruthie took Danny's hand and brought it to her chin as if she wanted to talk to it. "My mother just got a job and we have our own food now." Her eyes were filled with adoration and gratitude.

11

Watanabe Family Work

Subsistence farming on their fifteen-acre plot maintained the Watanabe family and Mr. Schmidt with virtually everything they needed. Resourceful planning and hard work provided the essential cash reserves that even the most independent and hardworking family needed.

A year after coming to the community, Mr. Watanabe was approached by Neal, the local plumber. "Would you dig out a septic tank and leach line for Jim's widow? It's totally clogged with willow roots. I told Jim years ago that there would be problems, but he didn't listen. Now he's dead and his widow can't afford for me to do the job, and she has no family in the area. She couldn't afford to pay you very much, but she needs the help."

"Yes, it would be my pleasure to be of help. Will you be able to connect the line again, and provide a chemical that will retard the root growth?"

"I can sell her the chemicals, but I can't afford to give them to her."

It was known in the community that when there was some particularly dirty or unpleasant task that needed doing, "That Japanese man could do it." They knew him to be both honorable and compassionate, and in hard times, this was not a common combination.

As time went by, Mr. Watanabe was also known to be particularly skillful in mending clocks, electric motors, and other such things. Of course, if you had a really good clock, you took it to the local jeweler. But Mr. Watanabe's work was always on the peripheral margins of the community's business. He provided a valuable service, but did not compete with the professionals for jobs.

John and Mr. Watanabe shared the yearly ten-dollar rent-al fee on ten acres of wild rosebushes, willow trees, Canadian thistles, weeds, and grass that was part of the Southern Pacific Railroad right-of-way. Uncharacteristic of Japanese of that era, they also had a cow that provided the milk for making butter and cottage cheese. The yearly birth of a calf meant there would always be milk, as well as meat for the table.

By 1937 the effects of the Great Depression had started to wane. The workforce of America was beginning to find jobs. Fewer people were in desperate financial trouble. The fear of spending a little money that had been put away for emergency needs was being replaced by a willingness to invest in much-needed repairs to homes, buying basic furniture, bedding, automobiles, and other items. That, in turn, put more people to work, which gave them money to spend. Whether Republican or Democrat, it was a fact that President Roosevelt's program of "Spending the nation back to work" was having a positive effect.

The impending conflict in Europe was signaling the nation that it needed to become functional. Private and government financing of businesses, development of resources, public works programs, and general faith in the ability of the nation's people to work and purchase products opened the job market for millions of people.

The "family grocery store" served people who lived within an eight- to ten-block radius. Generally, women did the grocery shopping on foot. Housewives would take their shopping lists to the store, and the weekly orders would be delivered.

Mr. Watanabe was renowned in the community for integrity, hard work, being polite, and thorough, and considerate. It was no surprise when he was hired to work in a local grocery store. He proved to be an accomplished butcher, as well as a good produce man. In an era when the roast you wanted to have for Sunday dinner was going to be cut before your eyes, it was good to have a man who knew how to slice the meat so it would provide the most tender and savory cut possible. "That roast is extra lean," he would comment as he weighed it and marked the price. "If you cook this piece of fat with it, you can make more gravy, and the flavor of the meat may be improved." The extra fat was added *after* the price had been marked. Customers felt they were being given a bonus for their purchase: a bonus in food, service, and consideration. They returned to the same store, particularly when the Japanese gentleman would be available to serve and deliver the groceries for them.

The store clerks picked out the lettuce, potatoes, tomatoes, peaches, and other items they were going to deliver to the customer's home. All customers wanted Mr. Watanabe to select and deliver their groceries. His influence increased the popularity and profitability of the store.

Most stores had a policy that bruised or partially damaged fruit and vegetables should be "passed off" on those who were not wary. Produce was displayed with the good side up, and put in the bag of the customer who wasn't watchful. A couple of poor-quality items could be delivered to someone's home. Mr. Watanabe changed that policy for the store that employed him. He placed "damaged goods" on a special counter, where a customer could select the best of the damaged, and buy it at a reasonably reduced price. They made their choice. He frequently asked, "Are you going to use it today? If so, this will be a better buy. But don't keep it until tomorrow, or it will be past its prime."

Customers knew the days Mr. Watanabe would deliver groceries and they delayed orders until he was going their direction. Occasionally he would add a special bonus to a purchase. The bonus might be a head of cabbage or lettuce, a pear, or an apple, et cetera, from his own garden. It was a special gift from his home to the home of the loyal customer. Both the store and the customer benefited. Father Watanabe was pleased to be able to share the fruits of his labor that were surplus to his family's needs. With the return to "good times," it no longer was imperative to raise or grow most of the produce the family needed. A few elderly people in the community were without family to care for them. Several of them had lost their savings in the bank failures that were part of the Great Depression. For them, the resurgence of the economy came too late. They were unable to resume work and had virtually nothing. Some of these people also needed help with daily living, because they were too infirmed to care for themselves. Neighbors helped, and so did Gran and Mrs. Watanabe. The Watanabe family helped by providing some of the fruit and vegetables they needed. Gran helped by dropping by to give a hand "tidying up the place." Ito and Danny made sure that eggs and an occasional chicken or rabbit was available for some tables. In a small community, people tried to aid each other when circumstances made it impossible to care for oneself. It was a community that had respect and concern for the less fortunate. And there were those who spoke out against people who referred to the Watanabe family members as "those foreigners."

There had been years when classmates came to school with all the water they wanted to drink as breakfast. Lunch had consisted of a slice of bread, and dinner had been boiled potatoes embellished with salt. When their fathers worked and had a bit of money, the first thing they purchased was tobacco. Kids could go hungry, but their dads would have their tobacco. Even though almost all households had a yard large enough to raise a garden, some of these people simply were not willing to plant, tend, and harvest. Parental leadership was lacking.

Ito and Dan gave one kid a pregnant rabbit thinking it would get his family started raising some meat. They learned later that it had been too much trouble to take care of the rabbit, so they ate it. That rabbit could have provided them with a litter of little ones that would provide Sunday dinners for several months. These, in turn could make a lot more rabbits that could be eaten or sold. There was plenty of roadside grass available for feed. All it would take was the time and willingness to cut and feed it to the rabbits.

"Don't be too disappointed, boys," Father Watanabe said. "There are some people who are unable to make a connection between planning and working for a goal, and immediate consumption. I don't know why, but they are just that way. Immediate hunger is also a compelling force. Your mother and I hope you will never face such extreme conditions."

In times of stress, Father Watanabe invited the two boys to join him in *A Way* meditation and then, later, the physical part of defending themselves against attack. "Remember, you must be at peace with yourself, and have no hatred for anyone who attacks you, if you want to be most proficient in your defense." They concentrated and practiced this "art of living" many times daily.

The boys were learning lessons about life, and so were some of the local residents.

12

Cow Hunting

There were times when the cows would wander their ten-acre pasture and not come in to be milked. Calling produced no results. A cowbell was placed on a large collar around one cow's neck in hopes the noise would guide the boys to the errant critters. The bell would clang with any of the cow's movements. But, on some occasions, the cow would stand motionless for seemingly hours on end. There was no audible sound to guide the boys.

This was terribly frustrating, and occasionally, the boys had to search for hours. This seemed to happen most frequently when it was dark and raining. Gran's admonition, "No use grumblin', get on with the job," would echo in their minds. They couldn't see the cows because of the frequent wild rosebushes that were up to ten feet tall and as large around. Also, there was a growth of willow trees that was about a hundred yards long and seventy feet wide. In the ten acres, there were many places for those cows to hide.

Father Watanabe said, "Compose yourself. Realize that the cows have not formed a conspiracy against you. What are they doing when you do find them?"

"They are just chewing their cud," Ito commented. He was annoyed.

"What do you know about a cow that's doing that?" he asked.

"They're content and don't like to be disturbed. Generally, they have had a good day of grazing and don't want to eat anything else for a while."

"Perhaps you should observe the cows more closely. Do they continue to chew when they are walking?"

"I don't know," Ito replied.

"Could you be more observant? We know that when one of her stomachs is full, she needs to belch up the cud for rechewing, so she can swallow it into the second stomach for digestion. She won't be hungry or active until she has completed that, unless she is forced to move. Be happy for the cows, because they are full and content. You may like to think more as a cow might."

Both boys protested, "But it is time for them to be fed and milked. We have to finish our chores and they won't let us."

"Is it possible that cows don't always keep the same time as people do? I ask these questions so you will understand that part of nature better. Remember our *A Way* training. Inner peace and tranquility are essential to turn negative forces into positive ones."

Gran's wisdom was added at another time, "No matter how difficult the task, ye should look for the fun that can be found while doing it. Ye both be good at games, so make a game out of what must be done."

The boys knew they would occasionally have to hunt the cows. It would help to know what areas the cows would *not* be in as well as where they *might* be.

They went during good weather to survey the situation. They kept up a running conversation between them. "The cow flops are the first clue as to where the cows are grazing."

"That looks like good grazing area because of long, green grass, but the cow flops are old. They aren't eating here. Those flops are overgrown with lush grass."

"They are grazing here. The flops are either fresh or old and decomposing to earth. There must be a smell or taste to the grass that the cows don't like when the flops were only a year or so old. The pasture is large enough to allow them to choose. It looks as if about two-thirds of the area can be eliminated each year. The cows don't even go there, except to walk through it. Maybe that's next year's area."

"There aren't any cow trails through the willow thicket, so we don't even have to go through there, but it would make a good hiding place. Wait a minute, I still have to remind myself that they aren't hiding from us."

So the boys did make a game out of finding the cows. They'd start on a day when it wasn't raining and it was fun to be outdoors. Ito initiated a different approach from their usual noisy blundering around. Stealth became their method of searching.

They spread out and tried to be as quiet as the cows. The boys became aware of changes in what they heard from birds, insects, wind through the rosebushes, and other sources of sound. Ito had particularly acute hearing. From a distance he could hear the rumble of the cow's belch as she brought up cud for rechewing. Try though Danny might, there was no matching Ito's ability to hear the slightest things that might tip off the cows' location. Ito could hear them breathing; he could smell them from two or three big wild rosebushes away. Ito's vision was as acute as his hearing. Later, Danny found out that Ito's night vision was almost as good as his daytime vision. During the day, they used hand signals for silent communication.

Ito and Danny never did like searching for the cows on wet winter nights. But their SSS (sight, smell, sound) searching technique, as they called it, was quick and successful. It was critical that the cows not miss a single milking, because milk production started decreasing almost immediately if they did.

The pasture area was over three city blocks long and nine other houses had property that shared a common fence with the pasture. The owners of two of these places each kept a cow, but there was no gate between the properties. The cows "socialized" over the fence, although they did not go through or over it. During a survey of grazing areas when rain was threatening, the boys found that a gap was forming between the second and third strands of the fence wire. This was where someone was regularly entering and leaving the pasture. A path led to the gap from the back property of the houses where Mr. and Mrs. Seal lived.

This discovery coincided with a gradual drop in the amount of milk the two cows were giving. Morning milk production remained the same. At first there was a shortage of about a pint from each cow. Then it became a quart and finally two quarts less milk per cow.

The topic happened to come up between the two boys. Since they had not been milking in the same barn, they supposed it was a natural thing.

Ito and Danny decided to spend a little time in the pasture an hour or so before the regular milking time. They found nothing strange. Then they went two hours earlier. Still nothing. Saturday arrived and they went out there at noon. Sure enough, they spotted Mr. Seal passing through the fence with a milk bucket, a small container of grain, and a milking stool in hand. The cows were eager for the grain treat. A few minutes later the boys walked quietly up to him. He had just finished taking two quarts from one cow and was in the process of doing the same with the other.

Ito said nothing. Danny said nothing. Mr. Seal said nothing. The boys just looked at him continuously as he stopped, took the bucket, the stool, and headed back to the fence. The boys put one foot on the second barbed wire strand of the fence and pulled up the top one so Mr. Seal could go through more easily. They followed him up to his house, still saying nothing, and really not knowing what they should do.

It was Ito who broke the silence. "We know you have no children, but are you or your wife hungry?"

"No, I have a good job. Everyone knows I work at night, and I figured no one would notice it if I took just a little milk."

"Do you really think no one would notice it if you steal a half gallon of milk a day from each cow?" Ito asked.

"Are you calling me a thief?" Mr. Seal angrily asked.

"We call you Mr. Seal. What do you call yourself?"

"Well, ahhhh ... I guess you want to take the milk home with you."

"That's probably a good idea. You can pick up the bucket anytime you want it. My mother is home during the day and she speaks very good English," Ito replied.

"You just keep the bucket, I won't be needing it anymore."

The boys walked home. "Why do you suppose he did that? There are lots of people in our area who are hungry, and they don't do that sort of thing."

Either of the boys could have asked that question, but neither of them had an answer.

13

The Bean Thief

Physically, Ito and Danny were hard as nails. This was a characteristic they shared with most of the boys and many of the girls in their community. Strenuous physical labor was a fact of life for youngsters at that time. Calluses that formed on their hands at age eight were still there years later. The skin wore off, but the protection against friction continued to develop.

During the summer, they joined the throngs of young people who flocked to the local farms, to harvest the yearly commercial crop of green beans. Mary remarked, "Danny, you will be earning a scandalously large amount of money for a boy of your age. How will you use it?"

"I don't know. Just earning it will be part of the fun." He thought for another moment and added, "It could just be fun to hold it in my hands for a while."

Danny and Ito talked about the money they hoped to earn, and what they would do with it. For about three to four weeks, there was money to be earned. The standard thing was for kids to buy their own clothes and school supplies. Whatever was left over would be something for them to discuss. The boys approached their impending wealth with similarities and differences.

Ito commented, "I'd like to have my own money to spend on birthday and Christmas gifts for my family, but I don't know how much that could be.

"I like that idea, too," Danny said. "Then, I'd like to support the church. The usual amount is referred to as a 10 percent 'tithe,' and that comes 'off the top,' before anything else."

"That's the way to do the figuring," Ito added. "Let's say, if we add 20 percent for the gifts, we'll have a better idea of how much we can spend for school supplies and clothes. Ten cents would be the usual price to be paid for a gift, fifteen cents would be extravagant, and twenty-five cents would be 'way over the top.'"

Ito and Danny presented their budget proposal to their parents. They were pleasantly astounded! Danny's mother, Mary, was aghast that such young boys could earn so much money! To her, having ten cents per month to "fritter away" on candy or movies was beyond her Depression-oriented reality. She said to Gran, "I'm afraid Danny may grown up without a realistic concept of the value of money."

Gran was not one to contradict Mary, but she murmured under her breath to herself, "That lad ... and Ito too ... will do right well in that respect, and all the others they face."

A bean yard society had developed over the years. Young or old, newcomer or longtime picker, it didn't matter. A person's place in the society was based on one simple factor: how many pounds of beans he or she picked in a day.

Rose had been the bean yard queen for several years. No one came close to picking as many beans as she did. She also provided transportation out to the bean field for eight other workers, including Ito and Danny. It was about a fifteen-minute walk from their homes to the pickup point. The boys paid five cents a day for the ride, but the second year was to cost ten cents.

The boost in price was something Ito and Danny talked over with Gran. "Tell me, laddie, how many days will ye be working this year?"

Ito replied, " We picked twenty-three days last year, and Frank expects the season will last three or four more days this year."

Danny added, "If we had a way out to his farm, we could hoe and weed beets and carrots for him at ten cents an hour before bean season starts."

Gran nodded. "I'll think on this problem and talk with a friend this evening. But tell me, would the two of ye be up to riding a bicycle that far, doing a day's work, and riding home?"

The boy's didn't have a realistic answer. Both had ridden their fathers' bikes, but just on short rides of a mile or two. They felt confident, but they simply didn't have the money available, and they felt sure their parents didn't, either.

The following day, Gran called the boys together. "The two of ye have been wanting bicycles for some time now. Ye, and we, have been thinking of the cycles as a toy; not essential transportation from school and work."

The boys' eyes sparkled with excitement. They knew that a new bike cost between a low of $24.95 to a high of $59.95. This was sobering knowledge.

Gran continued, "I have a friend who has 'a wheel' that belonged to her son. He quit riding it when he left home. It has been sitting for three years unused. Another bicycle is available from her sister's son. It has a smaller frame, but I'd guess both bikes would be a little large for the two of ye. Never mind that. Two dollars for each is the asking price if ye be interested."

"Wow! We can save more than that on transportation to the bean field during the picking season," Ito replied. His voice registered stress and excitement.

Danny added, "One problem: We need the bikes before we can pay for them."

Gran interrupted, "I told ye these ladies are friends of mine, and they will be happy for ye to have the bikes before they receive payment. I've talked with your father, Ito, and he is prepared to go with ye to look at the bikes to see what state of repair they are in. We know he can put most things 'right' that might need doing."

Two hours later Ito was riding a brilliant red bike that had yellow trim. The saddle had been lowered as far as it would go. It was "a stretch" for him to reach the pedals, but he could manage. Dan was in a similar position when he rode away on his blue-and-white bike. "We will want to clean, lubricate, and adjust all bearings to put both bikes in top condition," Father Watanabe volunteered. "But they are good for now, and your enthusiasm tells me that you are ready for a day out together."

Their destination was Frank's farm. They wanted to make arrangements for their first Saturday of work. They also needed to know how long it would take them to cycle there. By the time to boys arrived back home from the farm, they understood that cycling required its own form of physical fitness. From then on, they biked most places they went.

The pleasure they derived from cycling exceeded their fondest dreams. They didn't know it at the time, but they were laying a foundation for a lifetime of enthusiastic activity. They also learned the wisdom of working for something they honestly desired. Even more, a lifelong work ethic was developed. They treasured their bikes far beyond the work they had to do to pay for them, but they associated work with satisfaction.

After school was out, there were weeks when they worked for Frank. There were occasional days before bean season when Frank had no work for the boys. But that was okay, because they needed to work around their own homes ... and playtime was greatly appreciated.

Danny was an average bean picker. In contrast, Ito had quick hands, and a special eye for beans. He could pick more beans a day than almost anyone else. Danny always was happy to carry Ito's sack to the end of the row or empty his bucket there. While he did this, Ito would pick into Danny's bucket.

Each worker put his name tag on the burlap sacks in which he emptied his beans. At the end of the day, the sacks were tied closed with binder twine, weighed, and logged on the daily tally sheet. Weighing in was the big event of the day. Most pickers knew about how many pounds they had picked because they knew how many sacks they had filled. A sack usually weighed between forty-five and fifty-five pounds.

The pay scale was a penny a pound, if the picker stayed the whole season. That payment included a bonus of ten cents per hundred pounds. If the picker left before the season ended, when the beans were not so heavy on the vines and picking was not so good, the pay dropped to nine-tenths of one cent per pound.

During the first part of the bean season, a strange thing happened. One day, the bags of beans Rose filled were lighter than usual. The following day, someone else's bags were light. Mistrust spread throughout the bean yard society.

A code of ethics existed. You didn't pick beans from another person's row. You didn't mess with anyone's lunch or water jug. You didn't pick the culls (the overgrown beans that would be thrown out at the cannery). Most of all, you didn't touch anyone else's bean sacks.

The following days, several people had one sack that weighed less than normal. It was evident to everyone what was happening. Stealing beans was about as low as a person could go in that society. Frank, the farmer, simply checked the previous year's records to see who had improved his average pick by about fifty pounds. The next day one of the usual gang did not show up for work. The word got around to all the bean fields in the area. The guilty party could not get a job anywhere. The title of "bean thief" followed him until he was drafted into the army. Even at high school class reunions, he was referred to as the "bean thief."

The importance of picking beans to the youngsters in that community could hardly be overemphasized. In the Depression era, every source of income was critical. The short-term benefits were obvious. The integrating effect of people working together in the fields helped establish an additional and realistic basis for recognition and admiration. Respect for the prettiest girl in school, who also had the best grades, zoomed when she picked more beans than most of the workers. Some kids, who didn't do so well in school, picked a lot of beans. Their self-image improved measurably, because of their practical work success.

Among those who picked beans or hops, or who did other farmwork away from home, there was a special bond of respect. When kids came to school with some new clothes after the summer of work, everyone knew they had earned the money to buy them.

The second summer of bean picking and work on the farm had a great impact on the two boys. They felt competent to travel to and from their work, earn enough to pay for many of their personal needs, and as far as luxuries were concerned, they had their bikes.

The second consecutive year of "prosperity" made it possible for the boys to extend their social activities. They spent five cents each to go to the movies! The preview of coming attractions looked so funny, the boys invited Mr. Schmidt and Gran to join them, the boys' treat.

"Ye need not go to the expense of taking me to the cinema. I've muddled along without that luxury and can continue." Mr. Schmidt's answer was similar to that of Gran. The boys pleaded their case to be allowed to share the prospective fun with them. They finally went. The first film of the double feature was one of the forgettable cowboy films. The second starred Joe E. Brown,

91

in *Earthworm Tractors*. Excitement and laughter reigned supreme. It was the film they had come to see, and no one was disappointed. Later, Gran and Mr. Schmidt would occasionally go to a movie, perhaps once or twice a year.

Danny invited Teddie and Ruthie to see a Shirley Temple film. It was Ruthie's first movie, ever. She laughed until she cried. "Everything was so wonderful and happy. I know the movie is only a fairy tale and it had to end, but it was a wonderful dream world for me." Then a puzzled look came over her face. "Why did you invite me, and spend money on me. Are you sorry for me, or something?"

"Yes, and the same questions go for me, too," Teddie stated. "Nobody ever invited me to do things with them before this."

Danny replied quite simply, "We've had fun working together in class, and we always did a real good job. You're good company—both of you. Besides, I like you ... and nobody had to invite us when we were working in class. We just came together. It seems natural, now. Yes, the three of us just fit in. We've been a team since the second grade."

Emotional intensity was reflected in Ruthie's deep blue eyes and her wistful smile. She said, "I cried, because you wanted to take us. Now I'm crying some more, because you have made my fairy tale dream come true." What Ruthie had said was barely audible above a whisper; a positive sign that she was deeply emotional.

Teddy's brown eyes and quivering lips spoke volumes in their silence. In the semi-darkness of that fourth-rate cinema palace, with its pungent toilets broadcasting their fragrance eight aisles away, a fairy-tale kingdom had been created. This was where the luxury of crying and releasing long pent-up emotions could be revealed without fear, observation, or apology. An atmosphere of trust, comfort, companionship, and affection surrounded the three.

In a voice that was full-bodied, distinct, and articulate, Ruthie said, "Thank you!" And in turn, Teddie said, "Thank you."

Ito didn't go with them even though he had been invited. He commented, "You, Teddie, and Ruthie are a team at school and that's part of what you are celebrating."

14

Mr. Hill, Fourth Grade

Danny remembered Mr. Hill from his first day at the new school, as a second grader. They had talked together about Danny socking Cecil in the throat. Mr. Hill was still the school principal, and taught one of the two fourth-grade classes. He was the only man among seven women teachers, and most of the fellows needed a male role model to keep them from thinking that school was only a woman's thing.

Through Mr. Hill's actions and comments, boys learned that being polite and gentle with girls was not a "sissy thing." They also learned that being a boy was a good thing.

He took one boy aside and told him, "The last I saw of you was when you had mud all over your hands and face. Now here you are all spic-and-span." Both boys and girls came to understand that nobody needed to be clean, dainty, and polite all the time. Getting grubby during recess or the lunch hour was more than okay, it was expected. He taught boys and girls that sometimes it took an extra minute or two to clean up before coming into class, and that they should plan to do so. He acknowledged, commented, and encouraged, rather than lecturing.

Of course, everyone was to be on time, because every morning, he started class with an interesting personal story. A short and fun activity followed recess. A riddle or joke started the afternoon session. A short feature story, or item from the *Reader's Digest* or other sources, would follow afternoon recess. But he was not the center of attention. Class members were invited to share an experience, a joke, or tell a story. If students were late, they missed out. Everyone received what Mr. Hill called "wiggle room." There was less tardiness in his class than in any other teacher's class in the school. Kids wanted to be on time, but he could be really strict when it was needed. His words were carefully chosen to help the students understand that they had disappointed him, and that he knew they could do better. No one could remember a time when he gave a kid "the devil" in front of the other kids. He understood "why" better than anyone the students had ever met. He avoided trying to make students feel ashamed of themselves. Once the student and Mr. Hill both were clear why something was done, they could generally agree on other ways of doing things that would be satisfactory to everyone. He used mutual understanding, and the students responded to his concern for them.

Mr. Hill was an absolute genius when it came to finding ways and reasons to encourage students in his school, and not just the ones who were in his class. As principal, he tried to know something about each of the youngsters.

"Young Charlie, I hear that your spelling has improved greatly. By the time you are in my class, I'll probably use you as my dictionary when I need help."

"I'll bet you ask a thousand question every day," George said. "Why do you do that?"

"Do I really do that? Does it bother you?"

"You had questions about the fire drill we had a few days ago. I heard that you asked at least a dozen kids, and some of the teachers, too. Why?"

"I know what I think. What you and others think is important to me."

Kids in his class and in the school realized that his questions were not designed to embarrass anyone. When he asked, "What do you think?" he really wanted to understand. "You don't need to answer right now. Think about it for a while, and then let me know your reaction. Your opinion is important to me." In the course of an appropriate time period, he would provide an opportunity for people to reply, and even discuss the value of their views.

Students in the first grade would hang around him during recess, or lunchtime, hoping he would know they had improved in reading, And he usually did know. If he didn't, he would ask that youngster's teacher, so that he could mention it the next day. Consequently, the kids in school presumed he knew "just everything, good or bad," and they couldn't fool him.

Those who attended Mr. Hill's school learned that he was aware of successes outside of school. He knew that twin sisters helped a neighbor woman with the care of her home. The woman's husband had died and she had to work at housekeeping jobs for other people to feed her family. So the twins did dishes for her every evening, just to give her a break. She had more work than she could manage. Mr. Hill didn't pretend they were great students, but they knew he thought they were wonderful girls.

Wood-burning stoves were used for cooking and heating of most homes in the community. Some elderly people were unable to throw the wood into their woodsheds and stack it so the winter's supply could be put in there. A dozen boys would do the job for them in a couple of days and have fun working together. These older people often could not afford to pay for the help. They were not expected to. Members of the community tended to contact Mr. Hill, when the students at his school had gone out of their way for them. He expressed his gratitude, and told them he would be sure to praise the youngster for his or her kindness.

Yes, Mr. Hill knew how to encourage the youngsters in his school. There are many forms of success, and he made an effort to acknowledge them personally.

Playing marbles "for keeps" was against district rules, but it was done anyway. Mr. Hill complimented the kids who had the skills and luck to win. Their pockets would bulge with marbles before the school day was over. He started a marble bank where winners could deposit their earnings, and losers could borrow what they needed.

The borrowers had to pay for the marbles they received by doing special chores and odd jobs around the school. This could include picking up papers and trash, or erasing and washing blackboards. Erasers were cleaned, and easily reached windows were washed, as were grubby hand marks on doors, walls, desks, et cetera. Each borrower could select the type of work he wanted to do to "pay" for the marbles, and the time he would be free to work.

The marble bank's assets, in terms of marble deposits, were public knowledge. Names of the big depositors were posted where everyone could see them. The winners were encouraged to count out the number they had on deposit, and put them in big jars to display in the showcase. Counting thousands of marbles became too much trouble for the winners. Many decided to give them to the bank. But their winnings were always tallied. Merlin was the most consistent winner, and donated 3,871 to the marble bank. He was renowned for his skills and generosity.

Mr. Hill understood how effective the power of suggestion was on the toilet necessities for boys or girls. Going to the restroom was a natural need, and everyone knew it. Consequently, it was no big deal. No hand and finger communication was required. The students simply walked by Mr. Hill's desk, so he knew where his students were, and mutual nods were exchanged. No specifics were required. The need was cared for quickly and the student returned promptly. However, while Mr. Hill was giving instructions, no one left his class.

The fourth grade was the highest level in that school, and these students were the school's big shots. Mr. Hill emphasized their position of authority as well as their responsibilities to younger ones.

State laws required school fire drills. Twice a year, Mr. Hill arranged for the local volunteer fire department to arrive with the siren sounding. This added excitement and a touch of reality, and drama, to the situation. Older students were well aware that a fifteen-minute fire department response time was about as good as could be expected, even though the school was only a mile from the station. As soon as the fire bell rang in the school, a team of four boys went immediately from the class to the boys' restroom, to be certain that facility was empty. A similar team of four girls did the same for the girl's facilities. These teams checked the classrooms and office spaces as well.

The pinnacle of responsibility and prestige went to the two groups of seven students each, who manned the fire hoses. There were only two hoses in the hall, one near each end of the building. At the first sound of the fire alarm, immediate mobilization took place. The hoses were removed from their hanging brackets and stretched out so that no kinks would block the flow of water. Two students were to control the valve to turn the water on or off. Three kids manned the nozzle. The other two made sure no unexpected kinks formed in the hose along the way, and served as official communicators giving orders to turn the water on or off. It would be a mistake to presume that only boys got the hose assignments. All jobs were integrated except for those involved restroom checks.

Teams composed of two students each went to the other teachers in the building to see if they needed help. An additional five students reported to the school janitor to assist him.

The school was also equipped with four portable soda-acid extinguishers. Teams of three students each handled them. Each fourth-grade student had a post of responsibility and service. With two fourth-grade classes participating, there were enough youngsters for each position to cover for those who were absent. Mr. Hill also had his special bell that was extremely loud. He used it to signal all students and personnel to exit the building immediately, even if they were assigned some other task.

A large pile of trash and newspapers had been accumulating, and on a prearranged day the custodian put them on the ground in the middle of the play shed, well away from any burnable materials. It was set on fire and the fire alarm was sounded. The entire network immediately went into action. Actually, the volunteer fire department was out of sight behind the building.

In less than a minute, the school building was empty. The fire was located and the hose teams put out that fire. Students were instructed to never reenter a burning building. Their job was done when they made the school's firefighting equipment available for adults to use, if necessary. Since the fire was in the play shed, they put it out without having to go into any building.

In one and a half minutes the fire was out, and everything was under control. The kids manning the fire hose were in their element. They had done the job and the fire department didn't need to do a thing. A sense of cooperative achievement enveloped the fourth-grade class. Youngsters from lower grades felt cared for and secure. And they looked forward to the time they would be in Mr. Hill's fourth grade. Proud? The whole school, as well as the volunteer fire department, felt great pride. The two hoses had to be hung up in the play shed to drain the water from them, but this was done one at a time. The following morning before school, they were put back in place on their storage racks.

Occasionally, certain exits were blocked. Alternative evacuation routes worked without conflict or panic. Yes, Mr. Hill had guidelines for his school and his student to follow. His strategies were practiced, tested, rehearsed, and except for drills, were never needed. The fact that his plan worked so well surprised no one. After all, it was Mr. Hill's school, and his plan.

Mr. Hill had served in the Spanish-American War and he had war stories to tell. None of them glamorized war or military heroism. His history lessons concentrated on how much better off the world was when mutual regard and goodwill were substituted for conquests. Such lessons might be followed up by references to personal conflicts between students at school. It was during such lessons that the tension between Danny and Cecil finally lessened. The two boys were not likely to become friends, but they did cooperate well, when they were on the same fire hose team.

Mr. Hill was the right teacher at the right time, to aid the boys in their surging scramble toward manhood. His warm, caring, loving, and nurturing nature helped the girls feel safe, secure, and comfortable. He was also an outstanding teacher for the girls, and continued the fine work being done by the women instructors. But the boys *needed* someone like him guiding their school experience during that time in their lives. He was their first male teacher and he presented a masculine point of view dealing with many of the confusing issues in their lives.

Retirement age finally caught up with Mr. Hill, and he was forced to leave the school system. He worked as a real estate agent for an additional twenty years before retiring from work.

For many years following his death, succeeding groups of kids asked why their school was named after "that skinny old man" whose portrait hung in the main hall of the school. Parents who had been his students knew and understood why. The best answers came from men who realized how different school had become for them, once Mr. Hill had been their teacher. They also were aware that they had changed as well. A general reservoir of stories was common property among them, but each person told about things with an interesting and totally personal twist that was uniquely their own.

After telling youngsters about Mr. Hill, the storyteller inevitably faced one more question, "Why can't we have a teacher like Mr. Hill?"

His answer might well be, "There hasn't been another."
Another lingering question, *"Why?"*

15

Cows to the Bull

Ito and Danny had just started fourth grade, and at ten years of age, they felt humiliated by the task of taking the cows to the bull when they came in heat. But it was their responsibility.

"Everyone knows where we're going and what's going to happen." With a voice that could be heard three blocks away, Mr. Wright hollered, "I see you're taking the cow to the bull. She's sure bellerin' like she's in heat." And that darned cow did bellow.

The two boys believed that she joined in the conspiracy to make them feel conspicuous. Two years previously, John and Mr. Watanabe had agreed to skip a heat with one of the cows, so there was one cow that was giving milk, while the other was dried up awaiting delivery of her next calf. That way, the two households had a constant supply of dairy products.

For two young boys to control a randy and headstrong cow took some doing. There were times when she wanted to graze on special clumps of grass, and there were other times that she decided to hurry along. If they let her get up a "head of steam," she could drag them off their feet. The boys decided to make a "snoot cinch," which fitted around her upper muzzle just behind her nostrils. If she pulled against them too hard, it would cinch up tightly, but release when she eased off. It didn't go around her lower jaw, but through her mouth, and was made of small link chain. She didn't like it, but it kept her from running away, and dragging them along.

"I hope Mr. H answers the door this year. His daughter, Wanda, answered it last year and you know what that was like." Ito and Danny shared that hope. But, once again, fate seemed to conspire against them. Wanda was six grades ahead of them

100

in school. Whenever she saw them at the door with a cow, she always asked the same question. "What do you want?"

The answer was all too obvious. Danny pointed and said, "It's the cow."

"I'm not blind, I can see it's a cow, but what do you want?" She was intentionally making the boys as uncomfortable as possible, and succeeding. She seemed to thrive on this.

"She needs to have a calf and it's her time."

"Any fool can tell that from the way she's acting and bellowing. But what do you want me to do about it?" This girl just wouldn't quit, and both boys were flustered, embarrassed, and angry. It was time for *A Way* self-discipline to mitigate that anger.

"Maybe you could call your dad and tell him the cow is here for the bull." By this time, both Ito and Danny wished for a pair of one-inch-diameter holes in the ground to drop into and pull the earth over their heads.

"Well, tell me what you want the bull to do. Do you want the bull to screw your cow?"

With that word *screw*. Ito and Danny were beyond composure. In his mature years, Danny heard of women having "hot flashes," but he doubted if anything could equal the pressure-cooker feeling Ito and he were enduring.

She compounded this discomfort by saying, "I hope you have the money. In the animal world you have to pay the male for servicing the female. In the human world, you guys have to pay us girls if you want to do some screwing." She was outrageous, and loving it.

Her father came to a belated rescue. "That bull can kill you if you get in the pasture with him, so you stay outside of the fence. Just keep a hold on the long rope you have on your cow." Then the farmer opened a gate and the bull lunged in. The huge animal presented his magnificent self. He had been carrying on as much as the cow. He charged right up to the rear end of the cow and stuck his nose under her tail and sniffed great gulps of air. Then he arched his neck back as far as possible and wrinkled his nose as if something smelled awful. Or was that because it smelled so good? All this time, there was a red icicle coming from a hairy area in the middle of his belly. It came out a few inches

101

and then retreated, and it was always dripping. Then the bull mounted and made a huge thrust forward. The cow hunched her back and let out an *ooooph* sound and the bull was off her back. One great thrust and that was it! How much pleasure could he get in a couple of seconds? Then the bull took another sniff as he had done before, wrinkled his nose, and made another mounting lunge. In another moment he was back with all four feet on the ground.

"Good grief, don't let her piss!" the farmer cried. The cow was pulled out of the bull's area, and the farmer took a foot-long section of a shovel handle, and racked it back and forth across the cow's spinal column. This made the cow go swaybacked. The farmer was fearful that if the cow urinated or hunched her back, it might make the bull's deposits flow out.

On the way home, the loud voice called to them again, "I see the bull did his job. How many times, three, or four? Must have done a good job. That cow is a lot easier to manage than she was on the way to the bull." And both boys hated the man's continuing comments. He was still yelling when they were a block away.

Ito asked, "How would you like to have a set of balls like that bull has?"

"Not for me! How would you be able to ride a bike, run, or even walk? They'd be too much in the way. Besides, just think how much hurt you'd have if you cracked a set of those! You know, Ito, I can't figure it out. It was about all we could do to hold the cow from running away from us on the way to the bull, and look at her now. She's more interested in grass than ass. All that happened was that the bull rammed his dingus into her twice for hardly a second, and the whole thing was over, and all our effort and humiliation for a few seconds of breeding time."

"Yeah, it's about the same with the rabbits and chickens," Ito said. "It's over almost before it starts. But it isn't that way with all the animals. Remember when Kid's dog got to your dog, Stubby? He mounted her just the same as a rabbit or bull and pumped away like mad, and then he got off to the side only they weren't done. They both did some crazy turning and twisting and ended up rump- to-rump. And he stood there with his rear end twitching, his tongue lolling out, and his eyes rolled up and glazed over, and they were still stuck together."

"Don't forget, Stubby was acting crazy, too," Danny added. "Each time the dog would twitch, she'd almost bounce. He must have been pumping her full of that stuff as they were tied together. Remember when Don and Kid tried to pull them apart and both dogs were yelping?"

"Dogs seem to have had more fun out of it than the other animals. At least they are at it for ten to fifteen minutes. I wonder if men get stuck in women so they can't get out until they are finished. Or will guys be finished in a few seconds? It should be more fun if it lasts for a while." One mystery about sex was compounded for Ito and Danny as they observed various animals mating. Usually it lasted only a few seconds, except for dogs. But all the animals seemed crazy to do it. Maybe the boys would find their answers when they were older?

The boys and the cow passed by the house of a girl who was in their class. Five other girls were visiting. They all stood on the porch, gawking at the embarrassed fellows. "Where are you going with the cow?" Jill asked. Then the girls put their heads together and giggled.

In a loud whisper Jill said, "You shouldn't ask such embarrassing questions."

The boys could hear Sarah exclaim, "Bull! What for?" More giggling. "Oh! Well, how was I supposed to know?" In a taunting singsong voice, the girls shouted after the rapidly retreating boys, "We hope you enjoyed the performance. Next time tell us so we can go."

With beet red ears and subdued voices the boys replied emphatically, "NO WAY!"

16

John's Wreck

John thought, "At last! The realization of yesterday's hopes, and the key to tomorrow's dream successes, came together tonight." It had happened in a magnificent concert hall in Portland, the largest and most culturally affluent city in the state. The future looked as brilliant as a star on a moonless desert night ... hopefully, not as a meteor, not a falling star. Perhaps more like a comet that streaked through space, leaving a spectacular trail of light. This was not just in John's dream mind. The reality of the evening's performance suggested it was the beginning of a future, complete with recognition, fulfillment, and financial rewards.

The applause had been thunderous. The Mighty Twenty all-male choir had done it again. Their voices had captured the emotions and imagination of the concert hall patrons. Solo performers responded to their individual call to stage front and center. John, the baritone soloist, strode forward to a standing ovation that continued long after the one called for by usual courtesy and appreciation. The spotlights left him and then came back repeatedly, as the crowd continued their acknowledgment of his superb performance. Oh, the spotlights! They embraced the entire group, then focused again on John. It was a group triumph, but also personal acclaim seldom experienced by professionals, let alone amateurs.

Then it was time to go home. But for John, the stage and recognition were now a part of his home. He was familiar with both, because they had been paramount in his daily dream world of semi-reality. They had been a part of his environment. John had earned his living as a carpenter, but that was not where he belonged. He, and local admirers, had known this for years, and now many others were aware of it. Important and influential members of the music world had been in the audience. They knew and understood. A tentative contract had been offered to him. In ten days, there was to be a meeting to discuss his future, and to finalize the business arrangements.

The night was chilly and rainy, but nothing penetrated the glow of satisfaction that John and his wife shared as they started their drive home. Highway 99, the main arterial from Canada to Mexico through the Pacific states, had its normal flow of traffic. Careful drivers traveled at a slower pace, because of the rain and wind.

Heading south, the dance of thousands of tiny fragmented raindrop-mirrors reflected oncoming lights on the windshield of John's car. Wiper blades madly chased and erased these water-formed images. They were replaced a thousandfold. The rain-slicked highway also had big puddle reflectors. These relentlessly re-formed, were constantly shattered under the assault of vehicle tires, wind, and rain. Each mirror had a dazzling effect on the eyes of every driver.

Commercial drivers, who tried to maintain a schedule, pressed forward and were irritated by those who drove at a slower pace. Highway 99 had only one lane in each direction, and faster drivers seized every opportunity to pass the slow-pokes. But the dazzling water mirrors that reflected oncoming headlights were no kinder to the eyes of the professionals than they were to less experienced drivers. Each blinking of the eyes provided momentary relief. No one was exempt from fatigue, except those passengers whose eyes were closed, resting, or asleep. Pete, the driver of a northbound bus, was halfway through his extended shift. His replacement driver was ill, and that night, no substitute was available. In a little less than an hour, he would finish a double shift totaling sixteen hours, which would fatten his paycheck. His normal eyeblink speed had slowed, a sign of advanced fatigue. The lids stayed closed longer than normal, but no one was there to see it. The sudden appearance of taillights too close for comfort was a warning to Pete. Occasional moments of "driving by Braille," were signaled by the thumping of tires, as they contacted the rough shoulder of the road. This startled the driver and passengers into a momentary panic. "Sorry, folks, an obstacle in the road back there," was Pete's cover story. For the following five minutes he was on "adrenaline alert."

The passengers drifted back into the semi-comfort of travel-induced exhaustion. A false sense of security was reinforced by their isolation from the cold and rain. The bus was warm, and the musty smell of many people breathing the same air had a narcotic effect. This, combined with the sounds of tires on the wet road, and varied traffic noises, perpetuated the hypnotic effects.

The extra hours of driving, and the taxing conditions, continued taking their toll. Pete's driving errors were rationalized in his fatigue-shrouded judgment center. His foot was a little heavy on the gas pedal. "Well, an extra ten miles per hour will get us there quicker. None of the passengers will complain. Oops, I've got to watch that! That pass was a bit close. Those slowpokes make trouble for the good drivers." Stress-induced weariness and near exhaustion magnified the effect of the glaring water mirrors. A tragedy was in the making.

John was driving his first car, a 1937 Pontiac. The worst of the Depression had passed and John was working again. His world, and that of his family, had greatly improved. The World War I veterans' pension fund that Congress had passed, combined with a semi-regular income for two years, had allowed him to pay for their first new car. The heater kept the interior warm, and Mary was sleeping in the right front seat. She had shared the triumphant performance and might be reliving it in her sleep. He contemplated his dream and real worlds as he continued home.

His back had been broken, but it had healed. Mary was thriving in her new environment of a larger house and cherished neighbors, even though the household conditions were not up to modern standards. Her church activities and friends had surpassed her expectations. Gran was busy caring for invalids, engrossed in her grandson, and enjoyed frequent visits with Mr. Schmidt. The Watanabe family provided treasured companionship for everyone. John and Tsugio sought household repair jobs for people who couldn't afford to pay them. They valued their time together. Life was rich and satisfying.

John had told Mary, "It's fun being with Tsugio. In fact, it

106

is hardly work at all." Sagging doors, leaky faucets, plumbing and electrical problems, minor roof repairs, broken windows: all were part of their repair domain. "Tsugio and I will do that for you," John would say to a friend. Each was regularly employed, but they always joined together on those special occasions.

A bonus benefit had been that Tsugio's *A Way* philosophy was gradually replacing John's inner necessity for dominance and superiority with his son. He wondered if the cooperative relationship between Ito and Danny had shown him "the way" as well. He loved his son so much ... and he realized that he thought of both Danny and Ito as sons. And so did Tsugio. He felt a special sense of fulfillment as he saw them develop. Both men had agreed to talk with the boys about that, while they were working together on something special for Mary and Lili, Tsugio's wife.

The two men had a surprise project under way for their wives. A small enclosure had been built for an electrical water pump. The existing well on Tsugio's property had already been connected to the pump. In exchange for horseshoe replacements by Mr. Schmidt, Mr. Hadley had ploughed a furrow fourteen inches deep across the two properties. Danny, Ito, and their fathers had installed water pipes that connected the two households. All this was done without the wives' knowledge. Within a week, the women would have running water available in their kitchens. Other amenities would follow. Realistic opportunities, optimism, and enthusiasm had surged to the surface during the stage performance that night. He'd always had the voice to command attention, but expert musicians had said that his voice conveyed passion, warmth, sincerity, and personal joy in life seldom transmitted to such a large audience. His performance had been charismatic. John began to understand more about Tsugio's *A Way* philosophy. He realized that in his solos, he had been responding to the needs of his audience. They had shared a voice, yes, his voice, and his soul that sang eloquently with them, and for them.

As John continued south, he reminded himself, "There is no hurry. The general flow of traffic is fast enough. This is the section of the highway that has all the bridges that are a little narrower than usual. Be alert, keep to my side of the road, and

107

everything will be fine. Keep my eyes aimed to the right of the centerline, and when lights get closer, concentrate on the right shoulder of the road. Blink frequently to rest my eyes. Don't let the glare affect my driving."

Meanwhile, the memories of the recent success returned to John's mind. Success and spotlights were in the future.

"Spotlights, blinding spotlights! Two sets of them! Good God, they are headlights! That damned fool is trying to pass and there's no room, I can't go farther to the side."

Mary was suddenly awake! Why would John swear? He never...

John's car scraped against the concrete barrier of the bridge over a small creek. Nowhere to go ... no escape ... then confusion...

The sound of applause became confused with that of screeching metal being ripped and torn apart. Violent jolting, thrashing and twisting ... And then silence. The audience was quiet ... gone.

A cold, damp chill permeated John's consciousness. He knew something was dreadfully wrong. The sound of a strange orchestral instrument came closer. It had a wailing voice that was familiar, but not quite identifiable. People hollered and whispered in turn. The spotlights were back, but there was no ovation. John was lifted and moved. He was moving again. Now he identified the wail of a siren that seemed to accompany him, but he was not driving. Mary should be beside him. Where ... Then ... quiet. John heard nothing ... felt nothing.

Later there were other lights, and then the spotlights began again. John became aware of a strange sense of warmth that seemed to emanate from the spotlights. They were vaguely close. The audience spoke in gentle, respectful whispers. His head hurt terribly and his mighty chest, which supplied the bellows for his voice, seemed unable to bring forth enough air for even a whisper. Ghostly, featureless, shapes in white gowns and masks hovered around him. Strange. Ah, yes, the performance was over. He could relax.

A quiet voice asked in a matter-of-fact manner, "What about the lady?" There was no answer, just the felt vibration of a head moving slowly from side to side. Now John knew there was something terribly wrong! He wanted to reach across the seat for Mary's hand to reassure her. Ah, dear Mary. But, somehow, her hand was out of reach.

The spotlights started fading, and so did their warmth. The quiet sounds became less distinct ... then ... subdued. A spotlight dominated his vision with a brilliant red orb. This faded to yellowish hues and then merged and deepened into violet and magenta. The muffled noise of busy people faded into complete silence. The magenta light was gone; a black core dominated everything. A quiet vacancy ... and then, even that was gone. Gone ... gone. All gone. Nothing....

17

The Accident Report

The weary police officer knocked on the door at 3:30 A.M. He knocked repeatedly. This was a totally unpleasant task. No one liked to be awakened at such an unholy hour. The message he had to deliver, well ... Finally, a light was turned on somewhere in the back of the home, and noises came from within. From behind the closed door came an elderly woman's Cockney accent. "Who might ye be and what might ye be wanting at this hour?"

"Well, madam, there's been an accident." The door opened slowly. Danny had heard the knocking, and had arrived in time to see the policeman appear through the doorway.

"An accident, is it? And why would ye be callin' 'ere?"

"Is the man of the house home then?"

"No, if ye need to know."

"Would his name be John?"

"That's what I named 'im these many years ago. His father wanted to call 'im James Thomas John, but I put me foot down right hard, and said plain John is just enough."

"Well, it is John and Mary I should be talking to you about."

Gran sensed a sudden chill and gathered Danny to her side. There was nothing to say as the tragic reality was relayed.

The following morning, a Portland newspaper reported the huge success of the concert. A later edition carried the account of the tragic accident that took the lives of the acclaimed baritone, John, and his wife, Mary. The northbound driver of the bus tried to pass two cars and was unable to get back in his lane in time. John had swerved as far to his right as possible, but the bus ripped through the car and killed both occupants. No one in the bus was seriously injured.

Just hours before, Gran and Danny had listened to the officer's report ... it had been so early in the morning. They felt there must be some mistake. Someone must have been confused ... surely there was some error. The paper carried the story and showed photos. John's car was barely recognizable ... but it was real. Suddenly the two felt alone in an empty house.

Witnesses said the bus driver had been driving in an erratic manner that crowded other vehicles from the road. Company records showed that he was nearly through a "second shift," because the man scheduled to relieve him had failed to report for work.

Police offered the opinion that it was a clear case of negligent homicide and reckless driving. The district court agreed, and added the opinion that irresponsible company management had, in effect, forced the bus driver to work an excessive number of hours without proper rest.

The court awarded what was, at that time, an enormous sum of money. The amount was ten thousand dollars for the loss of each of the parents, and an additional ten thousand dollars in punitive damages to the couple's only surviving son, Daniel. The thirty thousand dollars were placed in a trust fund. It could be invested at the discretion of the trust, until such time as it became necessary for the purpose of education, survival, or other expenditures the court or trust advisers, deemed important. Gran had access to the funds to use or invest at her discretion. Other conditions notwithstanding, the total accrued value of the trust was to be turned over to Daniel on his twenty-first birthday.

The awarded sum appeared to be an enormous amount of money at that time. The case was of considerable social and legislative importance. Dr. Wayne, the dean of the law school, had championed the cause that had imposed corporate responsibility for such accidents. This was the same man who had been involved in the wreck in front of Danny's house several years earlier, and the same man who drove Danny home the day the boy had his big tricycle adventure.

Interest earned on the investment could provide daily living expenses for the two of them, at that time. Gran put things in perspective when she said, "It's a lot of money, laddie boy, but what's to replace the loss of two lives, and their care and love for you? Well, we have a job to do, and we'd best get on with it."

Danny and Gran had sat together, held hands, and looked deeply into each other's eyes. "You are the only close blood relative I have left, Gran, and I love you," the boy said.

As they continued looking at each other, Danny saw moisture form in Gran's eyes for the first time. Tears ran down her cheeks. Danny cried with her, and for her. He knew how he felt, but it was difficult to know how to console Gran.

Finally, she said, "Well, we've had a good blubber. Shed the tears ye have over matters of love, and not on hate or anger. But, not to worry, laddie boy, we each have our two good hands and a strong back. We've managed difficult times, and we'll manage this. And, after all, we have our Watanabe-Schmidt family."

18

The Watanabe Family Includes Danny

The newspaper photo had shown a car brutally torn apart ...
destroyed. The combined family, who were left behind, felt that
violence in human terms. One-fourth of their loved ones were
gone, and they were crushed by the impact to their lives. Gran
in her quiet wisdom sat with Danny, and said what needed to be
said. "We loved them all we could, laddie, and we still do. That's
why we'll carry on and do the best we can ... in gratitude for the
love they gave us. Nothing can take that away."

A calm determination saw them through those first days.
There were major life adjustments to be made. Gran continued
to provided stability, security, affection, and guidance. Danny
followed her work ethic. She had shown him how to make unpleasant tasks into positive experiences. Gran tried to maintain a familiar routine, which included meaningful time with
Danny. She assumed the household management chores, but
made no attempt to replace his parents. She and Danny had
already established a caring, loving, and intellectually stimulating bond, long before the devastating accident. In her sensitive
and supportive manner, she remained a positive force in guiding
his character, emphasizing integrity and respect. Perhaps more
than anything else, she remained "Gran," and everything that
name meant to the boy.

The Watanabe family, which included Mr. Schmidt, assumed an increasing importance in Danny's life. To them, he was
their second son in every way, and they adored him as they did
Ito. They also provided strong role models for him. They would
never intrude on the relationship Gran and Danny shared, but
they extended their nurturing care to Danny, in the same manner they had always done for Ito. Their strict personal code of
ethics was self-imposed, and by example, their behavior helped

others to understand that it was a valuable guideline for those who wished to follow it.

Ito remained Danny's best friend, but being Japanese in the community was not easy. Prejudice was rampant. The curfew sounded at 9 P.M. every night. It notified youngsters and non-white adults that they should be in their own homes. However, the boys were always too involved in their own activities, around their own property, to be concerned about the curfew or any inequities.

Danny frequently ate his evening meals with the Watanabe family. At the time, he didn't know that Gran and Mother Watanabe had worked out a calendar regarding where he would eat. It depended greatly on where Gran would be at dinnertime. Often, she was caring for elderly residents in the neighborhood. It was a rare occasion when Gran was not home for at least two hours in the evening. She valued her time with Danny, talking and studying Arabic.

"You have two homes, Danny," Mrs. Watanabe told him. "The first and most important is the one with Gran. The second is here with Mr. Schmidt, and us, your Watanabe family." During the years that followed the accident, the Watanabe parents and Gran often referred to Ito and Danny as their twins. In many ways, they were closer in temperament, interests, skills, and abilities than most blood brothers. In appearance, they were quite a contrast, but their mannerisms were uniquely similar. Few people who share the same blood ever achieved the level of comradeship the two boys enjoyed.

The willow thicket in the cow pasture was a favorite area for the boys. It provided them with a physical challenge that appealed to their sense of adventure. One favorite game was to climb to the top of one willow until it bent over and allowed passage to a second tree, and then to the next, without touching the ground. They could traverse the entire hundred yards of trees in this manner. It wasn't quite like Tarzan swinging from tree to tree, but it was their best option.

Another game was to make a tree house without using any tools except knives. They wouldn't allow themselves to use string, rope, nails, or wire. They stripped bark from willow limbs, and used that to secure branches in place. These were primitive perches well above the ground, and a makeshift roof was occasionally added to the platform. Still, when it rained, it didn't take much to encourage them to abandon the area and seek better shelter.

These perches were totally unserviceable within a week's time, but that was okay, because the boys wouldn't go back to them for months at a time. It was an occasional diversion that was enjoyed and abandoned in favor of different activities. It had been an imaginative taste of primitive life. They were unaware, and unconcerned, about the limited damage done to the willows. The trees were "volunteers," had no commercial value, and were thought to be expendable. Other trees and rosebushes were more than adequate to serve the needs of the birds.

The local millrace was a man-made canal that was used for floating logs downstream. From there they were dumped into the millpond for the lumber company. To get there, the boys had to cross the railroad tracks and another railroad right-of-way pasture similar to the one used by their cows. The boys had found a long section of a broken "pike pole." It had originally been used to help move jammed logs. The remaining pole was two inches in diameter, eight feet long, and had a metal tip and collar. It served the boys as a vaulting pole for crossing the fence between their properties. They used the shorter end for a chinning bar. It played a major role in their upper-body development, because daily sessions of "monkey activity" included swinging, kip-ups, chin-ups, and pull-ups. Their daily fitness routines were varied and fun. As always, they challenged their own abilities, rather than each other.

As community members aged, and needed assistance in order to remain in their homes, Gran spent more time away, and frequently stayed overnight. During such occasions, Danny was included in the Watanabe family.

With continuous exposure to the Japanese language, Danny's proficiency increased rapidly. He and Ito enjoyed playing word games during which they freely mixed English, German, and Japanese words within the same sentence. This became a household game. Mr. Schmidt joined in, although he proclaimed that he and the Japanese language were strangers. The adults accepted the fact that developing multilingual skills was potentially more valuable to the boys than to themselves. Gran and Danny continued to share English and Arabic.

The *A Way* philosophy and its practical application was another force that bound Danny to the Watanabe-Schmidt household.

Mother Watanabe often gave Mr. Schmidt massages to ease the pain of poor circulation, due to his cardiovascular problems. Ito and Danny observed how she worked with muscles, joint, and nerve centers, but Danny was more interested in her techniques, which, to him, seemed to be an art form. He would watch and listen to her explanations long after Ito had left to do other things.

At times, Father Watanabe came in from work and his head was tilted to one side as if his neck hurt. Mother Watanabe would begin a special massage on his neck and head. After some time, the tension would gradually diminish and his tranquil expression would be restored.

Danny became aware that Mother Watanabe seemed to be walking in the same manner as her husband. "Is it possible that you are experiencing some of the same pain as your husband?" Her nod and apologetic bow confirmed the boy's suspicions. "Would it be permitted for me to try your special massage technique? You could guide my hands and fingers, and tell me what to do."

He followed the procedure he had often watched. She sat in a chair, and leaned her head back into him. His fingers automatically followed the pathways he had seen her use on her husband and Mr. Schmidt. A few minutes later, her arms were crossed on the table, and her head was cradled in them. His fingers traversed the back of her neck, shoulders, and spinal column. He realized he had been successful, because she was asleep. A few minutes later, Mother Watanabe yawned, stretched, and was restored. "You have magic fingers, Danny. Please apply them to my husband and Mr. Schmidt the next time they need help."

Danny was delighted. "May I be allowed to help you if the occasion arises again?"

She bowed, and replied, "I am ashamed to be such a nuisance, but there are times when such help will be gratefully received."

And so the pattern began. Since Mrs. Watanabe had recognized Danny's natural skills and interest, she continued instructing him. Danny felt she was sharing a treasured gift, and he was pleased when there were opportunities to use it.

19

Throwing Knives

While Ito and Danny were still in the fifth grade, a circus came
to town. The boys entered the circus grounds, and were intrigued
by a sideshow sign indicating one act as DEAD EYE JAKE—KNIFE
THROWING EXHIBITION. They entered before his act began and saw
him preparing targets and laying out knives. During the exhibition, they watched his amazing skills and decided to approach
him between acts.

Dead Eye was pleased that two youngsters were so inquisitive, and talked with them between performances. "I always
hold my knife with the thumb up, *not* sideways, and the flat
of the blade must be parallel to the ground." He demonstrated.
"Here, you try the grip." He handed each of the boys one of his
knives. "Extend the wrist so the thumb is farther forward than
any of the fingers. That's right. Don't move or flex the wrist during the throw, or you will flip the knife and lose control of its
rotation. Throwing is done by the shoulder, elbow, and forearm,
but not with the wrist as you would with a baseball. Try throwing at that big target."

The boys were astonished that Dead Eye would take the
time to explain how to throw, and then actually allow them to
handle and throw his amazing knives. Ito threw first and the
knife impacted the target with the point aimed straight in. Jake
praised the boy for having followed his directions so well.

Danny was next. He threw, and the knife stuck in the target, but it had under-rotated. It lodged with the handle downward at about a thirty-degree angle.

"Both of you have done well, but do you know which was the
better throw?"

"Ito's is, because the blade is sticking straight in," Danny
volunteered.

"I agree," Jake said. "The force of Ito's throw had the point of the knife rotating into the target. With your throw, Danny, the point hit the target, but the rotation of the blade was not far enough along to make a deep penetration. Can either of you explain what happened with Danny's throw? Remember, it was good, but not as good as Ito's." The boys realized what a sensitive teacher he was. He was considerate with his praise, questions, and suggestions.

The boys looked at each other, but were unsure why there was a difference.

"Two things can go wrong," Jake explained. "When you begin knife throwing, the most common thing is to flex the wrist. The knife will spin and then over-rotate. It is pure luck if the point hits the target. That was not what happened with Danny's throw. It under-rotated." Jake handed another knife to each of the boys. "Now move back two steps and throw again." Both knives stuck, but Ito's had over-rotated. Dan's was sticking straight into the target. "As you can see, Danny, your half rotation distance is different from Ito's and mine."

"Gosh, I must have flipped my wrist on the second throw," Ito observed.

Jake smiled. "I said two things could go wrong. This was the second thing. You need to learn to judge throwing distances. Your first throw was at a half-rotation distance. When you backed up, the knife had farther to go and rotated more. To adjust for that, you must grip farther forward or backward, depending on the throwing distance, so the rotation of the blade is appropriate. For a full-rotation distance, you grip the knife by the handle. There are one-and-a-half-rotation, and two-rotation distances as well. Remember, in-between distances are adjusted for by how far forward or back from the balance point the knife is gripped."

"Get a move on, Jake, your snake act begins in one minute," the sideshow barker yelled.

Jake nodded, but continued, "I'm not trying to limit you or tell you what you can and can't do, but long-distance knife throwing of fifty feet is, for the most part, pure fantasy ... you know, Hollywood stuff. From that far away, rotation, impact, wind effects, et cetera, become almost impossible to control outdoors. Distances of up to thirty feet are manageable with reasonable accuracy and reliability, providing you have special ability and put in many hours ... perhaps years of training. Professionals seldom perform at thirty feet. It is too far for reliable results. But you may be exceptions. Practice at the half rotation distance, and don't flex your wrist."

"Thanks for taking so much time with us. We'll practice ... and come back next year."

"Good luck! You're the first two kids who ever asked me how to throw knives. Everyone thinks it is a sinister activity, but for me, it's recreation."

Kids in their neighborhood played games of Cowboys and Indians, complete with rubber guns, bows and arrows, and even rubber knives. Of course, only rubber guns were shot at each other. The rubber knives were not much fun, because there was no way to know whether they would have stuck, if they were thrown. Ito and Danny enjoyed these games, particularly the running and rubber guns. But Dead Eye Jake had tweaked their curiosity and imagination. They wanted to do knife throwing, but household knives were not available. Besides, they wanted proper knives similar to Dead Eye Jake's.

"Let's make our own knives," Danny suggested. "My father once made a hunting knife out of a worn-out flat mill file. He said dozens of those files were available at the sawmill, and the quality of the steel is super. We'd need to grind them to shape, and then temper the brittle steel. Grinding and polishing would remove the file teeth, and put on an edge and point."

Chief, a blacksmith at the mill, had made knives several times, but the boys wanted a different product. He gave them fifty of the worn-out files that had been accumulating for years.

"You know, boys, all the equipment you need for forging knife blades is in my shop," Mr. Schmidt advised them. "How are you going to proceed?"

Danny explained, "We asked the librarian, but she has nothing on the topic of making knife blades. She told us that such books are available on loan, from the state library."

"Would you like to read what my books have to say on the topic? Of course, they are written in German, but I'd be happy to be a translator and technical consultant, but I won't take your project away from you." Mr. Schmidt was obviously interested in helping.

"We'd like that, but you've never interfered or spoiled our fun. Never! We asked Father Watanabe for information, and he said samurai swords are renowned for their strength and sharpness. They have multilayer forgings. He suggested that we ask you about that."

Mr. Schmidt explained, "The original layering information for forging blades was based on the ancient Japanese process used for producing superior swords. The more times the metal was hammered flat and folded over, the better the blade became." There had been no information regarding a realistic guide to the number of folds needed to produce a superior product. The intended use for samurai swords was to slice off heads and other body parts during warfare. The boys had other things in mind. They would figure the folding problems later.

After talking with Mr. Schmidt and studying his books about forging and layering metal, the boys decided the basic way they wanted to work. Fundamental techniques were resolved.

Using Mr. Schmidt's equipment and working under his supervision, a file was placed in a bed of burning coal and the blower fan cranked to build up the heat. When a file became red hot, Ito used a pair of blacksmith's tongs to grip the file and hold it on the anvil. They wanted it hammered to about the thickness of a tin can. Ito used a sledgehammer to beat it flat. Danny was ambidextrous and swung similar hammers with both hands, and they set up a waltz rhythm. Even so, the metal cooled rapidly, and it had to be returned to the fire to keep it malleable.

When the metal was tin-can thick, it was placed against the thin edge of a bar that was clamped horizontally with a vise, and the first fold was made. This was repeated two more times, so that the folded metal was about the same thickness as the original file. The first cycle of three folds was completed.

"I'm loosing my grip on the hammers," Danny said as he massaged his forearms.

"Me too. I'm happy the metal has to be reheated so we have time to relax our grip." As Mr. Schmidt watched, an amused smile played across his lips. Ito added, "Milking and chopping wood helped our strength, but not for hammering. We need to relax our grip once the hammerhead hits the file. That way, the shock won't be so punishing to our muscles. But, Mr. Schmidt, why does the layering process make the metal into a stronger blade?"

"When you hammer a piece of metal flat, fold it over and hammer it flat again, you produce additional molecular layers of steel. Think of it as if it were wood. Which would be stronger, a piece of lumber a quarter inch thick, or a piece of three-ply plywood of the same thickness? Then compare that to a piece of five-ply that is still only a quarter of an inch thick," Mr. Schmidt replied, and added, "How many three-fold cycles do you want each knife to have?"

The two boys looked at each other. "Originally, we'd thought about a hundred, but that would take too long. Now, we don't know. It could take forever to make fifty files into knives." Ito added, "I read that makers of samurai swords sometimes worked two or three years forging one blade. We don't want to do that."

Mr. Schmidt suggested, "If we activate the wind-powered trip-hammer, it could do most of the hammering for you. That would be faster, and easier on your arms. We'd need to lubricate the bearing surfaces and release the brake. That might take twenty minutes, but it would be time well spent." The boys responded with grateful nods and broad smiles.

It took seventeen minutes for the trip-hammer to start operating. The windmill stood high above the ground, and the usual breeze was strong enough to turn the mill. The free weight of the trip-hammer was raised, the foot lever released, and the heavy weight came crashing down on the anvil and everything on it.

"You've noticed this cage around the anvil and hammer. When you are working with this equipment, nothing goes inside that cage except the metal you are forging, and the tongs that hold the metal. Never put your hand or arm through there." Mr. Watanabe had anticipated the use of the trip-hammer, and had brought a cow's femur bone home from the butcher shop. Mr. Schmidt gripped it with the tongs, placed it on the anvil, and then tripped the hammer release. The single blow shattered the bone into countless fragments.

"We see what you mean," the wide-eyed boys replied.

Mr. Schmidt gave additional instructions. "The hammer

must be directly above the anvil, in order to strike things that have been put in place for forging. This is the safety bar that will prevent the hammer from falling, even if you accidentally release the trip pedal." Then he put the file blade on the anvil and the hammer was released. The forge hammer delivered five strikes, and the file was as flat as a tin can in about a minute. The thin metal was placed back in the bed of hot coals. After the metal was reheated, the folding process continued.

Under the watchful eyes of Mr. Schmidt, the two boys developed their standard forging procedure. Safety was their first consideration. The three friends talked about the procedures they were following, and they soon had established a precise and consistent way of working. "This should speed our knife making," Ito commented, as he placed four more files in the bed of burning coal. Once at working temperature, they were flattened in sequence, and placed back to heat. By working on four files, there was no delay waiting for metal to reheat.

The boys' interest was in producing throwing knives. "They will require a temper very different from a hunting knife or file," their mentor said. "A throwing knife needs to be particularly tough. A razor-sharp edge is not important. In fact, it is not desirable. The entire blade has to withstand hard impact with rocks or metal and still not dent, crack, break, or chip."

During lunch, Mr. Schmidt repeated the question he had asked several hours earlier, "How many times are you going to fold that metal over itself? One time you said you thought a hundred cycles of three folds each would be about right?" They had managed to put five files through twenty-five cycles of three folds each.

Ito commented, "We haven't located any figures or suggestions about how many times it should be done. If we can produce a high-quality throwing knife without so much work, we'd like that. By the end of the day, the five files should have fifty cycles of three folds each, and we'll still need to try to hammer them into the shape we think will make good throwing knifes. After that, we'll grind the blades into their final shapes, smooth everything, and polish them."

"We like doing the work, but it will take a long time to finish the fifty files we have. We want to start learning to throw pretty soon. Maybe fifty cycles is enough," Danny added.

Again, the sly smile formed on Mr. Schmidt's face and he said, "We have time right now so let's do a little math together. We'll use this piece of paper to illustrate what is happening. We fold it over once and there are two layers. We fold those two layers one more time and there are four layers or leaves. We fold the four on top of each other and, the paper becomes eight layers thick. You did that with the steel file. When you finished the first cycle of three folds each, you had eight layers of steel. Keeping that in mind, how many layers of steel do you think you have already forged?"

The boys put their heads together. "It looks like simple math; eight folds times twenty-five equals two hundred."

"Not a bad quick number, but what did you overlook?"

Again the two boys looked at each other and a flash of insight passed between them. Finally, Danny articulated their realization. "We didn't start with one layer each succeeding cycle of three folds. We started with eight folds."

Ito carried on. "The first fold of the second cycle gave us sixteen layers, the next fold gave us thirty-two, and the third fold of that cycle gave us sixty-four!" And that's just doing two cycles of three folds!"

Mr. Schmidt nodded and added, "One hundred twenty-eight, 256, and 512 are the numbers for your next cycle of three folds each. I think it will be better if you do the math with paper and pencil."

This was the boy's first practical experience with geometric progression, and the numbers were staggering. At the end of five forging cycles of folding three times each cycle, 32,786 leaves of steel had been formed. Following this same procedure, 1,073,741,824 leaves had been formed at the completion of just ten cycles of three folds each! "How can there be so many? Each layer would be too thin to feel."

"You are absolutely correct. They become submolecular in thickness, yet each layer has density and strength. What does it really mean in terms of practical knife making? What have we learned from our calculations?"

"We can do fewer forging cycles. Several bench tests that

are described in your book show ways to determine differences between forgings."

The logic of Mr. Schmidt's questioning really opened awareness of geometrical progression to the boys. "Do you think we messed up on multiplying the numbers?"

As an answer, Mr. Schmidt blinked at the boys, and they blinked back. Then he added, "Even if you were a hundred million off the correct total, do you believe it would really make a difference in the quality of the blade? Let's talk about how you are going to test your blades, to find out if they are as good as you want?"

"First we have to temper the steel before testing it." Danny followed standard, recommended tempering procedures. He worked with white-hot and red-hot forgings, and tried both water and oil immersion procedures. The experiments also included temperature variation of the steel and the liquid, as well as slow and plunging treatments. Danny was more intuitive in this work, but Ito's immaculate record keeping made it possible to abandon some techniques and repeat or make slight variations, while attempting to find exactly what they wanted.

"Ito, perhaps we need to develop those bench tests that were described in the book, to check a blade before it is made into a finished product." Ito was the logical one to work with Mr. Schmidt on the bench test project, because he was much better at reading German than Danny. They started adapting special devices that could provide accurate and repeatable tests for all blades. Danny continued forging the blades made from files.

Their standard blade was eight inches long by an inch and a half wide and three-sixteenths of an inch thick at the center. It tapered to both edges. The standards they wanted to achieve called for the blade to stand five degrees of side deflection, not break, and return to its original shape. The blade was clamped in a vise at one end, and the jaws of a huge wrench tightened on the other. Ito could hardly move the blade. He put a piece of pipe on the end of the wrench to obtain more leverage.

A "sudden shock" jig was developed. The forged blade was clamped in a vise with the flat of the blade parallel to the floor. Four inches of the blade extended beyond the jaws of the vice. A "jig" was made that allowed a sledgehammer head to be dropped from various heights directly onto the last inch of the tip of the blade. Being able to withstand the hammerhead drop from five feet without distorting or snapping the blade was established as their standard.

Chipping of the metal was a harder test to set up, but a "punch" method was used. The forged piece was gripped in a vise with the thin edge up. A hardened center punch was anchored against the knife's edge. The hammer crashed down to hit the punch, to see if it could flake off the edge of the blade. Ito and Mr. Schmidt's jig, with the sledgehammer head drop technique, provided to be their standard, controlled, and repeatable hitting force. When a blade could pass these three tests, it was accepted for further development, and a "production standard" was set.

Danny started hammering the multifolded metal blade blanks into the prescribed shape they wanted for throwing knives. Ito assumed the task of keeping the quality-control records. He also undertook the final finishing of the knives.

When the boys had finished twenty knives, they temporarily closed down the forge. Father Watanabe had brought home a large number of cardboard shipping boxes. These were used to make targets, with concentric circles drawn on them with crayons. These were mounted on a backing of four bales of hay. At last, knife-throwing practice in the barn started in earnest. They began with a half-knife rotation, which was about twelve feet for Ito and fourteen feet for Danny. By noon of the first day, Ito had a sore arm. With that, Ito decided he would learn to throw left-handed as well as with his right. In this way, he could practice longer and double his skills.

During the following weeks, they finished their blades as throwing knives and were exceptionally pleased with the results. Each boy carried eight blades when they went out to the barn or pasture for throwing practice. To the boys, the knives had a good feel and balance.

"It's time to give the knives an acid test," Danny commented. "Because of the danger of the knife ricocheting around, I'd better do this test alone. I want to throw five knives as hard as I can, at that big piece of cast iron. That should wreck them, if anything will."

"That is a good idea, but throw from behind this sheet of

plywood," Ito advised. "We don't want a knife bouncing back into you."

As is the case when youngsters undertake a task, their immediate goal was not to produce knives, but to have some that were suitable for throwing. They remembered Jake saying that knife throwing was his recreation.

When they had the knives they wanted, they devoted hours to practice. In less than a month, each had lost several knives. They were throwing and missing targets out in the cow pasture among the willows and tall grass, and couldn't find them. Their cavalier attitude was that they could always make more. They enjoyed making the blades, and retrieved more worn out files from Chief at the lumber mill.

Danny confided in Mr. Schmidt. "With your trip-hammer, it is easy enough to do twenty forging cycles, and the blades are super. But I doubt if we need that many folds and layers for throwing knives. And as you said, the numbers are crazy."

Mr. Schmidt asked again, "Is there a possibility that too many heating and folding cycles could do more harm than good?"

This was one of Mr. Schmidt's ways of teaching. He didn't tell the boys how to do things. Instead, he asked questions that encouraged them to seek realistic answers. His inquiries could be related to many functions in life, not only to the one specific problem. They often applied it to ways of proceeding. "How much is enough?" "Is more of a good thing necessarily better?" "How do you balance the scales between instinct and knowledge?" "Theory and experience do not necessarily lead to the same conclusions." "Even when problems appear to have different answers, check carefully to identify possible errors." "How good is good enough?" "What are reasonable standards?" Each of his questions had many applications.

Questions from Mr. Schmidt encouraged the boys to seek their own answers. They remained dedicated to throwing their knives, but they returned to the forge and continued having fun experimenting and making blades. Once again, they exhausted the supply of steel files. Two cabinets held over fifty throwing knives on each shelf. This attested to the energetic devotion the boys gave this process.

The step after "layering" was to hammer each blade into the

rough shape desired. The idea was to taper forgings into beautiful "blanks" that required only minimum amounts of grinding, to achieve the desired shape and still preserve the steel they started with. This was all handheld sledgehammer work. Following extensive bench tests, they decided that they would do forgings with five cycles of three folds per cycle, which produced 32,768 molecular layers of steel for their standard throwing knives. Their testing procedures were primitive, but they were unable to detect a better result from twenty folding cycles, over those with just five. Twenty cycles seemed far beyond anything reasonable. They stopped making throwing knives at that point.

They were making items for their own use. Time was of no real importance, and their standard of excellence was set arbitrarily. What they made suited their physical, emotional, and recreational needs. Ito had etched each knife with the number of folding cycles it had been given. As it turned out, in all of their practice, they couldn't distinguish one with twenty folding cycles from one with five, without looking at the number.

Preliminary grinding, shaping, and sharpening of the knives had been done on one of those large sandstone wheels that was turned by foot treadle action. At this stage in blade production, additional heat could make an undesirable change in the temper of the steel. Grinding heat was controlled by a trickle of water running on the stone wheel while it was in use. Then the boys used a buffing wheel to do the final polishing. Their favorite knives for throwing were eight and ten inches long. Even a few six-inch specials were made that could be hidden almost anywhere. They spent less time testing them, but they figured the forging and tempering technique used on the larger blades would be appropriate for the smaller ones.

Some kids threw baseballs or footballs, played tennis, shot baskets, or concentrated on other sports. Organized games, teams, and leagues were formed, and coaches helped youngsters develop an understanding and skills through games. Ito and Danny had these opportunities and participated during gym class activities, but they were hooked on knife throwing. The fifteen-minute period of time they spent with Dead Eye Jake was all the coaching they would ever receive, except for what they gave each other.

They nailed together some pieces of lumber to serve as a new target, and followed Jake's advice. Gripping the blade and throwing with a rigid wrist were the first two things they practiced. "You're better at it than I am," Danny told Ito. It surprised neither of the boys that Ito had mastered that technique almost immediately, or that Danny occasionally lapsed into flipping the blade during the first two weeks. But Danny did develop the necessary skills.

They experimented until they found their personal half-rotation distance. "Danny, what's right for you is a good three feet farther from the target than mine. Maybe it's because you are taller and throw harder."

The boys practiced moving in and away from their basic distance, and developed an "eye feeling and a blade balance awareness" for just the right spot for throwing.

Danny could do most things equally well with either hand. He had found this out when he first started writing Arabic, which is written from right to the left.

"You're way ahead of me, Danny, when it comes to throwing left-handed. It's tough for me, but I'm not going to quit."

The next step was to locate the one-rotation distance. They gripped the knife by the handle, instead of by the blade, and then threw. "This is about the right distance for me," Ito announced. "Keep backing up, Danny. You'll find your distance farther from the target." Soon each boy became consistent. Ito was still having difficulty with his left-handed throws, but he persisted. "The next question is whether we should find our one-and-a-half-rotation distance, or learn how to adjust for the in-between distances. What do you think, Danny?"

"I'd like to see if we can become almost mechanical and consistent at each of the three basic rotation distances, including the one-and-a-half rotations, before we change our grips on the blade." They practiced for months.

The boys devised a challenge "Close your eyes, Ito, and I'll call the target." Dan led Ito around in the barn, where they had eight targets set at different distances. Each target had its own identification number, and they were placed in a semicircle. Eight targets, eight knives, and eight numbers. "Okay, Ito. Targets in this order: 1, 7, 4, 8, 3, 2, 6, 5. Set, throw."

Ito located and placed a knife in each of the targets in the correct order, but he still slowed down when he threw with his left hand, and the point didn't stick in very far. Dan was faster with the eight-knife barrage, and his knife penetration was greater. Target numbers were changed before each test, and the boy doing the throwing didn't know where the numbers were until he opened his eyes and reacted. To make the game more difficult, the distance from one target to the next was not always the same. Sometimes they had to grip the handle, instead of the blade. Other times, they took a few steps toward or away from the target to establish the right throwing distance.

The boys practiced the fast-draw game. They would whip out a knife, whirl from side to side, to find their target, and throw. It was during these games that Danny found that his hand was automatically inching up or down the blade, and seeking the balance point in order to achieve the right rotation for intermediate distances. Then the knife was away, always at full force. This gave him a major speed advantage over Ito. The adjustment was automatic for Danny from the very first. Ito needed to move forward or backward to compensate for rotational distance. Ito's dedication and work ethic produced the essential results.

They continued practicing throwing with either hand, as well as while standing, bent over, kneeling, or lying down. The target could be high, middle, or low, it didn't matter. The essential was to hit the target with point penetration at the maximum possible. Sticking the point in was their first priority. This was important from a practical point of view, as well as for personal satisfaction. When a blade didn't stick, it could easily bounce off and get lost in bunches of grass, bushes, et cetera, depending on where they practiced. Throwing was a major recreational activity for them, but they didn't like searching for blades.

As they became more competent, standards were set. A two-inch circle served as a ten-foot target, a four-inch circle for fifteen feet, and a six-inch circle for twenty feet. Before long, they abandoned targets larger than two inches.

Improvement was measured with the goal to be on target 100 percent of the time, at any distance, with either hand, and from any throwing position. As a point of fact, they were hitting within the two-inch circles at twenty feet and were consistently hitting the same two-inch circle at thirty feet. Reaching their standard for accuracy from a lying position was difficult. Twenty feet was about their limit when throwing from that position. Ito was the more accurate of the two boys with his right hand and Danny remained better with his left hand.

The two friends matured physically, and became stronger. They followed the same procedures for throwing from a two-rotation distances, and then beyond.

From the very first, the eight-inch knife was their favorite, although the ten-inch knife carried better in a wind, hit with greater impact, and consequently, penetrated deeper. With added maturity and strength, their ten-inch knife became their favorite for longer-distance use. The smaller blades had one distinct advantage. They made a neater package to carry. Frequently, they thought of Dead Eye Jake's accuracy distance limit of thirty feet, but that did not satisfy the boys. Their fantasy goal was fifty feet, but they concentrated on thirty feet and less.

This knife-throwing passion had started before the onset of puberty. It became a routine recreational activity. As their maturity and strength developed, they forged twelve-inch blades that were even better for throwing greater distances, particularly in windy conditions.

Targets on a pendulum made even a more difficult challenge. Then they rigged a sloping clothesline and hung a wooden target on a pulley from it. The challenge was to see how many knives they could stick in the moving target during its twenty-foot run along the line. One problem was that the weight of each succeeding knife affected the angle of the suspended target. Raising the high end of the clothesline increased the speed the target passed by them.

The boys did not throw at animals. Killing was not part of their fantasy. They would routinely throw together for a minimum of fifteen minutes daily, though never for spectators.

Although they had their throwing knives, they could pick up almost any knife, ice pick, or other sharp pointed object, sense its balance point, and throw it with power and accuracy. A screwdriver was a totally suitable substitute, and did not carry the stigma of being a killer knife or, officially, a "deadly weapon."

The boys had found their sport. Continual practice and

dedication increased their competence. As is usual among most people who develop skills, there comes a time when they like to demonstrate their abilities, and Danny was no different in this respect. Even the neighborhood kids had never seen the boys making or throwing their knives. However, Danny was strongly influenced by the Watanabe family. In a sense, they performed, but were not exhibitionists. They lived their daily life, doing their tasks at a standard that they knew was acceptable to them. Approval came in the form of personal satisfaction and recognition from within the family. A warm smile, the bow of the head, a gentle touch, a word or two: These were the ultimate acclaim.

Father Watanabe's *A Way* instruction continued, and seemed to fit in nicely with their knife throwing. A target was defined and a way, or method, of adjusting to reach the goal was developed, while maintaining composure. The boys expected to achieve their personal goals in life, and they understood how to work toward accomplishing them.

Competition was not the source of motivation within the Watanabe family, any more than it was with Gran. There was no need to be "as good as or better than others." Achievement standards were personal, and related to themselves. The qualities of character Danny admired so much in the family who had accepted him as one of their own, were ones Ito seemed to have inherited. Danny did his best to emulate them.

Knife throwing was an activity that increased the bonds of friendship and loyalty between them. They also found that it was an activity that relieved stress and tension. A source of satisfaction to the boys was the fact that none of their knives broke or chipped. The points did occasionally turn under a little when they crashed into steel or rocks, but for the most part they showed almost no signs of use or of abuse. And they certainly were used, greatly abused, and thoroughly enjoyed.

20

Bully Bill in the Sixth Grade

Two days after school had started, Bill enrolled as a new sixth grade student at Lincoln School. He immediately upset the balance of power, which had been established over the years. Before Bully Bill arrived, school disputes were resolved through shoving, scuffling, and lots of shouting. Punches were not thrown, because they could spoil friendships. Most "mad ons" lasted less than a day. Official administrative attention seldom was needed.

Bill was as welcome in the schoolyard society as any other newcomer had been. It was expected that he would become comfortable with his new classmates. But not Bill! He was mean. It was not enough for Bill to have someone "give up" in a fight. He wanted to inflict physical pain. Based on his general appearance and size, he was accorded a place in the middle of the pecking society. He progressively beat up kids who would never dare challenge him, or anyone else. His attacks seemed to happen every second week. Torn and bloody shirts, black eyes, swollen lips, a loose or broken tooth, and bruises, were evidence of his perverse nature.

None of the students could understand why he beat up Little Teddie, who was the most physically inept kid in school. Teddie challenged no one on the playground. He was always the last person to be chosen for any softball team and the one who was left, even after all the girls had been selected. But Little Teddie was Bill's target the last day of school in the sixth grade. It was not just humiliation he inflicted; it was physical hurt and abuse, including hard punches to the chest, stomach, and a cut lip. Then he threw Little Teddie to the ground and rolled him over, and over just to maul him as a bear might do. The rest of the kids didn't understand, and neither did Teddie, but that was Bully Billy's way. Danny felt ashamed of himself for not helping Teddie, particularly when Ruthie stared at him while it was happening. This was Teddie, their working partner from the second grade onward. They had been a team. Now they weren't. The hurt expressed in her pleading blue eyes told Danny that he had let the team down. She was emotionally depressed more than Teddy was physically hurt. A questioning expression on Teddie's face was also directed at Danny.

Why hadn't the rest of the class pitched in and helped Little Teddie? More important, why hadn't Danny? He couldn't even begin to explain why to Ruthie or Little Teddie. He supposed none of the classmates knew whether they could or should.

Danny tried to understand Bully Billy. Previously, school yard fights were generally between two kids. In the past, everyone watched, and no one was really hurt. If someone butted in, the two who were scuffling didn't get anything settled. The kids didn't have any experience dealing with a boy such as Bully Bill. Danny didn't fear him, but he was unsure of what to do.

The best Danny could do for Ruthie and Teddie was to promise them that Billy wouldn't get away with that the next year. But Danny learned an important lesson from that incident. Never break faith with a friend. No matter what you do to restore it, the blind and absolute trust that had once existed could seldom be replaced. Danny spent hours talking with Father Watanabe about this problem.

"The more I think about it, the madder I get. I wanted to go to Bully Billy's house and squash him. I hate what he has been doing to the kids, and particularly to Little Teddie."

"Yes, that is something all your friends would understand. Many would like to see you do it and I am sure you could. What was the worst part of the beating you saw?"

"It was the look in the eyes of Little Teddie and Ruthie. Would it have been wrong to interfere?"

"You must trust your instincts and best judgment when meeting such difficult situations. If you had interfered, would you have been robbing Teddie of his sense of manhood?"

"That was part of the problem I was having. Little Teddie just stood there and took the punches and accepted the mauling he was given. He would never have struck back, but he didn't even try to defend himself. When it was all over, everyone seemed proud of Teddie for being able to take all of Bully Bill's abuse. And everyone seemed to be ashamed of Bully Bill, and wondered why he picked on a guy who most of the girls could beat?"

"Did Little Teddie cry, or show himself to be a coward? You know from our defensive philosophy of *A Way* that negative energy needs to be directed elsewhere. Yes, I understand that Little Teddie was beaten, but the social energy of the group was with him. Think about these things. See if you find answers to your problems."

Danny remembered Ruthie saying to Teddie, "You were awfully brave to stand up to Bully Bill, and not let him make you cry. Not everyone could do that, and he can be so mean."

After hearing Ruthie's words, Little Teddie realized he had learned some things about himself. He could take a lot of punishment, and it wasn't nearly as bad as he had feared it might be. He wouldn't live in fear of Bully Bill anymore. He could take a beating and still not be whipped. It was almost as if he had won.

School was out and summer was ahead. There were lots of things to do, and Bully Billy was of no importance to Danny and Ito. The class would be in the seventh grade when they came back to school in about three months. Maybe by then, Bully Bill would have changed. If that didn't happen, Danny figured he might be Bill's next target. That didn't worry Danny, and it might do the kids at school some good if they saw Bully Bill get beaten, but would it help Bill? Whipping Billy might give some of the kids a feeling of revenge, but that wouldn't lead to self-respect or regard for others. Everyone knew that Little Teddie had gained a great deal of admiration, and that Bully Billy had "shamed" himself. Maybe things would work out when school started again. Secretly, Danny hoped Bully Billy would start something with him. He really wanted a chance to beat the bully. Danny was still struggling with his *A Way* philosophy that should have controlled such negative emotional feelings.

21

A Way

Ito's father had started the boys' instruction with the *A Way* discipline when they were in the second grade. He added information and techniques as they matured, and when they had mastered previous lessons. He worked regularly with them, to improve their coordination, balance, agility, muscular strength, and endurance.

He taught the boys personal defense. One technique he used was to have the boys attack him as viciously as possible. They were reluctant at first, but quickly recognized his agility and calm reassurance. He encouraged them to try everything they could devise, including fists flying, knees jabbing, feet kicking, and shoulder tackles. All were countered, diverted, and defeated without hurting the boys. He had no special name for his discipline of defense. He simply referred to it as *A Way of Life,* or *A Way* for short. He said, "This system utilizes no means of attack. Its sole function is to defuse a situation by redirecting anger, emotion, and action in a manner that is nonconfrontational, non-injurious, and respectful of the opponent."

After the attack had been diverted and neutralized, Father Watanabe repeatedly demonstrated his techniques. Then the boys practiced the same moves, until their reflexes became second nature. Variations in the means of redirecting an attack were introduced, and again, long sessions resulted in more complex reactions and techniques. In each case, the physical basics did not change: Angle, Base, Balance, Leverage, and Reaction.

For every moment Father Watanabe spent with the boys dealing with physical defense, he devoted far more time helping them understand the mental and emotional imperative to prevent physical conflict. "The mental side of *A Way* is the most important. We must strive for self-composure and inner tranquillity. It is not wise to meet force with force! Instead, react and redirect. It is difficult to achieve almost instant composure, as if one were clicking a light switch when fear, anger, or other emotions interfere. *A Way* failure can be expected if emotions are allowed to dominate our reactions. Normally, positive emotions such as joy, love, elation, and pleasure upset the essential internal *tranquillity,* when physical danger exists."

Ito had lived all of his life following the positive guidelines of *A Way*, so he lacked the strong contrasts that were so evident to Danny. The boys practiced the physical, mental, and emotional requirements of the *A Way* lifestyle daily. Control of the instinctive responses of fear, flight, frustration, and rage were difficult. The adrenal glands automatically flooded the circulatory system and this had to be countered. As with all instincts, they are part of human nature, and it was up to the boys to learn to adjust to them.

Mr. Watanabe said. "As you become more mature, you will realize that success in a fight, utilizing our *A Way* techniques, is really quite simple. However, *A Way* truly is about resolving problems and conflict without fighting. It supports a positive way of life that helps a person live a tranquil, secure, and productive existence. Avoiding conflict with dignity is far more important, and much more difficult, than winning a fight. Mastery of the technique is not evaluated by how many fights you have won. Success is determined by how many conflicts have been resolved, in which all parties emerged with a sense of dignity and mutual regard."

Throughout their training, Father Watanabe emphasized the underlying philosophy of *A Way*. "Remember, a person who trains only for conflict, expects to resolve problems in the manner in which he is trained. You should be able to defend yourself successfully from physical, mental, and emotional attacks. You are growing rapidly. Your physical strength and coordination have developed beyond your years. Your diligent attention to details of technique and daily practice will enable you to defeat any physical attack successfully. However, there is much that remains to be learned."

Ito and Danny developed competence and confidence. Without warning, one youngster might attack the other in the tradi-

137

tional youthful fashion. By following *A Way* techniques of redirecting the attack, the outcome was never in doubt. Occasional bruises, black eyes, scrapes, and lesser injuries did occur, but almost exclusively to the attacker. These minor setbacks could be expected in normal preteen activities, and in no way did they affect their bonds of friendship. Instead, it supported their mutual regard. It was important to their sense of boyhood, and anticipation of manhood, to win every fight, but confrontations were avoided. Some kids spread the rumor that both boys were "chicken" to get into a fight, but they couldn't figure out why they would be. Neither boy swaggered around and flexed his muscles, but their outstanding physiques were evident to anyone who looked past their loose-fitting clothing.

One day, Father Watanabe brought out a baseball bat, handed it to Ito, and ordered him to hit a home run. Ito's father's head was to be the ball. Ito and Danny were dumbfounded and frightened of what could happen. However, when they saw the expression of total composure on Father Watanabe's face, they realized that he was in no danger.

Ito approached, maneuvered, feinted, jabbed, and faked. Father Watanabe moved slightly to face the attack. Ito was quick, very quick, but when the swing was launched, so was Ito, and the bat followed him. A second bat was produced, and the two boys were ordered to attack at the same time. The results were predictable. Both boys ended up on the ground and Father Watanabe remained unperturbed, calm, and untouched, as he smiled at the boys he adored. He said, "A weapon may not always be an advantage." A lesson had been demonstrated. Ito and Danny realized there was still much to learn. But the fundamentals remained the same. Father Watanabe would attack the boys using a brawler's style, and each boy found he was able to redirect the assaults as readily as Father Watanabe. He, and one of the others, would launch such an attack and the defender remained successful, if he didn't make a mistake in his techniques. Mastering the instinctive emotional reactions were the more difficult factors.

The boys were about to enter the seventh grade when Father Watanabe said, "Do you know the young man Ted Hale, whose family recently moved into the house just west of Danny's? He and his best friend, Jimmy Knight, are in their last year of high school, and are part of the school's championship boxing team. They have offered to give you boxing lessons." Ito had a questioning look on his face, so his father added, "Boxing is a physical skill I do not know. Perhaps familiarity with the techniques may be of value to you. We do not shun knowledge and experiences that come from other sources."

Jim Knight did most of the teaching, including how to throw jabs, hooks, crosses, uppercuts, and counters. He taught the boys how to add power to the punches, how to snap a punch while rotating the fist from a thumb-up position to the knuckles-up position when it landed. Traditional boxer targets were identified, and these were added to the boy's knowledge about vulnerable pressure points, which would be accessible, with or without gloves.

On the defensive side, they were taught how to slip and deflect a punch with the right hand and, at the same time, step inside the opponent's lead and counter with their own left.

The concepts of boxing were interesting. Knowing a little about that discipline helped the boys become more effective with their *A Way* training. Of course, it really was Father Watanabe's system, but the boys were making it their own by continual practice and study. They benefited a great deal by being hit really hard by Ted and Jim on the side of the head, and in the chest and stomach. The boys knew that they did not want to experience very much of that type of punishment, particularly since they knew there was a better way ... *A Way*.

"Boxing seems to be terribly energy-inefficient," Ito said. "The economy of energy and personal tranquillity we have with *A Way* make me want to become even better at it." They resisted using their defensive system against Jim, although they were well aware of the multitude of opportunities they had to redirect Jim's aggressive punches, and send him flying.

The boys attended a few of the high school's boxing exhibitions against other schools. Ted and Jim were conference champions at their weight classifications.

Ito and Danny found it was exciting to watch the boxing matches, particularly because they knew Ted and Jim, and felt as if they understood a little about the sport. But it did seem

139

a crude and punishing way of fighting. They felt that a sport that considered beating the opponent into unconsciousness as an ultimate victory, was totally uncivilized and brutal. They preferred the less aggressive and more respectful method of using Father Watanabe's *A Way* techniques.

After six weeks, the school's boxing season ended. Ted and Jimmy went on to participate in baseball, and the boxing lessons ceased.

Father Watanabe resumed instructing the boys. "You now are mature enough to begin another phase of our *A Way* program. This places an awesome responsibility on each of you. It prepares you to attack, disable, or even kill your opponent."

Both boys were shocked by the concept. It seemed impossible that a man as gentle as Father Watanabe could know such techniques. It felt improbable that he could even contemplate such actions.

"This knowledge will help you control how you use the first part of our system. In essence, it is a follow-up on the techniques you already know."

The boys learned to apply the Japanese Death Lock, the Carotid Artery Choke, and how and where to deliver debilitating, and even lethal, kicks and chops. They also learned how to limit the force used, so the effects would be stunning rather than lethal. Again, practice and uncompromising mental discipline would help Ito and Danny become proficient and responsible.

Danny was continually reminded that the daily lifestyle of Father, Mother, and Ito Watanabe reflected the tranquil nature and philosophy of *A Way*. He had seen all three of them endure insulting verbal abuse, when he was positive Father Watanabe could have beaten the crap out of anyone. At first, Danny became livid with rage ... partly with Father Watanabe for putting up with such abuse. Instead, the Watanabe family endured indignity. Occasionally, an offender might apologize for his behavior later. This had a maturing, and sobering effect on Danny.

"It is with regret that I must teach you the final part of our *A Way* system. In my own lifetime, it became necessary to not only defend, but to attack in order to defend. This happens when you can no longer wait to repel aggression. It occurs when your calm and reasoned judgment tells you that to wait and defend invites defeat or unusual risk of injury or death to yourself or others. It is of the utmost importance that your inner peace and tranquillity prevail. If you become emotionally involved, you may become a fanatical death merchant who kills heedlessly and harvests his own disgrace and possible demise. Your responsibility for controlling the use of this discipline is without equal."

For the second time, Father Watanabe had said "our" *A Way* system. The boys were aware that this was no mistake. It was his way of telling them that the system was theirs, and not just *a* system. The complex philosophy and techniques of *A Way* were uniquely theirs. In addition to the usual body weapons of hand, elbows, knees, feet, head, and shoulders as deadly weapons, the boys learned to recognize and utilize even innocuous items in the immediate environment as weapons. "This discipline expands your responsibility to family, community, and culture. It must never be used, except when no other means will save you or others from death." Danny and Ito would never forget his penetrating scrutiny of their inner souls.

In her quiet and subtle way, Mother Watanabe had participated in the boys' training from the earliest days. Danny had been a dedicated student of her massage techniques, much more so than Ito. Now she added her own talents to those of her husband. Alternatively, she would ask one of the boys to help her in a demonstration. "Let your fingers touch and fly from one pressure point to others. Be sensitive to what is happening to the muscles controlled by nerves coming from the various parts of the spine. Applied properly, you will be able to relieve pain and stress in almost any part of the body, and from almost any cause. You will find it easier to locate and apply pressure, when the back is free from clothing. Also, it is more comforting and effective to have energy passing from your fingertips, to their bare skin. Indeed, the pressure points can be pleasure points, when touched in the right manner, and in the proper sequence."

Her calming and therapeutic technique had been utilized on Ito from infancy. She had started teaching him the techniques at about the time Danny's family had moved next door. As was the case with most lessons she taught Ito, she included Danny, who was far more interested in learning the discipline than Ito.

Her ancient charts were similar to ones Danny found in

Gray's Anatomy, many years later. Training and practical experience helped the boys understand where they should concentrate their finger and hand contact, and the amount of pressure to apply. "With practice and knowledge, you will find you can access these points, even when the person is fully clothed. It can be very helpful, but touching the bare skin is much better." Moving along the spinal column, she taught the boys dozens of pressure points. She explained that these techniques were used to relieve pain and induce relaxation. She called this technique "playing the piano on the spinal column." Mother Watanabe taught the boys dozens of other pressure points throughout the body. The boys became aware of stress characteristics that others were experiencing. They conveyed this by subtle movements or changes in the carriage of their body. A person's posture could signal discomfort. Later on, Danny could usually predict which of his classmates really needed glasses and he could relieve the discomfort associated with eyestrain.

One day it was obvious that Mrs. Fulton, one of Danny's teachers, was having a terrible headache. She was sick to her stomach. When the principal took over her class, Danny spoke with him and suggested that he might be able to help her. He recognized Danny's concern and sincerity. The boy was allowed to go to the teachers' room, where Mrs. Fulton was sitting in a straight back chair, with her arms on a table cradling her head.

Danny had knocked before entering, and assured her quietly, "I have been taught how to relieve pain, and if you will allow me, I am sure I will be able to help you."

Muffled groans and protests were accompanied by a slight nod of her head, and Danny began. He placed a finger of each hand on the top of her head in line with her eyes. "Roll your eyes upward and try to look right at my fingers. Concentrate on that point for a few moments." This produced obvious strain, but Danny proceeded. "Now look down as if you are trying to see your lips." Her head and neck strain started to relax. This sequence was repeated three times. Then with a light touch, he began the massage technique Mother Watanabe had taught him.

Danny exerted light pressure, starting at the bridge of the nose, then followed the eyebrows outward to the notch midway along the upper eye socket, and pressed there for a few seconds.

Then pressure was exerted along the eyebrow line, outward to the cheekbone, across the temple with increasing pressure, and around the back of the ear. He continued to the base of the skull, where the little promontories of bone extend downward. Then harder pressure was exerted around the base of the skull to the "knowledge bump" at the back of the head. Pressure and massage was continued down the large muscles to the shoulder blade. From there, the procedure began again at the bridge of the nose. This time, it followed the same pathway, only to divert to the two large neck muscles, and then moved downward to the point where they attached to the collarbone and top of the breastbone.

Within a minute, Mrs. Fulton had visibly relaxed. Five minutes later she was asleep. Danny left quietly and returned to class. A few minutes later, Mrs. Fulton was back. She smiled at the principal, and thanked him for taking the class, then nodded her appreciation to Danny.

At that time, he had no idea that some women developed debilitating migraine headaches during their menstrual period. In fact, he knew nothing about such female functions. After class, Mrs. Fulton proclaimed, "Danny, you must have magic in your hands and fingers. When I have this problem again, would you mind if I asked for your help?" A smile and nod of his head provided the reply she needed. When he returned home, Danny shared his experience with Mother Watanabe. Mrs. Fulton's urgent need for help occurred two or three days each month.

Sometimes weekend phone calls were made to the Watanabe household, asking for Danny to go to Mrs. Fulton's home to give her a massage. At that time, because of the expense, Gran and Danny did not have a phone. It was normal for Danny to be called two or three days in a row. During the eighth grade, the principal would occasionally enter the room where Danny was attending class, nod, and he would go to the teachers' room to give Mrs. Fulton her massage.

Occasionally, Father or Mother Watanabe, or Mr. Schmidt needed a massage, and Ito or Danny would be asked to practice the technique. The boys also gave massages to each other. Gran opposed such "mollycoddling," because "a nice cup of hot tea should set everything right." She was experiencing a great

143

deal of pain from "liftin' and shiftin'" one of the elderly women she helped. Mother Watanabe finally bullied Gran into accepting help.

From that time onward, there were occasions when Gran would acknowledge that a nice cup of hot tea *and a massage* would set her right. "It's the old age what's gettin' at me," or "I'm becoming a softie."

Massage became a topic of conversation at the dinner table one evening. Danny sensed there was some special agenda, but he didn't understand what it was. He looked at Gran, Mr. Schmidt, Ito, and his Watanabe parents. Father Watanabe stood to speak. This was an indication that a profound statement was going to be made that affected the entire family.

"Each of us has received massages from Mother Watanabe, Ito, and Danny. We have discussed this topic frequently among ourselves, and we have come to the conclusion that there is some special energy that we receive from you, Danny. We cannot define it, nor do we understand it. Perhaps we will call it a special magic, but it is a powerful gift that we proclaim."

With his head bowed in humility, the boy acknowledged the high praise, but he didn't have words to respond. He looked and Gran, she winked, and smiles flooded all their faces.

It was at the beginning of the eighth grade that Mother Watanabe taught the boys two advanced pressure procedures. "Your *A Way* techniques are wonderfully efficient and effective, but there may come a time when someone actually penetrates your defense and obtains a hold on you. Then you may derive benefits from what I call *Another Way*. As you might surmise, this technique is based on touching nerve centers you already know. You need only apply pressure from a slightly different angle and with increased intensity, to render your attacker almost totally helpless. You may also subject him to extreme and unsupportable anguish. Let me demonstrate with the 'funny bone' in your elbow. The feeling is familiar to all of us. You find that your arm feels numb, and you have a sudden loss of strength in the hand and forearm, as well as the unpleasant tingling sensation that results from momentary contact. Increased finger pressure for a few seconds can disable the arm for several minutes. The induced discomfort may be varied from mild all the way through to, and including, excruciating pain. I will stop at this point before you experience agony.

"Through your knowledge about pressure points to relieve tension and pain, you will have access to several vulnerable 'anguish points,' no matter what kind of hold an attacker may have on you. You must practice on yourself for months before you apply pressure to others. In this way, you will learn the direction and intensity needed to be effective."

Mother Watanabe was well aware that household peace and tranquillity can be greatly enhanced by assuring that sexual satisfaction and gratification is extended to both the woman and the man. Her own mother had taught her erotic techniques to arouse and satisfy a man, and also how to do the same for herself. It was the tradition that a woman should do this for her man, but he had no responsibility to the woman in this respect. If she was not satisfied when he was finished, it was up to her to "finish herself off."

She thought there should be a better way to accomplish this. She had taught her husband *A Better Way* and he asked her to teach the boys these techniques. She described, explained, and demonstrated the procedures without ever touching them or having them touch her. "You may think of this as an enhancement of the joy of life." To her and her husband the procedures were as natural as enjoying a beautiful sunset together. For the remainder of Danny's life, he would be grateful to her for her thoughtful and timely instructions.

22

The Beginning of DISKnife

There were still two months of summer vacation left, before Danny and Ito were to begin seventh grade. Because Frank, the farmer, had hired a man to help him on the farm on a full-time basis, the boys had not been needed as much for Saturday work. However, the growing season was at hand and there were weeding, hoeing, and other types of hard labor ahead. Danny had been counting on being employed as a means of helping Gran with the household budget.

During this period of indecision, Mr. Schmidt asked the boys, "What do you plan to do this summer? Are you thinking of making more knives, or are you finished with the forge?"

Ito answered for both of them. "We want to get as good at knife throwing as we can, but we don't need any more throwing knives. We seldom lose them, because we usually hit our targets. None of them have broken, and we have about eighty in reserve. Those could last a lifetime. We had fun producing the knives, but we've wondered about making a hunting knife."

"That's right," Danny added. "Remember Chief, the man at the mill who gave us the used files we made into throwing knives? He's a hunter, and we'd like to make a special knife for him. But first we need to ask him what would be needed to make it exceptional."

"Ah, yes. He's the man who is a Cherokee Indian. That sounds interesting. I'd enjoy watching you develop that project."

At lunchtime, the boys rode their bikes to the mill and talked with Chief. Danny felt doubly obliged and grateful to him, because once when Chief had heard that Danny was having diarrhea and vomiting, he had helped him. He walked nearly a mile from the mill through the railroad pasture to collect "cure all" weed to make a medicinal tea. Also, he had been a close friend of the boy's father.

Chief commented, "I was sorry to have missed you, when you came back for more worn-out files. Mr. Schmidt told me that you fellows made some good throwing knives from them."

"You bet we did! In fact, we made almost all of them into throwing knives, but we did save a few out for another project," Ito replied.

"I'd like to see them if you have a couple with you? Did you learn how to throw them?"

"We don't like to carry them with us. People get uncomfortable when they see big knives. They'd think of them as weapons, and wonder what we were up to. So we do all our throwing on our own property. The reason we came, is that we'd like to make a hunting knife for you, if you'd like one. But we don't know what would make a good knife into a great one."

"Good. I have more worn-out files to get rid of, and I'll drop them off on my way home from work. While I'm there, maybe you could show me some of your knife throwing."

Both boys were excited by Chief's interest in watching them throw, but they had never thrown knives with anyone other than their family watching. They had the notion that, because Chief was part American Indian, he should know everything about using knives as weapons.

Chief arrived shortly after finishing work, and the boys took him directly to the forge and foundry area. They showed him their two shelves filled with throwing knives.

"Wow! You do have a lot of knives, and they look professionally made. They sure don't look like files anymore. What happens when they hit a rock or something made of steel?"

"Sometimes they bounce, so step farther back and we'll show you," Ito replied.

In rapid-fire sequence the boys threw knives that banged into concrete, steel, and stone in the barn area. The knives were gathered for Chief to examine. "They look undamaged. Maybe they didn't hit point-first? I don't see any particular damage on the point."

"We seldom miss what we aim for," Danny replied with a wry smile. They walked into the barn and immediately planted

147

knives in their various targets. They threw from different distances and the knives impaled in close groups. They finished by throwing at moving targets on the clothesline. Distances varied from ten to thirty feet, and the boys didn't miss.

"I see what you mean! You've been on target every time, and with difficult throws."

"Can you tell us what design and features would make the best deer hunter's knife?"

"I'll do better than that. I'm butchering a yearling steer this weekend. I'll phone you before I start, and you can come over and watch as I skin it, and cut up the carcass."

That Saturday afternoon, the boys went to Chief's home. As he started skinning the steer, he explained, "This is the first irritation. I continually have to stop to resharpen this knife. The blade needs to hold an edge, when it cuts through tough hair. It is similar to cutting through steel wool. Here's another problem, the blade needs to be flexible and yet firm when it's used on tough tendons and ligaments. These problems are bad enough with this young steer, but they are much worse with a deer."

Chief continued, "Hunting knives have only one cutting edge, and it's annoying to have to turn the knife over when I need to slice in the opposite direction for a few inches. Crashing into bone should not damage the edge, but it does. It should slide easily through fresh flesh. To be a really good hunting knife, it should also be suitable for cutting tree branches and then for making a 'shave stick' to help start a campfire. The knife needs to be efficient and look manly. Eye appeal is vital. It ought to be easy to care for, have a nice balance, and feel comfortable. It shouldn't be heavy or in the way when it is not being used. These are things virtually every hunter and most campers would like to have incorporated into one knife. Unfortunately, no such knife exists. None really holds its edge when it is put to harsh or prolonged use. Professional butchers are always giving their knives a few swipes on a butcher's steel. I'd say that's the greatest problem, but there seems to be no help for that."

The boys expressed their thanks and headed home. Their heads were filled with design and forging essentials. They decided to make a knife that would cut in both directions. The last two and a half inches of the tip would be sharp on both edges, so it could do just that. With those considerations in mind they started designing blades.

The hunting knives they saw in stores had sharp points suitable for stabbing. They looked masculine, but appeared to be inefficient for the job of skinning or butchering. The boys' trial blade had a rounded tip nearly an inch in diameter, and broadening out to an inch and a half. It was sharp all the way to the handle of the cutting edge, around the tip and back two and a half inches from the top edge. The result was a totally unique-looking knife, and one that would prove to be remarkably functional for its intended purposes.

With the design determined, they considered the metal-tempering process that would give them the characteristics they wanted. All these features were radically different from their throwing knives. No sharp point for embedding into a target would be needed. To be a good skinning knife, it had to have side-to-side flexibility, sharpen easily, and hold that edge.

They first worked with their design using files Chief had given them. They made changes in the tempering process, but they were unable to achieve the essential flexibility. The mill file was suitable for throwing knives, but it was the wrong alloy for spring or flexibility. Of course, they went to their best source of information, and asked how to produce such a blade. Who else, but Mr. Schmidt? He led them to his storage shed, and asked the boys to remove two wooden boxes from one of the shelves. They were heavy and covered with dust. "Your wagon could be useful because those boxes are heavier than you will want to carry all the way to the forge." They appeared to have been sitting on the shelf for years. Content information was stenciled on the box: "One gross blade blanks, knife; spring steel; 14" x 1½" x ⬜". The name and address of the manufacturer were also stenciled.

Mr. Schmidt handed Danny a screwdriver. "These boxes have never been opened. As you can see, they were put together with screws instead of nails, so they would not break open as easily. Let's see what the contents look like."

The box contained rectangular pieces of steel. They had been dipped in Cosmoline to prevent rust, and were individually wrapped in waxed paper. Mr. Schmidt explained, "Those blade blanks are ready for shaping and sharpening and should make good knives. Do you want to do anything special with them?"

Danny explained, "First, we'd like to give one of them our regular bench test for chipping and breaking. Then we'd check the amount of flexibility before breaking or forming a permanent bend in the metal. Next, we'd sharpen it, to see how good an edge it will take, and how long it can be used before becoming dull."

Mr. Schmidt smiled and nodded. "Yes, you will be wise to make a complete blade, as a control model for comparison. You'll need several blades in order to make all of your tests. Then you can do your forging cycles and compare them."

This was the first time Mr. Schmidt had actually made a suggestion about how to proceed instead of asking questions. Ito and Danny looked at each other and realized that Mr. Schmidt had become emotionally involved. It was as if some dream from his past had been awakened.

"How long have you had those blade blanks, Mr. Schmidt? It must have been fifteen or twenty years." He nodded, and Danny continued. "You wanted to make knives years ago, didn't you?" Again their mentor nodded. "So why didn't you?"

"I was busy earning a living and paying off this property. Then I got sick and my heart wasn't so good. But maybe, it was because I was afraid to live out my dream ... to see if I could be expert enough to make something people would buy. So now, maybe we will join together and find out what your skills and my dreams can produce. Already, your design is unique."

He looked excited, but a little weak and uncertain. He sat down in his big chair in the foundry area, and watched as the boys began.

Danny lit the coal in the forge as they cleaned Cosmoline from six blade blanks. A drop test on the side of the untreated blank was first. It made a twanging sound when the drop hammer head hit the suspended tip of the blade. This action bounced the hammer head up in the air. The blank was not damaged. An increase in the height of the drop produced the same result. The weight was doubled. This had been enough to snap a throwing knife blade, which was both hard and brittle. The new blank flexed, but snapped back to its original shape.

With one end of the blank gripped in the vise, a long piece

of pipe was fitted onto the blade protruding from the vice. The pipe gave the leverage needed to bend the blade blank. After deflecting it ten degrees, it was released and the blank returned to normal. It was then placed flat against an untested piece, and they were identical. Thirty degrees of bending was required before the metal deformed and wouldn't return to its normal flat status, but even then, it didn't break. The punch test showed the blanks to be softer than used files, which was expected.

The next steps were grinding, polishing, and honing one edge of the unforged blank. The three needed to know how sharp the edge could be, and if it would hold that edge. A trickle of water on the stone prevented a change in the basic temper of the steel. It was not long before a rough edge had been formed. Then a change was made from the coarse stone to a fine one. The cutting edge of the blade started getting sharper. Finally a butcher's steel was used and a fine edge resulted. A few cuts through a piece of deerhide, with the hair on it, dulled the edge quickly. This blank had not been subjected to the folding routine the boys had used when forging their throwing knives.

The boys looked at Mr. Schmidt, and he nodded. "Perhaps this blade will be number one during the experimental phase of your work? Shall we let our book guide us toward making a more durable edge? "

"Our book" was a reference to the manual written in German, dealing with all types of topics concerning metallurgical processes and procedures. Danny labored through the text. The foreign-looking Old German type had him stumbling, and there were too many technical words that he didn't know. Ito was much better at reading, partly because he had a more extensive vocabulary. There were some underlined sentences that Mr. Schmidt had marked years before. The numbers on the packing slip, in the box of blanks, corresponded with some in the book.

Mr. Schmidt explained. "These numbers and letters identify the alloys recommended for producing outstanding blades. The other list is of recommended temperatures for immersion and emersion tempering, following forging the blanks into the desired shapes." The recommended temperatures and procedures were followed, and the edges became harder to sharpen. However, they stayed sharp longer. The quality of the edge was still short of what they were seeking.

"Now what do we want to do?" Mr. Schmidt questioned. But he already knew, because Danny was putting eight blanks in the forge, and was cranking the handle of the rotary fan to bring up the heat, so the forging and folding process could begin. "How many folding cycles do you plan to do?" Mr. Schmidt asked.

"Is it okay with you, Mr. Schmidt, if we experiment with your blade blanks?"

"We will think of them as *our* blade blanks. There are 288 of them, and how many will we use in my lifetime? We need to experiment to see what gives us the best possible blade. Are we agreed that we should produce a knife that is much better than anything currently available?" The intensity of his involvement showed in Mr. Schmidt's eyes, and in his voice. Making a superb knife was his great dream, and now they were trying to make that dream a reality.

"We share your dream," Ito replied. "I know it may sound foolish, but I believe we will succeed." Their unity of purpose dominated the atmosphere.

Two boys, who were thirteen years old, and a man in excess of seventy, shared an interest—even a vision. It became increasingly intense, as fantasy, pursuit, inspiration, and work were combined, to pursue a possibility.

"Our first question is, what number of folding cycles will give us the best results? Our threefold cycle produces 512 molecular layers of steel. Four produced 4,096. Five gave us 32,768. Six yields 262,144. Seven has 2,097,125. Eight resulted in 16,777,216. The number for nine was 134,217,728. Ten produces 1,075,741,824," Mr. Schmidt said. "All of these numbers are staggering, but we can do them since we have the trip-hammer."

"That will take eight blade blanks, and just for kicks, I'd like to do one with twenty folding cycles that produces that crazy number of over a thousand quadrillion—or whatever that number was. That will require nine blade blanks in all."

Danny and Ito started laying out the blade blanks. The two boys and Mr. Schmidt realized that they were holding their breath. The *whoomp—bang, whoomp—bang, whoomp—bang* of the forge started, and as one, Mr. Schmidt, Ito, and Danny started breathing again. The blanks were flattened, folded, refolded, and folded again. Reheating started the second cycle. They followed this procedure, and included forming the blank into the general knife shape.

Mr. Schmidt sat quietly in his chair, keenly aware and fully involved in every action. His ultimate dreams and ambitions were being flattened, folded, and forged—perhaps into the oblivion of failure. He sighed and thought, "Well, at last we have a genuine beginning."

The boys understood Mr. Schmidt's anxiety. He desperately wanted to participate, physically at the forge ... to be doing that part of the work. For most of his life, iron and steel had yielded to heat and the blows of his hammer. He had shaped it, and made it submit to his will, knowledge, and skill. Then had come the war that delayed and destroyed. He felt that he should have succumbed to the ravages of scarlet fever, which had left his heart incapable of even a modest amount of exertion. He had become inundated by the rust and dust of his former occupation. It had settled around him, and had formed a shroud of "no dreams, no enthusiasm, no future, and no reason to exist."

Then the Watanabe family had entered his life, and later, Annie Louise. He preferred that name to "Gran." Perhaps because he desperately sought someone his own age who was not "old." Annie had maintained the vigor, enthusiasm, and strength he lacked. He found the wrinkles and etched lines in her face appealing, even enchanting.

Danny was doing most of the forge work, and Ito was keeping the records. Ito etched on each blade blank the final number of folding cycles it had received.

The trio had worked right through lunch. It was two hours after dinnertime when the forge was closed for the night. One original blade had been done without forging, and nine blades remained to be sharpened and tested.

Mother Watanabe was indulgent when forge work was under way. By the time the three were ready to sit at the table, bowls of hot soup were waiting for them. This was her routine whenever she was told that a long project was in progress at the forge. Vegetables from their garden went into a big pot, along with rice, and her special herbs. This delicious dinner could be served within a few minutes' notice. Frequently, pieces of chicken or meat were added to the pot. Being late happened only on rare occasions, because everyone treasured family mealtimes.

Once dinner was over and dishes were done, Mr. Schmidt excused himself from the family gathering. He retired to his big chair near the forge, to relive the most precious moments in the past thirty years of his life.

The two boys had walked hand-in-hand with him on their way to dinner. In a jumble of words from both Ito and Danny, they said so many things. "You are fun to be with." "You know so much." "We love you." "This wouldn't be so much fun without you." "You help us make our dreams come true, too." "What do you think or know about...?" "Is it true that...?"

He had a purpose. He was needed and treasured. He was loved. He knew of no greater riches.

That night, deep, restful sleep renewed him, and he greeted the new day with vigor, and an enthusiasm, he had not known for years.

The three believed it was nonsense to bend the blanks any more than fifteen degrees to each side of their center. That was where they stopped, and the blades snapped back to the centerline without difficulty. All blades performed well when subjected to the weight drop, but it appeared that the blades with the lower number of folding cycles were not quite as lively in springing back from the shock.

"Perhaps we can count the number of rebounds before the hammer comes to rest on the blade," Ito suggested. The first few rebounds were easy to count, but the final ones became more of a chatter that couldn't be counted with any accuracy. Mr. Schmidt disappeared for a few moments and came back with a few pieces of paper. One was placed on the blade blank that was being tested. As the hammer was dropped, the paper was pulled across the tip of the blank. It was possible to count the number of impressions embossed into the paper. The fewest number of impressions came from the control blank that had received no forging at all. They could find no real difference when they compared the blade with five folding cycles with those having more. This included the one extreme one, with its twenty folding cycles.

The test standards were too crude to determine any variation in the chipping or flaking of blades that had received five folding cycles or more. The blades with three and four folding cycles didn't satisfy them, and they were abandoned at that point. No more work was done with relatively low numbers of folds. That left them with five blades for continued testing.

The punch test revealed that blades with the most leaves allowed the least penetration. These were the blades that were harder to sharpen, but they held a better edge. The group could determine no real advantage between a blade made with six forging cycles, and one with ten. The idea of a billion and seventy-five-plus million submicroscopic leaves or layers of steel per knife sounded unique to the two boys. Mr. Schmidt agreed that such a high number of leaves might be far beyond what was reasonably needed, but the idea of that figure delighted him. It certainly was unique. Ten forging cycles became their temporary standard.

The next experiments involved heating the remaining blades, and following various tempering techniques that had been recommended in Mr. Schmidt's books. Ito recorded each variation in the process, according to the number etched on the blade.

The next step was to temper each blade blank. Ito maintained his accurate record book. This kept the workers from repeating experiments they had already done. "Our test system is so crude, it hardly seems worthwhile to do it," Ito observed.

They had only one big wheel for grinding and sharpening of the blades. Ito was using it, and as he finished each blade, Mr. Schmidt honed a fine edge on it.

While they were doing that, Danny went back to the forge. Blanks that had been given three and four folding cycles were put to heat again. From no known source ... perhaps some form of inspiration or accident ... he made a few subtle changes, and some radical ones, in the forging and tempering process he used on the two remaining blade blanks. Although Ito usually did the record keeping, Danny carefully kept his own record of each step in this process.

He started retesting the two blade blanks. Flexibility was greatly increased. The blades virtually turned away the hardened steel punch. Attempts to flake off or chip the metal failed completely. A growing sense of excitement was churning in Danny's stomach. He realized, "These two blades are really different." Danny's hands were shaking when he took them to Ito and Mr. Schmidt. When Ito put them on the grinding stone, he commented, "What did you do to these last two blades? They are taking more time to sharpen."

"Let me work on them, while you help Mr. Schmidt put the final edge on those others."

The fact was that Ito and Mr. Schmidt were anxious to try the various new blades. Everything had been looking good from their tests. Soon, they took a strip of deerhide with the hair on it and started stripping and cutting it. Danny could hear sounds of approval and satisfaction coming from them. They even cut through steel wool and the blades would still cut. A piece of number ten copper wire was formed in a loop, and the blade was tortured back and forth against it. These tests dulled the edge considerably. Then they were back with the butcher steel, dressing the blade so it would shave the hair from Mr. Schmidt's arm.

"These are superior blades," Mr. Schmidt declared. "We can be proud to make such a knife as a gift. We could even sell them," he said as he warmed to the subject. His enthusiasm grew as he thought about it. And yet, there was something lacking ... something that was short of the dream he had cherished for much of his life.

Danny had put the finishing touches on the last two blades, and had started the standard torture test. Moments later when Mr. Schmidt became aware that Danny's hands were shaking, he asked, "What's wrong?"

"Nothing! Nothing, *Just look!*"

He repeatedly shaved hair from the deerhide. He repeated, "Just look!" He cut strips of leather and sawed through steel wool. Copper wire was cut through again and again. With a growing sense of excitement, the three sensed an approaching climax. Hesitatingly, and in an almost joking gesture, Mr. Schmidt put a little spit on his arm, and pretended to shave with the blade he had just used to cut the wire. *And it shaved!*

"Mein Gott, Daniel, what have you done! I cannot believe this blade. This blade must have a handle. I have never before seen a blade of such superior quality!" It was Mr. Schmidt talking with almost uncontrollable excitement. In his enthusiasm, he drifted off into German. "I will cast a handle that is worthy of such a knife. But what have you done to these two blades? And can you do it again? The whole world has been trying to produce such a blade, since the beginning of the Iron Age."

He took the other sample blades that had been made and said, "These are superior blades ... probably better than anyone else makes, but for us, they are scrap. You begin manufacturing blades, I will be making a mold in which we can cast handles on these knives." Then he showed a rounded zigzag pattern he had ground in the handle portion of four of the experimental blades. "This will be done more easily before the tempering and final sharpening and finishing. It will give the cast metal a form to surround, so the handle will never pull off, break, or slip. You may wish to drill three holes in each handle. Perhaps the holes should be half an inch in diameter."

"Mr. Schmidt, it's midnight. Maybe we need to go to bed."

He eyed the boys as if he were seeing them for the first time in weeks. And then he seemed to join them once again. "Yes, midnight. I was lost in the memory of my youth. That was a time when I dreamed I would be able to produce just such a blade. So tomorrow we will see if you can duplicate these blades. Do you have school tomorrow? Well, you boys go to bed. My mind is full of things to do."

Danny and Ito began to hear in their memories, what Mr. Schmidt had said during his excited departure, "... begin manufacturing blades!" In their minds, they had thought they would make a few knives, including one for Chief at the mill, some for the Schmidt-Watanabe family, and perhaps one for Little Teddie. "Manufacturing?" Mr. Schmidt was really serious.

"Mr. Schmidt is so excited he's forgotten that school is out for the summer! Perhaps there is more to this knife-making development than we had thought," Danny said. He added, "I'll have an early start to see if the other blade blanks can be made as good as these two."

Realizing Mr. Schmidt's excitement, and with his word *manufacturing* resounding in their consciousness, the duo stayed to drill holes in the handle portions of the remarkable blades. The

157

steel turned away the drill bits. They had to grind away the metal to make a zigzag pattern.

In the morning, Ito made up a jig to hold the blade blanks for uniform drilling. Then he lubricated the old drill press, and mixed some white water lubricant and cooling solution, to prevent the bit from burning. He made another jig to hold the blanks while the zigzag pattern was being ground into the handles. The handle would be poured around the butt of the blade.

Danny had eight blade blanks heating in the forge when Mr. Schmidt reappeared and seemed subdued. He certainly was troubled. "You must please forgive an old man for trying to impose his lifelong ambition on the two of you. From my early years, I have wanted to produce blades of the quality you lads did last night. I know it will be possible to sell every knife we could produce, and to make a huge amount of money. To me, the money is of no importance. All I need is right here in this home and family. But for pride and a sense of accomplishment, I'd like to be a part of a company that produces the best-designed and best-quality knives in the world! To achieve the fulfillment of such a hope at my advanced age is almost beyond imagination." Then he sat down in his big chair and looked searchingly at the two boys. Ito and Danny went to him. Their heads formed a triangle as they leaned together, and placed arms around the shoulders of each other.

Using his best Hamburger German accent, Ito said, "We will produce dis knife." The three were comfortable with each other. They were aware that they were making a formative commitment to produce hunting and skinning knives.

"Daniel, never let anyone see or find out how you produced those two incredible blades. That is an industrial secret worth more money than you can imagine. Everything about this knife will be known once companies find the quality. The blade blanks are available to anyone. They will analyze the blade, and soon know the folding technique, but they will not be able to discover the critical thing, which is your tempering process. No company will be able to match these blades, until they discover your tempering procedures. Remember, you are to tell no one!"

With those thoughts, Ito took one of the super-blades to show his parents. Danny took the other to show Gran. Yes, it was early in the morning, but everyone was up. Mr. Schmidt remained in his big chair, with one of the blade blanks in his hand, caressing it as if it were the hand of one of his long-dead children.

"Ye must have been 'aving a time, to be this early. Ye look proper pleased."

"We have the blade and the knife we want. Just look!" Danny replied and took a loop of copper wire and cut it in two with the blade, and then demonstrated that it could shave the downy hair that was forming on his legs.

"Well I'll be blowed, 'Ow did ye come up with that?"

"It's partly the steel. Part of it is our forging technique, but mostly it is the tempering process that just came to me from out of nowhere. Mr. Schmidt says it is an industrial secret and that I must tell no one. He says it is worth more money than I can imagine."

"I daresay it is! So what will ye be doing with it?"

"I guess we are going to start making knives ... lots of them, to sell. I need to go to the forge again, to be sure I can make this same forging and quality of knife blades."

As Danny left, he realized he had been sharing his news in Arabic and that Gran had been answering in her Cockney English. The boy wondered what Ito had told his parents.

Back in the foundry, a big three-person hug was shared. Ito commented, "Today we find out if this is a 'two-blade dream' or if we really can duplicate these super-blades."

Danny took the other blades from the previous night's work and started to put them in the forge coals as well.

"Perhaps those blades represent a part of the developmental history of our company? We can make many more blades, but those are part of how we got to this point." With that statement, Mr. Schmidt helped the two boys realize that they were involved in something more than just making a few knives. "Do you understand that you have here a revolutionary process? I have no idea of how important it will eventually become."

Danny started forging eight new blade blanks. He was so excited about the possibilities he was nearly beside himself. Drilling and machining of the blades would be the last stages before the tempering process. Both boys wanted the total process

159

to succeed, more for Mr. Schmidt than for either of them. When they showed the blanks to Mr. Schmidt, their hands were shaking. Mr. Schmidt remarked, "It appears as if I am not the only one who is excited about your new knives." His hands, too, were shaking. He continued, "... and I've been working with metal all my life. How old are you boys now, twelve or is it thirteen years of age?"

Ito said, "Maybe you meant Danny's new knives?"

"Without the three of us, there would have been no knives," Danny asserted.

Before lunch, eight blanks had been folded, shaped, drilled, ground, and were ready for tempering. Mr. Schmidt and Ito would test them, and give them their preliminary sharpening. Danny had followed the exact techniques he had used to forge and temper the first two superb blades. The torture test involved shaving the hair from a deerhide, racking the blade back and forth along copper wire, shaving more areas of deerhide, and then shaving hair from Mr. Schmidt's arm. The new blades were as good as the previous two. An instant explosion of joy followed.

Mr. Schmidt was not demonstrative this time. He simply looked at the two boys and nodded his head. "Yes, yes, I expected this. Now the world has a new standard for cutting blades, and they don't even know it yet. I will be busy organizing some things during the next several days. In fact, I may not be home at all."

"Did you tell Gran? She'll miss you."

Ito added, "We'll all miss you. What if we have some problems?"

"It is unlikely that you will face anything you can't overcome. Just open the second box of blade blanks whenever you like."

He didn't say why he was leaving, and they didn't ask.

Ito and Danny continued at the forge, turning out twenty blades in a ten-hour working day. Hand shaping the blades took about as much time as doing the ten cycles of three folds each. That was much harder work, because they had to hand-hammer the blade into shape. Ito stated, "Once the blade has been tempered, it takes twice the amount of time to finish it that it did before. I'm glad you can do the tempering after the shaping and preliminary sharpening are done."

160

By the time Mr. Schmidt returned, the boys had emptied the first wooden case of 144 blade blanks and most were ready for handles and final finishing.

Mr. Schmidt proudly arrived with a large piece of equipment that was being delivered to a special work area. It was a steel milling and drilling machine. He set up the mill and showed the boys how it was used to form and drill the handle shapes of the blade more quickly and accurately. He had spent many of his silver dollars for the machine, but thought little of it.

"Which one of you will become our expert at preparing the forged blade blanks for handles, do the final shaping of the blades, and returning them for tempering? After that, handles will need to be applied and the final finishing will be done." He looked at both boys and read their expressions. Both were anxious to operate the new machine. "Right! I expected that. We can use a few blade blanks while you learn to operate this wonderful monster."

Ito said, "We needed to open the second box of blanks. We finished the first box this morning. For those, all we need to do is make handles and put them on. They will be ready to give and sell after they have been polished and given the final sharpening."

"You've been busy while I was gone, and so have I." Mr. Schmidt was excited again. "Let's see what we can do with this mill." The remainder of the day was dedicated to learning how to do the primary operations of drilling and simple milling.

They were rare kids, who had embraced Mr. Schmidt's dream world with enthusiasm, and had worked to make it a reality. As was common among the three of them, smiles, nods, and hugs were rich forms of communication that asserted admiration, agreement, and esteem.

The boys did their knife throwing, but only in the confines of the barn. They did not want to take too much time away from their manufacturing. They did their regular physical fitness program and practiced Father and Mother Watanabe's versions of *A Way*. Each had a cow to milk, chickens and rabbits to care for, and a garden to tend. Both boys were grateful for the luxury of vacation time. This allowed them to pursue their work without going to school.

161

At the forge, and while making knives, they were speaking German. Danny was becoming more competent with that language. He could hardly differentiate between Mr. Schmidt's German and that of Ito. Most of the time in the Watanabe household, the boys were speaking Japanese. When Danny was in his own home, he and Gran were usually talking Arabic. It was a full and exciting time in the lives of the combined households.

A few days later, when Ito and Danny arrived at the forge, they could tell by Mr. Schmidt's expression that he was about to explode with his news. Then he displayed it, and announced, "DISKnife number one. I think this one stays here. We can make many others, but there is only one first." Mr. Schmidt had completed the negative mold in which the knife handles could be cast directly onto the blade. The research and product development stage of DISKnife was over. He had melted some of his silver dollars to make and cast that premier handle. It was beautiful. The name DISKnife was in the casting. Under the *D* was etched Daniel, Ito was under the *I*, and Schmidt was under the *S*.

"For the standard knife, I have a special aluminum alloy that is harder than most. It will polish to a silky sheen, resist scuffing, and of course it won't rust. That will help keep the knife lightweight and functional. If you do not like that idea, we will use some other material. But Danny ... Ito, some business things you should know. As I have said, you have a nonstandard process for tempering the steel. Keep that absolutely secret. Don't release that information to anyone, unless you want to give up the business." Again he had warned the boys to be particularly careful regarding the tempering process. Everything else could and would be copied once the reputation of DISKnife blades became known.

Production was the next project. Mr. Schmidt set about making more negative molds, so that many handles could be cast at the same time. The team became more organized as they started specializing. Each of the three had his own skills and responsibilities. Danny was forging and folding the blades, while Ito tended to their drilling and machining. Danny took the blades back to be tempered. Mr. Schmidt was their mentor, the business manager, and more. Casting handles on the blades was heavier and hotter work than Mr. Schmidt should be doing on a

162

regular basis, so Ito and Danny traded off doing the forging and casting handles. Mr. Schmidt took it from there. He did personal engraving on handles. Sharpening, buffing, and polishing took most of his time. In addition he did special engraving on some of the handles.

Mr. Schmidt asked the boys to engrave their first initial, *I* or *D*, on the handle of each knife they had actually forged, shaped, and tempered.

Ito was quick to react.

"I can't do that. I don't know how to do the tempering." Both Mr. Schmidt and Danny were dumbfounded. They had been preoccupied, and didn't realize that Ito didn't know the procedures, but then, neither did Mr. Schmidt.

"But, Ito, you have been here while I was forging and tempering blades. Haven't you been watching?" Danny asked with amazement.

"Mr. Schmidt said no one should know, so I haven't been watching," Ito insisted.

Danny hugged Mr. Schmidt and Ito. He was stunned when he realized neither of them knew the tempering process. He said, "We are family. We share our luck, our knowledge ... our fortune and misfortune ... everything. I am nothing ... *we* are everything." The tempering process was demonstrated, and Danny explained how it was discovered. It was evident that Danny had never considered the process to be his personal secret.

The first production blade was presented to Chief, along with a letter of appreciation, acknowledging his help in getting their knife making started. He was so proud of the design and its ability to hold an edge, that all his hunting partners were offered the use of it, as well.

There was an immediate demand for the knives. A few were given away, but soon DISKnife became a business that earned increasingly large amounts of money and renown, not only locally, but in other parts of the state. Some of the boys' "playtime" was redirected. Ito and Danny were forging, forming, shaping the handles, tempering, and shaping blades full-time. They would pour handles when they were needed to keep up with Mr. Schmidt's ability to finish the knives.

They were "in business." The revitalization of Mr. Schmidt

was amazing. He took over the all business management, including officially forming a corporation, ordering equipment and supplies, the price structuring, shipping, bookkeeping, and the initial marketing.

Ito and Danny had been aware that their system of folding blade blanks was slow and clumsy. It was okay when they were only producing a few knives, but now they were supposed to be in business and in production. With the forging system they were using, it took about an hour to forge one knife. They thought they should be able to do better.

"Mr. Schmidt, we are too slow forging blades," Ito declared. "By the way, we are almost out of blade blanks."

"Don't be concerned. Ten cases arrived two days ago. They are the same as the ones we have been using. Even the serial number is the same. The company looked up my name in their file. The manager said he wondered why it had taken so long for me to reorder. Anyway, he sent all he had in stock, and they will produce thousands more when we want them. I sent a money order for another hundred cases of blanks. They should last us for quite some time. But you think you are working too slowly. Have you any ideas about how to speed up the process?"

"We made a tool to begin the folding, but it still isn't efficient. See, these two pieces of angle iron form a *V* to start folding the flat metal."

"Yes, the idea is good, but the materials you used for a hammer and anvil are too light. It is time to use income money from our sales, to buy production machinery. I anticipated this problem, and a local machinist has a milling machine, and he is making the anvils and hammers we need. They should be ready in two days. In this case, it has cost us three of our knives. It's the old bartering system. I have a feeling he thought he had the better end of the bargain. We could have used our mill to make the changes, but the time is better spent in producing knives."

There was new reality regarding the value of their knives. In this state there were many outdoorsmen, and they were happy to trade considerable time and expense for one DISKnife.

The machinist milled three anvils and three hammers. Each anvil had a deep V-shaped grooves the full length of the blade blank. It was so heavy that a chain hoist was needed to put it in place. The largest unit was wide enough at the top to accept the flattened blade blank, so that it was centered above the bottom of the V. A single stroke of the heavy hammer, that was mated to the anvil, folded the metal to a narrow V-shape. The three anvil-hammer combinations were powered by a single electrical motor. A foot lever operated them, and just as they had with their original trip-hammer and anvil combination, a cage prevented the operator from putting his hand under the hammer.

The blank was placed under the original flat hammer on the flat forge, and was delivered several blows that flattened the metal ready for the second V-shaped anvil and hammer. For the final step, a single blow of the hammer folded the metal for the third time.

In this manner, the three folds were completed quickly, and the blade blank was ready for reheating, and to be hammered flat for the beginning of the next cycle of three folds each. This innovation significantly reduced the amount of time needed to forge a blank into a blade. It worked so well that the machinist was asked to make a second set of the anvils and hammers. Production increased so that each boy produced an average of twenty-five blades for each eight-hour day.

Mr. Schmidt commented, "We paid cash out of our company funds for the machinery to operate the second V hammer and anvil equipment. Obviously, it is well worth the investment. Your increase in production, over just a two-day period, paid for everything."

The second innovation in their search for efficiency was the installation of a controllable gas-heated oven to replace the old coal fire. It made it quicker to bring the blade blanks to working temperature, and eliminated the chance of overheating, which could burn the metal. It assured constant conditions for duplicating the tempering process. These were essential controls.

A one-horsepower electrical motor increased the speed of the forging process, by replacing the slower, and less reliable wind-powered forge. Hammers were raised quickly, and fell when a foot-operated trigger was released. Also, the new hammers struck with far greater force. Consequently, fewer blows were needed.

Efficiency, convenience, and safety were constant concerns.

An office-type swivel chair was the next operational improvement for each forge station. Ito and Danny could sit in the chair, and simply rotate from one station to the next. Steel blade blanks were at station one. Station two was the furnace. The flat forge was next, and that was followed by the three V forges. Then the blade blank was placed in a special anvil. It was made in the shape of the final knife. It had a heavier back, which tapered to a thin cutting edge. With this equipment, the rounded end, instead of a point, was forged. The thin edge on the upper two and a half inches of the blade was also roughly formed at this station. These changes produced an enormous increase in efficiency, and reduced the amount of grinding needed to shape and sharpen the blade.

The swivel chairs offered flexibility. The arm supports were extendable, and their rocking motion reduced physical fatigue. In the end, the number of folds used was more an emotional decision. They settled on a standard of seven forging cycles of three folds each. The 2,097,152 individual molecular leaves or layers of steel this produced sounded impressive, but also gave the essential results. The new equipment was so much quicker, that the extra time to forge the higher number of layers of steel seemed insignificant. They found it took only one hour to forge three blade blanks.

Although Mr. Schmidt chose to work twelve or fourteen hours a day grinding, polishing, and honing blades, he asked the boys to limit their working time at the forge to no more than eight hours a day. He added to his own time by taking care of the office work involving ordering supplies, correspondence, banking, and marketing. He was "in his element."

The sounds emitted from the forge had changed considerably. The boys could still use the windmill, if they wanted, but they became more accustomed to the staccato *bang, bang, bang* of the new and faster equipment, when compared with the *whoomp—bang, whoomp—bang, whoomp—bang* of the old windmill-powered forge.

Taking a cue from the earmuffs used in cold weather, Mr. Schmidt fashioned hearing protection. He also introduced the boys to goggles to protect their eyes.

Brilliant early-morning sunlight was pouring through the

open sliding door of the forge area. Danny was at work with the trip-hammer, and the furnace was heating blade blanks. The trip-hammer was beating its staccato rhythm as metal was flattened and folded repeatedly. "Ito, please come with me and look at Danny from this angle." The scene of the boy at the forge was in a silhouette. Strong backlighting showed the swirl of particles in the air. Each strike of the hammer kicked up more dust and tiny metal pieces. "Of course, you understand that some of that is going into Danny's nose, throat, and lungs."

"I know that when I blow my nose or cough up phlegm, lots of it looks black and ugly."

"The worst part is that you can't cough all of it up," Mr. Schmidt stated with conviction. "Some of it stays in the lungs and accumulates. It's the same with tobacco smoke, or any other kind of dust and smoke."

"So what do we do to protect ourselves?" Ito asked.

"Do you have any ideas?"

Ito thought for a moment. "Movies show cowboys using a neckerchief up across their face when the trail dust is really bad. That should help. Doctor movies show them wearing gauze masks for surgery. They fit snugly across the nose and mouth. Those should be better."

"Would you wear a mask of that type, if you had it?"

"Golly, yes, if I had one, and so would Danny."

"And so will I," Mr. Schmidt commented as he led Ito to a shelf on which several boxes of masks were located. He was fifty years ahead of industry, when it came to caring for worker health and welfare concerns. "I should have been doing this all my life, but I didn't really think about it. I bought these this morning, and if you come up with a better solution, please tell me. But today, we start wearing surgical masks."

A large room was added to the barn, and that was where the tempering of blades took place. It was totally isolated from prying eyes. It was intended to secure their special secret.

The DISKnife business was under way. They couldn't anticipate the many directions it would take. The enormous amount of money it would make seemed unimportant. The dreams, companionship, love, and devotion would last. They were involved, valued, and happy.

167

It was difficult for the trio to comprehend that within only three weeks, they had become a functioning corporation complete with a bank accounts, an extensive line of credit, inventory, and sales potential for everything they would be able to produce. The three workers shared smiles and hugs and a sense of great accomplishment. These were extended to Gran and Mr. and Mrs. Watanabe.

23

Puberty Awakens

The onset of puberty imposed essentially the same burdens and joys on youngsters of this community as it did in all similar areas throughout the nation. From one year to the next, the players changed, but problems and opportunities remained almost constant. Each succeeding year, youngsters felt as if they were the first to be faced with such uniquely demanding imperatives.

Seventh-grade girls started giggling, whispering behind their hands, and casting darting glances at each other, forming strange, secret, and silent syllables to be seen and understood only by another special girlfriend. And the sideways glances at various boys became a source of wonder and mystery to all the fellows. As was the case in every generation, guys lagged behind girls in this unique venture toward adulthood.

Uneasily, Ito, Danny, and the rest of the boys were aware that mysterious things were happening. But fellows remained primarily concerned with guy things, such as who could run the fastest, or who was best at marbles, top spinning, mumbly peg, football, or baseball, and all of the "important stuff."

Girls remained almost alien creatures. They usually had the best penmanship and were the first to recite poems, and other materials that were to be learned by heart. That was just the way things were. Girls were called on first although, secretly, Ito, Danny, Little Teddie, and occasionally a few others fellows would recite the memorized material to each other the same day it was assigned. Some boys had to wait several days, and sit through seemingly countless hours of listening to fellow students stumble through yet another effort to "get it right." Of course there were girls in the class who were really first, because they were brilliant and prepared. Away from school, girls seldom figured into the boy's activities. Before puberty, many of them were too good at non-roughhouse activities, and the boys couldn't compete with them in "girl things." The one place both groups often met was at the swimming hole on the millrace. A two-by-twelve-inch plank of fir served as the diving board. Girls did swan dives, jackknife dives, forward flips, and back dives, with a considerable amount of finesse for youngsters who had received no instructions, except from some older sister or friend.

The boys did belly flops, cannonballs, and folded jackknife dives, because they couldn't unfold before they hit the water. But this was the year for some strange changes to occur within Danny and Ito's age group.

Pauline showed up at the swimming hole along with some other girls. There was nothing unusual about that. But this year a lot of things weren't the same. Pauline was different. Girls had always looked a lot like boys with long hair, and sometimes with more delicate bones and pretty faces, but not now. Oh, the fellows knew about older girls, but Pauline was from their own class. Wow! She was something to see, with her chest filling out and tits all formed! When she climbed up the riverbank, even with her suit, you could see lots of curves and pink nipples and she looked different down below, too. She had just gone sort of "cushy" looking.

The combination disturbed the normal way things were "supposed to be." Ito and Danny were each aware of a strange sensation stirring in their groin region, and hit the water for fear someone might see them getting a hard-on.

Yes, puberty was creating its usual havoc in yet another generation of kids. Not only boys were having problems. There were other girls from their class who were making the same changes although they swam at some other place. Of all the girls at the swimming hole, Pauline's development was the most disturbing to Ito and Danny. They had never thought of classmate girls in such terms, but to them she was "sensational."

Danny and Ito were so naive; they hadn't a clue that the changes in appearance and actions on the part of girls signaled that they, also, were inundated by the pressures of puberty. They certainly were not aware that most of the young ladies of their age were about a year farther into that new emotional and physical world they were entering.

"Mr. Schmidt said we needed to get away from making knives and see what's going on in the world. Do you suppose he knew about Pauline?" Ito asked.

Danny shrugged. "I doubt it, but maybe he figured someone like her would show up sooner or later. One thing, I'd give up a lot of DISKnives for another look at her." Actually, the boys did give up some of their knife-making time, because they didn't miss an afternoon at the swimming hole as long as the days were warm. But Pauline didn't show up again and they were looking for her all the time. In fact, Danny didn't see Pauline so delightfully revealed again, except in his perpetual memory. She would remain a vision of exquisite beauty ... the personification of female loveliness throughout his life. How could an accidental few-second glimpse be so important? But it was!

Later that summer, Ito and Danny were sitting on a nice patch of grass at the swimming hole when the adult world also took on a new look. They had seen women all their lives. They knew women had tits and rounded bottoms, but they seemed so old and removed from the world of young boys that they were hardly women at all. Then the former musical director from the church, Miss Kelly, showed up at the swimming hole. Danny remembered her best, because of her frequent musical association with his parents, and coming to their home for rehearsals. Two-piece swimming suits were seldom seen in those days, but there she was with her flat tummy and bare skin showing around her middle, and a delightfully obvious belly button! From her feet up, she was so wonderfully rounded without being shaky or flabby, and her "back porch" did enticing things when she walked! She went right by the boys and suddenly turned.

"Danny, is that you?"

"Yes, Miss Kelly." Funny that Danny called her by her complete last name. At home, before his parents' death, they always called her Miss K.

She hadn't seen the boy since his father's death. She murmured something to the man who was walking with her and came back, nodded at the vacant area of grass next to Danny as if asking permission to sit with him. Then she gracefully sank to the grass close by in a nearly profile view. Her friend just stood there for a moment and then, apparently a little annoyed, went off in the direction of the water.

Miss K brought her chin to her shoulder, looked at Danny through long, black lashes, and started a conversation. The low, soothing tones of her voice were enticing. At that particular moment, looking and listening at the same time were beyond him. Large, dark eyes seemed to captivate his consciousness. Danny's eyes followed the direction of her gaze for a moment, only to return to get lost in her eyes. Then she seemed to glance downward toward her lap as if willing his eyes to follow hers. The boy's eyes embraced the roundness of her breasts that showed above her halter top, and at the wondrous valley between.

Yes, older women took on new dimensions. As she talked, gestured, and slightly changed her position, increasingly subtle and exciting changes were made in the way her breasts were cradled. Danny became aware that he had been staring at the creaminess of her curves and he had reached a full erection that was straining at his swimming suit. This was extremely embarrassing and he turned crimson-purple, but Miss K's eyes were fixed on his. She had an impish smile on her lips and she said gently, "It's okay, Danny." Her eyes shifted slowly to his crotch where he was trying unsuccessfully to conceal his bulge. It would have been easier if he were wearing boxer-type swimming trunks. Then her eyes came back to Danny's, seemed to go soft and misty, and she said, "You are young, Danny, but you are a man."

Miss K turned directly toward Danny and faced him fully with her hands on the ground. Then she brought her shoulders together as far as they could go. The top of her swimming suit slacked off a little from her breasts. They were unrestrained, but did not go saggy. They cupped lovingly to her body and the delicate pink of her nipples stood proudly to be seen and cherished. The boy squirmed to ease the pressure in his crotch. She murmured, "It has been nice being with you, Danny." She strode proudly away with a provocative and graceful undulation of her hips. His eyes couldn't leave Miss K's retreating form until she went into the water and swam downstream out of sight.

Ito had been sitting there completely silent. Unfortunately

172

for him, his view had been more from the rear until Miss K had turned, and put both hands on the grass to rise and leave.

"Wow! Was that really Miss K?" Ito was also having difficulty resolving the fact that the vision he had seen in a swimming suit was the same woman who had directed the church choir. At church she wore a long black choir robe, and it was startling what that robe concealed.

But Danny was too involved with his own thoughts, observations, and obsession to even answer. Yes, older women were really something! The loveliness of Miss K remained deeply embedded in his mind's eye as a consuming source of wonder, appreciation, and gratitude.

As Pauline continued to mature, she became one of the most beautiful girls in school ... and totally desirable. When Danny thought about dating girls, he was intimidated by his memory of her. Her face and figure had matured to match the enchanting nipple and breast contours that were etched in his memory. He feared the possibility of making a fool of himself, if he ever asked her out. Just dancing with her at school dances presented problems enough.

All the copulating that happened in nature took on a new meaning. Before, the boys were simply observers. With the onset of puberty, the boys realized they were potential participants. The antics of birds in flight, or a sparrow bouncing up and down on its mate that was sitting on a wire, the sight of a rooster dusting off a hen, were common to country boys. They had seen it for years. It simply meant that the egg that would be laid, would have a blood spot in it, and could be hatched into a chick. The buck rabbit frantically humping away on a doe had simply meant more bunnies would be born before long.

But now, things had changed for the boys. When it was time to take the cow to the bull to be bred, it was no longer a simple matter of helping the cow have a calf, it was the physical impact of the bull shoving a foot-and-a-half-long red icicle-shaped prick into the cow's pisser. They wondered where all that bull's "meat" came from, and how it felt to be the bull, and how the cow must have felt. The boys conclude that it must be okay, because both seemed anxious to do it. And they wondered where all that gism came from? During one breeding session, the bull shoved at the

173

same time the cow coughed. He missed his target and about a quart of gooey slime was shot all over the cow's back. Boys knew how babies were started, whether they were baby rabbits, birds, or people.

The antics of rabbits, chicken, birds on telephone wires, dogs, or the bull and the cow were always a little comical to watch, but it was becoming different for the boys. The reality of parents and the local teachers and preachers doing "IT" seem unreal.

Perhaps one of the most difficult things for boys to understand was the strange urge to become a part of that girl society. It had seemed so silly just the year before. Just how did a guy go about it? What were they supposed to talk about? You, for sure, couldn't talk with them about their tits and how their butts were getting rounded and cute. At least the boys thought they couldn't. Talking about clothes and makeup and hair was for sissies.

Boys hoped the girls would say something ... maybe about how their arm muscles were getting bigger or how much faster they were running, and important things like that. And because girls seemed to be smarter in social situations, some of them knew how to flatter a guy's ego and make him feel grown-up and manly. A few boys knew how to talk to girls and make them feel desirable, beautiful, and mature. Most boys were tongue-tied, and too intimidated to say much. Sometimes when Danny was working at the forge, his thoughts became obsessed with breasts. He remembered the first time he was aware of seeing a bare breast. It was Buna, the next-door woman, while she was nursing her infant daughter. Danny remembered how the mother and child seemed so close together and loving. But seeing Pauline and Miss Kelly created an entirely different reaction of surging emotional ecstasy that was new, exciting, breathtaking, and compulsively erotic. They were the first, and as such, the most cherished and unforgettable.

Danny realized something else: He and most of the boys called those wonderful female appendages "tits," but that seemed a crass term to him. In the very core of his existence, they were lovingly adored as breasts.

24

Bodily Changes, Seventh Grade, and Bully Bill

It wasn't just girls whose bodies started changing with the onset of puberty. Girls stuck out more and became curvy and rounded. Boys became more angular and muscular. Chests enlarged, shoulders broadened, muscles became more defined, and voices cracked.

Ito and Danny always had hard physical work to do. So did most of the boys in the community. Some boys delivered newspapers. Others chopped firewood, threw it into sheds to keep it dry, and stacked it so more could fit in the woodshed. Mowing lawns and doing other jobs to keep yards looking nice provided semi-regular money for a few. George's father painted houses, and his son assisted him. Occasionally a sidewalk would be installed, or a house foundation would be poured. Boys did part of that work and learned about the concrete business. Many of the fellows earned money working outside their own homes. The youngsters who did a good job developed a reputation within the community, and other people hired them.

For Ito and Danny, working for others was a thing of the past. Making knives provided an income far exceeding that of the adult community. Each of the boys could make two knives in an afternoon and evening period of time. Saturday afternoons were open and they could manage six knives each if they worked on into the late evening. The boys were not really interested in the economic side of knife making. Mr. Schmidt, and now Gran, took care of that. Their recreation required almost no spending money. There were occasions when they went to the movies, which cost five cents each. They didn't know how much they were earning, and they didn't care. Enormous changes had taken place in the economy of the nation, as well as in their town.

Young kids were working at jobs for wages their parents would have been happy to earn five years earlier.

Girls? They had the easy jobs, or so boys thought. They could babysit. Boys, in the luxury of ignorance, believed they just sat. Fellows didn't understand that in many cases, babysitting really meant preparing a meal, doing a sink full of dishes, changing and washing diapers, and a variety of other household chores that often were truly unpleasant. Some of the girls were terribly exploited and served as a weekly housekeeper as well as taking care of one or more babies.

But girls did have one distinct advantage over boys. If a guy invited a girl to the movies, he had to pay for everything. It didn't take the fellows long to discover which girls were too expensive to take out, or which ones would walk or ride the bus to go to the movies. And of course the big question was which girls would hold hands on the first date. Kissing? Well, that was going too far for many of the guys.

Kids living closer in town were giving parties, going to social events, and dating. Ito and Danny were socially retarded about girls. They looked, and looked, and looked. They did the same as far as talking was concerned. Seventh-grade dating was beyond them.

They spent hours talking and exploring ideas about girls and women. They devoured the bra and corset ads in the Sears and Montgomery Ward catalogs. Magazine stores had detective magazines that always featured a beautiful woman on the cover, with lots of legs and breast curves showing. Comic magazines also featured incredibly shaped women to go along with Superman, Batman, and similar heroes. They didn't buy magazines, but they looked when other kids had them.

"You aren't even reading the story," Bruce complained. "You just look at the pictures. It would be a waste of money to buy them, if I didn't read the story."

"I guess you are right, Bruce, but I do like the pictures." Danny didn't have the heart to tell his friend that he had read through three of the magazines. At that point, he realized that he knew the plot and what was going to happen, if he read only the first page. It was the same basic plot repeated again and again.

The energetic intellectual games and studies of the previous years were suddenly supplemented by the urgencies of puberty. And, of course, they compared what they saw in the magazines and catalogs with their limited experience looking at live examples. The girls at school came in an interesting variety of sizes and shapes. The ones in the magazines seemed to be all the same. Ito and Danny enjoyed the look of the live ones more. All this obsessive preoccupation with girls didn't cause the duo to abandon any of their activities. They just added watching and fantasizing about girls to the other pleasures.

The two friends discovered the rapture and temporary relief of "jacking off," something each boy did in total isolation. They heard all the horror tales associated with "doing it." These stories threatened boys with insanity, growing hair on the palm of the offending hand, warts and pimples, being weakened as if losing a pint of blood, and myriad other personal disasters, if they did it too much. But no one ever provided a definition of just how much was "too much." So, cloaked in ignorance, superstition, and secrecy, they went along carefully checking themselves, and everyone they knew, for telltale signs of overindulgence.

The hopes that Bully Bill would change during the summer were realized. But the change was for the worse. He devoted the first week of school to intimidating a dozen or more kids. He carried a little notebook with him, which he would consult. "Your appointment with me will be during lunchtime on Monday, September 9. Meet me behind the play shed at twelve twenty. That will give you time to eat your lunch. Then I'll beat the crap out of you and you'll probably barf up your lunch, if you haven't already done it. Now, don't disappoint me by missing school that day. I become angry when someone upsets my schedule. Then I hurt him bad."

After delivering that intimidating tirade, he went to the next boy on his list, and politely informed him that they were scheduled for a meeting. That was the beginning. The rest of the week, he swaggered around the school, bumping into guys he had notified, and reminding them. He would trip one, kick some in the butt, jab another in the stomach, twist ears, pull hair, spit on the cleanest kids, and generally terrorize them. But the code

177

of silence prevailed. A tattletale would be ostracized from the school yard.

Right on schedule, Bully Bill delivered his first beating to Lyle. A sense of schoolyard curiosity and excitement prompted many of the kids to watch. Lyle didn't try to fight back. He just covered up and tried to keep from being hurt too much. When the teacher asked how he got the black eye and cut lip, Lyle just murmured something about having fallen down.

To increase the anxiety of his next victim, Bill said, "You were scheduled for after school today, but I have another appointment. I'll reschedule you for tomorrow." His voice was pleasant and his words were business-like, but the look on his face was uncompromising and menacing.

Danny and Ito were unaware of what was happening with Bully Bill, because they were working with Mr. Bag, the school custodian, instead of being in the schoolyard. Little Teddie confided in Danny, "I'm glad I got my beating from Bill last year. He's bigger and meaner this year." Sadly, the comment missed its mark because neither Danny nor Ito paid much attention.

Two days later, Bill cornered Little Teddie. "I regret to say that I didn't do an adequate job on your behalf last June. I must apologize; I was distracted by the excitement of the end of the school year. I will make amends on Friday of next week. We will meet right after school at the usual place. Please don't keep me waiting. In the meantime I'll give you this token of my esteem." He slugged Little Teddie on his left ear and knocked him down. It appeared that Bully Bill was boiling mad at almost everyone. During the summer months he had grown bigger and meaner. He had also developed a lot of pimples, so all the fellows knew he was "jacking off" a lot more than he should. But he didn't seem to be getting weaker. Everyone decided that such consequences were likely limited to only one of the "bad things" that could happen at a time.

Bruce, was an underfed-looking skinny kid. He offered a concerned suggestion to Bill, "If you didn't jack off so much, you might get rid of a lot of your pimples." Bill's reaction was immediate and brutal. He started hitting Bruce as hard as he could. "Lay off," Danny said as he grabbed Bill's arms. "He was only trying to help you."

"I don't need his help or help from any of the rest of you piles of shit."

A day or two later Mr. Stewart, the principal of the school, called all the seventh-grade boys together and told them, "No matter how long you shake it and shake it, the last drop always goes in the pants. So fellows, when you go to take a leak, don't play with it too long." That was the extent of sex education to the boys in the seventh grade.

But Bill and Danny were on a collision course for a real fight. Danny was not afraid of Bill, but he didn't want to fight. When problems such as that arose, Danny usually had a talk with Father Watanabe. After all, he was his Japanese father, confidant, and friend. As usual, he presented Danny with many options.

"There are things you must, and must not do. These may be different from what you want and don't want to do. There are things that the other person will and won't let you do. There are standards your friends and society expect from you. Examine all these options in the light of caring and respect. Then you will know what to do. You have been training in *A Way* for years. Let your knowledge, good sense, self-control, and tranquillity guide you."

At noon the next day, Bill was coming out of the boy's toilet when Junior yelled, "Hey, Bill, it's one o'clock." This was the favorite way of letting a guy know he had left a button open on his pants after he had taken a leak. In fact, it was a minor triumph to catch a guy with a button undone. Finding a fellow with "two o'clock" could be the highlight for the week.

In his usual surly manner, Bill replied, "It'll be more than that before you get a suck!"

"Who'd want a suck from you? You've probably got more pimples on your prick than you have on your face." Junior immediately regretted his emotional outburst. He figured he was in for a real pounding. "Anyway, you always spoil all the fun no matter what it is."

Bill grabbed Junior and started pulling him toward the outside door. One thing Danny learned from Father Watanabe involved diverting tactics. Openly "butting in" on a problem might suggest a person was unable to cope with a situation. By divert-

179

ing attention, he could leave a person with his self-esteem as well as helping him out of a difficult situation.

Danny stood calmly by the door and explained, "Aw, come on, Bill. All he did was catch you with your pants unbuttoned and told you about it. You've caught me with one o'clock and thought it was pretty smart." Bill's attention was diverted.

"I don't have to take any of that stupid shit from you or any of the other shit heads around here. I'm going to 'fix' you good."

Bill and Danny were outside. The rain had just stopped, and there were big mud puddles all around them. Bill made a lunge at Danny. Following the lessons from Father Watanabe, of "Base, Balance, Patience, Leverage, and Inner Tranquillity," he redirected Bully Bill's energy, and the bully went crashing into a mud puddle. Bill came out sputtering and livid with rage. Danny offered Bill a handkerchief to wipe his face. He used it and threw it into the mud puddle. "Thanks for nothing, shit head! If you want your handkerchief, you know where to find it."

"Inner peace" prevailed. Danny shrugged his shoulders, started chuckling, and everyone else did the same. Bully Bill only got angrier. "Later shit head, later," he threatened, but turned away. He had some things to figure out, and didn't know just what to do at this point. He didn't understand how he had ended up in the mud puddle facedown, and Danny was just standing there as if nothing had happened. But then, nothing had happened to Danny, and Bully Bill was more than perplexed. It would take time to figure this one out. For the first time in his life he was going to have to lay off when he got mad at someone. He hadn't figured out why or for how long.

During that week, most of the boys took heart from seeing Bully Bill facedown in the mud puddle. He was vulnerable! But then it happened. Bill was in one of his mad periods and he knocked Chuck down. Chuck was being mauled and rolled over and over on the playground. A dozen fellows surrounded the two of them. At first, Bill thought he had a good audience, but Bruce spoke up. "Bill, you've done enough of that, and we aren't going to put up with it anymore. You've beaten us up, and from now on you are going to get hurt every time you have a fight."

"Oh, yeah! And who is going to do it? You, chicken shit?"

"We are! And beginning right now." Two boys grabbed each

of his legs and started pulling in opposite directions. The same was done with his arms. Eight boys were playing tug-of-war using Bill's arms and legs, and the legs were being given the "splits."

Bill was screaming with pain and was livid with anger. "Eight on one ain't fair."

"Figure on ten on one." Two boys took Bill's ears and started twisting them.

"Or twelve on one?" Two more boys joined in and each took a handful of hair.

"Now, One—Two—Three," the boys counted. With each count, Bill was swung higher and higher off the ground. On the count of three, everyone let go and Bully Bill went sailing through the air and landed with a thud. The breath was knocked out of him. Finally he gasped, "I'll get even with every one of you." He staggered to his feet and headed for Bruce, who just stood there, but he was not alone. The group of fellows moved toward Bully Bill. The bully started to retreat, but he stumbled backward over Little Teddie, who was kneeling behind him. Bully Bill hit the ground and on his back again. He was surrounded, and totally confused.

Each boy kicked him lightly with no intention of hurting him. "This is just to let you know we can get you down and hurt you, so don't mess with us anymore."

Bully Bill knew only one way to react—aggressively. "I'll get even with ... ugh!"

A heavy kick had landed in his ribs.

"That's just a sample of what you'll get the next time you even make a threat." As if acting with one mind, all the boys turned from Bully Bill and walked away.

Bill approached Danny the next day. "Did you put those kids up to that? It's not fair for all of them to jump me at once."

"No, I didn't know anything about it until after it happened. In a way it is a compliment to you. They know that they can't beat you individually, so they have organized as if they were a pack of wolves taking on a big grizzly bear. None of them wants to get hurt anymore. Your game hasn't been any fun for them. I know I'd do almost anything rather than face them as a gang."

Respect, the essential ingredient in all successful human

181

relationships, was conveyed to Bully Bill. He was a big grizzly bear. He liked that image. The pack of wolves had to organize to beat him. Father Watanabe certainly was right when he admonished Danny and Ito to always convey feelings of respect for the person, even if you didn't like what they were doing.

Big James said, "You've never picked on me, Bully Billy. Why?"

"Just look at you. I weigh 150 pounds and you weigh 265 pounds and are awfully strong. You're too big. Anyway, I don't like to be called Billy. That's a little kid's name."

"We are all going to call you Little Billy until you grow up and act like a man instead of a nasty little kid. Anyway, a difference in size hasn't kept you from beating up on kids who are fifty pounds lighter than you, and not nearly as strong. So now I'm warning you, if you pick on anyone else, I'm going to take you down and bounce up and down on your chest." Big James reached out a massive hand, clamped it around Billy's arm, and threw him to the ground. Then he sat on Billy's chest, but maintained some of his weight on his knees. Then he started easing his weight on down. "If I bounced up and down on you, it would squash your chest. I could squeeze your guts right out your asshole if I sat farther down on your belly. I waited a long time for the little kids in the class to stand up for themselves. Now they've done it, and they've regained some of the pride you've beaten out of them. They shouldn't have to fight you or be humiliated. It is your choice, but you'd better tear up your appointment book and tell everyone you are canceling." James stood up and walked away, without looking back at Billy.

Bully Billy had been overwhelmed and dumped on his back more than once during the past two days, and he didn't like it. "I'll have to do something different when I get mad," he said to Danny, "but I don't know what."

"If I had a great voice like yours, I'd start singing. All of us wish we could sing as good as you. Hard physical work helps me. If you asked Mr. Bag, I'll bet he'll let you wheel slab wood into the boiler room for heating the building."

"That's stupid! It's just hard work. What does it get me?"

"You're right that it is hard. You can think of it as work, or as a chance to use up some of your anger without hurting someone else, or getting squashed, or getting the heck kicked out of you. For Ito and me, it's fun. We've learned to make fun out of almost everything we do. It just depends on how you look at things. We don't think it's fun hurting other people."

"Yeah, I always figured the two of you were goofy. You can be sure, I'm going to get even with you for shoving my face down into that mud puddle."

Once the havoc created by Bully Billy had settled down, classmates started relating stories of their summer of "puberty awakening." Seventh grade was well under way. Boys who had not seen each other all summer had stories to tell and experiences to relate. A group of fellows from the other side of town passed on their favorite story, which involved inviting a new kid into their special club. Each member paid his one-penny dues, but there was a chance of winning all the pennies back by coming in first in the "circle jerk." It was "winner take all."

Handkerchiefs were used as blindfolds. At a given signal all the boys were supposed to whip out their pricks and start jerking off as fast as possible. The winner was the one to "come" first, and he won the pennies. After a short session of frenzied activity, the new boy would excitedly shout the infamous words, "I'm coming, I'm coming, I'm coming." And, of course he had won. When he removed his blindfold, he found all the rest of the guys pointing at him and having a grand old laugh at his expense. He was the only fellow giving it a whack. But it was all in fun, and they went off to play rubber guns or some other game, in which everyone participated. And he did win all the pennies.

Outside one's own special group, most of the guys pretended they didn't "do it." They thought they had invented the phrase, "Ninety percent of the guys admit to jacking off, the other 10 percent are liars."

Many of the girls had changed. Sweaters fitted differently. Dresses featured pleats or darts to make room for developing breasts and more interesting backsides. Some of the girls still wore the previous school year's dresses and it was particularly interesting watching them try to accommodate today's body into a garment that had no place for protruding and newly rounded parts. The ones everyone felt sorry for were the girls who hadn't started the metamorphosis from girl into young lady.

Boys who had sisters took special pride if their development was bigger or faster than most of the other girls. If the sister wasn't keeping pace with the rest, the boy felt as if he were being let down ... there must be something wrong with her and, by family association, with him.

For reasons none of the boys could understand, they expected more from their sister than they expected from themselves.

Seventh-grade English class was a special treat for Danny, because he sat behind Dottie. She appeared at the school from the "nowhere" of several other states and dozens of other towns. People were moving into this community, and they served their time as outsiders. Dottie was painfully shy, intelligent, and never spoke out in class, so most kids didn't pay much attention to her. But she certainly attracted Danny's attention.

Dottie's two dresses were exactly the same style. One was pink and the other was yellow. When Danny sat in his desk with the seat tilted up, he was in a position to look down the front of Dottie's dress, and the sight was both lovely and disturbing. The first day he found himself in trouble. The bell rang to end the class and leave the room. There he sat with a demanding erection, and nothing to do about it. It just wouldn't go away. The best he could manage was to carry his notebook over the bulge in his crotch, and limp away. He also was experiencing his first case of the "stonies," which felt much like a hard kick in the family jewels.

He immediately learned a valuable lesson. About fifteen minutes before class was to end, he had to sit back down and think about something else. Would Dottie come to school the next day? Would she wear one of her two dresses? Such questions and related problems had Danny in a dither every day. Without any previous conversation Ito said, "I guess girls are pretty important." He had sensed Danny's turmoil. Then he added, "Betty is the one that gets to me."

25

Expanding Adventures with DISKnife

Installing innovative manufacturing techniques and equipment, plus coordinating supplies and schedules, took time and effort. Production continued, although not always as efficiently as might have been ideal.

At the same time, Ito and Danny were just young boys and needed time off to pursue other interests. Mr. Schmidt, in his quiet and nondemanding way, encouraged the boys to take breaks from their knife-making routine. He was protective of their boyhood. "We are not hungry for money. Work should not rob you of the joys of youth. The forge and knives can look out for themselves. Life is not one-dimensional. Would you join me for a walk on the way to lunch?"

He regularly took a thirty-minute walk around the property to see what changes were taking place among the living things. Summer or winter, he stripped to the waist and carried his upper garment with him. When he returned, he put it on before entering the house.

"Why do you take your shirt off, Mr. Schmidt?" Danny asked.

"What does being alive means to you?" A puzzled look came over the boys' faces.

"Look at that honeybee. Is it alive or dead?"

"It's dead," Danny replied.

"Ito, do you agree and how can you tell? How can you be sure?"

"It looks dead to me. It can't move, or fly, or do anything bees do when they are alive."

"Exactly. Now, what are a few of the things you can do that a dead mouse or any other dead animal can't?"

The boys joined forces and answered, "Move, talk, smell,

see, eat, sleep, hear, feel, think, taste things, breathe, poop, and pee, and a whole lot more."

"You are right. Although there is not a strict separation, is there a difference between things you feel, and the things you do? For example, are you warm, just right, or cold, and how do you know?"

"I'm just right, and I know it because I can feel it," Ito replied.

"Would you two like to take off your shirts and tell me what you feel?"

The boys followed Mr. Schmidt's suggestion. "My skin feels little tingles and impulses, and funny sensations all over my back where the sun hits it," Ito observed.

"Does the front of you feel the same?"

"No, my chest is beginning to feel chilly, but it feels good."

"Me too," Mr. Schmidt replied and Danny nodded. Suddenly, Mr. Schmidt turned around to walk the opposite direction, and went into the field.

"Ugh! Something stinks." Ito had an extraordinarily keen sense of smell.

"Ah, yes. Now I can smell it. What does the smell tell you?"

"Something is dead."

"Yes, but what else does it tell you?" Mr. Schmidt asked the boys.

"It has been dead for a long time."

"What is it, a plant or animal?"

"Some kind of dead animal."

"A land animal or a fish?"

"Well, it isn't a fish."

"Do you think you can find it?"

"Yeah, it's over in that direction." Ito started walking.

"Is it close or far away, and is it a large or small animal?"

"We are getting closer, because the smell is getting stronger, but it must be pretty big to stink so much. Besides, there are some buzzards circling close to the ground. They wouldn't be there if it were just a rat, or something that size."

"Now you are beginning to think like a dog. Your senses are providing information. You are alive, and sensitive to your environment. A dog processes information a little differently from

186

the way we do. It may not be so quick to decide if something is good or bad. Let's see if we can locate that animal."

As the three companions neared the dead animal, they were concentrating on obtaining information. They already knew it stank. They turned off the "light switch" to that part of their sensitivity, so they could concentrate on other types of information. They were between the big patches of wild rosebushes.

Ito signaled for them to stop. "Listen," he whispered, "I can hear crows, magpies, and blackbirds squabbling over which one gets the choicest parts. That other bird may be the sound of the buzzards, but I'm not sure."

The companions eased forward as quietly as possible. "I didn't know there were deer this close to houses," Mr. Schmidt commented. "Have you boys seen any signs of them when you've been out here playing?"

"We've seen tracks and 'pellets,' or turds, but not deer."

"Tell me as much as you can about the remains you see."

"Well, it probably was killed by a man, because both hindquarters have been cut off and carried away. They definitely were not chewed off," Danny observed.

"That's right," Ito added. "Not even all the guts are gone, and that's what wild animals eat first. But what are all of those little white worms?"

"Notice the flies swarming around the carcass. Are they normal houseflies?"

"No, they are too big, and they make lots of noise ... more like a bee."

"Right again." Mr. Schmidt said. "They are commonly called blowflies. They seem to come from almost nowhere as soon as something dies. They lay eggs, which hatch quickly, and these become maggots that start eating dead flesh. They won't eat living tissue. The scavengers of nature are busy cleaning up things that die. That makes it nicer for us. A month from now, only the hide and larger bones will be left. Oh, yes, and the teeth ... they can last for thousands of years. We don't have larger predators in this area. But we are going to be late for lunch if we don't hurry. Do you think you'll be able to eat after seeing this?"

"Why not?" Danny jokingly replied. "We are just three dogs out gathering information." Then he turned more serious. "Maybe I understand a little about why you sometimes take your shirt off, even when it is cold, or rainy, or boiling hot. You use your senses to know and understand what's around you. You are alive."

They walked quickly to the house for lunch.

Sometimes Mr. Schmidt would lead the boys to look at the flowers, the trees, or his bees. Other times he would pick up a little of the earth, run it through his fingers. It was almost a caressing of the soil. He would smell it and let it drift back beneath his feet. "You know, this is where we come from and where we eventually end up. We should enjoy our passage through life, and be worthy of the gift of time while we are here. There is no reason to fear death, as long as we are sensitive to the experiences of the life we have. Rule number one is to enjoy the time you have in life."

On a warm and sunny day, Mr. Schmidt occasionally escorted the boys from their forge stations to a nice patch of grass, and would lie down to look at the sky and clouds. Perhaps they would spy a buzzard circling overhead and would marvel at how sensitive it was to its environment. The slightest movement of a few feathers was all it took to remain aloft for hours. This could be a time for conversation, or silence, or whatever suited their moods. Mr. Schmidt expressed himself most eloquently in German. At times such as these, he told stories about his past, and the dreams he had for the boys' future. "In a month you can earn enough money here at DISKnife to meet your bodily needs for a year, and more. For your mind and spirit to soar in the skies of the world with that bird up there, you must have the freedom from restrictive thought. Education will help your world expand.

"Always, there is work to be done. Never be ashamed to do what we are doing now. Many people may refer to us as being lazy. In fact, it renews our spirits and makes us stronger. This is activity, that must be done or we may lose our awareness of life. I was too busy for this when I was young, and so ignorant that I did not realize its importance. Now my bones are old, and the support of this grass and the ground is not as comforting as it was during my youth. Our greatest luxuries are time and health, not possessions."

As with most things in life, some of the seventh-grade school hours and days seemed to drag, as if the clock's gears were inundated in heavy grease. But the weeks marched along in "quick step."

Bully Billy occasionally was involved in a shoving match on the playgrounds. That happened with lots of other kids as well. Tempers would flare, but they were held in check. The kids would bump, shove, separate, and walk away.

At the talent assembly held in May, Gwen played a piano solo. It was some classical number by a foreign composer who had been dead forever. That was the way some of the kids described it, but they added that it sounded pretty good.

Next on the stage came Big James and Bully Billy and everyone wondered what was going to happen. Big James said, "I guess everyone knows that Bill and I had a little problem earlier this year, but we found we like to sing together, so here we are. It's okay if you laugh when something goes wrong. Our voices are changing. It happens to me more than it does to Bill, because he is more mature than I am. Anyway, I call him Bill now, and we are going to sing." Voices did crack a couple times, and all the fellows could relate to that. But there was a special quality to their voices, a mellow richness, and Bill seemed different. Enthusiastic applause encouraged them to sing a second song. Gwen had stayed on stage, and accompanied them on the piano.

Gangly-legged Millie tap-danced to an accompaniment by Gwen and the boys developed a new sense of appreciation for her. They had been reading and hearing about long-legged heroines in detective stories, and they had one right in their class! Well, maybe she didn't have all the curves the story heroines had, but they were beginning to develop.

Poems were recited. One kid brought his dog, and it performed some good tricks. Donald drew some big cartoon character while he was on stage. He sketched copies of Donald Duck and Goofy before drawing several characters of his own.

Gwen ended the show with a crowd-pleasing "boogie-woogie" on the piano.

The next thing the kids knew, the teachers were collecting books, having them clean out their desks, saying nice things about them, and handing out report cards. School was over until September.

Summer sun warmed the land, air, and water. Swimming provided an afternoon break from the forge for Ito and Danny. To get to the swimming hole on the millrace meant a bike ride. Sometimes the boys stopped where the logs were dumped from the trucks into the water. They watched the driver swing the big truck into position and off-load the logs into the water.

The boys watched the spectacle, and realized this was probably as close as they ever would come to being a part of the logging industry. Knife manufacturing was their trade. The logging and sawmill industry would do very well without them. They knew that their bean-picking days were over. In a way, Danny regretted that Ito would not pick again, because he was so quick and good at it. He would have been "king of the bean field" if he continued working there. A lot of prestige went along with that title. But then, Ito was good at everything he attempted. The boys recognized each other's skills, talents, and strengths. Each cooperated with the other in pursuing goals, and remained unconcerned about competition.

But they were at the millrace to swim. There were times when they would jump in the water downriver from the logs, so they could ride the waves made when the logs hit the water. Other times, they would leave their bikes and walk a mile or two upriver, tie their tennis shoes around their waists, and swim back down to their bikes. There were usually about a dozen kids who met there daily. Some had feet tough enough to walk barefoot over gravel, thorns, and whatever. Ito and Danny never could do that with any comfort.

The swimming maintained a healthy contact with kids of a similar age. Perhaps it was strange, but the boys never really talked with their friends and schoolmates about their knife making. Little Teddie could have talked about it, but he didn't. That part of their lives was private. When anyone did ask about knife making, they talked about their own private throwing knives. DISKnife did not enter into the conversation.

The worst of "the Great Economic Depression" was over. Most men who really wanted to work, and who had skills, were employed. Competition for picking up snipes, a common name for cigarette and cigar butts found on the streets and in ashtrays, had ceased. Few men were doing that in order to have smoking tobacco.

Riding the rails remained common transportation for men "on the bum." Railway boxcars were frequently seen with the doors open. Bearded and ragged-looking men might be their only cargo. "Where are those men going?" Ito asked Mr. Schmidt.

"Maybe they are going home. Is it possible some of them have been away for so long, they don't know where their home really is?" Mr. Schmidt's voice seemed to reflect a poignant, nostalgic, and wistful mood. Perhaps he was thinking about Germany and his long-dead wife and children. Ito and Danny didn't know, but they had become increasingly sensitive and aware of other people's feelings. Years of *A Way* training had been effective. So had Mr. Schmidt's time and devotion to their awareness of what it meant to be "alive."

Ito said to Mr. Schmidt and to Danny, "Your home is with us. It wouldn't be the same without either of you. We love both of you." His words were spoken softly with youthful affection.

Danny knew the truth of what Ito said and so did Mr. Schmidt. "Since my parents died, Gran and I have been more aware that we really are one family."

"Speaking as a family member," Mr. Schmidt replied, "would it be out of order to share a hug?" Then he continued, "This is what so many men lack. Men come to the side or back door of a house, and offer to work for a sandwich or any kind of food. Of these, many are really hungry, and willing to work hard for their meal. Others just want a free handout without any commitment or obligation. They eat first and then drift away. The hunger from being alone will never be satisfied unless you make a commitment. I know this only too well. For many years I lived an aimless, loveless life. Now I have you as my family."

The thought of Mr. Schmidt living that type of life brought tears to the eyes of the boys. Then he continued, "There are choices in life that each person may make. Often, the consequences may be enormous. In my lifetime, I have been both devastated and rescued. For me, life is better and happier than it ever has been."

One man "on the bum" was just leaving Gran. Danny asked, "Did he work for the food?" Gran replied, "Not to worry. I've never turned any person away. There were times in me life when a bit of food would have suited me just fine. We all need a helping hand now and again."

The two boys went to the homes of classmates. Prosperity, even luxury, was represented by a sack of tobacco sitting on an ashtray stand, along with a pipe or two, and paper for "rolling your own." It was unpleasant for them to be where people smoked, because the places always stank of stale tobacco. The two boys used to joke that it was nicer to spend the time in the "bughouse" than in a house filled with tobacco smoke.

Cheap brands of cigarettes cost five cents a pack and the expensive ones were ten cents. People who smoked littered the streets with their cigarette butts and empty packs. Some folks picked up the empty packs of the expensive cigarettes, and carried their cheap brand in one of them. This was an attempt to appear more prosperous than they actually were.

Often, women had a different concept of luxury. It might be a new handkerchief, a hat, fingernail polish, lipstick, a dinner plate, or a kitchen spoon. Regardless of the budget, the stores were full of items to appeal to the penny, nickel, dime, quarter, dollar, or many-dollar budgets. Many sales were to an impulsive purchaser. Others were based on agonizing desire that had built up over a period of time of being without.

The DISKnife was just such an item. The fact that it was superior to anything else of its type only made it that much more attractive. But just having enough money didn't mean a person could buy one. The supply was so limited that among some segments of the male population, ownership was almost the ultimate luxury.

A local cobbler made hand-tooled leather scabbards for the knives, following the motif engraved on the handle. When it became evident to him that demands for his scabbard would continue, he had tooling dies cast that would stamp out the basic design, and still leave surface area for custom tooling.

There were shooters, hunters, and killers. Many shooters never hunted. Shooting was their sport; the targets were not animals, and they had no desire to kill any animal. In the area where Danny and Ito lived, most young boys grew up with the idea of deer hunting. They had a .22-caliber rifle at their disposal from age nine onward. This was used for learning to shoot and for recreational "plinking." For some hunters, almost any bird or other small animal made a suitable target. "Plunking frogs" was a game. In the next breath, the frog shooters might complain that "skeeters" were eating them alive. Apparently, they didn't know or care that frogs ate huge quantities of mosquito larvae. Ammunition was a scarce item during the Depression, but some kids became so accurate with their shooting that a variety of small birds and animals were shot for food. "Make every shot count" was the rule of the time. Killer shooters appeared to take no pleasure in using their gun for purposes other than killing.

A firearm was thought of as a "man's weapon." Familiarity with shooting and continual practice during childhood years provided the US military with a valuable resource for the army and marines. In this semi-rural community, a "real man" had his family roots in Northern Europe. A pocketknife or a sheath knife was a tool that most men and boys carried almost everywhere they went. But a throwing knife was considered a sneaky weapon of those "others," who were characterized in the films as being greasy types from somewhere around the Mediterranean Sea or south of the border. Of course, some of the "insidious" Asians, as found in Charlie Chan movies or Fu Man Chu novels, always carried and used knives. Consequently, when it came to knife throwing, the boys kept mostly to themselves. Friends knew the boys threw them at various types of targets, but they didn't see it being done, and were neither interested nor concerned.

Men who owned a DISKnife carried it almost everywhere they wore jeans, Levi's, or sports clothing that didn't require a tie and jacket. Not many of the knives were available, and a saying developed in some areas, "I have my DISKnife, and he only has a Cadillac."

Little Teddie received a DISKnife and a pair of throwing knives from Danny and Ito. Once in production, he had been invited to watch the procedure, except for the tempering of the blade. Then Ito and Danny demonstrated knife throwing to him and he was astounded. Danny started showing him how to throw a knife. It was then that he realized, at least in part, why Teddie was so inept in all sports. No one had taken the trouble to show him how to do apparently simple things, such as how to hold a ball, how to step into a throw from the back foot, and all those things most boys take for granted.

Teddie's throwing knives were never used for throwing, and the DISKnife never went hunting. They were on display in his bedroom while he was a child. Later, they occupied a place of honor in his living room, even when he had a home and family of his own. Many years later he said they were his symbols of childhood masculinity and acceptance. This was during a time when he was having so much emotional turmoil based on physical and sports-oriented incompetence. He treasured their symbolism.

State law at that time required school attendance until the completion of the eighth grade or reaching age sixteen. Many people strongly urged Ito and Danny to quit school and devote full time to their knife-making business. Even with part-time activity, their income greatly exceeded that of most full-time adult workers in the community, including many physicians, attorneys, and bankers.

It would have been easy to become totally obsessed with producing knives and making money. The wisdom of Mr. Schmidt guided them away from that direction. "You two young men will attend university and also explore the world. Then, if you want to make knives, you will have the facilities, the experience, and the knowledge to continue making the best knives in the world."

Perhaps Mr. Schmidt was most vocal about the boys' future, but the other adults were adamant that education was more important in life than money.

What better way could there be for an individual to emphasize the need to have more than just one direction in life, than the example Mr. Schmidt set for the boys? "It is time for a day or two off. I'm not going to go anywhere, but I always enjoyed designing and making wind toys." And so he did. He resumed making one-of-a-kind, multi-activity units. This change in activity could last a day or two, or perhaps a week or more.

Wind toy bicycle riders raced around a track at various speeds. A remotely located wind-driven propeller powered them. Jointed acrobats performed on bars, rings, and a trapeze in their own miniature circus. Airplanes flew in an aerial competition of their own. A running horse led a parade of animals around and around a field. A cow followed the horse. Then came a donkey, goat, dog, cat, and chicken. The harder the wind blew, the faster the animals ran. All the animals had articulating legs. When a wind toy design was undertaken, he might take a couple weeks to finish it. That didn't mean he completely quit working on DIS-Knife projects. He took time off during work hours to do other things that he enjoyed.

His wind toys could have been produced commercially, but he had no ambitions in that direction. Each completed model was mounted on a pole about eye height and placed in the garden area near the house. They created a magical playground for the eyes and imagination. They also served the practical purpose of keeping birds away from the fruit and vegetables he was growing.

26

DISKnife Report and Lifestyle Changes

The DISKnife was not advertised and yet orders came in much faster than they could be filled. Mr. Schmidt had registered the trademark, which assured its unique identity. "Me best advice is to make no attempt to patent your steel-tempering secret, because that would require releasing details of that process," Gran suggested. "After reading through many pages of information on patents and reviewing patent infringement cases, it appears that companies with large budgets can essentially steal your process. They can read the information, make slight changes, and do what they like with it. If only the three of ye know how to temper the steel, others can't steal from ye what they don't know, unless someone observes ye or ye tell them."

Danny and Ito protested, "All our family should know," but Gran held up her hand.

"We all love our family unit and no one would do anything to cause a negative impact on ye, or the business. But it is best that the secret be known only by the three of ye."

"But what would become of the business if something to the three of us?"

"That is a possibility we don't want to contemplate. However, it would be a shame for the tempering process to be lost to the world. Each of you could write it down carefully, compare what you have written to be certain there can be no misunderstandings, and then we could put it in a bank safe-deposit box," Mr. Schmidt suggested.

The family unit agreed and the boys immediately followed Mr. Schmidt's advice. Gran had been planning ahead. "I'll see to the safe-deposit box in the morning. Now, we know it is possible for bankers to be corrupted as well as the rest of humanity. So now, laddie boys, here's another wee chore for ye. I'll be putting part of this information in three separate safe-deposit boxes in three different banks. One will be in our regular bank and one in each of two other banks in our next-door city. Write on three different pieces of paper, putting one third of the critical part of the tempering process on each of the sheets. Please be certain that all three sources of information are needed in order to do the tempering. That will make it more difficult for unscrupulous persons to obtain your secret tempering procedure."

Gran also undertook the task of compiling a record of orders and issuing a position on the waiting list. Orders arrived daily, and she would update that information, so a customer would have an estimate of his knife delivery date.

By mid-December all of the original blade blanks Mr. Schmidt had in storage had been used, and many times that as well. Their senior partner had become so swamped by blade production that Gran offered her assistance by taking over all correspondence, packing, and shipping, as well as helping with sharpening, buffing, and polishing of knives when needed. Revised innovations in production techniques and equipment, combined with coordinating supplies and schedules, took time and effort. But production of knife blades continued as their top priority.

During mid-December, Mr. Schmidt presented a business report. "Production has been 1,521 completed knives, with our cost being just under two dollars each. This includes new equipment. We have no knives in stock except for ones for personal use, and the two we maintained as examples. Of course, 'Number 1' is in our showcase."

Mr. Schmidt continued his informal accounting. "The company has in stock nearly eight thousand blade blanks and two tons of aluminum in five-pound ingots, which, as you know, are a good size for melting to cast handles. As a form of speculation, I have purchased two-thousand ounces oz. of .92 fine silver. It will be used for casting handles on special presentation knives. I predicted there will be orders for them within the year."

"Why not pure silver?"

"Good question, Ito. The small alloy added to the silver makes for a more stable material. Our silver dollar, half-dollar, quarter, or dime would be ideal, and their value is set. However, it is illegal to deface US currency. If we were to use .999 fine stock, I am certain that any engraving would wear away."

Heads nodded in understanding and appreciation.

"Let us look at the current financial status of our company. Our bank account shows a balance of twenty-one thousand dollars ... and we have no outstanding debts!"

All eyes had opened to the size of silver dollars, and a chorus of gasps dominated what otherwise was shocked silence. Danny broke the silence, "Ito and I would have to pick 2,100,000 pounds of beans to earn that amount of money!"

Mother Watanabe joined with her comment, "The new plywood company pays its workers seventy-five cents an hour. With the two of you working for them, you would need to work for fourteen thousand hours to earn twenty-one thousand dollars. Let's see, that would ... help me with the mathematics ... eight hours a day and six days a week..." She paused for a time. "Yes, it looks as if the two of you could earn that amount of money in just over six years. Yet your company has earned this in a matter of months. You should be very proud of your efforts, skills, and accomplishments."

The two boys protested, "We've been figuring this all wrong. We didn't do this by ourselves."

Mother Watanabe bowed to Mr. Schmidt and Gran and then nodded her pleasure. Her two boys recognized the contributions of the family members.

Mr. Schmidt, who had started the discussion about the company's financial status, added a shocking realization: "Keep in mind that we are dealing with just a six-month report. Also, our production for the first two months was greatly curtailed, because we were in a developmental period. It is apparent that the financial future of our company is ... may I say *brilliant!*"

The bean-picking season had come and gone, and Ito and Danny had missed it. They were totally committed to developing DISKnife, and their bean working days were over. For years they would miss the bean yard society and its comradeship. At the beginning of the school year, they talked with fellow students about who picked the most beans and other happenings. Strangely enough, throughout his life, Danny would calculate the cost of luxuries in terms of the amount of beans he'd have to pick to pay for the item.

The sportsmen of the nation quickly embraced DISKnife. It became a renowned, highly respected, and desirable item to own. As expected, Mr. Schmidt's prediction of special orders came true. The first such request came from a high-ranking official from the state police. Gran replied by mail that the firm did not make such an item. The official telephoned the Watanabe residence and was told the same thing. He persisted by coming to the house. Gran and Mr. Schmidt were in the middle of finishing some knives. They worked as the official described what he would like to purchase as a special gift for the state's governor. He explained by saying, "The governor is a hunter, and it is a little embarrassing for him to have the best blades in the world made in his state, and for him not to have one. In fact, the only one he has seen is owned by the governor of California!"

Gran had an outward disregard for the various levels of political influence. She might joke about a politician's level in the order of "cock-ha-doodle-do dome," but she could not escape her upbringing, complete with reverence for those of "higher birth." For Mr. Schmidt, designing and making special items suited his creative nature. It also validated the realization of his childhood dream. He brought out "Number 1 DISKnife," with its silver handle.

This complicated matters. The governor wanted a working knife, but the visiting officer wanted a special presentation model with a silver handle and an inlaid gold seal of the state.

Mr. Schmidt said, "All our knives are pre-ordered. At our present production rate, it would be about five years before we could get to your order. We understand that you feel an urgency in this matter, so we'll need to consult one of our two blade producers. When we first started out, we decided that all our regular production would be delivered according to date of order, without exception. I could take the time to cast a special silver handle for a presentation knife and inlay the state's gold seal. My part of the work would be a pleasure, and our pride in this state may prompt others to participate. But only two workers make the blades and know how to temper them. You will need to talk one of them into working extra hours."

"Well, I'd be happy to pay double or more, to get them done quickly."

"You misunderstand what I meant. We have only one price for our regular knives. The special silver handle and inlay work would, of course, cost more. Ito is walking this way now. You can see him through that window. Just tell him who you are and what you want. If he agrees to work the additional hours, you could have a regular knife within a couple of days. The silver handle special could take an additional day from the time you deliver the gold medallion."

Their visitor looked concerned. "The only person I see coming this way is a young Oriental boy."

"Yes, that is Ito. Our other blade producer is Daniel, the one who discovered our tempering technique. Tempering, combined with our multiple layering process, makes our blades superior to any others in the world, for both sharpness and durability. Danny and Ito are both thirteen years old, and they are in the seventh grade."

The officer and Ito met, and the request was presented. Ito understood that Mr. Schmidt wanted to make the special presentation knife. He simply stated, "I'm sure Danny would be willing to work overtime with me to make the blades," and then politely excused himself.

"My guess is that they will work during their noon hour to fill this order for you. This will be the first time an exception has been made in the timing of our order and delivery."

The officer had sat in quiet amazement, and finally reacted. "But they are only kids."

"You are right, but they also own and control this business."

"They are too young to quit school, so how do they manage?"

Mr. Schmidt couldn't resist the opportunity. "Let me brag a bit about the two of them. Ito, of course speaks Japanese. Your short conversation with him lets you know that he speaks English with an accent that is the same as is common in this state. He speaks German with a Hamburg accent, which is the same as mine. He reads and writes it better than most German students of a similar age.

"Danny's mother tongue is English which he can speak with your accent or the Cockney accent commonly found in London.

My best estimate is that he knows about five thousand German words. He converses with Ito and me freely, but not at Ito's level. He knows many thousands of words in Arabic, and can read and write it as well. He is fluent in Japanese and can also read and write that language.

"Now, those are just their 'outside of school accomplishments.' Teachers report that they are the two most brilliant students they have ever encountered. Beyond that, they are outgoing with other students, adored by most, and I'd wager they could defeat you or any of your officers in hand-to-hand combat. But you would be hard-pressed to find any youngsters their age who are more anxious to avoid conflict. Now, let's get back to the two knives you want. When will the gold medallion be delivered?"

"How about now?" The officer handed a small container to Mr. Schmidt. The gold seal that he provided would later be inlaid into the silver handle. The arrangements were concluded. No one was happier than the officer, except for Mr. Schmidt. It vindicated his investment in silver. Most of all, his dream of highly placed officials wanting his knives had come true.

Two weeks after receiving his presentation knife, the governor started placing special orders for knives he wanted to present as personal awards to friends and selected official visitors to the state. The letter attached to the order stated, "I will take great personal pride in being able to present such an item that is totally unique, and is only available in our state."

Mr. Schmidt made a handle mold that contained a round blank area in which a disk of the state seal could be inserted. The disc could be cast in gold, silver, or other metals, and inserted in a handle that could be cast in almost any metal. A duplicate of the governor's signature was made in the mold. The governor was advised of the delivery date. His order was at the end of their list.

Sometimes orders arrived with specially engraved disks to be inserted in the handles. Mr. Schmidt explained that no matter what the order might entail, there was only one quality of blade, and that was the finest in the world.

Gran and Mr. Schmidt became increasingly involved with the special orders. They combined their artistic and creative skills on a series of knives for the US State Department. The government supplied a particularly hard gold alloy for the handles and leather scabbards. These knives were to be presented to dignitaries of Muslim nations. Ito and Danny enjoyed the challenge of developing and producing the longer, curved blade that was in keeping with the traditional Arab style. The State Department provided a gross of longer blade blanks that came from their regular supplier. These presented a challenge, because the final shaping process did not fit the existing forges. It was back to the old and slower method of hand hammering to produce the curve to the blade.

Danny commented, "This procedure is inefficient. I can make eight of our regular knives in the time it takes me to shape the curved blade. I timed it, and this isn't fair to our regular customers who have been waiting for months for a knife."

Four days later, Mr. Schmidt presented the boys with a different hammer and anvil. It was designed for making the curved blade. This new forging equipment was necessary, because it was inefficient and labor-intensive to change from one set of hammers and anvils to another. "I charged the costs to the State Department." Mr. Schmidt explained. "They did not complain. In fact, they commended us for being resourceful in fulfilling their orders."

While the boys were making these curved blades, Danny commented, "Someday I'm going to go to Arabic-speaking countries, and it would be nice to have a few blades ready as special gifts. I can pour the silver handle on them and do special engraving later, when needed."

"Good idea!" Ito replied. "Is it okay if I make some with you? Tomorrow is a holiday and we normally wouldn't be making our regular knives."

When Gran saw the curved blades and unique handles, she was pleased. "So ye are making something else unique! Would ye mind if I put a little fancy work on the blade? I'd leave the handles for your own expressions." Gran's Koran verse selections sang the praise of peace, justice, and humility. She utilized her knowledge of Arabic, and outstanding calligraphic skills, to inscribe meaningful verses from the Koran. This surprised and delighted the US officials, as well as the recipients. As one potentate was reported to have said, "We have received knives with handles and scabbards made of precious metals and encrusted with jewels, but only from America can we obtain such a blade!"

The team was dedicated to producing their standard knives to distribute to their customers who were on their list. Although they enjoyed making their regular blades, they took extra pleasure producing specialty items. These were made during added working hours.

For Mr. Schmidt, special orders fulfilled a lifelong ambition dating back to the days when he had gone to Solingen to study knife-making techniques. He was the guiding light behind the enormously successful and profitable DISKnife business. Each time unique orders came in, Mr. Schmidt glowed with pleasure. His original dreams had been realized and compounded, beyond measure. He stroked the unique knives with a delicate touch usually reserved for a child's cheek.

Gran saw Mr. Schmidt looking carefully at one of his legs. He explained. "I've no more hair to shave, and I like to test my blades from time to time." With that, they burst into laughter.

Mother and Father Watanabe occasionally assisted in knife finishing. This increased as Gran and Mr. Schmidt became more involved in finishing presentation knives.

Gran and Danny continued their word games in Arabic, telling and creating stories of their own, in the fashion of the Arabian Nights tales. This time together was accompanied by the sounds of buffing, engraving, and honing knives. Gran spent some evenings away, helping and visiting with her elderly friends. Financially, it would have been easy to hire someone to replace her, but she separated assistance with living, from assistance with chores. The money would not be missed, "But 'elping out is part of who I am, so I lend a hand when needed."

After each forging was completed, Ito and Danny would pause, grab a few throwing knives, and embed them in wooden targets from distances ranging from ten to thirty-five feet. This would be followed by a huge yawn, a moment of stretching, and perhaps twenty-five push-ups. Their exercises relieved work-induced fatigue and tension.

A *Way* practice was a continuing part of their daily fitness training. It included regular instruction and supervision by both

Father and Mother Watanabe. The boys had installed a chinning bar just at the entrance to the forge area, and at least twice daily they did their maximum numbers of hanging leg lifts, and alternated that with pull-ups or chin-ups.

"There are many different worlds of activity to discover. You must have holidays that will help you expand your knowledge and provide different types of fun. Last year you cycled to a forest camp. Will you do that again this year?" These guiding thoughts came from the four main adult influences in their world.

Shortly after selling the first DISKnife, it had been obvious to Mr. Schmidt, the Watanabe family, and Gran that income problems were a thing of the past. By the time the month and a half of production innovations had been completed, it was possible for the combined households to net an average of sixty dollars for each hour Ito and Danny worked producing knife blades. Of course, that was only part of the job. Handles had to be poured, and finishing of the knife needed to be done. The completed product and a leather sheath, had to be posted to its new owner.

The limiting factor in their income was how many blades the two boys produced. Recently the boys became aware of the increasing use of the phrase "*Vorrang haben vor.*" Mr. Schmidt, of course, was using that phrase. "*Yori juyo na*" came from Father and Mother Watanabe. Roughly, both expressions were translated into the English word "priorities."

One evening Ito and Danny returned late from milking the cows. The critters had not come in at the regular time, and the boys had to go out and find them. It had taken them an extra hour. Gran put the idea directly to them. "It's the choices ye have regarding the lifestyle ye want, laddie boys. Ye no longer need to be messing with cows unless ye want to. The hour ye spent at the milking could have been used at the forge, and ye'd have earned enough to buy a hundred gallons of milk. It's the same with the garden. In days past we hadn't the choice. We needed the milk and the garden produce to eat. We needed the chickens, eggs, and rabbits as well. We now 'ave money a plenty to buy what's needed. Ye 'ave priority and lifestyle choices ... your choices. Ye need not change, unless ye 'ave a mind to."

Ito and Danny nodded their understanding of the words and

realized they needed time to think and discuss what the impact of such changes would be. The boys thought about their gardens, chicken, cows, rabbits, chores, time, fun activities, and other activities.

A word or two and body language served as a type of "shorthand" discussion. Garden-fresh fruits and vegetables meant better taste. They wanted to continue that part of their life. They felt a need to dig in the soil and run their hands through the earth. They treasured that Mr. Schmidt had helped them feel a bond with the earth. Chickens were not much trouble, and they helped keep the garden free from insects. They would keep chickens. Rabbits were an interesting and meaningful part of their past experience and food, but they were not needed. It was about time to take one of the cows to the bull. "I don't mind if I never have to do that again!" Danny exclaimed.

"And I don't mind if I never have to chase a cow down in the pasture on a wet night, either!" Ito added. They would be pleased to have that part of their lives finished.

At that moment, getting rid of the cows sounded awfully good. No more trips wading through the mud to bring in cows that refused to come when called. No more having to shovel cow flops off the floor of the barn. At least an hour a day less time would be needed for milking and associated chores. No more churning butter, no more making cottage cheese. No more spending an hour each evening delivering milk. That sounded good. Hold on! They thought. Prosperity had not reached everyone. Danny had been delivering a quart of milk to a man, his wife, and her sister since he was in the third grade. They were church friends and Danny's mother had made it a personal commitment to supply them with a quart of milk daily, and sometimes a special treat of cottage cheese and butter, when it was surplus. These friends could not afford to buy these things, and would not accept a gift of money to help them purchase their own. They were money-poor, but not poor in spirit or dignity. Milk, fruit, vegetables, and chickens that might be surplus to one family, were gratefully received by others. Danny had continued these deliveries even after his parents' death, because his mother would have liked him to do it ... and he liked doing it. "I could pay for the milk and maybe Little Teddie would deliver it?"

Ito nodded his head, "Yes, but *we* can buy it, not just you. Another thing, Teddie lives only a couple of blocks from the store and their place, and I'll bet he could use a little extra spending money. How much should we offer him?"

The arrangement worked perfectly for all parties. Mr. May, the man of the house, had been an accountant, but he had to leave his work because he had developed palsy. His mind remained absolutely clear, but his hands and body shook so much he couldn't write.

When Little Teddie started delivering milk, Mr. May opened the world of bookkeeping to the boy. It was a natural course of study for a boy who loved working with numbers, and was gifted in that area. "Remember, Teddie, being an accountant can be the next logical step after becoming a bookkeeper. The pay is better, and you might find the work more challenging."

When Ito and Danny arrived home from school the following day, the cows were gone. It seemed funny that such a big hole was left in their day. A few days later the rabbits and hutches were also gone. As originally planned, the chickens remained, because they were good at keeping garden bugs under control. And, if you didn't eat them, they were almost no trouble. Besides, the eggs were good. They continued keeping a garden and fruit trees, and Mr. Schmidt continued to enjoy keeping his honeybees.

Danny and Ito worked an extra hour a day at the forge, but no one was concerned about the extra money that was coming in. No one seemed particularly interested in buying much of anything. There was not a car in either household, and that suited everyone.

The outward signs of what Danny's late mother would have called "scandalous prosperity" were not to be found. Danny remembered when he first heard and learned that big word, *scandalous*. It was when he had told his mother about "doing IT" to Beverly Jean and using the "f-word." That seemed to have been so long ago.

Gran dealt with the family income. Danny wore cords, Levi's, T-shirts, and tennis shoes, and rode his two-dollar, second-hand bike. Whatever he needed was available, but he really didn't want all the "stuff" that many kids thought they had to have. Ito's needs were similar to Danny's. "We have our throwing knives and the pleasure of making DISKnives. School studies, and working with Mr. Bag, are more like recreation. For us, fun is doing things, not having stuff. What else could we want?"

Father Watanabe added to his treasure of silver dollars, and he buried them at various places on his property. The financial lesson of the Great Depression remained etched in his mind: Don't trust banks. But he and Mother Watanabe made a variety of investments that they felt represented secure opportunities for growth. Gran's prodigious reading skills and innate ability to research and analyze the stock market guided them, and most of the money earned by DISKnife production was also invested in stocks and bonds.

Gran and Danny spent some of their income to equalize the rent on the homes of nearly a dozen of her favorite elderly friends. All were having difficulty meeting the increases. "We've more than enough money to help them live where they are, and even decrease or eliminate their rent so they can have a little spending money. They needn't spend their last days in poverty." This also applied to Grandma Skelen, who was more than a hundred years old, and still living on her own ... and continued raising flowers. "Being able to assist a few friends is me own form of luxury," Gran admitted. Then she added her timely phrase when she wanted to share a special treat with Danny, "Not a word, not a word to anyone." In earlier years this had happened when she had a piece or two of hard candy to share with the lad.

Danny nodded his understanding, hugged Gran, and said, "The feeling is even more delicious than candy, isn't it!"

It seemed almost impossible to believe that four years earlier, near poverty had been a reality in both households. The animals and a garden were part of a lifestyle they all knew, understood, and treasured. However, desirable changes were taking place, and lifestyle adjustments were being made.

Perhaps the philosophy of the two households could best be summarized by the framed needlepoint, that hung in the living room of Gran and Danny's house:

DO YOUR POSESSIONS POSSESS YOU?

27

Eighth Grade

The new school year began, and Ito and Danny were finally in the same classroom. They were eighth graders, "seniors," and it was the last year they would be in that school.

There was another kind of learning going on this year. Because of the obvious physical changes in fellow students, talk switched to differences in development. Cruelty in conversations came in many forms and from many sources. It was often posed in such questions such as: "Why haven't you...? Why don't you...? When are you going to...? What's wrong with me...?" These were beginnings to sentences that deal with puberty-oriented feelings of inadequacy. Differing rates of maturation, and the variety of body types, imprinted self-image and personality characteristics that would last a lifetime. Big James hated the question, "Why are you so big?" He was well over six feet tall, weighed 265 pounds, and was only fourteen years old. Even though he always had top grades in all his subjects, those at school only asked about his size, not his abilities. There were just two boys who could run faster than Big James, but they didn't ask about his athletic accomplishments, only his size. He would have been happy to give up everything else, just to have normal height and weight.

The other side of the coin was Don, who was the smallest kid. "When are you going to start growing?" He would hear kids say to newcomers, "He's one of the strongest kids in the class." Then they would add those three hated words ... "for his size."

"Where'd she get such big tits? They're bigger than our milk cow's." Or, "When are you going to grow some tits? Boys have more there than you do." "What's she wearing a bra for, when a couple Band-Aids would do?" "Falsies!" "His prick is so small, he couldn't find it, and pissed his pants." Such cruel remarks passed as humor, and they didn't always come from other kids. Parents and other adults were known to make similar "smart" remarks. Were they trying to be clever, or were they attempting to cover up their embarrassment that *their* child was somehow different or sub-standard?

Twice a year school officials weighed and measured kids, to monitor their growth. They would consult the "normal height to weight ratio charts" and send students home with the reports. Implications were that underweight children were undernourished. Parents were presumed to be doing a good job of providing for the overweight youngster. Body type and hereditary factors were completely ignored.

Bruce was one such youngster. He knew he was underweight. The term *skinny* had haunted him all through school. He jumped up and down on the scales, hoping to make them show that he was really heavier. Another time he bent over and pushed as hard as he could on his right knee, hoping to make the scales show a higher number. He wore a pair of his father's shoes one year and filled them and his pockets with sand. Nothing he did overcame his genes.

In order to increase his height, Don created his own version of "platform shoes." He saved all the money he earned, and purchased three pair of stick-on soles, which he put on his shoes, one on top of the other. His next step was to cut a section out of an old car tire and nail additional "heels" onto his shoes. His final innovation was to glue pieces of cardboard an inch thick to his own heels and cover them with his socks. The sweetest words he could ever imagine were those that said, "My! How you have grown!"

In their own groups, boys speculated, bragged, and were ready to demonstrate and measure the size of their cocks to see who had the longest one, whose was the biggest around, and every other conceivable comparison that might give the bragger a slight advantage in the headlong race toward completed puberty. Voices cracked and deepened. Fuzzy down appeared on chins and upper lips. Guys loved to speculate about needing to have a shave pretty soon. Adult "humor" of the day suggested that the youngster should put some whipped cream on the fuzz and let a cat lick it off. Insensitive cruelty accompanied the push to "grow up."

Most fellows in the eighth grade suffered from ignorance and misinformation about so many things involving girls. They wanted to appear sexy and desirable to all the girls, but they didn't have a clue. Boys only knew what appeared manly and desirable to themselves, and presumed it would be the same for girls. So they swaggered and flexed their muscles. They talked in a way they thought was sexy, or tough, or whatever way suited what they were pretending to be. But for most of them, this was too much of a strain, and they settled down to being whatever they were, and hoped that would be okay.

Bully Bill had quit physically pounding his classmates, because he knew the kids would gang up on him. Even worse was the idea of his guts being squashed out his "bung hole" if Big James sat on him. He controlled himself better than before, but he still hadn't learned to manage his mouth. It became his weapon of choice. Poor Little Teddie, who had endured humiliation because of physical incompetence in games of strength and skill, suffered yet additional and ultimate degradation. Bully Bill accused him of not even being able to get a hard-on.

The following Saturday, Teddie invited Ito and Danny to go to the Sunday movie, his treat, and then ice cream and cake at his house afterward. The boys met him at the theater entrance and were amazed at how nervous Teddie was. Joe E. Brown had the lead role in a comedy. In addition, a cowboy film, the news, and a cartoon were shown. Ito and Danny didn't often take time to go to the movies, and they had a hilarious time.

It seemed as if Teddie didn't really enjoy the films, and the boys wondered what was up. When they got to his place, he led them to his room, where he had stashed away a mail-order book on human anatomy. It contained a line drawing of a woman's lower parts. It looked pretty ugly to Ito and Danny. It was Teddie's fantasy aid. He begged them to watch him, so they would be witnesses for him the next time Bully Bill said he couldn't get a hard-on. So they watched as he did a two-finger caress job on his diminutive member. It stood upright, about the size of a woman's lipstick, and after a short period of special attention, it spurted forth with a vigorous rapture that carried Teddie's seed thirteen feet across the room.

"Promise you'll tell everyone, please promise ... well, not the girls."

Ito and Danny did tell all the guys. And they also told them they'd better not get into a shooting-off contest with Teddie.

The school had a gymnasium, which was separate from the schoolhouse. It had been built twenty years earlier. A good floor had been laid and sanded, but never finished. An ultra-conservative board of education chose not to "fritter away more good money" just so kids could have a place to play. Their games could be done outside or in the play shed that had a dirt floor. When it was too wet outside, they could stay in their schoolrooms and study. After all, they were there to learn, not play. An almost worn-out basketball had been a hand-me-down from the high school. A swarm of about fifty kids would push, shove, and wrestle to get the ball to take a shot. This melee took place surrounding the basket. Of course Little Teddie was not in the crowd. The basketball rebounded past the key and no one scrambled after it. Teddie was at center court when the ball hit him in the chest. He grabbed the ball without dropping it. Then a playground miracle started unfolding. No one, including Teddie, figured he'd be able to throw the ball in the air as far as the basket. With an unsure grip on the ball, and unsteady feet, he took two awkward, lunging steps in the right direction, and just heaved the ball toward the crowd under the basket. The impossible happened! The ball arched upward, cleared through roof trusses ... there was no ceiling in the building ... continued its flight, and dropped directly through the metal hoop without touching anything. It couldn't be referred to as a "swisher," because there was no net! It really was a miracle, because he was a sure bet to miss nineteen out of twenty uncontested layups. But Little Teddie became known as "Long Shot." The girls thought it was because of his long, center-court shot. But the boys knew better. Long Shot Teddie had found a new sense of belonging, and manhood.

And Long Shot found a new comfort zone in his life. He continued being neat and precise when he did his math papers. The columns were always in order and he was accurate. He simply did not make mathematical errors. On some class projects, he,

Ruthie, and Danny continued being a team, as well as devoted and supportive friends.

The three remained in the same group, and were joined by Ito, throughout their last year of grade school. Although they shared most things, the real origin of the title *Long Shot* remained obscure as far as Ruthie was concerned.

Ray was a year older than his classmates in the eighth grade. He had been in the class a year ahead, but he missed a year. As Ray said, "I was running with the dogs before I got polio. We were stealing milk bottles, siphoning gas, swiping bikes for a ride and then dumping them, and stuff like that. We figured we weren't doing anything really bad, but two of the fellows, went from one thing to the next, and ended up being sent to reform school."

Well, polio knocked him flat. Ray was going to wear a leg brace for the rest of his days, and he had to make a new life. Instead of feeling sorry for himself, he won the admiration of all the students by being one of the smartest kids in class. He carved airplanes out of black walnut wood. Many of them were used by the military for aircraft identification training during World War II.

Most of all, he built his own radios. He started with a crystal set and went on from there. During lulls in class, his index finger and thumb would straddle the index finger of his left hand and he would practice the Morse code alphabet, as if he were using a key. Ito and Danny became curious about what he was doing, and asked him. He gave the two boys a copy of the code and soon they were doing the same thing. It wasn't long before they were sending messages back and forth during class. That didn't last long. Mr. Rob, their teacher, interrupted them with his own tapping. His message was, "Do not disturb other class members. Yes, practice, but you should do it quietly." He knew the code, too.

A group that began learning Morse code quickly developed that included most of the class, and Ray was at the center. There was a special bond among kids who went over to Ray's house, and started learning radio construction and theory, and of course, they continued their code practice. They strung wires from houses to barns, to outhouses, and to garages. Then they would "talk" with each other. Little Teddie was part of that group and really belonged. It took some doing, but three of the fellows and Ray built two small transmitting stations. One was at Ray's home and other went to Junior's home. They could talk back and forth anytime they liked. It was only a few years later that these skills became valuable tools in the US military.

World War II was rapidly approaching and Ray desperately wanted to join the navy. That was out of the question because of his physical disability. "I know I couldn't serve aboard a ship because I have the deformed leg, but there are plenty of shore stations where I could be useful. Heck, I taught enough fellows and a few girls how to build and operate radio communications facilities. I could do it in a naval training facility as well."

But it wasn't just for his special skills and intelligence that his fellow students looked up to him. When his leg brace started irritating his skin, he quickly switched to using crutches for a period of time. He developed powerful arms and shoulders. Only Ito and Danny could beat his time for the twenty-foot rope climb. Ray was the number one man on the small-bore shooting team that had been organized for teenage students before the beginning of the war. He particularly excelled with a pistol. He won the admiration and respect of people who knew him.

He kept pace with the development of radio, electronics, and small electrical appliance repairs. These hobbies were to become a source of income when World War II shortages made it essential to repair rather than replace such items.

One thing all the boys knew was that they wanted to screw girls, lots and lots of girls. At least they thought they did. They had decided that in the seventh grade. Now they were big eighth graders! They felt they had waited long enough. This imperative possessed much of a pubescent boy's consciousness. It was a wonder they learned anything in school. Some of the girls in their class were pretty classy, but they seemed more like sisters. A nice guy wouldn't want to do anything bad to one of them.

Another thing they knew was that they didn't want to knock up some girl, and have to marry her. The holy grail of possessions for boys at that age was a rubber. It was supposed to guarantee that she wouldn't get pregnant. First the rubber and then the girl, but the dilemma was where to find such an item that was so absolutely essential to the realization of manhood.

Guys knew drugstores sold them, but they were out of sight behind the counter near the cash register. Most boys were too embarrassed to even consider asking a male clerk for some. And what would he do if a female clerk waited on him? He'd just have to run. Besides no clerk would sell rubbers to a kid. Having a rubber became a status symbol to boys, and was on a par with owing a Parker 51 pen, a Ronson lighter, and a Rolex watch. The leather of the billfold of a fellow who had one became embossed with the round ring that proclaimed to his fellow students, "I have mine." And in most cases, that was where it remained. It was a good thing, too, because most of them would have deteriorated beyond any serviceable function long before they could have been put to the test. The girls were not supposed to recognize what had formed that circular impression.

"Gosh, Danny, who do you suppose makes those rubbers?" Ito asked.

"Darned if I know, but I'll bet women don't. What could a man or woman say when they are asked about their occupation? Do you suppose he'd says that he makes cock-rubbers to keep women from getting knocked up?"

Some fellows had big brothers who would supply one for a fee. One older brother offered to sell them to anyone for five dollars each. But five dollars represented picking five hundred pounds of green beans, and for most fellows that amounted to as much as three to five days of work. As often as not, an older brother's attitude was, "I had to wait for mine, you can wait for yours."

Earning spending money was a daily activity for many boys. Clay was resourceful and established a regular Saturday- and Sunday-morning circuit on his bike, collecting beer bottles. Stubbies, or the small-sized beer bottles, brought five cents for two of them, and full-sized bottles were redeemed for a nickel each. A handlebar newspaper delivery bag was hung over the carrier rack on the back of his bicycle. It served as a place for the bottles he collected.

The best location for finding bottles was at "pecker-point." That was the place local lovers went for a few beers, and a place where the car was not in view, and where a guy had a chance to "get some." Empty beer bottles were thrown out the windows, and the more successful fellows decorated a conspicuous tree branch with a well-filled rubber as proof of their success. Clay found many of these and, when he was lucky, the individual package in which the rubber had come. These he took home and carefully washed out. Once they were dry, he sprinkled talcum powder over them, rolled them up, put them in their packet, and sold the treasures to his classmates. Of course, most of the guys knew they were used, but that added to their mystique. Maybe the new owner hadn't been "there," but IT had!

So Clay became a success. He had learned several good business lessons: Find an item that is in great demand, and then supply it. Keep expenses and business risk at a minimum, and maintain a high profit margin.

For some of the guys, one of the terrible burdens of developing puberty was a mother who was a nosy busybody. Under the pretext of making everything clean and tidy, this keeper of order inspected drawers, nooks and crannies, and all possible hiding places a boy could devise. Nothing was private or safe from her prying eyes. She knocked on the bathroom door, if her son was spending too much time in there. She was fearful he might be "having a go at it." Such mothers were known to creep into their son's bedroom when he was sleeping to inspect his trousers and billfold for naughty things. Underpants were carefully inspected, and sniffed, for foreign matter before being placed in the washing machine. Privacy was impossible.

Boys had wet dreams! What glorious experiences, and yet what frustrating disappointments they provided! These nocturnal emissions occurred when young men were asleep. Everything seemed so real! "She" was always lovely and available. Just before he got to put it in, a glorious climax was reached. Then he was awake with a gooey mess, and still had not screwed a girl. Ugh! Some fellows started wearing shorts to bed with toilet paper stuffed in the front to catch the gism. Shared information gave everyone the scoop. If a fellow jacked off often enough, he was not likely to have a wet dream. At the same time, the wet dream was so unexpected and so erotic, most boys wanted to have them. Boys didn't know if girls had similar experiences, or even if they shot off as boys did. There was so much to learn.

Perhaps the greatest mystery of that era was how to get a girl "in the mood." Heck, boys were always in the mood. They saw movies about men giving women diamonds, perfume, candy, flowers, and stuff like that. "Funny," Ito commented, "if a guy gives her money, she is a whore, but if he gives her other stuff, she falls in love with him, and then it's supposed to be okay ... at least after they're married. But then, sometimes he has to give her things if he messes up." Danny shrugged his shoulder, made a questioning gesture with his hands, and shook his head.

Many parts of life were terribly confusing for eighth-grade boys. They didn't know if life held such complications for girls, but the girls knew. It was called *pregnant*!

28

Biking Holiday

Bicycle riding was important to Ito and Danny. Compared with walking, cycling provided rapid and nearly effortless transportation. But the cycles offered so much more. A sense of freedom, mobility, and joyful activity were part of their need for big muscular recreation. The previous year, Mr. Schmidt had suggested the boys take a summer vacation. That way their lives were not totally focused on DISKnife work and school. Kid, a classmate, joined Ito and Danny on a bike camping trip to a forest camp about thirty-five miles from their homes. They had no lightweight camping equipment or supplies, but they had managed bedrolls, a bunch of canned food, and three loaves of bread. To make sure they didn't go hungry, Mother Watanabe had hidden a five-pound sack of uncooked rice in Ito's sleeping bag and added pancake flour mix and homemade butter. A kettle and a frying pan were their only cooking utensils. Mr. Schmidt and Mr. and Mrs. Watanabe had taken over their extra duties of caring for the chickens, the garden, and the boys' other chores. This year, the boys planned the same basic trip.

"I just realized that you didn't take any plates or cups with you last year," Mother Watanabe said. "What did you use?"

The boys smiled and Ito replied, "Our first meal was a can of beans each. We saved the cans and they became our drinking cups. Kid ate from a tin pie plate. I ate out of the kettle and Danny used the frying pan. It was okay, but we'd like pie tins this time. That surprise bag of rice came in handy last year. We soaked it for several hours, but it still took forever to cook over the campfire, but we ate it all!" As before, eggs were packed and survived the trip unbroken.

The route was familiar. The first fifteen miles were paved, and then they were on a gravel road. It was rough going with

217

wheels occasionally skewing sideways into a chuckhole filled with gravel, but the boys were accustomed to such road conditions. However, the added weight and awkwardness created by their luggage made the riding more arduous. As they neared their destination, *it* happened!

They were about to cross the wagon bridge over Little Fall Creek when they looked down at the swimming hole and the large, rounded boulders at one side. There they were. The boys could hardly believe their eyes. Four young ladies were sunbathing and each one was completely naked. Every boy's fantasy lay out there on those large rocks. Two were sunny-side up, and the others were just the opposite, with everything showing ... absolutely everything! A fifth naked water nymph had started climbing out of the water, and the trio thought they could see partway into her! The boys really did not have the experience or sophistication to deal with their good luck. They just stood there gawking from less than thirty feet away.

The boys were in plain sight, and yet were completely ignored, as if they weren't there. Finally, the boys rode on across the bridge, and went to one of the forest camp's open-ended shelters. That was where they had planned to spend the week. Their decision to stay there was reinforced by the commanding view of the swimming hole. Actually, they were a little embarrassed by having spent so much time looking at the girls. But embarrassed or not, when they sat at a table to play cards, not one of the boys had his back to the view.

The young ladies obviously were older than the boys. They represented quite different body types. Two of the girls probably were sisters. They were heavy through the hips, their breasts were pendulous, and their nipples were not "proud." On the contrary, they pointed down as if looking at their toes. Another of the five appeared to be thin, and seemed to need a bit more filling out. She was freckled, even across her flat tummy and small breasts. Her nipples appeared to be seeking a way to see what was under each of her armpits.

The fourth girl looked more like the boys imagined all girls should look from their experience with magazine illustrations. Everything was proud, firm, and exciting looking. She was petite, with small and exquisitely formed portions to taste and savor in their mind's eye. The observant trio decided she was a neat package.

The boys had a tough time keeping their eyes off the fifth girl. She carried the bloom of youth, combined with robust amplitude. Large red nipples rode on top of breasts that would require two hands to contain one of them. They floated freely on her rib cage, and yet did not appear to be heavy or weighted down … they were proud ones. She seemed deeper through the hips instead of being wide. What her breasts did up front, her backside did to the rear.

Using a cliché of the time, the boys reckoned that they "wouldn't kick any of the five out of bed." Of course, each boy fantasized and expressed his choice by giving each girl a number from 1 to 5. Kid figured he'd prefer the two sisters and the skinny one. Yes, he wanted all three! "I'd like to line them up in a row and give them a couple strokes each, until they said, 'Enough.' Little did he realize that one woman was more than a match for three boys.

Ito's fantasy involved the larger girl with the "ample breasts." He wanted to put a nipple in each ear and snuggle his face deep down between those large mounds and hum and blow bubbles. He didn't need encouragement to continue his unbridled erotic adoration. Ito volunteered that he already knew Danny's choice was for the littlest one with everything in such gentle and graceful proportions.

The boys stayed at their camp and played a card game called "slap." They found it difficult concentrating on the card game. Those girls were still lying on the rocks or swimming less than thirty feet away. They couldn't figure them out, nor the two older women, probably mothers of the girls, who were not over sixty feet upstream from the guys.

The heat of the day began to dissipate and the swimmers left the big boulders where they had been sunbathing. They swam across the creek, joined the women, and then they all left.

Kid started the other two thinking with his sage observation, "I saw everything they had to offer, and it was wonderful, but I didn't even get a bone-on. What's wrong with me?"

Ito and Danny looked at Kid, at each other, and just shrugged and shook heads in unison. Neither had they. This really seemed strange, because on rare occasions, those unexpected peeks that showed just a little, or maybe a little bit more, triggered an immediate reaction of considerable consequence. They were relieved to find that while they were sitting and talking about the girls, they "rose to the occasion."

The boys enjoyed sweet dreams that night, but it wasn't of sugarplums dancing in their heads. Each had prepared for what might happen. Toilet paper had been stuffed in the front of their shorts. The wet dream factory did not let them down. All three experienced nocturnal emissions, which were triggered by the day's visions.

The next day the three took their bikes for a ride on the Cow Horn Trail. The first mile was slightly uphill and reasonably straight. Then the trail became too crooked, narrow, and steep for cycling. They hid their bikes in a deep patch of dogwood and fern, and hiked on without them. The trail went upstream and away from the water. Ito's keen hearing was first to pick up the sounds of girls splashing and talking. Around the bend and well below them they spotted the same quintet, and they were all wearing the same thing: skin!

Ito and Danny decided to do a commando crawl to see how close they could get to the girls without being spotted. Besides, they wanted a closer look. Kid said he wasn't interested in getting any closer and would just stay behind. Ito and Danny crawled downhill as quietly as they could. They stayed in the undergrowth of ferns and dogwood, and behind fallen trees, until they were close to the creek. At no more than thirty feet away, one of the girls picked up a rock and threw it right at the boys. They had been spotted!

"Cowards, why don't you quit sneaking around? You've seen us, why don't you let us see you? We dare you to take off your clothes and come on in."

Ito and Danny didn't have the maturity or self-confidence to oblige. They stayed low and made a hasty retreat, being as careful as possible to avoid having their faces seen. The girls took off in pursuit, but not having shoes or clothing to protect their bodies from underbrush handicapped them. Each boy was ashamed of himself, not for peeking, but for being discovered when they thought they were being invisible.

220

The three headed for their bikes, and started back to camp as quickly as possible. They were grateful to have their bikes for their retreat on the last two miles. They hurriedly started a fire and were getting ready to cook pancakes when a car rolled up to their campsite. The girls piled out and wanted to know where they had been. The trio pretended innocence, and said they had stayed around the creek and their camp. The girls concluded the three boys couldn't be the ones, because they had seen only two guys along the river. Also, it was too far for them to have hiked all the way back when they, themselves, had just arrived by car. As the girls left, they said they hoped they could find the guys who were peeking at them, because they were going to "pants them" and take their pants back to town. The boys figured they were lucky to have gotten away with their expedition, and that they had not been identified.

The trio returned home at the end of the week, refreshed and knowing they had experienced an unprecedented fantasy ... one that had come true. Even so, it was a "happening" they chose not to share with others ... except for Mr. Schmidt and Gran. They relived the trip's highlights many times together, and in their private memories.

29

Mimicking Others

From the time Ito and Danny were in the fourth grade, they were consciously mimicking the speech patterns of others. This was not to ridicule anyone, but to communicate more accurately. They both had a good ear for slight variations in inflection and people's tone of voice. Rhythmic cadence and word order were critical, if a person wanted to sound like a native speaker. Babies learn a language that way. Since the two boys were busy learning foreign languages, sounding right was important. This essential goes far beyond simply learning vocabulary and grammar. Both boys were learning German by association with Mr. Schmidt, and Danny was also learning Japanese from the Watanabe family. They understood the importance of subtle variables that identical words could have contrasting meanings.

Mr. Watanabe said, "When speaking on the phone, no one should be able to tell your race or ethnic group." The boys listened carefully, and mimicked what they heard. They spent a lot of time learning Hamburg German from Mr. Schmidt and the school's German janitor.

It may sound easy to learn extra languages, but it isn't. Between the two of them, Ito and Danny could readily substitute an English or other word for one they didn't know in another language, but this didn't work when talking with most people. There were times when Danny would become confused, and begin to stammer over words in Japanese and German, and occasionally in English. The best solution was to emphasize Japanese, until he was thinking in that language. This took years of concentrated effort. Gran, as well as Mother and Father Watanabe, diagnosed Danny's problem as trying to crowd in too many language variations at the same time. For Danny, English was his mother tongue. Arabic was close to being a second mother tongue. He had been exposed to, and used both from early childhood. But Japanese and German were totally unknown to him during his formative preschool years.

Danny's relationship with Ito and his parents had become one of family, not by birth, but by choice. It was only natural that he would concentrate on Japanese as his first truly foreign language. German was useful when talking with Mr. Schmidt and the school janitor, but English would do as well. He focused on Japanese as a foreign language, and expanded his English vocabulary and spelling in the same manner as other students in school. Gran and Danny continued with their Arabic study games. Meanwhile, he became functionally literate in verbal German, but with major limitations. Father and Mother Watanabe made up dozens of cards for him to study. These were placed in holders that were located at his DISKnife workstations. Repeated glances at them fixed them in his memory. This helped him develop knowledge of word characters, along with his spoken vocabulary in Japanese.

Ito's mother tongue was Japanese, but English was commonly used in his home, and he spoke it at school, and with other kids. It was essentially a second mother tongue. Mr. Schmidt used German with Ito so frequently that the boy readily adapted to it as a usable language. In effect, it was Ito's first foreign language. The boys' Hamburg-born mentor was proud of the youngsters' accomplishments with his native language. Ito spoke, read, wrote, and lived German, with the Hamburg accent.

Ito and Danny had started hanging around the school janitor shortly after they began attending that school as fifth graders. Mr. Bag always had interesting repair projects to do, and the boys liked watching and learning from him. He served as the school carpenter and fixed chairs, desks, tables, a broken door, or whatever else needed mending. He was also the electrician. When a light switch or almost any other thing went bad, he repaired it. About the only thing he did not repair were lightbulbs. In those days, people didn't just replace everything with new. Since replacements were not in the school budget, he repaired most broken things. Plumbing was a frequent problem in the old building, so the boys learned basic plumbing.

Most of his exclamations were spoken in German. Mr. Bag

was ten years younger than Mr. Schmidt, but they were both born in Hamburg, Germany. Each had come to the USA when he was thirty years old. It took the boys just a short time to master some of the custodian's exclamations, and copy his tone of voice.

The boys' vocabularies increased markedly as Mr. Bag spoke German with them. He reinforced what they were learning from Mr. Schmidt. He said they were learning to speak like "Hamburgers," which brought a smile to their faces.

Listening skills and a good memory were basic tools the boys needed to learn to speak and understand a foreign language. Continual practice and familiarity made it easier to converse and learn more. As an eighth grader, Ito had a good command of conversational Hamburg German. He was far more advanced than Danny.

The two boys found that they learned things in quite different manners. "Why are you writing down those vocabulary words?" Ito wanted to know.

"That's the way I learn them. I write them down a few times and then I sort of 'see' them and how to spell them. After a time, they are just there in my mind, when I want them. Maybe I have a visual memory. Don't you do the same?"

"I'd never thought about it, but I seem to remember things just from hearing them. Words produce a special music of their own. That is what stays in my memory. Maybe one of the reasons you have some difficulty with Japanese is that we don't have an alphabet to guide your memory. But how do you read and remember Arabic? Do those squiggly lines represent letters in an alphabet?"

"Oh, yes! They have most of the same sounds we have in English. In Arabic, we don't write the vowels out except for *alif,* which is our letter *a*. They don't have the letter *p* and substitute a *ba* sound for it. Maybe I started developing my visual-oriented memory when Gran began teaching me to read and write Arabic."

"Funny, Ito, we've known each other all these years, and we've just discovered this. It's no wonder you can remember almost word for word what a teacher says. You sound like Mr. Schmidt when you speak German. Do you read the German Gothic script very well?"

"Not really," Ito replied, "but it's getting easier. At first it looked confusing to me and I didn't study it. I'm really more interested in being able to speak and understand it."

"That's strange. For me it's easier to learn the words by reading them, and then I put the sounds to them. That's my visual memory."

Gran had a large, old map of London, and nearly a hundred picture postcards of the city. Visually and mentally, the two boys "visited" Parliament, Hyde Park, Gran's childhood home in London on Reynolds Road, and other places in London that were significant among Gran's memories. In a similar fashion, they visited the harbor in Hamburg, the zoo, and other public areas courtesy of memory trips, supplied by Mr. Schmidt. The maps of the two cities helped the boys feel personally familiar with some sections and streets, and brought reality to the memories of their adult mentors.

As Europe prepared for World War II, political forces in the United States began to organize and take sides. By law, the US was to remain neutral, but sentiment leaned in support of Britain, France, and the other nations with whom the USA had been allied during World War I. Germany was portrayed as the "bad guy," in the impending international struggle. Even though Mr. Schmidt was a German, he was okay, because he had been in the community a long time and was "one of us," even though he spoke with a funny accent. Mr. Schmidt had become a fixture in the community, and was totally accepted.

Child labor laws were not strict, if they even existed. The boys contributed to the school's maintenance, and felt a real sense of accomplishment. When asked why they did that sort of work, the answer was simple: "We like working with Mr. Bag. He's a good friend and we learn a lot from him." Gran, Mr. Schmidt, and the Watanabe family encouraged to boys to continue working with Mr. Bag.

Respect was an important bonus that Mr. Bag received from the boys. In many ways he was a teacher. From time to time he might need an extra set of hands to help with a project. The boys always were ahead in their studies, so he could get them out of class to help him almost anytime, but he used genuine restraint. Except for the truly rare emergency, repair projects were scheduled ahead of time, such as before or after school, or during lunch period.

When Danny had free time during class, he studied Japanese or German vocabulary, reading, and writing. Ito followed the same routine in his pursuit of the German language.

Other students found their own way to occupy spare time. Little Teddie had a book with complicated math problems in it. Ruthie read novels about nurses. By the time she was in the seventh grade, she was studying manuals that outlined nursing procedures and medical practices. She and Danny learned the names and shapes of the bones in the human skeleton, as well as the main muscles. Danny helped her learn many of the nerve pathways, which he had studied with Mother Watanabe, as he practiced her *Other Way* techniques. However, he did not share that special knowledge with Ruthie.

Don liked to draw. He specialized in cartoon characters and caricatures of fellow students and teachers, to the delight of all. But there was a more serious side to his drawing as well. His pencil or pen-and-ink studies of students captured a likeness and mood with an economy of strokes. This fascinated Danny so much that he frequently sat beside Don, and tried to emulate his technique. Don's work possessed a sense of movement and flow that was life-like. Danny's attempts were tight, structured, and labored. There was no difficulty identifying who the subject was supposed to be, but Danny's efforts didn't please him. He realistically commented, "That's the difference between genuine talent and work. It's like the difference between pleasure and pain ... and what I produce is pain, but I have fun trying. We are amazed by what Don creates."

Lois took particular pleasure in learning poetry. She occasionally recited a poem in class, and sometimes she recited a poem that her classmate Doris Ann had written. What the kids didn't know was that she often composed music to go along with the poetry.

The kids who had the most difficult time were those who needed physical activity, and found it a torture trial to be confined to their desks for prolonged periods of time. Skinny Bruce was a bundle of nervous energy. He wiggled, squirmed, shifted, slouched, sat upright, and tried everything to become comfortable. Because of this difficulty, Bruce was usually one of the last to finish reading assignments.

Mrs. Fulton had been Danny's teacher. That was when he first offered to give her massages when she experienced migraines. Now she taught some of the eighth-grade subjects, including English. She had always seemed young, fresh, and closer to her students in age, when compared with most of the other teachers. Among other things, she was an avid reader, knew about monks in some of the early monasteries, who studied standing up or walking through the gardens. She offered this opportunity to her students. A section of the classroom was designated as a quiet area, and the section near the windows and along the back was available to students who needed to move around while studying. A traffic pattern was established to help avoid collisions. Occasionally a foot might be put out to trip one of the walkers, but that was not common. Mrs. Fulton didn't "sweat the little things." Mostly, the students managed their own discipline problems, because the room and the people in it were friends. Skinny Bruce blossomed in this environment and started catching up academically.

The faculty of the small school was aware of how financially impoverished their school district was, but they didn't complain about it among themselves. They shared successes and solutions involving individual students.

Visitors to the school often wondered what was going on with so many students out of their seats, and such a variety of books and activities going on at the same time, particularly in Mrs. Fulton's room. But achievement scores on standardized tests quieted any negative comments. Mrs. Lombard had been officially retired from the school years before, but that didn't keep her from coming to school daily. She had no assigned classes, but she filled in and assisted wherever needed. As she said, "I still teach here, it's just that I no longer receive a paycheck." One of her pet projects was developing a school library. When anyone in the community had books or magazines they no longer wanted, she would survey what was received, and make suitable material available to students. She took pride in finding special material that would be of particular interest to selected youngsters. She was the teacher who had directed the atten-

227

tion of Ruthie and Danny to a collection of medical journals from the local doctor's office, when they had entered the sixth grade. Without question, this encouraged Ruthie's lifelong devotion to nursing.

That year of school was remarkably memorable, because for many of the students it was their last. The "Great Depression Years" had a powerful influence on the direction many of them took. School personnel encouraged everyone to go on to high school, although state law said they could quit school after completion of the eighth grade, or when they turned sixteen years of age. Parents often guided their youngsters into jobs as they became available. The logic was to "get a foot in the door while the door is open." Confidence in the economic future of the country had been devastated by the Depression.

Mrs. Lombard, and her library work, helped kids find areas of special interest that developed into occupational goals. Most of the teachers joined her in emphasizing that getting married and having babies was only one of many options available to girls. If they applied themselves to their studies, and developed marketable skills, they could find opportunities in exciting and rewarding careers. The roles and potentials for women were expanding, and so were their options if they were prepared.

30

Mr. Schmidt: Philosopher and Friend

Ito and Danny had been best friends and fellow adventurers in the mysterious trek toward puberty, and soon would enter the hallowed halls of high school. Mr. Schmidt had been Ito's personal tutor, friend, and companion from his earliest memories. The love, respect, interest in life, and feelings of viability he experienced with the boys and the Watanabe family helped keep his mind active and vital, long after doctors had predicted he would die. The boys didn't recognize his teaching methods at that time, but he seldom gave a direct answer to any questions they had. He would associate the question with things they knew and then, through a series of his own inquries, would guide them as they found their own solutions. All three shared a common curiosity, and the need to continue the learning process. Most topics interested all three.

His typical way of responding to most inquiries was, "That is a fascinating question, why don't we look for answers?" And he did mean "we." Ito and Danny were certain that he already knew almost everything, but it was fun to find answers with him.

When their questions related to making knives, his personal metallurgy library, which was written in German, helped them learn to read and understand the language, and look for solutions in their inquiring minds. He would read in German, saying, "It says right here that..." and "You understand that means we should..." Then the three would explore the potentials they saw. Successful or not, they would read and study, to see if they had followed all the directions completely and correctly. They also considered other options which had not been detailed in his books. He encouraged them to add the essential question, "I wonder what would happen if...?" Then together, they would investigate alternatives carefully and safely, to find out where they might lead. Ito, continued to keep accurate records of their findings.

Danny had followed that procedure of "what would happen if," when he discovered the tempering process that made DIS-Knife unique among knives.

Some of life's most important lessons were learned through Mr. Schmidt's guidance. "When you articulate a question, you remove it from the vague unanswerable arena. In that way you may increase your perspective about the problem." "The larger the number of people who join in seeking information, the greater the variety of potential solutions. Many of these may be valid, while some might appear correct, but should require further study."

The research process which was intended to investigate a topic, was interesting and usually revealed more possibilities than they originally sought. For the trio, the pursuit of knowledge was also a pursuit of mutual pleasure. Gran had instilled the same investigative curiosity in Danny from early childhood, and Mr. Schmidt reinforced it.

The boys could talk with Mr. Schmidt about any topic, including the five bathing beauties. His eyes sparkled as he said, "Oh yes, you are lucky lads. I should have been there with you . . . and many years younger. Even to hear such a story pleases the inner eyes of this old man. Never be ashamed that you appreciate the beautiful things of nature."

"We don't understand what was wrong with us when we were looking at those girls. We looked at them for a long time and didn't even get a bone-on. It wasn't until we started talking about them that it happened," Danny confided.

"Perhaps several things happened. Have you ever seen a mature young lady completely naked before?"

"Gosh, no!"

"All of a sudden you saw five of them. Absolutely wonderful, but what was your reaction when you came upon them?"

"Well, we could hardly believe our eyes. Then we started feeling . . . kind of funny, as if we shouldn't be there . . . sort of ashamed, almost as if we were peeking."

"So, in addition to being surprised, you felt embarrassed. Quite natural."

"We made remarks about wanting to screw this one or that one. We were kind of ... well, I don't think any of us was proud of what we said. It was like we were, maybe even ... it was like dumping dirt on something lovely."

Ito agreed with what Danny said, and added, "They all had the same equipment, but the arrangements were different. We looked and talked about that."

Perhaps you were involved in an intellectual evaluation of the five ladies?"

"Maybe, but I hadn't thought about it that way," Danny responded. "Anyway, the funny thing was that each of us had different ones we liked best. They were all beautiful, and we kept looking at one, and then the others."

"Interesting. Tell me, did you finally quit looking at the others and concentrate only on the one you thought was the best?"

"I know I didn't," Ito replied.

"Me neither," Danny commented. He paused in thought and added, "I guess Kid didn't either. I don't know how to explain it."

"I believe you have explained it quite well. You were taken by surprise, and then felt guilty for looking. Later, you felt disrespectful for expressing your natural sexual bravado. That was followed by an intellectual evaluation, and discussions concerning what you were seeing. A selection and preference process came next. But this was continually being interrupted by your response to the many forms of loveliness you were seeing, and only thirty feet away. Your sense of loyalty to your primary choice became confused under such circumstances. It is natural for a person to reach a saturation point, at which time the mind and emotions were on 'overload.' That was when you left the bridge and went to your camping place. After a diversion, you placed yourself in a position so you could indulge your beauty receptors. As I understand it, you started reacting, sexually, after the young ladies left."

"Yes, that's what seems so crazy," Ito insisted.

"Remarkably normal, given the circumstances. The glories of nature and man arouse the human spirit. At the height of our capability to appreciate such grandeur, it is enough to be aware of it, and we feel uplifted to be in its presence. We don't have to do anything about it. This includes a sunset, breathtaking scenery, creative artwork, and music. It also includes the human form, both male and female.

"People often find that what is before them stimulates responses that motivate the then to do something about what we have seen ... that is, to react physically."

The two boys looked at Mr. Schmidt with some confusion about his words. Each thought through what their friend had said. Over the years, they had learned to do that. They wanted time to internalize and emotionally understand his words and wisdom. As a result, they came to understand themselves, and others, better.

Later, while the boys were producing blades, Mr. Schmidt spent time sitting in his big chair, watching them at the forge. Then he would follow them and watch them pour handles. It was obvious to the boys that Mr. Schmidt was not well, but he continued tempering the blades, and was elated over the complex process which he was sharing.

Mr. Schmidt was aware of his failing health, and because of their mutual love, he wanted to assured the boys regarding his intentions. "I hope you both understand that I don't want to spend time in a doctor's office or in a hospital. My family, my dreams, and our knives have been realized here. My life is here, with all that I value." He took a knife, tortured the blade against a length of copper wire, and then shaved the hair off a piece of buckskin. He stroked the handle and blade and then whispered, "DISKnife is *the* knife." Each stroke emphasized the special bond he shared with the boys and the product.

The boys were aware of the fragile nature of human life. They stopped what they were doing, picked up the knife Mr. Schmidt had been holding, and Danny said, "Each knife represents the strength of your character, our appreciation for your wisdom and guidance, and the love you have given us. We love you."

Three foreheads came together to form their bonding triangle, as arms encircled each other's shoulders. Each shared the strength and love of the others. This gesture was also a triangle of discovery, joy, and triumph. They were at ease expressing

232

their honest emotions and thoughts ... no reservations, no hesitation, and no restraints.

In those days, such words were uncommon, particularly among men. A man might proclaim his love to a woman when he asked her to marry him. Possibly, that would be the first and last time she would hear those cherished words. The boys and Mr. Schmidt were able to express themselves in words, as well as hugs, glances, and body language.

"Mr. Schmidt, Ito and I know we would never have made knives or anything like that without you." He nodded as Danny added, "You are such an important part of our lives in almost every respect. We have been so lucky. I know of no one who has such a guide and friend."

He replied. "The two of you have made my knife-making dreams come true. You have also replaced the children I lost so long ago."

"One thing I regret," Ito commented, "is that we were never with you when you were making wind toys. They are so much fun to watch. I'd like to learn how to make them. It's just that we've been up to our ears making knives."

"Me, too." Danny offered. "After we finish these two blades, and you temper them, will you show us how you design and produce mechanical parts that make wind toys move?"

"Yes, we can do that. In my locker are twenty or more designs that I drew, but have not made. The plans for the ones we have outside right now, are also there. You are welcome to look at them, and make any or all of them. But I'd guess that, once you look at the plans, you would want to design and produce your own. Your imaginations are expanding, and it is a joy to see you discover your own abilities. So much lies ahead for you two dear boys."

It wasn't long before Mr. Schmidt completed tempering the last blades the two boys had prepared. He worked confidently and followed the instructions precisely. He restated, "This is easy work that I can do from now on. It is a delight to do it, and this really completes my lifelong ambition. How is it that the metalworkers of the world never thought of this process? The industry waited for your young, inquiring mind to be the innovator."

Gran had engraved an elaborate *S* on the blades in Old English, Old German, and Arabic. Mrs. Watanabe had designed a Japanese "chop" identity for Mr. Schmidt, and that was also engraved on each of the blades before it was tempered. The handles were poured in presentation silver.

The occasion was emotionally charged when Mr. Schmidt received his two personalized knives.

31

Dead Eye Jake Returns with the Sideshow

The boys were delighted when the circus and sideshow returned to town after a two-year absence. Dead Eye Jake was with them and performed his knife-throwing act. Near the end of his demonstration, he glanced at his audience, spotted the two boys, and had a puzzled look on his face. Then he snapped his finger and thumb, remembered them, pointed, and they shared huge smiles.

When he was finished his act, he left the stage and went to talk with the boys. "I remember the two of you from ... what was it, two or three years ago? But you have grown. Did you ever do anything with the knife throwing we talked about?"

"You bet we did! First we made some throwing knives, in fact, over eighty of them. Here, we brought a set of eight for you." Danny handed them to Dead Eye Jake as Ito continued talking. "We've been practicing daily since then. We are really grateful to you for getting us started on the right track."

"Well, use the knives you brought for me, and let's see what you can do with them. You first ... is it Ito? Yes, you first, Ito."

"May we use your background target?" Jake nodded, and Ito embedded eight knives deeply into the center of the target from a distance of thirty feet.

"Wow! That's a better than I can manage." Jake pulled the knives from the target and handed them to Danny. "It's your turn ... I'm sorry, I can't remember your name." Danny backed away from the target, off the stage, and was about forty feet away when he unleashed alternating left- and right-handed throws that cluttered the center of the target. "I wouldn't have believed it if I hadn't seen it. The distance is beyond the capability of anyone I know who throws for accuracy. I know of no

235

one who even attempts to throw at that distance. To do so with both hands is even more astounding." He nearly staggered as he grasped the reality of it.

"Ito throws with his left hand as well. Show him." Danny collected the knives and handed them to his friend.

Ito walked toward and away from the target, and threw on the move. All knives were embedded within a two-inch circle. Then he gave the knives to Danny who threw underarm and sidearm from varying distances, and also had a two-inch grouping. Danny threw a paper plate across the big target area and Ito skewered it in midair.

The sideshow manager was watching. "I could put the two of you to work, and you could make good money traveling with us. How old are you?"

"Thank you very much, but we are only fourteen years old, and our parents want us to continue with school. Besides, Danny and I have a business making knives."

"Yes," Dead Eye Jake commented. "They made the knives they are using."

Danny added, "Mr. Dead Eye taught Ito and me how to throw a knife. We wanted to thank him by giving him some of our throwing knives and one of our hunting knives. The hunting knife is called a DISKnife, and is made with our unique method and design; tempered to be what some people claim is the best blade in the world. It's intended particularly for hunters."

Dead Eye tested the DISKnife edge with his thumb. "I'll say it's sharp!" Ito took the blade and tortured it against the piece of copper wire he had with him. "You can even do a dry shave with that blade right now."

The manager laughed at that statement. "Not with my beard, I couldn't! And after ruining the edge with that copper wire, that's ridiculous."

"Five dollars says the boys are right," Dead Eye taunted, as he handed the DISKnife to the manager. He had a genuine belief in what the boys said.

"It *was* your five dollars, and it is going to be mine." The manager laid the blade up against the stubble of his cheek, pulled the skin tight with his other hand, and grimaced. The blade glided smoothly down his cheek. He rubbed the area and it was stubble-free. He shaved across his chin and exclaimed, "Well, I'll go to hell. You could sell a blade like that!"

Ito simply replied, "We do."

Still unconvinced, the manager said, "There must be some con about that wire across the blade. Give the wire to me." He sawed back and forth on the wire until he cut it in two. "Now we'll see about shaving." He laid the blade on the other side of his face and stroked. "I'll be double dammed. Sell me one of those."

"At our current production rate, it'll be five years before we make yours."

"I could be dead by then. How come Jake gets one?"

"We made one for him when we first started producing the knife. We've been waiting for him to come back," Ito replied.

The manager turned and started to walk away.

"You forgot to pay the five dollars," Dead Eye Jake said.

"I'm getting it now, but remember that knife throwers, snake charmers, sideshow boxers, and wrestlers are a dime a dozen. Don't push me for your money."

"He's okay," Jake said. "He's just miffed that he can't buy one of your knives. He's straight down the line with everyone who works for him. He doesn't pay a lot, but he always pays, and on time. Well, my act is scheduled straight through until midnight, and then we pull down the tents and drive north, so this is good-bye. Ito, Danny, it has been more of a pleasure than you can imagine. I'll remember both of you, your outstanding knife-throwing skills, and I'll cherish your gifts. You've made me feel quite important ... as if I were a part of this miracle knife of yours. By the way, I'm happy you are going to continue with your education. I was in university when the Depression hit and I had to drop out to earn a living. I've been saving little bits of my income, and this is my last tour with the circus and sideshow. I'm going to finish my education."

"We figured to look for you the next time your circus comes to town. Now I suppose we'll never see you again."

"Never can be a long time, and full of surprises. Besides, now I know your names and the name of this town. I'll look you up, if I get back this way. Who knows, I might need more throwing knives or a DISKnife."

Both boys were happy Dead Eye Jake was going to be able

to do what he wanted. They were already aware that the excitement and glamour of the circus was mostly tinsel, sawdust, grubby living conditions, and hard work.

Handshakes all around were accompanied by words of gratitude and respect from the two boys. "We meant it when we said we would never have started our knife business if it hadn't been for you."

"I'll use your throwing knives in my act, and your DISKnife will be featured as one of the 'Technical Wonders of the World.' I'll make a big speech about it and the two of you. Then I'll take bets on being able to shave with it, just as I did with our manager. I should be able to get a dozen challengers at each performance. But won't the blade ever need sharpening?"

"Yes, but about forty swipes against a butcher's steel will return the edge."

They waved as they left, and the boys looked at some more of the sideshow attractions before the circus started. Suddenly they left and headed home. There would be other circuses, but there was only one Dead Eye Jake.

"Gran, could we ask for a big favor? We'd like some special presentation engraving done on a blade for Dead Eye Jake. He's leaving town around midnight and probably won't be coming back, because he is returning to university. That gives us about seven hours to complete a knife and one hour to deliver it. We have an untempered blade that is ready for engraving?"

"Aye, laddie, and what will ye be wanting on it? I'll begin straight away, when ye conjure up the message and the design ye want."

Ito and Gran nodded and the Danny said, "I'll heat some silver for the handle." Ito was talking to the back of Danny's head, because Danny was already on the way to the forge.

While Danny was at it, he made up a group of three knives. The boys had found that the time waiting for a blade to reheat between folding intervals allowed them to work up two other blades as well. There was no special hurry.

Danny had finished forging the blades when Ito arrived. "Does this design suit you? Gran can complete the engraving in about two hours. That leaves us lots of time to temper the blade, pour the handle, and to buff, polish, and sharpen the blade. You know, I'd like to put a gold medallion in that silver handle."

Danny nodded. "Mr. Schmidt needs to be in on this as well. I'll deliver this blade to Gran and you go look for him."

"Is someone looking for me?" Mr. Schmidt had just entered the forge room. Excitement prevailed! Of course he knew about Dead Eye Jake. He went to his special locker and took out a gold disk. He studied the design Gran had made, nodded approval, and said, "I'm sure I can make up something that will go along nicely with that. Would your mother and father like to join in on this project, Ito?"

Ito ran to tell them what was happening. Six hours remained. It was a good lesson for the boys ... marshal all your forces before attacking a problem. Ito's parents smiled, nodded, and assured the boy that they would prepare an appropriate presentation case for the knife. "Would you like to have the case made from teak or local black walnut?"

"The knife is locally made, so local wood is our choice."

Ito's father nodded his approval.

"I have silk and velvet in red, green, and gold. Would you care to make your choice?" Ito's mother inquired. Ito smiled at his mother, placed his hands together, and bowed. It was his way of thanking her and honoring her judgment in the matter.

This was work both parents had done before. They had collaborated previously when presentation cases were needed for special knives.

The entire extended family was joyfully involved in the "spur of the moment" project that, once conceived, seemed important to all of them.

As the oldest member of the household, Mr. Schmidt met with the sideshow manager to make arrangements for the presentation to be made to Dead Eye Jake. This was so unique a happening that he arranged for all performers and crews to be there.

At the end of the final circus performance, Dead Eye Jake received his presentation DISKnife and an additional standard knife. The third knife of the three Danny had forged that day, was a surprise gift to the manager.

Jake talked to the audience for about two minutes, telling

about first meeting the boys. He had the manager demonstrate the capability of the DISKnife he had received. The two boys gave what was their first public display of knife throwing, and were rewarded with resounding cheers and applause.

Ten minutes later, the circus workers and performers were involved in their routine of tearing down the tents, packing costumes, and preparing for their departure. Gran and the Watanabe household visited with Jake for a few minutes before he had to join the others.

The circus left town with many individual performers sharing a sense of warmth and personal value. In a small western hick town, "one of their own" had influenced the lives of a family, and positive things had resulted. There was an added feeling of pride in the broader influences of their traveling circus.

32

High School Girls & Year One

On Monday morning Ito, Kid, and Danny started their first year of high school. Almost immediately they saw the five bathing beauties, who were juniors or seniors. A month later, the boys went to their first school dance. They bumbled and stumbled as they tried to sweep the girls around the floor in the fashion of Gene Kelly or Fred Astaire. They were inhibited. Holding hands with a girl was new. Having body contact! *Wow*!

Ito's big-busted fantasy girl, Bobbie, asked him to dance. Immediately, he was aware that she had a lovely smile, dimples, a delightful voice, and exciting hands. He was so shy that he could hardly say a word. But she snuggled up against him and he was enveloped in the cushions of her breasts, and against the firmness of her tummy and thighs.

It was obvious that Ito's dream girl had him just where she wanted him. She massaged him with her body without remorse, and brought him to a full erection with no way of hiding it. Ito had the presence of mind to be right by the chairs when the record ended, so he could immediately sit down, to hide his bulge.

"Well, Ito, do you like me better with my clothes on or off?" Bobbie asked.

Poor Ito could only stammer, "You're wonderful both ways, but it's awfully difficult for me to dance with you because..."

"Well, you'd better get used to it, because I'm going to dance with you two or three times every school dance. If you don't keep coming to the dances, I'm going to tell everyone 'everything,' and I'll make up some lies to go along with the truth that'll really embarrass you."

"You won't need to do that. I've never touched a girl before and you are so ... exciting. The fact is, I don't know how to manage myself."

"Ito, you really are a nice guy, and you make me excited, too."

Danny's dream girl from the camping trip looked at him intently. He didn't know her name, but he said, "I was one of the guys that was looking at you when you were swimming and sunbathing. I'm sort of sorry, well not sorry, but well, ah ... heck."

"Didn't you like what you saw?"

"Gosh, yes! You were beautiful, but we were not supposed to see you that way, and it was pretty sneaky of us the second time. The first time when we stopped on the bridge, well, that was one thing. The second day, when we crawled down to the creek ... that wasn't very nice of us. But we had to do it."

"Well, let's dance. You know how I look, and now you will know how I feel. Besides it's okay. If you hadn't wanted to look at us, it would have been hard on our egos. Speaking of hard, what is that poking into my leg? Oh, it's okay, but you are going to have to keep up against me for a while, or everyone here is going to see it."

So they danced and after a time, his erection eased off. Then it was possible to dance not quite so closely. Finally she left Danny and danced with fellows who were in her class, not just a lowly freshman. Danny wondered just how much girls knew about boys, and who told them? She never knew how complete and painful her revenge had been. Any case of the "stonies" is painful. Local wisdom suggested that straining hard to lift an object was supposed to provide relief, so Danny picked up Ito repeatedly, but it didn't help.

Kid, who actually was a year older than Ito and Danny, was having a great time with Lois, the one they had called the skinny girl. She had a charming way about her that had Kid completely enchanted, and they started going steady. The girls they thought were sisters were occupied with young men their own age. Ito, Kid, and Danny were just kids.

The following day, the two boys reported all the details to Mr. Schmidt when they assembled at the forge. "Yes, yes, nothing could be more natural," he said with a twinkle in his eyes and a chuckle in his voice. "Learning to become a woman is as difficult as learning to become a man. I think you were helping each other."

Ito continued going to the school dances, and Bobbie helped him become a good dancer. She also kept him pretty agitated, and not only at the dances. She would see him in the hall, take his arm, and walk with him to class with one voluptuous breast squeezed up against his upper arm. Finally Ito realized that she was enjoying herself, and it was not just a case of "revenge." The first part of the freshman school year was a great experience for all three boys. It didn't seem to bother Bobbie or Ito that he was younger or smaller than she.

Ito and Danny continued reporting their experiences with the girls to Mr. Schmidt, and he continued to share his kindly reflections. Ito had much more to tell, because Bobbie was really interested in him.

"Do you think you love her, Ito?"

"Gosh, I don't know. I'm awfully young. She's the first, and only woman I've held hands with, and walked with, and danced with, and it's exciting. I know I have feelings for her."

"That sounds like something special to me," Mr. Schmidt said. "Maybe it isn't what you might call 'settle down and get married' love, but first love is memorable, and most people treasure it for their entire lives. It is not foolish, Ito. Enjoy every moment you can, and be sure to tell her how you feel. It may be difficult, but it is most important that she understands how much you treasure her. Although she is older than you, you may be her first love, as well. Men and women both need to be loved, but women need to be told they are enjoyed and special, much more frequently than men. I don't know why, but I am absolutely sure it is true."

Pauline, Danny's special girl at the local swimming hole, had continued to develop. She was one of the most beautiful girls in school. Danny was totally intimidated by her presence. Her face and figure had matured to match the enchanting nipple and breast contours that were part of his indelible memory from years earlier. He feared he might make a fool of himself, if he ever asked her out. Trying to maintain control while dancing with her was difficult enough. She was lovely and her personality matched the rest of her. Danny told Mr. Schmidt about her.

"Yes, I remember those feelings. For me, her name was Helga. She was not in a swimming costume, but she was wearing an off-the-shoulder Bavarian blouse that was intended to reveal the upper contours of her breasts, and the valley between. I was quite young, and she wanted me to see that she was becoming a woman. It is unlikely that she had any thoughts of romance with me, but she needed to be recognized. To my regret, I failed to tell her how charmingly lovely she was. When you next see Pauline, will you tell her?"

"Gee, Mr. Schmidt, I don't know if I could do that."

"I understand, but it could mean so much to her. Particularly if you tell her with the adoration I see showing in your eyes right now."

Mr. Schmidt continued to help the boys understand themselves and the complicated circumstances involving human relationships. "You are never playing the fool when you express yourself honestly. Admiration, affection, and esteem are food for the souls of all people. Be generous ... but above all things ... be sincere. Sometimes the person may laugh, but that will be because they have difficulty dealing with their own emotions. It is not meant to ridicule. We all need to know that we have qualities that are admired and appreciated. It may be embarrassing to express our admiration, but our reluctance is more than compensated for by their gratitude."

33

Mr. Schmidt's Death

Mr. Schmidt died peacefully in his sleep. There was no evidence of struggle that would indicate differently. He was ready, but not anxious, to depart from surroundings where he was loved, honored, appreciated, and had fulfilled many of his life's ambitions and dreams.

He had shared his final wishes with his family. "Make no fuss or bother about me when my time comes. I'd like best to be put here on the land where we have our garden, but the officials won't allow that. I've asked. So, anyplace that is permitted will suit me. I've made my own box out of simple rough-hewn wood grown on this land. Don't let them impose a commercial casket on you. Remember the love and appreciation I have for my family. I'll welcome those who wish to stand beside my grave site. If you chose to sprinkle a handful of soil on my grave, let it come from our own garden."

Ito and Danny had learned to express their feelings, and to tell loved ones how important they were. They had shared those special experiences and sensitive emotions, whenever they could. The three had done so many things together, but the boys would never be finished telling Mr. Schmidt about their love and appreciation for him. They would continue doing this by the way they fashioned their lives, and with their memories of him.

Gran and the Watanabe parents had their own adult ways of dealing with the death of Mr. Schmidt. Perhaps they had more experience. It was obvious that they missed him greatly. They, as Ito and Danny, were grateful for what had been, and did not feel it was appropriate to mourn his death. Together, they celebrated his life, but when they were alone, there were times when each of them wept. When major questions came up throughout their lives, they would hear Mr. Schmidt's familiar words, "Why don't *we* look for answers?"

It was after dinner on the second day following Mr. Schmidt's service that a man arrived at Gran and Danny's house. "I have here a letter for you from Mr. Schmidt. I'm to remain here to answer your questions."

Gran took the letter, read it, blinked twice at Danny, and handed it to him. Moments later, Danny looked back at Gran and returned her blinks. "Well, laddie boy, what do ye think?"

The man stood uneasily. He doubted if they had read the entire letter so quickly. "If I may be of any assistance reading the letter, I'll be happy to help."

"That is thoughtful of you, but there is no need for concern. We understand completely what Mr. Schmidt wrote." Danny continued, "We know that Mr. Schmidt was right when he said that we should install an indoor plumbing system including a toilet, tub, shower, and water to the kitchen sink. As he suggests, the time saved would more than compensate for the expense."

"Yes, and we've needed a new well and a septic system for years," Gran added. Then she turned from Danny and addressed the man who had brought the letter. "The letter says we should talk with ye about the work that needs doin'. So what 'ave ye to say?"

"Mr. Schmidt and I worked together on three different plans as to where to construct the bathroom addition. He thought you should look at these plans and make any suggestions you wish. I'm sure I could incorporate any additions and changes without difficulty." He handed three sets of plans to Gran and Danny. "I can explain any of the drawings and specifications that may seem unclear."

"No need for that, me son was a builder, and I spent many an hour reviewing and revising just such plans. Ye 'ave yet to mention the cost of such a project."

The builder held another paper. "Mr. Schmidt said you would get at that soon enough. Here is his second letter."

Dear Annie Louise and Danny, who are such vital parts of my dear family,

For several years I have wanted to express my love and

appreciation for both of you, in some lasting way. The proposed project should provide years of pleasure and added convenience to your lives. The construction plans were started years ago, with John's help, but were terminated with the death of Danny's parents.

Del is a good and honest workman, and we have settled the accounts for the work he proposes to do on your house. He was paid in silver dollars in advance, and they were some of the last I received when I sold my home to our Watanabe family.

I may not be here to see this work completed, but I know it is a worthy project that will pay dividends in comfort, gracious living, and more discretionary time for both of you.

> With my love,
> Hannes Schmidt

Mr. Schmidt's letter was dated two days before his death.

"May we phone you tomorrow with our decision? The lad and I will need to look at what the plans offer. Have ye a beginning date in mind, and an idea about how long it would take to complete the work?"

"The list of materials is similar for all three plans. It is loaded for delivery in the morning. A well-drilling rig is scheduled to begin work three days from now. Four fellows will be working with me, and we should complete the project within three weeks."

A broad smile blossomed on Gran's face. "Aye, laddie, a good wallow in a hot tub of water would set me up just right. Three weeks did ye say?"

The DISKnife production continued after school and on Saturdays. Mr. Schmidt's chair in the forge room was physically empty, but it was filled with more memories than the boys could count. Ito could sense when Danny felt lonely. The two boys would come together, arms reached around their shoulders, and they could "will" Mr. Schmidt to be there with them. This was not some imagined psychic experience or phony "return from the dead" happening. It was simply two boys cherishing the memory of someone they adored.

Two weeks later, Gran turned on the hot water at the kitchen sink and murmured under her breath, "Thank ye, me dear old friend. Ye gave us the luxury of your friendship during your life, and now this gift. Since I'm getting on in years, I'm happy to dispense with the walk to the little house to do me business."

Gran may have missed Mr. Schmidt more than anyone else. They had devoted untold hours together designing and engraving presentation knives, as well as their daily involvement working on the constant demands of a growing business. They also were from the same age group. The popular music and literature of their era were essentially the same. They shared many memories of the great events that happened during their lives.

"Danny, me lad, ye should know that the one thing Mr. Schmidt feared was becoming an invalid who would require care and attention, and not being able to do for himself. He died where he wanted and in a timely fashion." Moisture formed in Gran's eyes ... and in Danny's, too. So they hugged, missed Mr. Schmidt, rejoiced in his life, and were grateful to have shared the years of memorable experiences.

34

Internment

Ito and Danny were still in their first years of high school when the Japanese nation attacked Pearl Harbor. Unprecedented changes took place throughout the world. High school boys knew they would be headed for the service, unless they were physically unfit or deferred, because of work in essential war industry or farming. The local industry was logging or sawmill work, and there was almost no chance of getting deferred for those lines of work. There were older men to fill those jobs. Locally, farmers' sons sometimes were deferred, but infrequently.

The usual thing for a young man to do was to enlist in the branch of service he wanted to join, before he turned eighteen years old. Otherwise, he would be drafted into the branch that needed to fill a quota, and usually that was the army. A few fellows figured to make some money during the war and joined the Merchant Marines. Those who thought they were getting a "safer war" in the Merchants Navy simply were ignoring the facts and statistics.

Those who enlisted before they were eighteen were usually allowed to remain in high school until they graduated, provided they were in the second half of their senior year. Otherwise, they were taken shortly after signing up.

For Ito and his family, the war with Japan produced no conflicts in loyalty, any more than it did with people of German or Italian ancestry. They were Americans, just as Danny was American, even though his father had come from England. However, such arguments carried no weight against the tide of fear and hatred for the Japanese that increased as one Japanese success followed another in the Pacific. The Japanese forces piled death, defeat, and humiliation on the US armed forces. There was little opposition from the good, white American population when orders were issued to transport Americans of Japanese ancestry to internment ... let that read "concentration camps." This was done, ostensibly, to protect sensitive war industries from the possibility of sabotage. The Japanese, being Orientals, were believed to be less trustworthy, simply because of the color of their skin, and the slant of their eyes. People from obviously different racial and ethnic backgrounds were not to be trusted. That mood of many US citizens was easily fostered by propaganda and news releases about war losses.

In retrospect, one can wonder how internment camps could be set up so quickly in remote areas. Within the first three months of the war, most Americans of Japanese ancestry were being, or had been relocated. There was virtually no opportunity for them to make arrangements for proper care of their belongings or property. They simply were ordered to pack a few things and be ready to leave on a specified date. Security personnel were present to enforce the orders. The procedure had worked in Nazi Germany, when dealing with the Jews. Similar tactics were instigated for transporting the Japanese Americans within the USA, except the American compounds were not intended to be death camps.

In Danny's small town, it didn't dawn on anyone that the Watanabe family would be interned. Everyone knew them. They had earned the reputation of being a valuable and responsible part of the community. They had their place, and were not a threat to anyone. Town leaders filed appeals, as probably happened in many other small towns, and even in large cities, along the West Coast of the nation.

When the Watanabe family received orders to report and be transported, Danny felt there was a mistake, and the state governor would be able to correct the order. The governor recognized the name immediately and promised to use all means available to him to countermand the order. His voice registered the bitterness he was experiencing when he phoned the Watanabe household and reported that his efforts had resulted in a frustrating and irrevocable denial. Even the governor of the state, who had benefited from his DISKnife association with the Watanabe family, was powerless in the face of the federal orders.

Included in the official arguments supporting the transportation of the Japanese, was the statement that it was done for their own safety, because of strong anti-Japanese feeling expressed by the general population. As increasing numbers of American servicemen were injured, captured, and killed, resentment and hatreds were expected to build. It seemed possible that local law enforcement agencies would be unable to protect the Japanese living in the community.

Successful war tactics require the dehumanizing of the enemy. Posters used in Europe showed a German storm trooper grasping an infant by the legs, and bashing its head into a brick wall. The shape of the German helmet, and the prominently displayed swastika, easily identified the culprit. In the United States, the friendly Chinese were depicted as being kindly people with a friendly smile. The Japanese were portrayed as being brutish, with sinister features, and no sense of honor or decency.

When such propaganda tactics were successful, it became much easier to eliminate the enemy, as if one were destroying ultimate evil. It helped to increase enlistment, motivate the military, and made it easier for civilians to tolerate and accept the internment camps for the "others." In fact, the US Constitution had been suspended!

Danny and Gran asked to be allowed to go to the internment camp, but that was officially unthinkable. They went to the train station as a family. Conflicting emotions were tearing Danny apart. The unreality of what was happening defied all reason and sense of fair play. The hope for rescue had vanished with the personal phone call from the governor. An underlying sense of personal loss was accompanied by growing awareness of frustration and consuming rage. This was America! Justice was assured for all. It was there in the Constitution. Danny had read the document repeatedly, and he could find no provision that allowed the government to deprive people of their rights without due process of law.

Father Watanabe understood Danny's emotional turmoil. The train had arrived and people were boarding. A huge family hug ensued, and Danny's composure was shattered. "I don't know how I can put up with this injustice ... and losing you. I feel the need to lash out and smash thing ... how am I going to put up with this?"

251

Father Watanabe gentle gaze riveted the boy's attention. He said, "There is *A Way.*"

Still protesting, he complained, "I'm still a kid. I don't know enough."

Three Japanese family members looked at the boy through the train window. He saw the words formed on Ito's lips, "You have *A Way* and you have Gran."

Mother Watanabe's words were formed. "You know much more than you think. You are my second son ... an additional one we chose to have. Our love is eternal."

Then there was no more time for additional messages. The departing of loved ones so common during wartime was absolute. It could not be further delayed, nor recalled.

Gran and Danny faced the necessity of making another major adjustment. They were just coming to terms with the death of Mr. Schmidt. Now the Watanabe family represented another irreplaceable loss they had to learn to accept.

"Danny, me lad, the strength and security ye find among your loved ones, never expires as long as ye have a good memory. Ye have not been one to delay telling them of your love and respect, so there are no regrets on that account. We will continue to make the best of the future and treasure the past. Now we will write and receive letters. We will look ahead to a time when we will have our family with us again."

Danny took over all aspects of the knife production, except for the final finishing and office business. Production fell to about forty knives per week, but this still provided an enormous income.

Mr. Schmidt's gift of household improvements liberated Gran and Danny from the obvious inconveniences of heating the house and the water. Electrical appliances did that. But the most inconvenient of the old living conditions had been that the toilet was "out back."

Increasingly large numbers of women entered the defense industry's workforce. Many husbands were in the service, and there was a greater need for older women to take care of those who were even older, and infirm. Gran was away from home more hours than previously. As she had in the past, she occasionally slept at the house where she was working. Danny didn't know how she managed taking care of the knife business, along with everything else.

Equipment used for engraving, buffing, polishing, and sharpening were all within the home of Gran and Danny. The evening hours from six to nine were ones that Gran and Danny spent together. Dinner, doing dishes, and finishing knives gave them time to talk, continue with the Arabic study and word games, as well as creating adventure stories in that language. Gran cared for "her people" following a regular schedule that fitted around her first commitment, which was to Danny.

Of course, when the war first started, people in the United States figured they'd "kick the butts" of that miserable bunch of little "slant-eyes," who didn't know how to make anything of good quality. You could see their stuff in the cheap stores ... mostly junk. It was unbelievable that they had come up with an airplane that literally flew circles around the US fighters. Everyone knew that a six-foot-tall, 200-pound American football player was a lot tougher and stronger than some little 120-pound "midget," who had to stretch to be five feet two inches tall. How could he possibly fly a plane against an American? But they not only could and did, but they won a high percentage of the time during the early days of the war. Their toy-sized tanks and miniature soldiers swept the fields of combat; British, American, Dutch, Australian, or Chinese, it didn't matter. For a period of time, they were tougher, better trained, better equipped, had combat experience, and had a combat code the Allies did not match.

At the same time, Nazi Germany, under the leadership of Adolf Hitler, began slaughtering over six million Jews. These were some of the brightest, most ambitious, creative, and capable people in Western Europe ... in the world. They represented an invaluable natural resource. They were not only totally wasted, it required additional resources to exterminate them. With reasonable utilization of that human resource, it was likely that the course of the war in Europe could have had a different ending.

When it became apparent that the Watanabes would not be returning to their home for some time, Gran acted as their agent and rented their house to one of the many families who continued to come to that area seeking work in the wood products industry.

Gran and Mother Watanabe exchanged letters weekly. They never expressed bitterness. Nonproductive work and living conditions were a cause of distress. Worse yet, the American government held all of them in contempt. Most devastating of all was that their family had been decimated by the loss of Mr. Schmidt, and then their separation from Gran and Danny.

Danny and Ito, who had shared virtually every thought and action since first meeting, found they lacked the skills and maturity to bridge the physical gap of distance between them. The thought processes of wanting input from Ito continued, but by the time the letter was written and an answer received, the intimacy of sharing was gone. Danny found he was filtering out thoughts and editing small things, so that only important things were written. Previously unknown barriers were developing, and neither boy knew how to deal with them. Telephone communication among camp internees and the "outside world" was virtually nonexistent.

At the internment camp, Ito found himself in a strange situation. For the first time in his life, he was among youngsters and families who looked similar to him, and who shared so many cultural traditions and customs, and even the language! In fact, Ito experienced cultural shock.

Racial and ethnic prejudice in the USA, was also rampant throughout the war and postwar years. Segregation and underutilization of the capabilities of Negro, Filipino, Chinese, and other minority service personnel was the standard, rather than the exception. "Let them do the dirty work that involves long hours of drudgery, but don't really trust them. Let them be the mess cooks, man the garbage details, load the ammunition, scrape the paint, and clean the latrines. When it comes to combat, it's okay to send them on particularly hazardous missions, because there are plenty more where they came from, but remember, never quite trust them."

That attitude permeated the US military hierarchy and was supported by many of the enlisted men. "Do you want to risk the lives of the good white officers who are commanding those who are less than trustworthy? Do you promote some of unworthy ones to become noncommissioned and even commissioned officers? If we do that, we would have good white boys having to salute and follow orders issued by their racial inferiors." Yes, racism was alive, thriving, and growing disastrously in the United States, both in military and civilian life.

The need for Japanese-speaking military intelligence personnel was critical in the Pacific. Hawaiian residents of Japanese ancestry were the primary source for such personnel. There were usually checks and cross checks of their work, because you could never tell when one of *them* might be working for the enemy. As far as mainland Americans of Japanese ancestry were concerned: forget them. For some reason, they were considered far less trustworthy than those who had lived in Hawaii.

Ito and Danny were both nearing fifteen years of age and were in their first year of high school when Ito was interned. Although they did exchange letters, they never saw each other again. Among the few things Ito took with him to the internment camp were a dozen of his throwing knives. These had to be smuggled in, because they represented weapons. The ignorant general public didn't understand that a butcher knife, screwdrivers, ice picks, and even table knives, in skilled hands, were equally deadly weapons.

Ito, and many of his fellow internees, came to the conclusion that there was not much sense in going on through a segregated school system that provided little opportunity for a future. Many of these young men decided to enlist in the military as soon as possible. Sixteen years of age was the minimum. At that age, parental permission was required.

The army was faced with a basic problem of what do they do with thousands of young Japanese American volunteers whose parents were in internment camps. From the military point of view, there was a question regarding their suitability for service, their loyalty to the USA, and also, who would be assigned to train and command them.

The army, in its collective wisdom, did train and assign several groups of such questionable personnel. Among them was the 442nd Regimental Combat Battalion, and they were utilized as a totally expendable resource. From Anzio onward they were given the worst of the combat assignments. Whatever looked or

255

had proven to be particularly dangerous was just the right assignment for them. By war's end, they were the most decorated unit in the US military, and they had paid for that distinction with their life's blood. Individual acts of heroism were simply not reported, because so many of them were witnessed by comrades who could not report them. They, too, had been killed. Throughout America, no other segment of society received such a high percent of communications from the War Department, telling of wounded and dead, fathers and sons. And the telegrams came before and after Anzio and Cassino, because they were perpetually being replenished with more volunteers from the internment camps. They continued to be assigned the most difficult and deadly combat missions in Europe. Because of their personal codes, these men would do nothing to dishonor their families or their nation, the United States of America. They served without hesitation.

To further disrespect and degrade these loyal Japanese American servicemen, when wounds were so severe that they were discharged from the military, they were frequently returned "home" to internment camps!

35

Captain Jacobs

Mrs. Clark, the school secretary, was a diminutive package of dynamite, in the best sense of the word. She entered Miss Turner's second-period English class of sophomore students and spoke with her. Miss Turner went to Danny. In her usual efficient and friendly manner, she said, "The principal would like to see you immediately, but don't worry, it isn't anything bad."

Students who were summoned to the principal's office usually had feelings of apprehension. The questions scrolling through Danny's mind were, "What did I do? What didn't I do? What did or didn't someone else do that I'm supposed to know about?"

"Captain Jacobs, I believe you already know Danny," the principal said. "I'll leave the two of you here. When you are finished with your business, Mrs. Clark will take care of the arrangements for each of you to carry on with your day."

"Hi, Danny! I am Captain Jacobs now, not Dead Eye Jake, but I'm the same person. The army took me out of university and I've ended up in charge of forming a 'special forces' unit.

"I know about Ito and his family being interned. I even tried to pull some strings to bring them back here for the project I have in mind. It seems as if 'the powers that be' had a single-word vocabulary, 'Negative!' Then they expanded that response with a reply consisting of two words, 'Case closed.' So, tell me about yourself. Do you still make knives and are you continuing to throw them?"

"Yes, to both questions. But, of course, I'm farther behind on knife deliveries than ever before. For every knife I make, dozens of new orders come in. Even if Ito were here, we still couldn't keep up. You see, Mr. Schmidt died, and he was our inspirational guide, and a major work partner. What's up with you?"

"I need ten thousand of your throwing knives that are durable as your DISKnife. The throwing knife design is perfect, but we think we need the sharp and durable edge as well."

"You want ten thousand of them! They would be quicker to produce, because I wouldn't have to pour handles for them, but about all I could produce in a twelve-hour day would be sixty knives. The blades would have to be ground, buffed, polished, and sharpened. I'm still in school, which would cut me down to about fifteen blades a day. I could produce another sixty on Sunday. Let's see, if I dropped out of school until I completed the order, I could produce something like 420 blades a week. That means it would take me the better part of twenty-four weeks to do the job, provided nothing went wrong. How soon do you need the throwing knives? Can you tell me what this is all about? In any case, if it is part of the war effort, I'll do whatever it takes."

"Before I go into details, you should know that some of what I'm going to tell you is classified as top secret, and should go no farther than you and Gran."

Danny gulped, hunched his shoulders, and nodded. "Understood."

"I was reared in a swampland area of the Deep South. Army 'brass' overheard a few of us swamp rats talking about where we grew up. They had the radical idea that we might form a special group, one that could be particularly effective in some of those pesthole islands in the Pacific, and the jungle areas of southeastern Asia.

"Special jungle training seems impractical for an entire army of men. However, these same army officers surmised that one or two specialists, within each platoon, could greatly enhance morale, and the survival potential among the other men. Specialists could teach others to cope with the creepy-crawly unknowns, and the realities of swamp life.

"My personal background involving boxing, wrestling, knife throwing, snake handling, and being able to make almost anyplace home for the night, provides a rare combination of expertise. An additional plus is my experience running a small-arms shooting gallery.

"We have a select group of 'swampies' who know how to survive, and even prosper, under conditions where most other people would die. We are pretty good at not getting mosquito-bit-ten, when everyone else does. We know how to survive on water extracted from plants, so we don't get dysentery. And I'm teaching my boys how to kill using silent weapons. We will take two types of manufactured weapons with us. As you might guess, your knives top the list. We want them to have a Japanese identification 'chop' on them. Our other weapon is top secret.

"When we do noisy killing, it will be with their own stuff exploding. Not many of us expect to survive, but we figure to have a rowdy old time of it, while we are playing with the enemies' minds, and undermining their morale. The program calls for these lead men to be adept at stealth and silent killing. One of the most demoralizing things that can happen among any military force is to have men killed when no known enemy is facing them. We need your throwing knives to be among the weapons that our specially trained men will use. We are already training with knives that follow your design. The problem is that they chip, break, shatter, and become dull too quickly. That's where we would like your help. The men need to have absolute confidence in their weapons. My personnel had already heard about your DISKnife, and when I showed them the one you gave me, and demonstrated it, their reaction involved overwhelming confidence."

"I'm willing, but is there time enough for me to do the job?"

"I've cleared it with your principal for you to go to your workshop, so I can see what you have there, if that is okay with you."

Twenty minutes later they were in the forge area. Danny made up eight throwing knives using his multiple layering procedures. "That looks straightforward enough. I'm not a foundry man, but I didn't see any secret technique for making the blades hold an edge."

"That's right. What I have shown you are foundry and forging techniques. Any company that wants to spend the time and effort can accomplish that. The tempering process is unique, and I demonstrate that to no one."

"Right, I expected that. I'd like to bring a top foundry man here from the large company that could do everything but your tempering. You can show him your process of making and folding the blade. In a short time, his firm should be producing all the blades we need. We'll ship them here for tempering, and then return them to his factory for finishing. You will keep control of your tempering process, and we will get the knives we need. How long do you think it will take you to temper ten thousand blades?"

"Probably a week or two at the most. I'm not certain. The numbers are staggering. The slowest part of my job would be heating the blades, but then, simply handling ten thousand blades is beyond my comprehension. I could be a couple weeks off on my estimate. I lack the experience and the statistical basis, to be accurate about that."

"Three weeks would be perfect. We hope that's realistic. The company we have in mind to make the knives has already supplied us with copies of the ones you and Ito gave me. We use those for practice throwing, but as I told you, they chip, nick, and snap too easily for our purposes. And the points fold over! About 10 percent of our group shows outstanding throwing capabilities. Fortunately, they are also the best at shooting. We won't receive any publicity, but we expect to be diabolically effective. It is imperative that we have good throwing knives."

Before leaving, the captain said, "The factory rep, where the knives were made, and I will be here at your place by 0800 hours tomorrow. I've cleared it with your principal for you to stay home the remainder of the day. See you then, and thanks. Oh, yes. You didn't ask about pay for your work. I'll see that you are well compensated."

When Gran returned, Danny explained the situation to her. She replied, "So what troubles ye?"

"Am I being unpatriotic by not giving the tempering process to the company that is going to make the throwing knives?"

"Captain Jacobs is your friend, and he needs knives for a special military mission. Is that correct?" Danny nodded. "Is he going to get them according to the present agreements?" Danny nodded a second time. "Will he receive them on time?"

"He will, if the company sends them to me for tempering, well before they are due. Captain Jacobs is a forceful and resourceful personality. My guess is that the knives will be ready for me within two or three weeks. Captain Jacobs and his men, should have the knives at least one month before their departure date."

"Fine! So what be the problem?" Gran asked, although she felt she knew the answer.

"He said I'd be well compensated for my work, and for my expertise. How do I charge him? Is it unpatriotic to accept any money at all?"

"Ah, yes, now I understand. Ye be caught up in the conflict involving friendship, patriotism, and money. Henry J. Kaiser is building ships with a 'cost plus 10 percent contract.' No matter what the item, all contracts have a profit margin included. The value your process adds to the knife far exceeds the total cost of the product, without it. Would ye be happy to allow the manufacturers and the captain to decide the compensation?"

Danny and Gran shared eyewinks as an affirmative part of their special, and comfortable, communication. Danny left the house and went to the forge area, did his self-imposed workout on the chinning bar, and spent fifteen minutes throwing knives at his moving targets. Then he tempered and finished the throwing knives he had started when Dead Eye Jake was with him. He liked to think of Captain Jacobs by his former, or circus, name.

Danny experimented with the throwing knife blades, making them razor-sharp. Upon completion and sharpening, Danny put on a pair of buckskin gloves and did some throwing. He soon concluded that the shape of the blade needed to be altered so his hand would have less chance of being cut while he was throwing. It was evident that one razor-sharp edge made the knife far more versatile. Two extremely sharp edges were a liability, when the knife was to be used for throwing. Even one sharp edge could "bite the hand that was using it." An alternative was to have a multipurpose knife separate from the throwing knives.

The following morning, Danny's two visitors arrived promptly at eight o'clock. Gran was introduced. The man with Captain Jacobs was named Mr. Arnold. When it came time to finish the blades, they would be with Gran. They went to the target room, where Danny had left the knives he had made the previous evening, and had started another set of DISKnives. He worked as he talked with the two visitors.

"Would each of you please put on these heavy buckskin gloves? Handle the knives with care, because they are extremely

261

sharp. Select your target and see how the knife feels when you throw it," Danny suggested.

Danny left it to the captain to give Mr. Arnold instructions about throwing knives. Captain Jacobs threw first as a demonstration. "Stop! Don't throw!" Captain Jacobs commanded. "Now I know why you insisted on the glove. Just look at it! The heavy glove leather is nearly sliced through."

"Take another glove and try this knife," Danny interrupted. "You see, it still has two sharp cutting edges, but they are asymmetrical. Grip it with the fatter edge."

"That is better," the captain said as he threw the knife, "but it's still risky. Even a minor cut on the hand, in our prospective environment, could disable the operative for weeks, or even lead to death by infection." Mr. Arnold still had not thrown a knife.

Danny handed the captain the third of his knife designs. One edge was "shaving sharp" and the other was benign. "Better still," the captain said, "but the weapon remains a hazard to the user. Careless handling, or use in an emergency could decommission the user. Thanks for a lesson well taught. The old wisdom prevails. Good throwing knives must not injure the thrower. This demonstration leaves no doubt that throwing knives cannot be general-purpose knife as well. But, we still need it to be DIS-Knife durable. The classical bowie knife design, combined with DISKnife strength and sharpness, would fulfill our general-purpose needs and be an ideal close-combat weapon. We still must have our throwing knives that won't let us down. For now, let's only talk about out first priority, the throwing knife."

Mr. Arnold had been nervously handling the various knives. "Call it skepticism or professional curiosity, but I still find it difficult to believe the sharp edge on these blades can stand up to the type of abuse the captain has described."

Danny pointed to the throwing knives and suggested, "Help yourself. Subject any or all of the blades to any reasonable test you like. Then check them for sharpness. After that, submit the blades to any unreasonable test you devise." Then Danny added, "You might use this electrical engraver to sign your name on the handles of the blades I just finished. That will assure you that you are receiving the same blades you saw being made. After tempering them, I'll join you later where Gran is working."

Thirty minutes later Danny rejoined the two visitors and Gran. He handed the blades to Mr. Arnold. He identified each by his own engraved name, and then Danny finished the knives with limited grinding, polishing, and sharpening.

Later, Mr. Arnold said, "I can't believe what I've done to these blades, and they have not nicked, cracked, chipped, bent, or really become dull. I repeatedly banged this blade's edge on that anvil, and it's still sharp enough to whittle wood. Many things I don't understand. One is how you're able to achieve such a sharp blade on a knife that has a rust-free blade. Tell me, would you sell your tempering process to me for one million dollars cash?"

Danny and Gran looked at each other, smiled, and simultaneously shook their heads.

"Would five million prove to be more interesting?"

"The process is intellectual property that Gran and I own jointly with the Watanabe family. They would have to be consulted regarding any decision. That would be relatively easy. But the process also represents the realization of the lifelong dream and success for Mr. Schmidt. Contacting him is no longer possible.

Captain Jacobs interrupted, "Danny, two dozen of my men are joining me on a trial expedition in a Brazilian rain forest in three weeks' time. Our first priority is to have reliable throwing knives. The second involves making a dozen of the larger, and a dozen of the medium-sized bowie-type knives for us. It makes more sense to choose one or the other based on jungle experience, instead of speculation."

Gran and Danny nodded that they understood. A few moments of consultation was all that was needed. "They will be ready for you within ten days, providing I won't need to work too long on the throwing knives. Where should they be delivered?

"We'll collect them," Captain Jacobs replied. "Phone me at this number to confirm when they are ready. Now, Mr. Arnold, what did your company charge for producing the special order of throwing knives?"

"We charged twenty-five dollars for each knife. We warned you that no knife we could make would hold up to the abuse you specified. It would be reasonable to double that price, if the throwing knife could meet your performance demands. Yes, I'd say you could pick them up at the factory for fifty dollars each, and that's an extremely reasonable price for the product and the service."

Once again, Gran and Danny blinked at each other. "That is an enormous amount of money, particularly when I'm sure we won't be able to provide a scabbard for the knives."

"Leave that to our leather tanners and workers in the Chicago stockyard area. They are working up special boots and soles for us."

"Right. Mr. Arnold and I are happy we came. Are we agreed that, other than the fifty bowie-type knives we have already talked about, Mr. Arnold and his company will do the knife manufacturing, and Danny will temper all of the blades? This includes the throwing knives. Transportation of the products will be provided by the military. One last thing, our chances of success might be compromised by any conversations about our plans."

During the following three weeks, a variety of vehicles delivered various-sized boxes and collected others. Then Captain Jacobs arrived. After greeting Gran and Danny, Captain Jacobs expressed his concern. "The throwing knives you made are holding up just as the ones you gave me while I was still with the carnival, but the ones Mr. Arnold's company made are not reliable, even after you tempered them. Do you have any ideas about what may be wrong? As you can see, blades have bent, cracked, and chipped." As he spoke, he showed Danny three examples.

Danny replied, "I'm no expert, but my guess is that they took a shortcut when it came to layering during the forging process. When we first started making knives, defects of that type showed up when we did only a couple series of three layers each. Just look at these." And Danny took several blades out of Mr. Schmidt's locker to be examined.

"They show about the same types of problems," Captain Jacobs observed. "Anyway, I can't take my men out with defective equipment. What do you suggest?"

"If I could watch their process during the forging stage, maybe I could figure out what went wrong, but I'll bet they aren't layering the blade blanks enough times."

"I was hoping you might say that, because I have a military

264

aircraft scheduled to fly us to the knife factory two days from now. I've cleared the time with your school authorities. They will allow you to miss up to a week of classes."

"That's fine with me, but what would you like to do in the meantime?"

"My men used the DISKnife you gave me during the circus days, and all of them preferred it to the bowie-type design. They liked both sizes of knives, but given their choice, they would carry what they referred to as a genuine DISKnife along with the throwing knives. This preference was based on their practical experience in the field, where they would usually prefer to carry less weight, rather than more. I asked if they would like to keep one bowie type, as well as the DISKnife? Their response was that, if they were able to have a second knife as a backup, they would like the same thing, the DISKnife. Three dozen of us will be operating independently for months at a time, without contact with other Americans, or access to supplies. I'd really like to have each of us equipped with the 'genuine item,' ones you have made yourself."

"Originally, you talked about somewhere near a thousand operatives. What happened?"

"Oh yes! They are still being utilized and integrated into standard platoons or companies. They are great for the moral support and expertise they provide. The brass called that one dead-on. My select group of three dozen men will be independent operatives. Enough said."

"Understood! You will have two DISKnives for each man." Three dozen of the standard blade blanks were immediately put in the oven to heat. In a few minutes, the *bang, bang, bang* of the trip-hammer sang its song of thin, thinner, and very thin; fold, flatten, fold, flatten. Gran was alerted that production was under way, so that she would be ready.

Around noon, Gran delivered a huge kettle of Mulligan stew, and two homemade loaves of dense, dark bread. "Ye can dip into that as suits ye fancy. I'll be ready to do me bit with knife finishing, whenever ye say."

Before he quit for the night, a weary Captain Jacobs had watched the entire process of making a dozen knives, except for their tempering. Not all the knives had been ground, sharpened, and polished, but Gran would work on them as Danny started making more.

Two days later, Captain Jacobs and Danny boarded the military aircraft for the flight east. With them were DISKnife packages ready to be put to use.

It was fifteen-year-old Danny's first flight, and the pilot invited him into the cabin. The flight procedure was explained, so he knew what to anticipate. When they hit turbulent air, the beginner already knew what to expect. The sudden drops or increases in altitude were fun, instead of frightening.

Following the flight, Captain Jacobs and Danny met Mr. Arnold at his knife factory. The captain held several of the knives Danny had made, and an equal number the factory had produced. They met with Sean, the foreman of the blade making section of the factory.

Sean was defensive when he was shown the blade failures. "Well, what do you expect? These blades have obviously been subjected to abuse beyond reasonable expectancy."

"You're right," Captain Jacobs agreed. "So have these, and much worse as well. Young Daniel here made these. As you can see, they show none of the failures that are evident in the blades made here."

"Then you must be mistaken about how they have been used. We make only first-class items here. No one can do better."

"We appreciate your pride and confidence in your careful work, but you might learn a thing or two from this young man."

"From a snot-nosed kid like that! I've forgotten more about working with metal than he'll ever know." His face was flushed, as he glared at Danny.

Captain Jacobs showed every sign of being aggressively angry and protective, but Danny put a gently restraining hand on his arm. The boy said, "We both know you are absolutely right. Even so, you might like to check a few things we have with us." Having said that, Danny took one of his throwing knives and pounded the blade into the machined surface of the faceplate of a lathe. Then he followed that with repeated jamming it against a cast-iron surface. Finally, he used it as a chisel and attacked a hardened bolt, using a hammer to provide added impact. "Check the point, if you would, please."

"Well, I'll be gone to hell! What's the trick?" He was totally frustrated.

With a smirk on his face, Captain Jacobs replied, "No trick, just this snot-nosed kid's technology. Roll up your sleeve and show me your forearm. Ah, nice and hairy." With one gentle swipe, the captain shaved a two-inch swath. From hilt to tip, he racked the cutting-edge blade back and forth along the metal surface of the lathe bed. Captain Jacobs shaved another section of Sean's arm. This was done with one of the throwing knives Danny had sharpened.

Danny clamped the blade in a convenient vise and whacked the side of the blade a good solid blow with a five-pound sledge-hammer. "This is for testing resistance to snapping and the springiness of the blade. Here, give it a good wallop, yourself."

"No need, I'd call anyone a liar if he told me he had seen what I just saw. I still don't believe it, but there's the proof. What did you do that we didn't? Will all of your other blades take that amount of abuse?"

Danny, Captain Jacobs, and Mr. Arnold picked knives at random and attacked the cutting edge against steel and handed them to Sean to test himself. "Well, I see I've made a 'proper mess' of the throwing knives I made, so how do I set it right?"

Mr. Arnold replied, "If time were not a factor, I'd have you fly back to the West Coast, so you could watch Danny work for a day or so. That's not practical under the circumstances. He'll tell you what he needs as a shop facility and you set it up for him. And while you are doing that, set up enough facilities so we can have ten thousand throwing knives ready to ship within two weeks. Danny will do the essential tempering."

"We could do the tempering here ... oh, not unless we know how."

"Right, and that's the problem. We don't know the process, and Danny is not willing to release or sell that information. We will need to operate twenty-four hours a day until this order is filled. Remember, you have two weeks and the clock starts to-morrow. Please, get it done."

Danny was left with Sean, and the foreman showed the youngster the facilities he had. One blow of the mighty hammer flattened a blade blank paper-thin. It was turned and squashed flat again. That was demonstration enough. Danny sketched the V anvil and hammer he used for doing the first of the three folds before returning the blade to the main anvil. "I don't know if the striking force of your big hammer is too great to allow the leaves of the metal to form their individual molecular layers after folding. I've been working with a force that takes six blows to form the blank back to its original thickness. After that, the blank goes back to be heated and the process is repeated."

Sean asked, "How many cycles do you complete, before you form it into its final shape?"

"We settled on seven cycles, consisting of three folds for each. We couldn't tell the difference between seven and up to twenty cycles, but by the time we dropped to five, blade failure started showing up."

An hour later, a V hammer and anvil combination was set up, as well as the smaller flat hammer and anvil. Then, Danny demonstrated his technique for hammering the blade into shape without cutting a large portion of the blade blank away. "We want to maintain as much of the original metal as possible." Then he drew the shape of the final stamping shear that did the rough trimming. An hour later, that piece of equipment was ready to be used.

Eighteen of the best workers in the facility assembled, and Sean introduced them to Danny. "Now, Danny will show you what you are going to make, and how to make it. I had put you to the task of making an inferior product, and I take full responsibility for that. Each of you take one of those throwing knives that Danny made, and submit it to any form of torture you've a mind to, short of putting it in the furnace." He demonstrated by bashing and smashing it into steel and the concrete floor. "Now take a look at the damage done to that knife."

A murmur of astonishment came from the men. "It's like we had been digging into soft pine lumber," one of the men said. "But what's the use of these blades?"

"Is it okay to use one of those wooden packing cases as a target?" Danny asked. Sean nodded, and Danny drew an oval to represent a head and added a neck. Small circles were marked for eyes and an Adam's apple. "If you want a silent kill, you do this." Six knives were instantly embedded deeply into the neck area around the black dot that represented the Adam's apple. "One blade would do. The victim wouldn't even get out a whisper, before dying. If you want to terrorize the enemy, do this!" Danny launched a single knife that found its mark in the eye he had drawn in the head shape. "If the knife's impact is too great, it will penetrate into the brain. Make no mistake, these are killing weapons, when put in the hands of trained experts." Gasps and then silence prevailed.

Sean outlined the project. "Starting now, we will be working 24/7 on this project … three shifts of eight hours each until ten thousand of these blades are finished. We will ship twenty-five hundred to Danny, in four separate shipments, so he can be doing the essential tempering. They'll be shipped back to us for the final sharpening and polishing. Each of you is an expert with years of experience, but you are asked to follow his procedures *exactly*. Don't improvise or take any shortcuts. We have time enough on this project to do everything right, but there isn't time for even one mistake!"

The remainder of the day, Danny made throwing knives, and each man followed through with him individually. In the meantime, the machine shop was producing the needed hammers, anvils, shears, and other equipment. Danny had never seen such quick and accurate work being done before. By two in the afternoon, three additional stations had been established, and Danny was able to watch each man at work making a blade.

"You men are great! You are master craftsmen! I hope you won't mind that I have watched. I have so much to learn."

"Don't you worry, Danny, we'll have these knives in your hands for tempering ahead of time," Sean said. "We're getting a head start on it right now. Within a couple hours we'll have all six stations operating. Right, lads?"

A man named Oscar added, "No shortcuts taken by any of us. We work rapidly, but carefully, and we take pride in our work."

When Danny boarded the military plane to return home, seven hundred throwing knives were on board with him. Danny designed a Japanese "chop" that was a symbol for "Dragon Slayers." This was stamped in the metal of the handle. He started tempering them soon after he arrived home, and they were sent to Captain Jacobs on the return flight.

Three days later, the captain called. "We've done a demolition campaign on those knives that just arrived, and they are virtually like new. Every man in the outfit threw and abused them until their arms were sore. We will enter our special assignments with the best equipment in the world. Three dozen of us who will ... well, never mind. We are individually grateful to you. Thank you, Danny."

"Remember that Ito and I would never have gotten started in this direction if it hadn't been for you. We were just a couple of little kids in a no-name town, and you took the time to talk with us, get us interested, and showed us how to throw knives."

Danny hadn't developed a heavy beard, but he did shave about once a week. He had made up two special knives with a blade two inches long. He used his for shaving. In the final shipment of throwing knives, Danny addressed a small package directly to Captain Jacobs. The package contained the second razor-knife. He had made one for Captain Jacobs and had saved one for himself.

An old business card arrived by mail that modestly identified the sender as Dead Eye Jake, renowned marksman with both knives and firearms; handler of all forms of deadly snakes; boxer, wrestler, and accomplished circus performer. It carried the message, "Thanks. The razor-knife works wonders for me. Look at your bank account. I hope to see you after the war." It was signed "Jake."

Jake and his group of "swamp rats" or "swampies" remained an unfinished story for Danny. He knew that military action was taking place, but he had no access to any information. He had been warned that even the military would have no communications with them, or know about that special forces unit, until the war was over, and then, only if some of them survived.

When Danny read news reports about the operations in the Mariana Island Group, including Guam, he could imagine Jake and some of his special services personnel, being involved in stealth operations. The same could be said for Indonesia, but he didn't know. Gran and Danny read the newspapers but they didn't find even a hint or clue.

Guadalcanal was one island that made news headlines repeatedly. Gran read everything she could find dealing with that part of the Pacific War. "I keep hoping to find a line or two that might give us a hint about your friend Dead Eye Jake or some of his team. I guess it is best if nobody knows about them."

Dan nodded and added, "He said that the less heard about them, the better their chances of being effective and surviving. But I'd like to know that he's okay, wherever he is."

36

High School Continues for Danny

More than a dozen of Danny's classmates had been in school with him since the second grade. New friendships were formed as youngsters entered the school, but Ito was irreplaceable.

The days were dominated by news of war in Europe and the Pacific, even though the reality of war was "over there," not here. However, mobilization was everywhere. Air raid wardens were organized. High school students started manning stations to spot aircraft. Scrap metal became a "hot commodity" with drives to retrieve aluminum pots and pans leading the way. The propaganda films showed the pots going through one door and leaving as airplanes. Iron and steel was also needed. Decorative iron fences around small town city halls were salvaged and supposedly made into tanks, ships, cannons, and other war matériel. A report documented that the fences were never collected, and had been left to lie rusting.

Rationed items included car tires, gasoline, meat, and sugar. Hollywood went to war in many ways. Hero actors, who never served a day in the military (such as John Wayne), lifted our spirits. In contrast, Jimmy Stewart actually piloted a bomber over Germany for a greater number of missions than required. Bob Hope, Bing Crosby, Dorothy Lamour, and thousands of other stars devoted time to entertaining at military bases at home and abroad. Even modest-sized towns had a USO organization. Young ladies served as hostesses and servicemen flocked there to dance, be entertained, receive snacks or a meal, and perhaps get a date. Literally millions of military personnel were "displaced persons" on any given day.

At the high school Danny attended, girls spent countless hours rolling bandages for the Red Cross. It was a satisfying way for girls to fulfill their compelling desire to contribute to the war effort. For a girl seventeen years of age or older to join the military required an enormous amount of independence. An undercurrent of sentiment suggested that the military would subject a nice girl to many experiences that a potential wife and mother should not have. In effect she would become a "fallen woman." Women were expected to be virginal, guys, not. It was difficult for the nation to adjust even to women entering work in the defense industry.

Danny knew he had played an unsung, and secret, part of the war effort when he made knives for Captain Jacobs, and his men. But fourteen- or fifteen-year-old students were in a quandary regarding their future.

One of the most appreciated differences between grade school and high school life, was having passing periods between classes. Eight years of having to ask a teacher for permission to go to the toilet were over. Only an emergency would create that situation.

At the beginning of the third year of high school, over 150 new students entered the school. Many of them seemed to be exotic, because they came from states most kids knew only by name. The solid core of the classmates, who had been together since the first years of school, and had relationships pretty well established, were now outnumbered.

Many students from out of the area seemed unique. Girls came from Nebraska, California, Iowa, and other states, which previously had been only names and shapes on the map. Local guys thought of them as being mysterious. Others from Arkansas and New Mexico were not really different, because some classmates had previously come from those states.

Juanita was startlingly exotic. None of the class had ever seen anyone even similar to her, other than in the movies. Her family was Basque, but she had grown up in Seville, Spain. Juanita was breathtakingly beautiful. Her flawless olive-colored skin was the envy of everyone. It served as a background for eyes that were the darkest imaginable ... and the whites were the whitest as well. Deep black lashes nearly swept her cheeks, and her equally black hair was wavy, and came down to her waist. Prominent cheekbones emphasized hollows and dimples. Exquisitely shaped lips completed the picture until she smiled.

273

Then her eyes danced. Beautifully white and even teeth seemed to express a gracious welcome, and her entire face lit up with joy. Any form of facial makeup would have detracted from such perfection.

But that wasn't all. Her neck was not just long; it was elegant and supported her head in an aristocratic fashion. At the same time, there was nothing snooty or aloof about her. Juanita's clothing was rather severe, in that it was formfitting but offered no seductive suggestion of what was obviously a fine body. Probably every boy in school found some excuse to pass through the girl's gym area during third period, when she was there wearing the standard blue gym shorts and white blouse. Even in that commonly worn outfit, she was more enchantingly exotic.

Mrs. Walt, the English teacher, also taught Spanish. She had Danny assist Juanita with English. Her logic may have been that Danny knew foreign languages, or because he was always up to date with his class work. In any case, Danny was the envy of all the fellows.

As was usually the case, a person who intended to teach someone else learned more than he taught. Juanita was totally immersed in the English language, except at home. Danny was able to help Juanita, and at the same time, he was becoming familiar with a few hundred Spanish words that sounded similar to their English equivalent.

He quickly learned that Juanita's family exercised nearly absolute control over her life. Her grandmother walked her to and from school. For her to have a date was impossible, by typical school standards. Grandmother was in sight at all times. Juanita attended school dances during the year, but she was taken there. Grandmother supervised her dancing, and Grandmother took her home. Juanita was "old Spanish" ... lovely, exotic, desirable, and totally unobtainable. If a fellow held her too closely while dancing, Grandmother went out on the dance floor to establish the "proper distance" between the two. Anyone who wanted to dance with Juanita had to ask Grandmother for permission. No boy was allowed to hold her hand as they walked on or off the dance floor. He was required to offer her his arm.

Juanita and Grandmother represented a level of refinement that appealed to almost all of the kids. They represented a cultural elegance that transcended the stereotype of a logging and farming community. The boys often felt clumsy and uncultured, but they strived for improvement. Grandmother was familiar with Danny, because Juanita had told her about his helping her with English lessons. He was allowed certain liberties in talking with Juanita in a social setting, such as the dance, that others were not afforded. He was learning a little Spanish and that helped, because Grandmother spoke only limited English.

Grandmother was in her early fifties, which seemed terribly old to high school students. However, she appeared and acted youthfully. In addition, she was a beautiful woman.

When Danny first asked Grandmother to dance with him, she was truly surprised and delighted. He began learning how to hold a woman, so that they could dance together with grace and elegance. He experienced the thrill of sweeping and sophisticated movements, the coming together and parting of two dancers, the subtle brushing of bodies as they crossed paths, the shared body and musical rhythms passing from hand to hand, or hand to shoulder, hip, or back.

This was so different from the typical routine of grab, hold, and squash her up against the body so her breasts, stomach, and thighs catered to the demands of raging hormones. There was a sense of regal grace in her posture and movement. This transported Danny into a different level of body awareness. Dancing with Grandmother was a mystical and rewarding experience, and by dancing with her, he learned how to dance with Juanita. Instructions were so subtle and unspoken they were unnoticeable to others. Grandmother taught him, and Juanita helped Danny practice. Both enabled him to discover that "elegant" could also be uplifting and erotic. A new form of passion was revealed through and for the dance, and not just for the body of the partner.

Danny became aware of many new areas of understanding for words such as *elegant, refined, graceful, and exotic.* He developed an appreciation for the functions of the "Old World chaperone." She guided not only the young lady, but also the young man, through the shoals and pitfalls of lust, without destroying the intensity of passion and mutual attraction.

Grandmother explained relationships to Danny, "That

which is too easily attained, is often lightly abandoned. You will treasure Juanita as she is. You are not ready for a permanent commitment and neither is she, although you both may think you are. But, you certainly are ready for the joyful enchantment of life that a sweet romance can shower on you. Its effect is adorably sublime, and memorably beautiful. There is room in your life for an almost unlimited number of such experiences, which uplift the soul. However, one bitter experience can damage, or even destroy, your ability to embrace and treasure the beauty of delicate relationships."

Danny attempted to commit the wisdom she offered to memory, and incorporate it into his life. Emotionally, he didn't understand it all, but he was subliminally aware that he wanted to preserve that part of the beauty in his life.

As was often the case during those unsettled times of World War II, things changed without warning. One day Juanita was gone. What a stressful word, gone! Nothing else could be added ... just *gone*. "Gone," was the only explanation.

The school had no transcript for Juanita from her previous school. Even a year later, there had been no reply to the transcript request. Checking with the owners of the house in which they had lived provided scant information. They had paid the rent in advance and still had nineteen days before the next month's rent was due. The owners of the property had been told they were leaving. That was all. The post office had no forwarding address for them. Neighbors said a medium-sized truck was used to move their household items, but there were no markings on the truck that might help identify a moving van line. "They," for Danny, meant both Grandmother and Juanita.

At the following school dance someone brought one of the Ink Spots latest records; at least it was new in that area. Its title was "Address Unknown":

Address unknown,
Not even a trace of you.
Oh! What I'd give,
To see the face of you.

The huge vacuum the disappearance of Juanita and Grand-

mother had left in Danny's life amazed him. They both represented Old World cultural enrichment. Perhaps Danny was
particularly vulnerable, because of a combination of influences.
Students of his age group were falling in and out of love with
the intensity and regularity of Hollywood's leading stars. But,
Juanita was someone so wonderfully special. She was a study
partner, someone to look at and adore, just because of the sheer
beauty of her. She was an uplifting presence, whose smile made
his world dance. She was a person Danny could adore, but not
yet feel the necessity to possess.

Shortly after Juanita had gone, Danny had to deal with
another of those unbearably lonely words, *killed*! Ito had been
killed in Italy. Officially, KILLED IN ACTION and nothing more. Final, empty, completely devastating, none of the circumstances
of his death were revealed. Within two months Mother and Father Watanabe were also DEAD. Because Gran and Danny were
not their blood relatives, they were only informed of the deaths,
but not any of the circumstances. At least, in the case of Grandmother, Juanita, and other friends, *Gone,* did not mean "killed"
… did not mean "Dead."

Dealing with the concept of *killed* had been imposed on
Danny from the time of his earliest memories involving that
car wreck. What *killed* looked like was etched in his mind. His
parents had been *killed* in a violent car wreck. He had not complained that he had not seen them before they were buried. As
Gran said, "They don't look like themselves. It is nicer to remember them as they were the day before." He had seen what *killed*
looked like.

Mr. Schmidt *died,* which was different. He had talked with
Ito and Danny about what it meant to him to die, and how he
thought of it as a good thing. The boys knew and understood the
difference. He had used up his life. His last years with the Watanabe family had been joyful and fulfilling. And Danny knew that
he and Gran were included in his concept of the Watanabe family. Mr. Schmidt had said that so often. The boys were not ready
for him to die, but they accepted the guiding wisdom he offered
in such a personal and emotional matter, just as they had so
many times when dealing with other realities.

The violence of *killed* sometimes showed up in war newsreels, but it usually was "sanitized" by editing what had happened. Religions attempted to help the living deal with the finality of death, and for some, it helped. Through their talks, Gran and Danny kept his mother and father alive in a sense of appreciation and good memories.

"Immortal soul" was a concept that seemed okay for a life that had been used up, such as Mr. Schmidt's. *Killed* left too much of a person's life unexplored and unused. The childhood inquiry "Why?" simply had no viable answer when it came to *killed*. Gran and Danny sat and looked at each other. Moisture formed at the corners of their eyes and then tears ran down their cheeks. Words simply did not come. What was there to say? They put their foreheads together and cried. "Closure," the psychologist's term for acceptance of someone's death, simply did not come. Too many needed facts were missing. In Ito's case they had no information about where, except that it happened in Italy. Why and how also remained unanswered. For Mother and Father Watanabe's deaths, there was an equal amount of "No Information Available." Only blood relatives had access to such information, and there were none in the United States. So Danny established the Watanabe family within the "library of his mind," a place reserved for treasured memories. They joined his parents and Mr. Schmidt. It was there that the *killed, died,* and *gone* could reside. They continued to add viability to his life. One thing Danny and Gran were grateful for was that Mr. Schmidt did not have to suffer the indignity and trauma of seeing his Watanabe family so thoroughly dishonored. They, along with thousands of other Japanese Americans, were imprisoned in internment camps in the country they had come to by choice, and were happy to respect and serve. And Mr. Schmidt did not have to deal with the deaths of a second, and deeply loved family.

Three categories of loss had become well established in Danny's consciousness: *Gone* suggested there was hope for a possible meeting in the future, or at least, a continuation somewhere to be shared with others. Juanita and Grandmother represented that to the young man. He treasured the intensity of Juanita's eyes, as she concentrated on study topics she discussed with Danny. Such contact was etched in the boy's memory. The sudden dance of excitement and joy that radiated from her smile, eyes, and entire being when she grasped an idea could highlight a day ... even a lifetime. Perhaps she had inherited that from her grandmother, who was another treasure. To Danny, she represented beauty, grace, dignity, and statuesque nobility that transcended age. Seeing and knowing her removed the fear of "getting old" from Danny's life.

Dead left a vacancy in the lives of those who remained, but it was not a tragedy. Death was the natural conclusion of a life that had been completed. Such was the case with Mr. Schmidt. He had told his family that he was ready. He was not anxious to do so, but it was his time.

Killed was the most stressful. That concept represented a terrible waste, lost potential, and destruction.

Those who were gone, dead, and killed still maintained a viable and treasured place in Danny's memory.

37

Pre-Navy

Gran, Danny, and the Watanabes had thought of themselves as being one family. The truth of their relationship was thrust upon them when they were not all transported to the internment camp. When Ito decided to join the army at age sixteen, Danny had been told to finish high school. In no uncertain terms, he was advised that there would be no chance that he would be assigned to that "Jap Regiment" that was being formed and trained. Besides, "There will be plenty of war for you to fight after you graduate." It certainly looked as if there would be.

Two years later, Danny was ready to graduate from high school, and the tide of the war had changed enormously. Germany had surrendered the month before graduation. Continuing Allied success in the Pacific made the world aware that sometime within a year, the Japanese home islands would be invaded. An enormously bloody invasion was expected, with extremely heavy casualties on both sides. Military authorities expected several million Allied casualties, and in excess of twelve million Japanese would die before the Pacific War was over. An epic number of wounded would totally exceed any possibility of providing reasonable medical care for them in Japan, on hospital ships, or at hospitals that were being established on American occupied islands that surrounded Japan.

Young men who wanted to select their branch of military service needed to enlist before their eighteenth birthday. A week before Danny's eighteenth birthday, he received a phone call from Teddie Long Shot and little Ruthie. Ruthie did the talking. "Teddie and I bumped into each other at the drugstore, and we wonder if it would be okay if we came out to see you pretty soon?"

"I'd like that. It's about a mile. I could bike there in five minutes and save you the walk."

"Mother will let me use her car," Ruthie explained.

"Teddie knows my house, so he can give you directions."

"I know where you live," Ruthie replied. It seemed funny that she would know that, since her home was a couple of miles north of town. But that thought was temporarily sidetracked.

"Come along laddie and give me ha' 'and tidying up." There was little to be done. Gran was careful, but not fussy, about housecleaning. Seven minutes later, Ruthie and Little Teddie arrived.

Ruthie's voice still had that breathless quality, but it grew stronger when she looked at Teddie, and he involuntarily took a deep breath to clue her into doing the same. "The three of us have birthdays this month and it would be fun if we got together for dinner and a movie. We worked together on lots of class projects during grade school, and even a few times in high school. This might be our last chance to be together for a long time."

Danny's mind raced back in time to the second grade, when the three of them presented their first project. Ruthie could hardly be heard, and Teddie had whispered, "Breathe," as he took great gulps of air. In many respects she was that same shy little blond girl with startling blue eyes, and a waif-like expression. He knew that under her shy exterior was a sensitive and competent person, who got things done.

"Danny, could I see where all those eggs came from?" For a moment the boy was puzzled. Seeing his expression, she added, "You remember ... all through the second, third, and fourth grades you brought me a hard-boiled egg for my lunch, and sometimes a piece of chicken. Other times you shared a sandwich with me ... or an apple, or something to go with my slice of bread lunch. But you always had an egg for me."

"That was my mother. I told her about your father being gone, and that it was pretty tough for your mother to earn a living. Anyway, she always added something in my lunch sack for you, until you told me your mother had gotten a good job and you had your own food."

"Both of your parents were killed in that car wreck. I never did get to thank your mother for caring for me, or your father for the many times he rode his bike all the way to our house to give us a chicken or rabbit. But the chickens and that Big Red Rooster you told us about, may I see them?"

"We still keep a few chickens, but that Big Old Red Rooster is gone."

"Where did he go?"

"That was nine years ago, when we were in the third grade that I told about him. Even that tough old guy couldn't live forever."

"Did you 'put him in the pot,' like you talked about back then?"

"No ... he and one of the younger roosters had a proper 'go' at each other. The young one finally 'chickened out' and limped away, but the poor old guy went off and squatted down in a corner. When I went in the pen without a bucket or stick to keep him off, he just stayed there and looked at me. I knew then that he was about done. To give him his respect, I turned and ran out as if he were chasing me. He was still in the same place the next morning, but he was dead. I dug a deep hole and buried him."

Little Ruthie's eyes welled up with tears. "He may have been ferocious with people, rats, and other roosters, but he took care of his family, didn't he?"

Danny nodded and wondered what had happened to Ruthie's father. Why hadn't he been around to help take care of his family during the worst of the Depression? Maybe he had been killed in a car wreck, too.

Teddie and Ruthie had been fidgeting for some time, and the three friends knew each other well enough to realize when something was in the wind. He had a hint about what it might be when she mentioned birthdays on the phone, but he was anxious to know what they were up to.

"You knew I'd like the idea of the three of us having a dinner together and then going to the movies. You are two of my best friends, but that's only part of why you are here, what's the rest?"

This time Ruthie nudged Teddie forward. "What are you going to do about the service? Are you going to wait to be drafted, or sign up?"

Danny relaxed. That was an easy one to answer. "My choice is to go into the navy. I phoned Chief Bell at the recruiting office.

He's going to be in his office all day Friday and will see anyone who shows up. No appointment is necessary."

It was Teddie's turn to nudge Ruthie forward. She took a deep breath and asked in a firm voice that showed strength and resolve, "May we go with you? Teddie and I would like to enlist at the same time you do. I know I can't go to boot camp with you fellows, but they send recruits away from here to have their physicals and to be sworn in. We could at least do that together. Then recruits go home for a few days to await orders."

It felt so good to Danny when he enfolded his two friends in a big threesome hug. He hadn't done that for a long time. "What do you want to do in the navy, Ruthie?"

"I talked with Chief Bell, too. He said I could train to be a corpsman and, if I'm any good at it, they might send me to nursing school to become an RN. That's what I'd really like."

"We know you are smart enough, and that you are a good worker. Teddie and I will bet on you. What do you want to do in the navy, Teddie?"

"I probably wouldn't be good at anything except keeping mathematical accounts. Chief Bell said they need sailors who are good at that, so that's what I'm hoping for."

"What about you, Danny? You'd be good at everything."

"It seems as if we have all talked with Chief Bell. He said he had no way of judging my language capabilities, but that Naval Intelligence could use anyone who could read, write, and speak Japanese or German. He didn't know about Arabic. There is a military language school at Monterey, California, and he could make out the papers that would head me in that direction right after boot camp."

"Is it okay, Danny if I use your phone to call Chief Bell to make sure about Friday? While I'm calling, you might show Ruthie how you make a DISKnife. Kids at school don't know about that."

"I've heard about DISKnife," Ruthie said, "but what does that have to do with you?"

As they walked to the forge area, Danny explained how he, Ito, and Mr. Schmidt had started the business. When he came to the chinning bar at the entrance to the forge room he said, "Go on in and look around. I have a little job here before I join you."

He and Ito had put that bar up years before and had always followed their routine of doing maximum pull-ups and chin-ups when entering and leaving that area. Danny continued that commitment even though his partner could not.

Teddie had been running at full speed. He panted, "Chief Bell said we'd better be in his office within two hours if we want the navy. Recruitment policies have just been changes and he needs to have us on the train tomorrow morning for Portland, or you and I are headed for the army. We have papers to fill out and that sort of thing. Ruthie could go anytime she chooses, because there's no draft for women."

"Nuts to that," Ruthie exclaimed. "I'm going with you! We can have our dinner and movie in Portland. Boy, I'm excited. This will be my first time to be more than twenty-five miles from home!"

Both boys nodded agreement. Danny mentioned his bicycle camping trips, which actually were only thirty-five miles from home, but there was no time for small talk. Ruthie phoned her mother, Teddie phoned his parents, and Danny told Gran about their imminent trip to Portland.

The next thirty-six hours whizzed by, almost in a blur. Three hours with Chief Bell, the written tests, train tickets, hotel assignments in Portland, papers to fill out and take with them, packing, the train trip, and the whirlwind excitement of it all left the three friends nearly exhausted. "We get our dinner out this evening with the navy paying the bill," Ruthie observed.

At the induction center, the first order of business was to line up and wait, even though there were only four other guys there. Ruthie was the only girl. More paperwork was processed and finally it was time for the physicals. "Women first," the corpsman in attendance said.

Ruthie was escorted into the inner examination office. The corpsman returned to the outer office. He halfway complained, "They keep me busy when they do exams on guys, but kick me out when a good-looking woman goes in."

Later, Ruthie came out. She was wide-eyed, pink-cheeked, and flustered. "That was my first complete physical exam and they checked everything ... and I do mean *everything*!"

"Okay, you raw-assed recruits, it's your turn. Get into that office and strip until you're 'mother naked,' and do it on the double."

In short order, the guys understood what Ruthie had meant when she said the doctor checked "everything." They were left with no secrets and no dignity. It was their first physical *ever*. X-rays and blood samples were added, and then they dressed and returned to the office where Ruthie was waiting.

There were no chairs, and a sign read, DO NOT LEAN ON THE BULKHEAD (wall). After about thirty minutes, they were given orders. "You will be here at 0900 hours tomorrow, not five minutes earlier nor one second later. The officer in charge will inform you of your status at that time. You will then find out if you have the honor of joining the United States Navy, or if you are rejected and relegated to a life with one of the lesser services. Dismissed."

The three were feeling adventurous and decided to try eating some Chinese food. "If we don't like it, we still have money we planned to spend on a good dinner." This was Teddie's logic. Danny realized that some of the dishes were wonderfully similar to ones he had eaten with his Watanabe family. Each dish was different, strange, and delicious to his two companions.

They found what turned out to be a "skid row" movie theater that showed continuous films, one after the other. The films were interrupted by live vaudeville performances featuring a couple of strippers. They didn't realize what they'd gotten into, but once they had paid for entry, they stayed through three films and two of the stage acts. Some of the vaudeville performances were fun. Teddie asked, "Do you think those strippers are pretty?"

Ruthie replied "I think they may have been pretty when they were much younger. Now it looks as if their life has become difficult for them." More could have been said, but it was kinder to leave it at that.

The hotel the navy sent them to was not a "flophouse," but it was far from being a luxury establishment, as seen in films. The clerk accepted their vouchers. He muttered, "Three people in two rooms, and it's the good-looking doll who is alone. What's wrong with those guys' hormones?"

Ruthie was reluctant to go to bed. She seemed uneasy, and Teddie and Danny understood. Sleeping in a hotel room away from home was new to each of them. At two in the morning, a

285

pajama-clad Ruthie stood outside the guys' room, knocking on the door.

"I couldn't sleep. I've never been by myself like this before. Maybe I'm a little scared."

"I guess all three of us are a little uneasy. It isn't like being at home, and Teddie snores."

"Do I really? I didn't know that." Teddie admitted.

"No, not really, but it was something to say."

Later, Ruthie felt more comfortable. "I can go back to my own room now, and I'll be okay." They shared a full-body, three-people hug, and then the fellows walked Ruthie to her own room.

"Gosh, I didn't realize it before, but Ruthie is all grown up, and has all the right equipment," Teddie observed.

"You're right! But she's always been second-grade little Ruthie to me. Disturbing, isn't it, to have been so shortsighted? Thank goodness that hug didn't last much longer, or my flagpole would have been standing straight up."

"Yeah," Teddie observed, "and with you it would be difficult to hide." Teddie had come to terms with the fact that his diminutive member was not going to attract much attention.

For years Ruthie had felt totally secure, comfortable, and mostly uninhibited when Danny was around. That represented a level of trust that could not be violated.

In the morning, the three young recruits stood outside the induction office door until their watches showed ten seconds to 0900 hours. Danny reached for the door handle and heard the door lock being opened. The three entered, closed the door, and stood at attention. "Right! That's the navy way!" they were told. Five minutes later, Ruthie was called into an inner office. She returned with a big smile. "Boot camp and then nurse's training!" She was flushed with excitement. Hugs were exchanged.

"You next." A finger was pointed at Danny. The interviewing officer said, "I have an English translation here of a Japanese document. Read it to yourself and then let me know when you are ready to translate it. Take your time. I have other work to do here at my desk."

Dan spent a minute with the document and said, "I'm ready now, sir."

"Now?"

"Yes sir." And Dan did translate it, complete with explanations regarding the nuances that implied things other than those that were directly stated.

"Can you do that well with German?"

"I think not, but I do speak freely with German-born citizens of the United States. They tell me I have a Hamburg accent. That's because I learned if from two German friends who were from Hamburg."

"And it says here that you manage Arabic. How well?"

"I read and write it as well as I can English. I speak and understand it as well. The problem is that I have never had a conversation with a native speaker in Arabic, so I don't know if they could even understand me, or if I could understand them. I might be speaking it with a Cockney accent."

"Well, no matter, the demand right now is for competent and trustworthy Japanese-speaking, reading, and writing experts. I'm scheduling you for boot camp in San Diego and then to the Monterey Language School. They'll soon sort out what the navy wants to do with your skills."

Dan returned to the waiting room and was greeted with anxious smiles. They read his expression and rejoiced when he said one sentence, "San Diego boot camp and then Monterey Language School."

"You!" And a finger was pointed at Teddie. A nervous smile twitched on his lips as he stepped forward with a determined stride.

Three minutes later he appeared ashen-faced and totally dejected. "I'm 4-F forever. No branch of the service will take me. I have a heart condition. Well, I should be used to being rejected by now. No one ever wanted me on a team in school. I was always the last one chosen. But this is the first time anyone ever told me my heart wasn't any good, either. But heck, yesterday was my first physical."

"You were the number one choice on our team, Teddie. Danny and I wouldn't have wanted anyone else. No one could have done for us what you did." Ruthie captured his hands in hers. Then she carried them to her lips and face and held them there. "For ten years you belonged with us and you always will ... in our special group." The vibrant intensity of her eyes penetrated his pall of dejection. She would not allow him to continue feeling rejected. "You are so good at one thing, numbers, that there isn't room for you to excel in others. I swear you are an absolute genius in mathematics. What you want to do with that is up to you."

"Maybe so, but I wanted to be good at something physical."

"Do you know anyone else who was nicknamed Long Shot?" A secret smile passed between the two boys. They both knew it had nothing to do with having sunk that one long shot in the basketball gym, when they were in the eighth grade. That was one secret they didn't share with little Ruthie.

The trip home from Portland provided time for reflection among the three friends and study partners. They appreciated their time together, and realized that each had been heading toward different lifestyles and careers for several years. A school-age romance between Ruthie and either of the two guys really had not been a likely event, given their various prospects and ambitions. Perhaps they cared for each other too much to play games with their relationships.

Instability was a hallmark of the time, but Ruthie, Teddie, and Danny had maintained more than just an illusion of unity. The fact was, that they had only once shared the same class since they had entered high school. But the "young child" remains a part of every person's entity. In that respect, they were a "trio for life."

38

High School Graduation and Mrs. Bass

Seven students who had been together in Mrs. Bass's third-grade class were about to graduate from high school. They felt mature and grown-up as they talked about various things, including good and bad teachers. Anna Marie said, "I wonder where all that food came from, when Mrs. Bass gave us that third-grade party?"

The group had nothing but blank stares instead of answers. Anna Marie said, "I'm going over to the grade school and ask her. That was a big thing in my life and I never told her. I'm not sure we really thanked her for being such a wonderful teacher for all of us."

"Let's get our class together and go to see her. It's only about five blocks away." From a total of twenty-nine kids who had been in the class, there were only twenty in the graduating class.

The following day, they filed respectfully into Mrs. Bass's third-grade classroom, the same room she had shared with them nine years earlier. The shelves were empty. Those wonderful books that filled spare time with adventures for her students were in boxes on the floor. She dropped something in one box and they could hear her say, "That's it. That's the last of it." Her mood seemed to be hovering between resignation and despair.

She still had not seen the students who had entered her room silently.

"I have to go now, I'm sixty-five years old, and they say I'll be too old to teach next year. I've spent much of my life here in this room with youngsters, and it seems so strange to just be too old to be of value to anyone." She shook herself, squared her shoulders, and stood up. It was then that she realized she was not alone. Her glorious smile radiated from her face and a twinkle returned to her eyes. "You wonderful rascals! You have caught me muttering and feeling sorry for myself, just like a crazy old woman. You know, we have one more thing in common. Today is the last day of school for you in this district, and it is for me as well." Smiles were exchanged, and then her former pupils felt a little embarrassed. They didn't quite know what to say or do.

"Well, don't just stand there," she said. "Take your seats so I can take roll just one more time, and find out who is absent. Now, let me see. Harold? Oh, yes, he joined the army last year and so did Sidney. No, I'm wrong! Harold joined the navy. It was Sidney who joined the army. He sent a postcard from Italy showing him with a scrap yard full of German tanks that had been destroyed." She came to a third empty seat. "Now, Big James was very bright boy, but his parents wanted him to start working when he finished grade school. He's replaced three men."

Danny realized that Mrs. Bass knew so much about so many things, but above everything else, she understood people ... particularly her people ... and her students would always be her people. Seat by seat and pupil by pupil, she called everyone by name, and knew what each had been doing or where they had gone. "Merlin, you scallywag, you are in the wrong seat again, and you know it." Mrs. Bass and Merlin shared a smile. It had been their private game nine years before, and they had enjoyed it then as they did now. This would be the last time, but she remembered. "You were the all-time marble champion of this school. I don't remember how many marbles you left in the school bank, but it was enough to let many youngsters play who could not afford them."

Mrs. Bass lingered for some time at one empty seat. "Poor little Lucy Johansson, she was so young. It was childhood leukemia, you know."

But they hadn't known. She had become a name from somewhere in the past, and for many of the group, they had all but forgotten even the name. But Mrs. Bass remembered, and in so doing, made each of her former students feel cherished. "There are twenty of you left in our community now, after only nine years. We have lost one person each year. I wonder how many of us will still live here nine years from now?

"Danny, did you ever thank your mother for the chickens she gave us for our class party?"

"I didn't know ... I didn't know." And now it was much too late to thank her. All he knew was that one day some of the chickens were missing. When he told her, she had replied in her own way, "They were needed elsewhere." This was her way of saying some people were hungry and those chickens could be spared. She always seemed to be a little embarrassed when she was recognized for doing something particularly nice or meaningful for others.

"The potatoes came as a gift from Mr. Hadley, and our local dairy gave us the milk. Pete's father grew the corn and peas, and I made the cookies. It was a nice party and it did my heart good to see you stuff yourselves. There were two necks and three popes' noses left over, do you remember?"

For this reunion, the girls had made oatmeal cookies and the boys brought homemade ice cream. The first party had filled empty stomachs. This party filled and would continually refill a soul's need for viability, and to know that others remembered.

High school graduation for Danny's class took place that Friday evening. It often has been said that if you have seen one graduation, you have seen them all, but commencement services were often meaningful to those who were graduating, and also to their loved ones. Danny and his classmates shared the excitement of the occasion. Gran was there and beaming with pride. Chief, the sawmill worker friend who had given the boys the files, surprised Danny by attending. It was heartwarming to see their fourth-grade teacher, Mr. Hill. This was an opportunity for his former students to tell him how valuable his influence was. He had been instrumental in helping so many young boys become aware that it was okay to be a rough-and-tumble boy who got dirty on the playgrounds. This helped them feel a surge of manhood. And then, one after another of the grade school teachers were discovered among the group of those who wished the graduates a successful future, including Mrs. Bass.

The happy glow of the occasion was saddened by the awareness that most of the fellows expected to receive their orders to report for military service within the next few days. Yes, the war in Europe was over, but the Pacific War against Japan was predicted to last an additional year or two, perhaps more.

Awkward hugs and cheek-to-cheek kisses were exchanged

among students who had never hugged or kissed each other before. Guys exchanged overly strong handshakes, because they lacked the words to convey their regard and best wishes for the future.

The security provided by the "cocoon of school associations" had held its annual rupturing ceremony. It had started twelve years earlier with a core group. During those years, it shed some parts, as kids move away and others were absorbed. The community had grown from twenty-five hundred to over five thousand in just six years, and that "school cocoon" expanded enormously. But that process was at an end for these classmates. There was an eerie awareness among some of the graduates when they realized that if they returned to school, they would be required to register at the main office as a guest on campus. This no longer was their school. Other classmates escaped the confinement of the institution with the enthusiasm of the Arabian Nights djinn free from the captivity of the bottle. For most of their lifetime, they felt they were disciplined and regulated prisoners of the school system. Perhaps a few would never look back, but for most of them, these had been good times, with precious associations. It had been so good to see former teachers at the graduation, but for Danny, there was a major sense of incompleteness. One valued teacher, Mrs. Fulton, was not there. Perhaps she was suffering another severe migraine.

Although there were friends and memorable teachers sharing this evolution from high school into uncertainty, he felt an underlying sadness. Those who had given him life, and four who had enriched it, were missing and deeply missed. Representing all of the combined love of those dearest to him was his treasured Gran. She sat proudly, glowing with joy, and gave a wink and a nod to her adored bonny laddie. She had always been able to ease those difficult moments. Through her, and memories ... his loved ones were there.

39

Pauline

Danny finally made the phone call that had been delayed for years. His heart was pounding, and his breath was shallow and jagged, when the phone rang.

"Pauline? This is Danny."

"Yes, I know. After all of these years, this is the first time you've ever called me.

"I've been intending to call for a long time, but..."

"But what? Do you need something?"

"I guess so ... at least I need to talk with you about some of our years in school together."

"You could hardly say we were together. I've always sensed we've had a barrier between us."

"That's part of what I'd like to talk with you about."

Almost immediately her voice softened. "Would you like to come over? It would be easier for me to talk with you in person than on the phone."

"I'd like that. How soon?"

"About an hour. Would you mind if I ask you some really personal questions ... some that all the girls you knew at school, would also liked to have asked?" He hesitated, but agreed.

Danny took a hot shower, shaved, put on some deodorant, and tried to relax. In his mind, he had a long-overdue monologue with Mr. Schmidt. "You suggested years ago that I tell Pauline about the time Ito and I saw her at the swimming hole." In Danny's mind there was no need to repeat the vision of loveliness the two boys had beheld. It was time to do as Mr. Schmidt had suggested. Thirty minutes after their phone conversation, he started cycling.

Pauline greeted Danny at the door. She invited him in and

nodded toward a seat by freshly baked cookies. Nervously, she asked, "Do you want to go first, or should I?"

Danny still wanted to put off telling her as long as he could. "You first."

"Little Teddie told us after we graduated that you, Ito, and Mr. Schmidt started the DISKnife business, and now there's only you left, and why did you keep it a secret?"

"Gran is my father's mother, and she and I do all the knife work now, but there was no secret about our making knives. Any apparent secrecy wasn't intentional."

"Everyone says that you have made an enormous amount of money ... so much that you could buy almost anything you wanted, including nice cars, several houses, and everything. But look at you! You wear plain clothes, like most of the other boys, and you continue to ride that old bike you must have had for ten years, and it was old when you got it. And..."

"Stop a minute," Danny interrupted. "I'll forget some of the things you want to talk about, unless I answer them one at a time. I guess Gran and I do have some money, but I don't know how much. She keeps track of that. Neither of us wants a lot of stuff and we're used to things the way they are. Expensive clothing wouldn't make me feel any better ... probably, just less comfortable. I think the guys have it right: Levi's or cords, and T-shirts are easy to care for. About my old bike—when Ito and I bought our bikes, they represented dreams come true for each of us. My bike still gives me a lot of pleasure, and good memories as well. Besides, it cost me a hard day of work in the bean fields, and it remains a good means of transportation. So far, neither Gran nor I feel the need or a desire for a car. It'd be handy if I took girls out, but I don't."

"Yeah, I know." Pauline remained a little puzzled but continued, "Everybody liked you even though you were the smartest person in school. And that included the teachers. You have always been polite to everyone, and went..."

"Just a minute again, Pauline. As far as being smart is concerned, there are all kinds of smart. Fred knows a lot about welding and is good at it. I don't. I've never even tried to do it. Ray knows more about radios than the rest of us put together. Gwen and Rita are amazing with their music. Lucille and Ann are great at managing social events. They have a way of making everyone feel welcome, comfortable, and important. Eddie learned more about farming than I ever will. Elmer recognizes hundreds of flowers and plants and even knows their Latin names. He also knows how to grow and propagate them. No one in our class is better than you at settling problems, when people get on each other's nerves or have deep-seated disagreements. Jesse didn't graduate with us, but that doesn't make him dumb. He can figure out how mechanical things work better than any of us. He just doesn't read worth a darn. But he's really smart. Teddie is a whiz at math, and we've always relied on him to be certain our calculations are correct.

"I do have some advantages in schoolwork, and I can thank my Gran for that. She started me off as early as I can remember, by playing games with me that involved learning. This was based on languages, creative storytelling, memorizing words, poems, and stuff like that. Studying and learning new things, which many kids think of as work, she made into part of the fun in my daily life."

"Well, you always finish your assignments in half the time of anyone else. What's more, you remember it all."

"My Gran is an absolute whiz at reading. She explained to me that fast reading and comprehension are inherited skills, and should not be confused with intelligence."

"Maybe you don't call it intelligence, but I do, and so does everyone else. It must make it easier to learn everything when you can read so fast. You went to most of the school social functions including the dances. You danced with most of the girls who didn't have dates, but the only one you made a fuss over was Juanita, that girl from Spain. Also, it seemed as if you were about as interested in her grandmother as you were in Juanita. Can you explain that?"

"Going to school plays, the carnivals, and dances was fun. You girls taught me how to dance and Juanita's grandmother taught me how to dance in a different style ... one that I feel has a special elegance to it." Danny paused and his eyelids fluttered in reminiscence. Nearly a minute went by before Danny continued, "In different ways, Juanita and her grandmother enchanted me. I hated it when they left, and I tried every way I could think of to find where they had gone. Also, they were teaching me Spanish. In any case, I like both ways of dancing."

Pauline confessed, "I wish someone would remember me in that dreamy mood."

Under his breath, Danny formed the words, "I remember, and so did Ito." This would have been a good time to tell Pauline what he wanted to say, but she still wanted to ask more questions.

"But about the dances and other social functions, it seemed to me that all of us went to the dances to have a good time. Some went with dates and others of us didn't. I didn't have a date so I danced with the girls who didn't have dates. It wasn't romantic, but it was fun. I enjoyed myself."

"All the boys say you were the strongest and the best athlete in school, and yet you never went out for any of the team sports."

"I don't know about that. There were plenty of guys who were good at sports, and they were really strong. I have my own type of sports activity that I do at home. Spectators are not necessary. I take about forty-five minutes a day keeping fit, and that is all the time I can spare. A good team member should devote as much time as the coach thinks is needed. For some sports that could take over fifteen hours a week. I didn't have that much free time available."

Pauline protested. "You worked during lunch hour and Saturday mornings with the janitor, and you don't even get paid for that."

"My work with Mr. Bag taught me a lot of practical skills. Besides, we are friends, and it is great being around him. I'm lucky enough to be able to work with someone I really enjoy and not have to earn money for it. If I didn't do that, there still wouldn't have been enough time to be on a school team. Besides, he helped me learn and practice using German."

"Back in grade school, you, and all the rest of the boys, were being pushed around by Bully Billy. He was mean and hurt a lot of the kids. When you did take him on, you let him off too easy. Everyone wanted to see you kick the living crap out of him. He had it coming. Why didn't you?"

"Beating up on Bully Bill might have seemed right at the time. I really wanted to lots of times. I even started to, but Mr.

296

Watanabe taught me to control myself and not be aggressive. If I did have a fight, I was to use the least amount of force possible to protect myself, and always leave the other person with as much self-respect as possible. I really wanted to hurt him. When I had his head in my hand, I wanted to shove his face in the muddy water, and hold him there until he started to gurgle. Then I envisioned clubbing him on both sides of his face, so he would have two black eyes. I was filled with rage and wanted to hurt him so much that he wouldn't be normal for a week. Look at me now! My fists are clenched and my voice has gone harsh and tight. He still gets to me. Anyway, I was about to do some of those things when I glanced up and saw the look in Ito's eyes. I was violating the trust and tenants of the *A Way* lifestyle, and I had to stop."

"I don't understand what you mean by *A Way*," Pauline protested, "but you mentioned self-respect. Bully Bill didn't show Little Teddie Long Shot, Bruce, or Chuck, or any respect."

"Were you there when those same kids ganged up on Bully Bill, and laid him out on the ground? They came close to really hurting him, and they taught him fear. He never picked on anyone after that. Those kids developed their own sense of self-respect. They also realized the strength they had when they organized. They resolved their own problems."

"That kind of makes sense, but we still wanted to see Bully Billy punished. Anyway, we knew you lost your parents in a car wreck, and then Ito was killed and his parents died, and they were like family to you. We knew these things, but we still didn't understand you. You remain a puzzle to all of us ... *and you didn't date any girls.*"

"So you want to know what's wrong with me, right?" He laughed nervously, but a concerned frown dominated his expression.

Pauline blushed but asked Danny straight out, "Don't you like girls?"

"While I'm talking and have the nerve, I'd better tell you why I phoned and wanted to see you. It's easy for me to remember when, where, and how you totally fascinated and enchanted Ito and me. That's what I wanted to tell you about. I finally got up enough nerve to phone."

"What are you talking about? You hardly ever gave me a second look."

"I couldn't. You were just too…" Danny paused, as he had when he spoke about Juanita and her grandmother. Moments passed, and then many more.

"Danny! What's wrong?" Alarm registered in her voice.

"I'd better back up to the summer before we were in the eighth grade. The place was the swimming hole on the millrace. Enticing parts of you didn't quite fit in your previous year's swimming suit. When you scrambled up the bank in your wet swimming suit, you had to bend over and use your hands. Ito and I just happened to be where we could look right down the front of your suit and … aw heck … the contours of your enchanting breasts and pink nipples … well, I never expect to see anything more captivatingly lovely in my life. We were so excited and embarrassed, and kind of ashamed, too, because we thought we shouldn't be looking, but we did. We had to."

"So you saw everything I had, and you weren't interested anymore and…"

"Golly, no! We didn't move and hoped you would never stop diving and climbing back up that bank. Those first looks remain devastatingly vivid and memorable. That's why I've always been afraid … or embarrassed to be around you, except in a group. It would have been awful to make a fool of myself, or do something that might show disrespect for you.

"Anyway, when Ito and I went home from the swimming hole, we told our friend Mr. Schmidt about seeing you. He knew it was a rare and wonderful experience for us. He suggested that we tell you how beautiful and memorable you were. That was over five years ago and I didn't know how to tell you, and I hope I haven't made a mess of it now. Anyway, that's what I wanted to tell you. Now you have become even prettier, smarter, and have developed a great personality. Everyone admires you, and so do I." He paused for a few moments and was nearly out of breath. Then he continued, "Does that sound as if I thought all there was to you was beautiful breasts?"

Pauline left her chair and went to where Danny was sitting. Her eyes were misty and she appeared to be a little confused. "I wish I had known this a long time ago. Girls are never very sure of themselves. I know I was always comparing myself with other girls, and with movie stars, and never knowing for sure how boys felt about me. It is all so confusing. Now I can see the answer in your eyes, and in the way you look at me. And it's wonderful to hear the words! I always thought that when you turned away from me when we were talking, and wouldn't really look at me, that it was because you didn't like what you saw. I couldn't figure out what was wrong with me."

"Believe me, there was *never* anything wrong with you. You will always be one of my most cherished visions. The summer after we were seventh graders, and even now, telling you what I saw, the way I felt, and the effect you had on me ... it's nearly impossible, but I promised Mr. Schmidt I would tell you someday. He was probably right. Ito and I should have shared the intimacy of our feelings, emotions, and observations many years ago, but we just couldn't ... and now it's too late for Ito."

Pauline became nervous and her fingers fidgeted with the top button of her sleek white blouse. "If you don't mind ... maybe I can ... would I be too bad to want you to have a second dream vision of me?" As if her fingers had a mind of their own, they were undoing each of the seven buttons on her blouse. She studied Danny's eyes as he watched her intently. Excitement dominated his very being as she slipped out of her blouse and stood for a moment in her bra. But this was not a strip tease Pauline was doing. She did not hesitate as she unhooked the back of her bra and let the shoulder straps fall off her arms.

An implosive "OH!" sucked a huge amount of air through Dan's mouth, and his lungs filled to the bursting point. Pauline stood there doing nothing ... not trying to wiggle or jiggle, bounce or seduce. She saw Danny's excitement increase, but she also became aware that his expression included gratitude, an appreciation for her beauty ... and adoration.

She simply turned slowly from one side to the other and absorbed his expression. Then she put on her blouse, but left off her bra. "Now I know the answer to my doubts, and I have my own vision and memory to last me all my life. Young girls need to think someone finds them lovely, and becoming older does not decrease that need. I'm realistic enough to know that my looks will go to pot when I get old, but I have my memory of how you reacted to me just now. That means more to me than you can know. Your expression was not just lust, but some of that was there as well."

"I'm happy that lust wasn't all you saw while I was staring at you. It certainly exists, but so does the appreciation and realization that the younger memory of you shares an equally memorable vision." Danny continued to look at Pauline and became embarrassed when he realized he was staring. "I just want to remember how you look today, to go along with how you looked back then. You are lovely."

Pauline's face was radiantly beautiful. "I'll always treasure what you said, Danny. That explains about me, but why didn't you take out any of the other girls?"

Danny tried to explain. "Our classmates started going steady a year or two ago, and they plan to get married after graduating, or when the guy gets home from basic training or boot camp. When the war is over, most of the girls will get jobs and then start having kids. That's the common dream and they've been preparing for it for two years or more. Am I right?" Pauline nodded.

Danny continued, "My plan is to graduate from university. That will take four years after getting out of the service. How fair would it be to take a lot of a girl's time in high school, and then say, 'Bye for now, I'll check back with you in six or eight years.' After such a long time, we'd both have changed and might not have the same feelings. We might even have found someone else.

"Anyway, I have early visions of you, which are enhanced by memories of you in the school play, wearing your Pep Club sweater, reciting a poem in class, walking to school, dancing with me and watching you dance with other guys. And now there is today! I was scared at first, but now things seem okay. I needed to come, not just because of a promise, but because I wanted you to know and understand."

She looked at Danny with eyes that again had turned misty. "And all these years I thought you hardly knew I existed. I always felt I was just one of your classmates, not someone special."

"'Someone special' wouldn't begin to describe you! And not just because you have a pretty face and a great figure, I remember that you almost always included some of the least popular girls and fellows in activities you started at school. That helped us feel as if we might be 'someone special,' too. Remember when Peggy and Rita got into a real tangle of hurt feelings with Anita? Who was it that sorted it out so that they became better friends than ever? You, of course! I don't know what you plan to do in the future, but whatever it is, you will make the world around you a much nicer place."

Tears began to fill Pauline's eyes. She rushed to sit beside Danny and faced toward him. "I need to be hugged and held ... you have made me feel so good." She sobbed with pleasure as she snuggled close to him and rested her cheek against his. He was resoundingly aware of the hammering of his heart, as his body was flooded with adrenaline-laced blood in response to dramatically erotic sensations.

At that moment, the crunching of gravel in the driveway signaled the arrival of a car. Pauline quickly left the davenport, collected her bra, and went to another room to reassemble her clothing. She was quick enough that she was able to greet her mother at the door, and go out to help bring in a few packages and two pieces of luggage.

Pauline spent a few minutes talking with her mother before they entered the living room and she introduced Danny. The young man was happy for the extra time to compose himself. After welcoming him to her home, Pauline's mother asked Pauline, "Have you finished setting out your things for packing? We need to leave in three hours, and we mustn't arrive late." She smiled and said a brief good-bye to Danny, then left to finish the last of her preparations to leave.

"I'd better go," Danny said as he started for the door. Pauline went to him and put her hand in his. "I have some time before I leave, and we have some unfinished things to say. You were answering my questions and I don't know if I have any more. You have made me feel incredibly desirable. I'll remember your visit ... and inside I'll always be as I am right now."

Pauline accompanied Danny to the door, they shared a hug that perhaps sealed their memories, and the young man pedaled away on his old bicycle that somehow had become a royal chariot in Pauline's eyes.

Pauline would always remain unchanged and enchantingly

301

lovely in Danny's eyes. He now knew that it was much more important that she was so ... in her own eyes. Once again, Mr. Schmidt had been right ... but it would have been almost impossible to tell her when they were just starting the eighth grade.

As Danny was pedaling home, he reflected on the wisdom Juanita's grandmother had expressed: "...You are not ready for a permanent commitment, although you may think you are. But you certainly are ready for the joyful enchantment that a sweet romance can shower on you. The effect is adorably sublime and memorably beautiful. There is room in life for almost unlimited number of such experiences, which uplift the soul."

Danny arrived home from his visit with Pauline when a phone call came from Little Teddie. "I can't go into the navy with you, but the city hired me as a bookkeeper. Mr. May has been teaching me accounting practices since I started delivering milk to his home. We have spent about thirty minutes together almost every evening for the past six years. Today I passed the first of two examinations needed for state certification as a public accountant. Mr. May said I could pass the final exams, but that I should have some practical bookkeeping experience before becoming a CPA"

"Wonderful, Teddie! What a great start to a career of doing the type of work you are so good at, and that you like. Have you called Ruthie?"

"Not yet, but I'm going to right now. I just wanted you to know first."

"How about Mr. May? You must have told him."

"Not really. He told me. The local officials went to his house and talked with him. They said that if I met his standard, they knew I'd do a good job for them."

"Ruthie is going to be as excited about the news as we are. Maybe we can celebrate with dinner and a movie."

That night, Danny's dreams were a confusion of emotional responses, gratitude, and visions of loveliness involving a young sprite in early puberty and a more mature woman, both of whom were enchantingly etched in the depth of his being.

40

Mrs. Fulton

For a number of years, Mrs. Fulton had suffered severe headaches, from two to four days each month. It was during seventh grade that Danny became aware of her pain and had offered to give her a massage using the procedures Mrs. Watanabe had taught him. They had been so beneficial that Mrs. Fulton had continued to ask for his help both during school hours and on weekends. At school this had been no serious interruption in Danny's education. He kept well ahead in his classmates, and time away from the classroom seldom exceeded fifteen minutes.

The grade school and high school were less than a block apart. Mrs. Fulton's time away from her class averaged twenty minutes, and that was covered by the grade school principal. As principal, he welcomed the opportunity to get to know some of the students and also to remain semi-active as a classroom teacher. Mrs. Lombard, the retired teacher and self-appointed librarian at the grade school, was happy to take over Mrs. Fulton's class at a moment's notice.

Saturday and/or Sunday treatments took time away from making knives, but helping people was part of Gran's way of life, and it seemed the natural thing for Danny to do as well. He didn't even consider not responding when Mrs. Fulton called for help.

The first time the boy went to Mrs. Fulton's home, her husband had been there and he spent nearly an hour talking about his wife's life as a student. She had skipped two years of grade school and finished four years of high school in three. Most students graduated from high school when they were between seventeen and eighteen years of age. Mrs. Fulton was only fifteen. She immediately enrolled in "Normal School," which was a teacher training college. At the end of two years, when she was not yet eighteen years old, the state issued her an elementary school teaching credential.

Danny had been in the first class Mrs. Fulton taught, and during that first week, she was given her first headache massage. These debilitating headaches continued to plague her. She consulted her doctor, tried the medications he prescribed, and all of the "over-the-counter" pills that were advertised.

During one appointment with her doctor, he asked, "It is of little comfort to you, or me, to know that I have dozens of patients ... mostly women, who experience the same monthly problems you have with headaches. All of them have worked out some form of strategy to get by during the most difficult hours. How do you manage?"

"You know Danny, the extremely bright orphan youngster whose parents were killed in the car wreck?" she asked. The doctor nodded. "He gives me a massage and within minutes I'm asleep. Five minutes later I am awake and feeling 100 percent."

"Then, why are you here? You found something that works, so use it."

She explained, "But Danny is one of my students."

The doctor queried, "So?"

"Well, how do I pay him? How much should he get?"

"Many doctors used to say that a patient should pay what the treatment is worth to them."

Mrs. Fulton studied the doctor's eyes to see if he were serious, then smiled and admitted, "I don't earn that much money."

"Then be happy that he isn't greedy. In rare circumstances, inexplicable gifts, talents, or even the very presence of the person, can alter the course of a person's life. Barriers between mysticism and science are not as rigid as we might imagine. In your case, he must seem to be a miracle worker ... and in fact, he is."

The first massage was given five years previously, when she was almost eighteen and Danny was thirteen. During all that time, the boy had met her husband only once. Very little conversation passed between Mrs. Fulton and Danny outside of classroom hours. She was always in a state of agony when he arrived, and was comfortably asleep when he left a few minutes later. Gratitude registered in her eyes whenever she looked at him.

It was while Danny was in high school that Mrs. Fulton

304

visited Gran. She talked about how helpful Danny had been throughout the years when she had one of her headaches. Gran commented, "Ah yes, lassie. I know a wee bit about headaches and such problems although I seldom suffer from them. When I do, Danny promptly puts me right."

Mrs. Fulton vigorously nodded her head and declared, "Exactly! But how do I compensate him for his time, labor, and treatment? The doctors charge me and don't help, even though they try. Danny resolves the problem in a few minutes and I feel wonderful for twenty-four hours. When I try to pay him, he refuses and says something about Mrs. Watanabe. I suppose that would have been Ito's mother. I understand Ito was killed in Italy and his mother and father died in the internment camp a short time later."

Gran searched Mrs. Fulton's eyes before commenting, "Giving a helping hand to those who need it has been a way of life around here." It was as if nothing else needed to be said. The conversation was essentially over.

As Danny and his classmates became more mature, they realized that the age difference between themselves and some of their teachers was only a few years. Some high school boys and girls were becoming engaged when they were only sixteen. Fellows were coming home from military basic training or boot camp to be married. The pace of life was accelerating.

Graduation ended high school routines and Mrs. Fulton's headache massages would stop, because of Danny's imminent order to report to the navy.

The merits of the various branches of the military had been a topic of conversation and controversy since the start of World War II. But eventually, the topic of death surfaced. From ancient times to the present, the one thing that virtually every man feared the most was the thought of being killed before he had "Really Lived." That fear was universal, and "Really Lived" was easily translated into one common concept: to have had sex with a woman. It was one reason why prostitutes locating adjacent to military bases were so prevalent.

However, those who indulged in sex with a whore were usually terribly disappointed. The women were, by definition, wanting money and the customers needed physical relief. Both were easily supplied, but the men were also seeking emotional security, and a feeling of being of special value to a woman. Few prostitutes were emotionally prepared to meet such needs.

By the time Danny's classmates had graduated, the majority of the fellows had acquired that desperately needed billfold sign of manhood, a "rubber." Many of the condoms had been in wallets so long that the latex had disintegrated and they were totally worthless for the intended protection. One local drugstore got a jump on the market and created a lifelong group of loyal customers by giving each of the local male graduates a "three-pack" of condoms. To alleviate any embarrassment, the fellows only needed to ask for his gift as a graduate. In fact, "graduates" became the common local name for that commodity, and that name remained in use for many years after Danny had left the area.

Danny was not surprised when he received a phone call from Mrs. Fulton the day following his visit with Pauline. "Danny, would you be able to come over right away?" This was the way her requests for help had always been phrased. He left immediately. Mrs. Fulton met him at the door of her house. She was dressed in a skirt that was fashionably short and a low-cut blouse in a flowery pattern to keep it from being transparent. The top button had carelessly been left unbuttoned, or was that intentional? It was obvious that Mrs. Fulton was not suffering from one of her headaches.

"Perhaps I should have told you, Danny, I am moving to Seattle. I have been in school almost all of my life and I decided to see what the rest of the world is all about. I have a job with Boeing that starts next week. Professional movers are to be here tomorrow to handle the big things, but I need a little help with a few items that are on high shelves and must be available for packing. I didn't know who else to call for help. Is that okay with you?" He nodded in reply.

She sat on an office-type desk and talked for a few minutes, although there were constant distractions. Bare skin showed above rolled stockings on her crossed legs. As she uncrossed her legs, white underpants were glimpsed. One hand kept playing with the second button down on her blouse. When she leaned over to wipe an imaginary spot from one of her shoes, that second button was undone and she was facing Danny directly. The upper curves of her full breasts were wonderfully revealed. No longer a boy, but eighteen years of age, the physical reactions were the same as they had been when he had first seen Dottie during seventh-grade English class. Danny dropped to his knees to relieve the strain on the front of his trousers, but she saw the situation.

"The shelves I need help with are in here," she said as she left the room. Danny followed, hoping to regain his composure while she wasn't looking.

She led the way into her bedroom. Danny noticed the bed-spread and blankets had been removed and the sheets were neatly folded back. She went into a large, walk-in closet. "It is in here that I need help ... the boxes are on the top shelf."

She knelt in front of some boxes that were on the floor. Her skirt slipped right up to the top of her legs and another button on her blouse released itself. As her elbows went back, her blouse opened fully and she uttered, "Oh, my! I'm coming apart aren't I?" But she didn't do anything to repair her situation. Instead, she looked directly at Danny's bulging pants. "You also appear to be having difficulty containing yourself?"

In an acute state of turmoil, Danny gulped out, "Yes, I guess I am," and squirmed to relieve the pressure.

She moved a hand as if to close the front of her blouse, but when the hand dropped away the blouse was still open and so was the center of her bra! She climbed up on the second step of a short ladder and asked Danny to take two large books she handed down to him and to put them on the floor. As he did so, her breasts were face-high and she leaned a little toward him. "Oops," she said as she went slightly off balance and leaned fully into his face with her hands clasping his head to her cushioning breasts.

The young man had had an erotic thrill just the previous day when he had been with Pauline. But the circumstances were different. Reality was wildly better than fantasies. "I think we'd better do something about your discomfort, don't you?" She stepped down from the folding ladder and released his belt buckle and buttons of his trousers. The straining erection shot out through his shorts and her hand clasped it for a moment. Then

307

she removed her skirt and panties and invited him down on top of her right there on the floor of the closet. Again, her hand took his penis and a terrifying urgency called for it to unload itself.

She apparently was aware of this as well, because she wasted not a moment in opening herself to receive its full length and the urgent message it contained. Youthful enthusiasm and total inexperience maintained him well within her despite her thrusting and squirming. The force of his ejaculation was something she felt, and her reaction was more than responsive. The strength of a young erection does not melt away as rapidly as that of a more mature man, and she continued enjoying her captive slave long after it had released its contents.

Everything seemed to be over too quickly. Danny thought about how the cow and the bull, the rabbits and then the chickens had reacted. They didn't last as long as he had, and it was so thrilling and felt so good. Then he realized that some animals didn't quit after just one release. He waited and delighted in the sight and feel of her breasts and her legs around him and how unlikely this situation actually was. He was right. A human could do it more than once!

The second occasion was not so desperate. He could sense motion within her. The lubricated smoothness of her formed a type of seal around him, and each outward movement produced a vacuum that seemed to draw him inwardly with greater force. He responded to little endearments that escaped from her lips; lips that always before had been reading stories to the class, taking roll, correcting mistakes, and giving directions. He felt erect nipples dancing across his chest. He wanted his lips around them, but couldn't reach them while he was still within her.

Then it was the time to really enjoy her breasts. He could look at them, touch them with his hands, explore their contours from every angle, and marveled at the fact that the nipples had been soft a few moments before, but were becoming rigid and her whole body responded as his tongue and lips surrounded them. As he continued, her hips started circling and thrusting once again, even though he was not within her. And he learned from his teacher. A woman has many erotically responsive zones. And so he continued and she responded magnificently.

A few minutes later, Danny was once again rigid, and she

308

was as eager to receive him as she had been the first time, per-haps even more so, because now she knew of her capability of reacting to the young graduate with whom she was sharing her body. But the floor was becoming hard on her back, so she rolled over on top of Danny. This exposed her breasts more fully and he could see their delicious form and shape alter as she moved and pivoted around his erection. He could see his manhood dis-appear and reappear in the confines of her body. This was so thrilling that once again the trigger of his need was caressed and tantalized into a delightful star-filled explosion.

When she dismounted, stood up, and helped Danny to his feet, he presumed they were done, although he was reluctant to stop. Then she turned her back and clasped his arms around her, one hand to her breasts and the other to the curly hair where he had been probing and enjoying himself so much. She guided his fingers within her and it was strangely thrilling to explore her in that fashion. Apparently he found another trigger for her pro-gressive response, because respond she did!

She dropped to her knees and, still holding one of Danny's hands to her breast, drew him down as well. The back of her hips was nestled in his lap and the vision of the bull and the cow, and the rabbits again flashed through his mind. These stimulating thoughts and the intimate contact induced another hard-on and the entry from that position was equally possible, and delightful! He could hold and fondle her breasts and that continued to be exquisitely thrilling to him. By raising and lowering the height of his hips, he elicited more writhing reactions from her. After a time of delight and anticipation, the pounding release once again manifested itself.

Who knows how much longer this could have continued be-fore one or the other of them would have surrendered to fatigue or become sated. The strength and endurance of youth in such matters can be a marvel.

Always before, when Danny had given her a massage for her headaches, she had been fully clothed, and the massage had only involved her head, neck, and upper shoulders. This time she was unclothed and did not have a headache. Danny started "Playing the Piano" of her spinal column in the manner he had been taught by Mother Watanabe years earlier. The technique ensured that the woman was completely fulfilled even though there was no sexual contact.

It was at that time that Danny realized and understood the enormous power he possessed at the tips of his fingers! Mrs. Fulton simply expired into a vat of awareness and fulfillment.

Later, they felt the need for gentle care and gratitude, but especially the tenderness of holding and snuggling. And so they shared that as well. This was enough. Not too much and not too little ... precisely enough. Danny had discovered peace without hunger and joy without regrets. One sexual aspect of life had been experienced in many forms and in no way had it been found wanting. Continued life was greatly anticipated, but he had escaped the fear of "being killed before really living." That fear had been put to rest.

Eyes searched eyes and lips smiled at each other, but words were not spoken until Danny stepped out the door, and only one word reached his ears, "Graduation." The door closed and Danny took his bike and started home. He contemplated what words might have accompanied the one word he had heard. Well, he certainly had graduated in more ways than one, and perhaps the gift of her body would be the grandest graduation gift he would ever share.

Danny arrived home after dark. The tantalizing odor of a vegetable beef stew greeted him. "It's on the stove now and I'll join ye at table anytime ye be ready," Gran called to him.

It would take Danny only a short time to get ready. Stew was one of his favorite meals.

As they sat eating, Gran's wry smile repeatedly appeared and disappeared. "Well, what is it, Gran?"

Gran's eyes twinkled. Her reply was a simple statement of fact, "I see ye 'ave had a woman, and it's time for that to be happening. Your father would be happy for ye, as am I." Their conversation was in Arabic, but an unusual expression of joy was evident in Gran's voice. This reflected her pleasure in knowing that Danny had experienced that form of elation before he departed for the uncertainties of military service. "I'll do the washing up, Danny. Ye will be exhausted, but totally at peace." He went to bed shortly thereafter, and he slept as never before.

The young man was up early. "Gran, how many of the

curved-blade knives would you like ... you know, ones intended for Arabic inscriptions?"

"I would be a pleased to keep me hands and eyes occupied with me favorite form of creative and artistic recreation." Gran could take up to a month to create some of her special blades. Other times it might take only a day or two.

Danny worked an average of sixteen hours a day at the forge and foundry, and turned out fifty knives for finishing daily. His schedule was dictated by a need to be sure Gran had an adequate supply of the blades she chose to engrave. He worked ten days straight, and five hundred DISKnives were ready for Gran to finish and ship to anxious customers.

"You know we've money enough to last us both for several lifetimes."

During the long hours of work, the young man thought about the wonderful events that had been crowded into just a few hours. Danny and Mrs. Fulton had shared deep feelings of tenderness and gratitude. Their relationship had been improbable, agonizingly erotic, and amazingly fulfilling. It had been the most meaningful type of gift they could share. She had led the way into a world that entailed a more complete appreciation of the uniqueness and grandeur of life. A short time before that, he had visited Pauline. The time had been so compressed, along with the pressure of his work, that he had become disoriented. Would the sensitive encounter he shared with Pauline somehow be diminished because of the complete sexual union with Mrs. Fulton? He had such limited experiences that he didn't know. As he was busy at the forge, he realized that his memory of Pauline was as vivid and enchanting as it always had been. He had continued to cherish his visions of Dottie. The bathing beauties Ito, Kid, and he had ogled at during the bicycle camping trip remained excitingly intense. One reality had not diminished the others. His engaging preoccupation with Juanita and her grandmother had formed a different reference and awakening, but remained compellingly etched and precious to him. It seemed as if these realities were enhanced. He was aware that in matters of the mind and emotions, comparisons were not necessary, or appropriate. Each was treasured, complete, and separately fulfilling.

311

For many years, Gran had reminded Danny that as long as memory lasted, people and experiences were sustained ... even when that event was separated by the great gulf of death. Would it be less so with other treasures of his mind?

Danny longed to talk with Mr. Schmidt. His kindly wisdom, in virtually all matters, would have comforted the young man. His mentor had counseled, "Cherish the past, enjoy the present, and anticipate an enriching future. Your mind is similar to an expanding library. Pages, chapters, and volumes are continuing to be recorded in your memory as you experience life. A good index is essential if we are to keep our memories in order and viable." From that time onward, Danny thought in terms of "the library of his mind." The luxury of time offered Danny the opportunity to review his memories.

Mrs. Fulton wrote to Danny six months after she and her husband had moved. "I no longer have headaches. 'Playing the Piano' on my spinal column may have been responsible for this amazing relief, but I suspect the completeness of my experience with you is the answer. I learned from you the glorious ability to respond more fully to a man, and subsequently to my husband. Thank you for the years of wonderful treatments. Perhaps we will think of our time together as graduation gifts for both of us!"

41

Report to the Navy

"You will have between forty-eight and seventy-two hours advanced notice of the time you are to report here for assembly and transportation to boot camp. Your travel orders will be sent to you by mail. These orders will include vouchers for your transportation and food to this induction center. If overnight lodging is necessary, it will be provided. Probably you will be sent to San Diego, but that is not guaranteed. You could be sent to Great Lakes, or hell itself. Your ass belongs to the United States Navy, and the navy's wisdom will prevail in all cases. If you miss your appointment here with us, it had better be because you are confined to a hospital or the morgue. Otherwise you will spend your first fourteen days in the brig on 'piss and punk' (bread and water). Thereafter you will be first in line for every shit detail the navy has to offer. Don't fuck up on this! Have I made myself perfectly clear?"

That was the departing lecture Ruthie, Danny, and the others received when they went home to await their call to report for recruit training. "That sailor really talks rough," Ruthie observed. "I know the words and a lot more that are as bad or worse, but I didn't expect to hear them from a man who has a public relations job. I was tempted to tell him, 'Up yours!' That probably wouldn't have been good for my career." A smirk of mirth had spread over Ruthie's face as she spoke.

Danny had roared with laughter. Once again, he was given the message that little Ruthie was emerging from their cocoon of childhood innocence.

The young man was enjoying the memory of that incident, as he put blade blanks in the furnace for heating. He had no worry about Gran having enough money to live on for the remainder of her life. She had assured him there was much more in the bank, and in stocks and bonds, than she could ever spend ... and for him, as well. But she did love working with the knives and he wanted her to have as good a supply on hand as he could manage. Among Gran's favorite presentation knives were ones with a curved blade on which she had engraved Islamic scriptures in Arabic. Completing this knife had taken countless hours of creative inspiration, artistic dedication, incredible skill, and resourceful knowledge.

Danny poured a few silver handles that made up a part of their special "presentation line" of knives, but his primary concentration was on making their standard DISKnife to fill orders that had been placed up to four years earlier.

Three days later, Danny received a phone call from Ruthie. "I received my orders to report to the induction center three days from now. Have you been notified?"

"I'll check the mail, just a minute ... yep, I'm scheduled for the same time. It says 0800 hours report time. This means going up the day before. They have me scheduled on the train north. Is it the same for you?"

With a touch of humor in her voice, she replied, "Yep. It looks as if we will be traveling together, and I also have an overnight with the 0800 hours reporting time. My mother is going to take me to the train. We can swing by and pick you up." Arrangements were made, and Ruthie added, "It looks as if we aren't going to have our movie and dinner with Little Teddie. He's away at a conference and won't be back until after we have reported." A few minutes later, Danny returned to his knife making.

On his last day at home, Danny closed the DISKnife operation and covered everything that Gran would not be using. Mr. Schmidt's chair remained unoccupied since his grand mentor and friend had last used it. Each time he passed it, he felt a special ... almost spiritual aura enveloping him, but this time there was an encompassing invitation that seemed to say, "Come! Sit with us. Ito and I are now dead to this world, but we live in your memory." Once again, it seemed as if foreheads came together and they shared another three-person hug. A few minutes later, Danny realized that he was sitting in the chair and the two heads he had felt pressing against his were his hands in which he was cradling his own head. He became aware that tears were flowing down his cheeks, but not for Mr. Schmidt, who had convinced the two boys that he had used up his life ... it had been time for it to come to an end. He had shared his dream of producing knives with the world's best cutting edge and he felt his life was complete. He had the love of his families and had been a positive influence for his two young partners. He had given and received and sensed a satisfying fulfillment.

Danny's tears were for his best friend, Ito, who had been killed somewhere in Italy. He was just one of millions whose lives had been taken in another of mankind's follies. It was comforting to Danny to believe that he could return to the chair near the forge, and reestablish a spiritual reunion with his two dearest friends.

Then it was time to close the place. The last thing he did before locking the door was to do his exercise routine on the chinning bar. He completed a list of chores that Gran requested. And they sat together and enjoyed a final visit. They learned their quota of new Arabic words and followed their usual routine.

"What will ye be packing?"

"Eight throwing knives and a change of clothing, a shaving kit, and my jacket. I have my little Japanese dictionary that Ito gave me, but I'm leaving the Arabic one here. I will be able to keep on learning while waiting around. The navy will be providing for all my needs and most of what I have with me will be returned here. They may let me keep my knives, but I'm not counting on it."

There is no adequate way for loved ones to part ... they just do it. This was the first time for Danny to be the one who was going, and he thought it was much easier than being the one left behind. He had almost no control over the new adventure. Ruthie's mother was at Danny's house on time. Final hugs, kisses, and words were exchanged. Then only hand waves could be given, and they were soon no longer of use. A similar scene took place at the train station. It was a surprise when "Little Teddie Long Shot" arrived to see his friends on their way.

For the first time, Ruthie and Danny sat and held hands on the train, just the two of them. Always before, Teddie had been part of the working trio. This was different, but not romantic.

They were giving and gaining strength through sharing this experience.

In Portland, they went to the same Chinese restaurant and to the same hotel. "I'm okay now," Ruthie said when she was about to go to bed. "If you have any problems, wake me up and we can be together for as long as you like," she added.

They hugged and Danny kissed her on both cheeks. She took his face in her hands. "I'd like one right on the lips, if you don't mind. I'm old enough, you know."

After the kiss, Danny's eyes were wide open. "I'll say you are!" With that, Ruthie closed the door and Danny went to his room. He thought, "That was a genuine revelation! The way she kissed, and the way she hugged me sent a powerful message. She wasn't inviting me to spend the night with her; she was just telling me in no uncertain terms that little Ruthie had grown up. She just wanted me to know. She was in control of herself." And Ruthie had added an element of "sizzle" to his awareness. It was comforting to Danny to realize that his two classroom partners from the second grade onward were okay, and not apprehensive about their futures ... nor was he. They had prepared the best way they knew how for what was to come, but who could predict the future?

42

The Navy

At 0800 hours sixty-three new navy personnel mustered at the induction center in Portland, Oregon. Three of them were women. Ruthie and Danny had been classmates and study partners from the second grade on through high school. It was early June 1945 and the war in Europe was over, but military and political experts predicted that it could take a year or more of deadly combat to defeat the Japanese.

Ruthie and two other young women had signed up for a four-year hitch and were scheduled for training to become registered nurses.

Danny was one of the sixty men who had enlisted "for the duration plus six months." The two school friends had mistakenly presumed they would have a chance to tell each other about their destinations and to say a final farewell.

The tough-talking petty officer third class assumed a stance of authority that displayed his two hash marks on the left sleeve of his jumper. That he had been in the service for over eight years and held only a third-class rating, suggested that he wasn't overly ambitious or that he had screwed up too many times. He growled, "No talking among the ranks. You three, split tails, into that next compartment, *now!*" The women were gone.

"Now you little Mommy's boys, hear me well. Your asses now belong to the United States Navy and right here and right now I am the navy, so even the hair on your balls is mine. You will be told what you need to know and when you need to know it. There will be no smoking, talking, or sitting. You are not to lean on the bulkhead. Stand on your own two feet."

Danny took out his small Japanese pocket dictionary and resumed his study. For him, time passed quickly, because studying was one of his lifetime pleasures.

"You, yes, you there with the book ... what are you reading?"

"It's a Japanese dictionary. I'm improving my vocabulary, sir."

"What are you, some kind of Jap lover?"

"Three of my dearest friends ... really family ... were Japanese. They are dead now. But there is a nation full of Japanese who are our enemy. I hope to be able to help our country defeat Japan, and deal with them afterward." There was no response.

After two and a half hours of standing on first one foot and then the other, fidgeting became obvious to the deaf and blind. Finally, instructions were given: "Six men who are forceful and responsible, step forward, now." Twenty-seven men came forward. "I said six men. Numbers one through six are painted on the deck. One leader is to stand on each of the numbers. The remainder of you form in groups of ten behind the leader you choose. You will be a part of that group until the navy changes your assignment in San Diego. Your leader will receive orders from the navy and you will receive your orders from him. Everything you do from now on will be in those groups of ten. Line up on the numbers. Group one will now go to the head. You will be back here in five minutes at which time group two will go. At the end of thirty minutes, all of you will have been to the head. Then we will go to the chow hall."

It felt like first grade all over, but without needing to raise the appropriate finger. Group one was at the head when the petty officer went over to Danny. "Jap dictionary man, I thought you would have been scrambling for one of those leader positions. No balls, huh?"

"I have much to learn that the navy will teach me, sir. I hope to be a good student and learn 'the navy way.' If the navy decides I should assume a leadership role, I will try to be worthy of it. Until that time, I'll do my best to support designated or authorized leaders. Right now, you are the navy's representative. I'm trying now to learn how to support you in your position of authority, sir."

"I didn't ask for a lecture from you, so shut up."

Thirty minutes later all personnel had been to the head. Sixty men followed the petty officer to the chow hall, ate, picked up their belongings, and marched to the train station.

The train passed right by the pasture where Ito Watanabe and Danny had played, hunted cows, and did much of their growing up. He could see the Watanabe home, his forge, and the foundry building where the two boys had made their throwing knives and the DISKnife. It had achieved national renown as the best knife blade in the world. The house he had called home since halfway through the second grade, quickly disappeared from view. Gran probably was there at that time finishing a knife or two. The next three road crossings were familiar. One led to the log dump, the second was the way to the old swimming hole. The third was the road to the forest camp where Ito, Kid, and Danny had seen the five girls skinny-dipping. From there onward, everything was unfamiliar territory. It was obvious that his world had been confined and sheltered. He thought about Kid, who was in Italy with the army, and Ito who had died in Italy. Seeing the world was a fine adventure, but being killed overseas....

Dan presumed that almost every person entering the military service dreamed about being a hero, a surviving hero. Those thoughts occupied Danny's mind for a short while, but he was more inclined to be a doer rather than a dreamer. He believed his language skills with Arabic and Japanese, and to a lesser degree with German, could be useful to the navy. Since the war had become primarily a Pacific Ocean conflict involving Japan, he continued his study of Japanese. He practiced composing letters and documents. He worked on vocabulary and wished he had a Japanese-speaking companion.

Bragging could be expected, because most of the men wanted to impress fellow recruits with their achievements. Academic accomplishments were of little interest. Talk about sports and girls dominated the conversation. It wasn't long before some of the glamour wore off the reports of athletic achievement.

"My school subscribed to the ten top newspapers in the state and I followed all the teams that were covered," one physically unimpressive fellow reported. He proceeded to run down the list of football teams throughout the state. League champions and the all-star players in each league were named. State championship competition was held in basketball, boxing, wrestling, and track, and the guy named them all. A quieter guy might say,

"Yeah, I took second," or "We had a good team this year." The better the athlete, the less bragging he seemed to do.

The topic that demanded the most attention involved romantic conquests. Guys showed photos of their girlfriends, and some became dreamy-eyed. They spoke about their plans to get married during leave after boot camp.

One particularly loud and caustic fellow, whose physical bulk matched the size of his mouth, was quick to jump on anyone's cherished memories or dreams for the future. "Hey, fellows, take a look at this poor sucker. He's engaged to be married. Tell us, are those her tits or just padding?" There was no reply. "He can't answer such a simple question because he doesn't know. Now, look here," he continued as he took out his billfold and removed a rubber, "I've used between seven and ten of these every week for the last four years."

From near the end of the train coach a burst of laughter started and swept toward the bragger. "What's all the laughter about? Don't you believe me? I'll whip the ass of anyone who calls me a liar." An anonymous voice from the far end reported, "We all believe you. It's just that one guy said you must have been spending a lot of money on jacking off."

"Okay, who's the smartass?"

The sports academic whiz responded, "You should remember him, but then you just got a glimpse of him before he decked you. You lasted only seven seconds in the first round in boxing. He took just thirty seconds to put you flat on your back and pin you in wrestling."

Cheers and jeers sounded throughout the train car, but they were quickly subdued when the kid who had won the state boxing and wrestling championships stood up. "Never make fun of a guy who has guts enough to try. In any sport you never know how the next competition is going to end. Maybe I was just lucky." He walked half the length of the train coach, shook hands, and added, "I'm proud to join the navy with you. I shouldn't have shot off my mouth."

"I've been doing a lot of talking myself. The fact is I'm still a reluctant virgin, if you don't count jacking off as losing one's virginity."

"My bet is that most of us are reluctant virgins. Let's see a show of hands ... the hand you use the most." Almost every hand went up and a spirit of comradeship was kindled that supported them during stressful times while they were in basic training. Danny had heard the request, but he kept his eyes and both hands on his dictionary. He translated the word *graduation* and then *present* and smiled to himself and remembered the gift his former teacher Mrs. Fulton had given him ... his first woman and his graduation into manhood.

Most servicemen have dozens of stories to tell. The company commander's first lecture was given outside the barracks in which they were billeted. "It's perfectly normal and natural for you men to have a 'wet dream,' but if I catch any of you men manufacturing a wet dream, I'll send you back to your first day of boot camp." He was an ex-physical-education-teacher and coach who had spent his first two years in the navy in command of the obstacle course at boot camp. He was lean, mean, and what the recruits thought of as old ... probably in his mid-forties. Each day he had offered a challenge to new recruits. "I personally pledge that anyone who beats me on this course will serve no extra duty, nor stand watch while in boot camp." He ran that course five to six times each day. All the high school and college athletic hotshots who had gone through training during those two years had figured it was an easy way of getting out of duty. They'd just take on the old man and whip his ass, but no one had managed to do it.

The first order of every day was to muster and march. The chow hall was a favorite destination. Everyone felt an obligation to complain about the food, but it was better than most recruits had eaten at home. There was no limit to how much anyone was allowed to eat, except one's own capacity, and the time the company spent in the chow hall.

The company's next stop was the obstacle course. This morning was no different from all the others. The commander reissued the challenge he had presented the first day. Half of the company had figured they could beat the old man. In short order, he demonstrated why no one had succeeded. From the number of breakfasts that were vomited during and following the effort, everyone learned not to eat so much or take it easy on the obstacle course.

One of the most memorable days for all servicemen of that era was the day they got their "shots." Vaccinations and inoculations were given for everything possible.

The "Navy Way" was to strip to the waist and walk through a narrow doorway in single file. Three needles were planted in the right arm triceps and two in the left so quickly that no one had an idea of what had happened until he looked. Occasionally a man simply passed out. A few steps later, syringes were attached to the needles and the appropriate amount of the contents was injected. Those who did pass out were injected where they lay and the next two "boots" were ordered to pick the man up and carry or drag him clear of the area. But the worst was yet to come! Each arm ached as if it had been "baseball bat battered."

When everyone had received the shots, the company was mustered, the platoons formed, and it was off to pick up dummy rifles. From there, "the grinder," or exercise area, was the site for the next daily activity.

Can any boot forget the rifle drill of "butts, muzzles, butts, chest?" The agony produced by swinging those rifles with so grossly abused, needle injected arms was excruciating. A question could come to mind regarding the enemy: Was it the Japanese, or the navy?

Rifle drill was followed by semaphore drill ... "Able, Baker, Charlie, Dog," et cetera, during which each arm was swung to the appropriate position to indicate the letters of the alphabet. Then push-ups and squat-thrust exercises were ordered. As was always the case, there were those who goofed off as much as possible during these and most other activities.

Many lessons were learned on the grinder. The navy actually did know what it was doing. The first moment of the activity truly was torture, but the following minutes became progressively easier. The harder a person worked during the arm activities, the less pain he suffered later on. The goof-off experts prolonged their agony into the following twenty-four to thirty-six hours. Every officer and man had gone through the same injections and someone had discovered that strenuous activity mitigated the pain in a comparatively short time. Even those who had not endured hard physical contact, found they could fight and function through such discomfort, when necessary. They found that they could "tough it out."

The boots dreaded the thought that the navy would subject them to the trials of the obstacle course, but that was their next challenge. At the conclusion of the course was a thirty-foot-long barrier of 150-pound sandbags. Each bag was suspended on lengths of chain that left about ten inches of space around it. The only way to complete the course was to use arms and shoulders to bull one's way through. This was difficult enough without having recently finished the series of inoculations.

The previous evening, Danny and half a dozen other boots had pooled their ignorance. They concluded that knowledge, skill, and necessary techniques for taking the obstacles, were all important if they hoped to beat their chief on the obstacle course. They needed to be close enough to their commander to watch how each obstacle should be taken. By concentrating their attention on how the chief ran each obstacle, they were less aware of their discomfort.

Daily recreational passes were issued. Danny and two other boots listed their destination as the obstacle course. "Why do you want to go there?" the company commander asked.

"We want to see if we can develop the skills and fitness needed to give you a real challenge. Obviously no one has so far."

"So you want to kick the old man's ass? Well, I'll go with you and we'll see if I can help you learn some of the techniques."

"You want us to beat you?"

"Any instructor or teacher worth his salt, wants his students to excel."

The trick with the cargo net was to contact as few rungs as necessary while climbing, bellying over the top, and descending still under complete control. The ship passageway and ladder obstacle required timing, and coordinated use of arms and legs when racing up one set of ladders, swinging through hatches, and then down the other set of ladders. The technique had to be learned and practiced, and the chief demonstrated and instructed.

"I'll go slowly so you can see how your hands and arms lead your feet and legs." They would practice taking each obstacle until they became coordinated and efficient. The course required

323

speed, endurance, strength, coordination, technique, natural ability, and an almost obsessive desire to improve.

It was obvious to the boots that their company commander had been a good competitive athlete even though he was smaller in stature than many who were under his command. Charles observed, "At first I didn't realize that our chief really wants us to beat him, because he abhors the thought of being beaten. One thing's for sure, he's not going to roll over and play dead for us. We're his first to command through boot camp. He wants his chief's rating and that depends on how well our company performs on all aspects of our training. Let' support him."

The first platoon was composed of recent high school graduates from the Pacific Coast states, and this included Danny. The second platoon was made up of high-school-age fellows, as well as a remarkable number of men in their late twenties and into their mid-thirties. Most of them came from Arkansas, Oklahoma, Texas, and other southern states.

During the train ride from various home areas to boot camp, most recruits had established a recognition factor involving geographic familiarity and accent. When they came together at boot camp, everyone was seeking a level of security. Prejudice was rampant. Okies and Arkies would put each other down, but joined together to form a core of regional solidarity representing the solid South. These men ranged from "hicks from the sticks," to men with brilliant minds, as well as some fine athletes. In that respect, they were little different from men from other regions of the United States, except for so many older men.

During their first few days in boot camp, those southern boots were more interested in refighting the Civil War than getting on with the war against Japan. They didn't have much opposition from those "damn Yankees" from the West Coast. That war among the states was too remote in time and location for the West Coast boots to be overly concerned about it. The North had won and the western part of the nation had not been a battlefield nor even deeply involved. They were just territories that represented about half of the landmass of the current nation.

The recruit company commander was selected from the southern group. Bushburger was his name. Allegedly he had attended a military school instead of a public high school. Simply being chosen to command made him hateful. He had done nothing to distinguish himself from the other boots. In fact, his appearance was less than impressive. He carried a layer of lard around his body, even his face. This had the effect of making his eyes squinty, and he was referred to as "pig eyes." Pimples ravaged his face and shoulders. His high-pitched, squeaky voice lacked any suggestion of authority or self-assurance.

About halfway through the second week of training, Bushburger supervised the early-morning muster. Following usual procedure, the company commander then took over to proclaim the scheduled activity for the day. Having done that, he ordered, "Bushburger, front and center with all your gear."

There stood Bushburger with his sea bag packed. "Why are you leaving this company, Bushburger? Speak up. This company and the neighboring companies need to hear you."

Bushburger mumbled, but he could not be heard.

"Speak up, Bushburger. Tell us why," and he whacked him across his ample backside with a piece of line, or rope.

"Well, I got caught."

"Hear that, men? He got caught. Tell us what you got caught doing."

The weak voice reply was, "Playing with myself."

The line again made a resounding whack. "Speak up!"

"Playing with myself."

"What part of yourself?"

Finally, in a loud and high-pitched voice, Bushburger virtually shouted, "I got caught jacking off in the head, but everyone else does it. Why pick on me?"

Bushburger departed to what a blind man might think of as a clapping of hands, but the noise was a result of a circle being formed by one hand impacting the palm of the other hand ... a mocking symbol of masturbation. A lesson in humiliation had been presented along with the imperative lesson not to get caught.

At morning muster, the company commander spoke to those under his command. "Two incidents happened yesterday. First, you witnessed the Bushburger departure. That is of little consequence to you or the navy. The second gives me as great a sense of pride as the first gave me a sense of disgust. Men, I've been waiting over two years for someone to beat me on the obstacle course, and it finally happened. I'm proud of these three men." Danny and his two training partners, one from Oklahoma and the other from California, were summoned forward for recognition. "Youth will be served, provided it is combined with training, dedication, and knowledge. The navy will provide challenges for all of you, both physical and mental. When you apply yourselves, you will become better than your teachers. These three men will be exempt from all extra duty and watch assignments for the remainder of their time in boot camp."

Recreational time was extremely limited. Hand-washing laundry, writing letters home, or spending a few minutes to read *Rocks and Shoals,* the manual of navy regulations, were considered suitable activities. Time available was usually forty-five minutes. What almost every serviceman yearned for was extra sack time, but additional sleep was not part of the "Navy Way," a term that was becoming increasingly familiar to the boots.

Even though they had regular exercise periods on the "grinder," Danny continued his routine of pull-ups, push-ups, leg lifts, bar dips, et cetera, that he had done since childhood. The company commander also allowed him to practice his knife throwing in a special activities area.

Two trips to the rifle range confirmed that kids who grew up with a rifle available for "plinking around" did not automatically make expert marksmen, but the general standard was much better than that of service personnel who did not have such opportunities. Less time and expense were needed to develop combat readiness. Danny was one of a group of fourteen chosen for special rifle training. But the navy made no pretext of making riflemen out of their seamen.

Rivalry among the services existed, even during wartime. The physical training needed to be an efficient marine, was considerably different from those essential to be a top-quality sailor. Without any doubt, the marines' physical conditioning was far tougher than that of the navy. A turret gunner or an engine room mechanic doesn't need the types of skills and physical competence required for a good jungle fighter.

Both branches of the service tried to provide realistic training for the jobs their personnel were expected to perform. The same could be said for the army, air force, and coast guard. A good ship-based navigator did not need to be an expert, or even be modestly competent as a rifleman. By the same token, a battle station four decks down in the engine room with temperatures at 120-plus degrees and no possible escape if the ship went down, requires its own form of stamina, physical and mental toughness, and courage.

A good marine needed to be trained as a tough and aggressive fighter. In most cases they were. Naval personnel, who delivered marines to Pacific islands, were happy to set them ashore and get the hell out of there. Many sailors voluntarily left their landing ship to help off-load equipment and supplies and assist wounded back aboard, but they were not riflemen. With luck, they and their ship would return to sea.

A universal failure among the military could be attributed to lack of respect for other branches of service and the jobs they were required to perform.

To foster desirable appreciation for the marines, naval personnel arranged for a special advanced training squad from the marine base to give the boots a demonstration of combat tactics. To perform well required self-confidence and perhaps realistic arrogance.

Expert rifle marksmanship was demonstrated, and most boots believed the navy did not require enough time and effort at the rifle range.

Combat bayonet techniques were demonstrated with the bayonet in the hand as well as with it attached to the rifle. Navy personnel were happy not to be the enemy.

Close-order marching drills brought cheers from the observers. One boot commented, "That has about as much to do with fighting as the marching band has to do with the score of a football game."

The marines did calisthenics, ran the navy obstacle course, and engaged in hand-to-hand combat. They were good at everything they did, and navy personnel showed their admiration.

Then a cocky marine corporal spouted off, "If you little sailor boys want to toughen up, you'd better transfer to the marines and we'll make men out of you, if anyone can. We will be happy to take on any of you in any challenge you would like."

From Danny's company came the comment, "Too bad Bushburger isn't here." This summoned a wave of laughter throughout the company.

That blatant disrespect was too much for Danny's company commander. He replied, "Pick your best three for the obstacle course including yourself. Two of my men and I will run along with you." Danny was not included. It was navy, 1, 2, and 3. The forty-plus-year-old company commander led the way.

Graciously, the commander said, "You marines made a good showing and we understand that this course is different from yours. This one is included in our navy training. The outcome would likely be reversed if we were using your course."

Then Danny was called forward, and the company commander asked, "Sailor, have you ever handled one of these bayonets before now?"

"No, sir."

The commander handed one to Danny and the young man felt the balance and weight. "Do you think you could do something with that weapon?"

"Yes sir!"

Bayonets and knives, ranging from butcher knives to knives from the mess hall were spread out and a variety of targets were placed in the performance area. Screwdrivers were also mixed in among the knives. Although it was news to Danny, it was obvious that the company commander had prepared a response or two for the challenges he had anticipated.

The bayonets were larger, heavier, and far clumsier to handle than any knife Danny had ever thrown. Yet he had been committed to the challenge. Multiples of two knives penetrated deeply into each target from a variety of ranges and they had been thrown with both left and right hand and from standing, lying, and crouching positions. The reaction was explosive and predictable. Even his boot camp buddies were unaware of Danny's knife-throwing skills.

"Now for a little hand-to-hand combat," the company commander suggested. Danny stood there, a questioning look was on his face, and an index finger pointed to himself as if to ask, "Who, me?" However, in his mind the *A Way* training he had received from Father Watanabe asserted itself ... base, balance, inner tranquillity, leverage, and reaction.

A marine stepped forward to accept the challenge the company commander had presented. "How do you want it, swabby?" the marine asked as he moved in on Danny. About the only obvious thing Danny did was to relax as if nothing would happen. The marine attacked with speed and energy, all of which helped propel him upward, over, and down on the flat on his back with the wind knocked out of him.

A second marine stepped forward and said, "Stupid attack, Jason," to his buddy who was beginning to collect himself. The second marine circled, feinting, starting to attack and then withdrawing in order to figure out Danny's defense and offense.

Danny simply stood there as if he were ignoring the marine. He didn't even bother to keep the attacker in front of him, only casually keeping him from being directly behind. The lack of concern angered the marine, and he finally initiated an ill-advised attack. He, also, was launched following a similar pathway that Jason had taken. Danny stood there, as if he were waiting for grass to grow on asphalt.

A third marine came out, fists clenched, and assuming a boxer's stance. This was familiar to Danny from the days when Jimmy and Ted had started trying to teach him boxing. Danny didn't raise a hand. The boxer moved within range and flicked a piston-like series of left leads that missed, because Danny moved his head as if it were on a pivot. A heavy right was launched for Danny's solar plexus. This punch made contact with Danny's right forearm, which swept it by his body and partially turned the boxer. Danny stepped slightly to the right and his right arm snaked around the boxer's neck, the right forearm across the boxer's jaw, grasped his own left forearm, and the left hand went to the back of the boxer's head. The Japanese Death Lock was now in place and the leverage was so great Danny could easily have broken the struggling marine's neck.

In fact, the boxer struggled so fiercely, Danny was afraid the marine might break his own neck. Danny dropped the right forearm down to cut across the right side of the marine's neck. The hold became a Carotid Artery Choke. Within thirty seconds the marine was unconscious on his feet. Danny set him down gently and released the pressure.

The blood surged back to the boxer's brain and he sat there in a semi-stupor wondering what had happened to him. Finally he staggered to his feet and said, "I thought I was dying."

Danny made his first comment since the combat started ... just two words, "You were."

This was the end of the "performances." Danny's boot camp company commander spoke out once again. "None of our men knew, until they marched here, that they would be treated to the fine performances by our marine guests, or that they would be invited to participate.

"But we must give credit where credit is due. These boots were not trained to perform as they did by the navy. A challenge was issued to them three weeks ago to master the obstacle course. Three individuals accepted the challenge. They used their own free time to reach the level you have observed. You saw two of the three run that obstacle course. The third participated in knife throwing and the hand-to-hand combat demonstrations.

"The knife throwing and hand-to-hand combat techniques you observed were a result of individual initiative, and training, prior to entering boot camp. Where they came from, frankly, I don't have the slightest idea. But they represent a small part of what is right in this country we serve ... individual initiative and dedication."

The petty officer continued, "I believe I can speak for every man here and our countrymen, when I say that we honor and respect our brothers in arms, the United States Marines. We are proud to serve with them and, by God, we sure as hell are happy to have them with us, rather than against us."

The marine corporal stepped forward. "I shot off my mouth, made a fool of myself, and dishonored my fellow marines. No excuses offered. It will not happen again. Our sincere respect is offered to the United States Navy and to the people of this nation."

Ten navy companies of about 250 men each had been watching the exhibition. When they assembled and marched away, crispness and pride were evident in their steps and body language, which had not been there before.

During that night Danny rushed from his bunk to the head, choking back a load of vomit. He staggered around, wretched his stomach completely empty, and passed out on the deck of the barracks on his way back to his bunk. That was where the guard on watch found him. He called the other guard, and they carried Danny to his bunk and put him in it.

Danny staggered around after a fitful night. A blinding headache and distorted vision made it difficult for him to walk. People's heads seemed to change shapes in front of his eyes. Heads became contorted sideways into oblong comic strip representations. The morning muster was held.

"Anyone for sick call?" This was the standard procedure and there were those who were suspected of malingering in order to get out of physically demanding duty.

Two boots, who had been steadying Danny on his feet, stepped forward. The commander took one look and said, "Take him to sickbay right now! Take him directly to the doctor, do not, NOW HEAR ME, DO NOT WAIT IN LINE!" Another boot was being escorted to sick bay in the same manner as Danny. He went to the doctor on the right side of sickbay and Danny went to the left side. Both doctors spoke the same two words. *"Ambulance now!"*

43

San Diego Naval Hospital

Two stretchers were loaded into the ambulance: Danny on the left side and the other boot on the right. It was a red-light run all the way. During that ambulance ride, Danny went in and out of sessions involving weird shapes, bizarre dreams, and strange exhilaration that seemed to follow the wail of the siren as its pitch changed. A persistent headache and developing backache added to the unreality of the situation.

There were several sections to the hospital. The two stretchers were unloaded at a section, which was posted, ISOLATION The wards within the isolation unit were further segregated according to disease. Danny was taken from the left side of the ambulance to the closest ward. His ambulance companion was taken from the ambulance to the other ward. Each ward was posted MENINGITIS!"

Two medical programs were being undertaken, one traditional, and the other experimental. Dan was placed in the experimental ward, which was proving to be remarkably successful with a death rate of less than 10 percent. Later, Danny heard rumors that more than 50 percent of those who received traditional treatment were dying.

Many memories were not fully formed during the first days in that ward. Danny remembered being flat on his stomach stripped naked and having a buxom blonde pinning his legs down on the table. Two other nurses were anchoring his arms and a fourth was lying across his buttocks. Two doctors were giving orders and probing up and down Danny's back.

A small pinprick was vaguely felt and then Danny became progressively numb and he lost awareness of the cushion of the buxom nurse's breasts on his legs. His mind continued to wonder, "Why am I naked with all these women here?" But he didn't care.

It had been reassuring to be aware of the nurse's presence. At least that constant comfort had not abandoned him. A second pinprick was followed by the awareness of friction along his spinal column that seemed as if it would go through him and into the table where he was lying. But there was no pain and the backache had abated.

Later, but he didn't know how much later, Danny was aware that his butt was being used as a pincushion, and that he had a gaggle of pills to swallow. There was some talk about sulpha drugs, penicillin, and vitamins. Danny didn't know if these were medications he was being given or not. But he did know he was feeling much better.

One arm was strapped to a board and fluid was being dripped into a vein near the inside of his elbow. He remembered asking the buxom blond nurse if she could give all the shots on the same side of his butt. He wanted to have one side to lie on that would be comfortable. The shots produced a deep ache that felt as if it were a bruise.

Danny was unaware of time-related factors. There seemed to be no day or night. There was no memory of going to the toilet—no bedpans, no flasks, and no trips to "go on his own." Meals were not served, but he wasn't hungry. His was a world consisted of needles, pills, and disorientation. Then there was a new memory, a bed bath. His face and ears were washed. Then his neck, armpits, and back received attention. The nurse skipped to his feet and legs and washed them. She handed the washcloth to Danny and smilingly ordered, "You finish the rest."

A time came when Danny became aware that there was a wall clock in the ward. He wondered why it was not a twenty-four hour clock. The navy was supposed to keep time on a twenty-four hour basis ... none of that silly A.M. and P.M. business. How could one tell if it were day or night?

Later, Danny noticed that the top two buttons of the nurse's "V-neck" uniform were unbuttoned. Deep cleavage and lovely mounds were visible. His eyes followed her every movement as she leaned forward, straightened the sheets on the bed, and generally fussed over him. Danny was aware of a level of excitement in the pit of his stomach, and a little lower down as well. The nurse observed the beginnings of an erection.

She was delighted and said, "You really are much improved. You will be well enough to leave us within a few days." Then she commented to the doctor, "He is attentive, alert, and his eyes focus clearly now." She smiled and buttoned the top of her uniform.

Patients in this ward asked what was wrong with them. A vague response told him what he already knew, "You have been sick with a headache, backache, and dizziness." Later they were told that it was spinal meningitis, but it was not classified beyond that.

Danny felt a level of guilt for using doctor time and hospital space, and contributing absolutely nothing to the war effort. He was a liability instead of an asset.

Following his initial recovery in the San Diego Naval Hospital, Danny hand-carried his assignment and personnel papers to what was called the "Parkside Hospital." When departing, the doctor said, "You are the lucky one, the other fellow who came in with you in that ambulance didn't make it. You were the last two who confirmed that the experimental treatment for spinal meningitis is no longer experimental. What you received will be our standard from now on."

The Parkside Hospital had been the scene of a World's Fair and Exhibition about thirty years earlier. It had become what essentially served as a holding area where marine and naval personnel were assigned when they did not need conventional hospitalization and yet were not considered fit for regular service or discharge. It was a recuperation area adjacent to the San Diego Zoo. Daily zoo parties were conducted to that extraordinary facility. Bing Crosby, Bob Hope, Don Ameche, and other Hollywood personalities of that era hosted busloads of military personnel at the Del Mar race track. Transportation and entry were provided without charge. Hollywood personalities frequently served as hosts and hostesses to the hospital outpatients.

The huge barracks in which Danny was billeted was filled with rows of double-decker bunks crowded in end to end. Most of the men housed there were marines who had survived Guadalcanal, Iwo Jima, Okinawa, and other notoriously deadly Pacific island engagements. Danny felt as if he were an intruding impostor among men who truly were heroes and victims of war. The living hell they had endured often escaped from the confines of shattered minds and bodies. Nighttime screams of terror and pain were common, but no one complained about the noise. No nation was equipped to mitigate this turmoil. At times, it appeared as if the dead heroes were the lucky ones. Danny could do nothing other than to feel compassion and express his deep appreciation.

A particularly heartwarming incident happened the last day of July at about two in the morning. A huge roar of joyous noise awoke everyone. The lights were flipped on and a marine was racing up and down the aisles of the barracks shouting, "Look! *Look! Look!* I'm alive again, I'm *alive* again!" He was displaying a rather modest-sized erection.

The full extent of the story was not known, but a report indicated grenade fragments had ripped through his hip and groin. Extensive surgery had saved the marine's life, but had left him impotent. Fellow marines did their very best to help him during recovery stages. They took him on liberty in the Philippines where he was stationed. He was introduced to scores of local women, who were among the world's most appealing-looking, kindhearted, and enthusiastically responsive women. He simply could not respond.

He had become increasingly depressed and was transferred to the Parkside Hospital. He retreated into a world of noncommunication. For nearly two months he had not said a word. Now members of various marine divisions surrounded their fallen companion and rejoiced with him, that he had risen from the dead. He gripped his precious erection, agonizingly called for a nonexistent woman, and then started stroking himself. In a few minutes his efforts were rewarded with some twitching, throbbing, and finally ejaculation. "It works. *It works*," he cried. And he did cry, but not alone.

Renewed hope and vitality surged throughout the barracks. The mute victim had become a vocal winner. Two-hundred-plus men were also better, more willing and able to contemplate their own future. They had all shared the burden of his anguish, and his personal resurrection became a cause for group celebration.

Each man was better prepared to face the day. The marines billeted in that barracks experienced victory without having to kill enemies and without having to face death again.

It was in the company of these marines that Danny felt a flood of sympathy and modest understanding for what they had done, endured, and what they represented. A few marines started using Danny as a sounding board for some of their concerns and fears. They no longer felt invincible or invulnerable. They knew the indiscriminate and impersonal nature of combat. Their bodies had been violated by pieces of metal and, in some cases, by fire. Some war victims had been inundated by blood and body parts of friend and foe as well as their own.

"We are not cowards, but we don't want to go back. Mainland Japan is on the horizon and we don't want to be there. We've done our share; let someone else do the next one. God forgive me, but I don't want to recover and then be sent back to the Pacific. The flyboys over Germany did their time in hell and had the chance of going home after a set number of missions. I figure every day on Iwo should count as a flying mission. We are in the USA, and they should let us stay here. I don't want to recover until they are ready to discharge me." These were some of the feelings that were expressed.

"I was hit in the head and before I passed out I saw an eyeball in my lap. I remember wondering if it had come from me or some other unlucky bastard."

"We were loading one corporal onto an LSM and he wouldn't let go of an arm that was clutched to his chest. He thought it was his ... but he still had both of his own."

The accounts were gruesome and agonizingly real. Danny had the luxury of being able to quit listening and go elsewhere. For the combat victims, their experiences were like a loop film, which played endlessly on the projection screen in their mind until someone or something turned off the projector in their brain.

When Danny resumed his own personal fitness program, he was dismayed to find how really weak and out of condition he was. A few of the marines from the huge barracks joined him in the fitness program. They were advised that a proper gym was available. At that same time, Danny's sea bag and his belongings caught up with him, including his throwing knives.

Danny found that a half-mile run required an enormous amount of effort, and that thirty push-ups taxed his capabilities. He then realized how ill he really had been.

More marines joined the physical program. Soon, over a hundred men from the barracks began recreational swimming in the huge outdoor pool. Many of these men had been isolated personalities. Danny wondered if their bunks had become their foxhole of security. No officer or noncom was going to order them away into danger. These men had proven their bravery. It was not a question of valor. They had been pushed beyond that fragile line. They were now voluntarily venturing out into a world of recreation, which literally was "re-creation."

For some of the men, swimming and zoo parties were their first voluntary post-trauma activities. At that time they didn't know that *their* war was over. Combat had done to them all it was going to do. They were waiting to reach as nearly a complete level of recovery as possible. Then they would be discharged.

Half a dozen of the men were career marines. They were serious about knife throwing as an extension of their military preparedness to meet all emergencies. They followed Danny's instructions and learned basic techniques and they would become competent with dedicated practice. A bayonet proved to be a clumsy throwing weapon, but they were determined to master it.

"We could have used you on Iwo, but we are glad you didn't have to do that bitch." Such words signaled comradeship that made Danny feel included. It was the ultimate compliment.

Entertainment at the Parkside Hospital included nighttime outdoor movies. On August 7, 1945, the night's film was interrupted by the announcement that a new type of bomb, an atomic device, had been dropped on Hiroshima with particularly destructive effects.

According to Japanese sources, the continuous raids over the homeland by B-29 bombers, plus air force and navy fighter aircraft, had created total havoc among systems of transportation and communication. Because of that, it was three days before Japanese officials started arriving in Hiroshima to assess the extent of the destruction caused by just one bomb.

Devastation was so enormous that officials had no means

of comprehending what had happened. Rescue workers, who had no concept of the danger, were accumulating lethal doses of radiation. Even years later, the total physical impact of that single atomic weapon would not be known. However, military records, which were released immediately after the war, listed the Hiroshima death total to be 78,150. An additional 51,408 were injured or missing. In this case, missing included an unknown number whose bodies were so totally consumed in the explosion and fireball that no traces were found. By the time radiation poisoning had taken its toll, the death toll would increase enormously.

But before this information could be accumulated and understood, the Nagasaki bomb was detonated. The date was August 10, 1945. Listed casualties included 23,753 dead and 43,020 injured. It was understood that, at best, these figures were only informed estimates. Many Japanese sources openly challenged the official figures and expressed conviction that the number of killed and injured was double or triple those released.

At that time, no one really understood the impact this would have on the world, but every action that would lead to the defeat of Japan was applauded among Allied Forces and nations. Then the world waited. The United States had demonstrated its ability to bomb any target in Japan it selected, and to do so almost unopposed in the sky.

Immediate postwar Japanese Army documents indicated that 198,961 people had been killed by air attacks on the homeland using conventional incendiary and explosive devices. An additional 271,617 had been injured, and 8,064 were listed as missing. It was emphasized that these numbers represented only those killed, injured, and missing by *conventional bombing and strafing attacks.*

Five days after the Nagasaki bombing, Japan accepted the surrender terms. The jubilation in the marine barracks where Danny was stationed was surprisingly introspective.

Groups of men who had invaded and fought on Saipan, Guam, Guadalcanal, Okinawa, Iwo Jima, and other islands questioned, and tried to assess, the importance of their part of the war. Three or four men would start talking. Others would join in, and before long there would be as many as thirty men assembled, but some only listened. Others wanted to do nothing but talk. Then the numbers dwindled as individuals drifted away.

Danny sat and listened. The only thing he offered was his attention and regard. Finally, one sergeant said, "Every time we start one of these bull sessions, I tell my stories and accounts about Guam. You've all heard them enough times to tell them word for word. And I'm still right where I was about understanding this damned war." Most heads nodded in agreement that they had done about the same thing. "Maybe we need a new perspective on the whole thing." Again heads nodded, and one marine said, "Hey Navy, you've always said you weren't there so have no right to comment, but do us a favor and give us a different 'take' on the war." Again, his fellow marines nodded their heads.

"Well, okay, but throw me out of here if I start getting out of line. You guys did the fighting and bleeding while I was in high school, boot camp, and then the hospital. You know, and I've been listening, but I also read a lot, which may give me a different perspective. Let me start out by expressing my admiration and gratitude for..."

"Yeah, we already understand that by the way you act around us. But get to the point."

"Let's start at the end of the war and go backward. We know that the Hiroshima and Nagasaki bombs convinced Hirohito and other Japanese officials to surrender. The first question might be, 'Why didn't the brass use those atomic weapons in the first place and make the entire island hopping unnecessary?' We need to realize that the first atomic weapons test took place at Alamagordo in New Mexico on July 16, 1945. Twenty-two days later, Hiroshima was leveled and three days after that it was Nagasaki's turn."

"Yeah, but why did they fart around those twenty-two days?" A murmur of approval of that question spread through the group, which was increasing in number.

"I can give you some information, but you will come to your own conclusions as to why so much delay. Scientists in New Mexico needed some time to evaluate what had happened. They found that steel beams had been vaporized and that temperatures created were said to exceed those found at the center of the sun! Some scientists estimated the explosive force exceeded the combined power of all the bombs dropped on Hamburg during the entire war."

"So why the delay?"

"The decision about deploying such a weapon was a tough call. President Truman requested expert scientific information and opinions. Many of the men who helped produce the bomb strongly objected to its use. World diplomats were consulted about the topic."

"It's easy to sit around and talk when your ass isn't on the line," one marine declared. A murmur of approval spread throughout the group.

"Agreed! President Truman certainly understood that. It seemed likely that the whole world would argue the point for hundreds of years to come. The sign posted in his office stated, THE BUCK STOPS HERE. It was his decision, and this time his ass was on the line when he made that call. But you fellows had secured pieces of the Japanese Empire before the first atomic explosion took place. Let me emphasize that before the Hiroshima and Nagasaki bombs were exploded, scientist were not certain that those bombs would work."

One marine commented, "I'm damned glad they did. From what we saw on Iwo and other islands in the Pacific, the war on the Japanese homeland would have been incomprehensibly devastating to us and them." Almost unanimous agreement was expressed.

"You've been in the service long enough to understand logistical problems when it comes to getting things done. The weapons had to be produced, organized, and packed for shipping. Your favorite transportation company, the navy, had to deliver them. As you know, it was a long and time-consuming sea voyage. Then favorable weather conditions were desirable in order for maximum effect and evaluation to take place over the target area. Of course, there was even the question of whether or not that device would work the second time. It is redundant to say that both bombs worked even though they were of different types.

"A B-29 delivered the bomb, and it flew from the island some of you helped take from the Japanese. That may answers the question of whether or not what you did was worth the cost.

"But let's back up even farther. What happened to the twenty-two-thousand-plus Japanese who were on Iwo Jima? How many were killed or killed themselves, and how many survived? Official numbers indicate that less than two hundred lived. They were the men who were too incapacitated to fight or die at their own hands. But the Japanese would not surrender. You are a part of the 15,800 US wounded and some of your personal buddies were among the 4,800 who were killed. That works out to six hundred of our forces dead per square mile of Iwo. The Japanese paid 2,625 men killed per square mile, and they lost the island. To make the numbers more vivid, nearly six Japs and one American died for every football-field-sized piece of land. Then you would need to add four Americans wounded on the same field. That is a hell of a price to pay for eight square miles of volcanic ash and cinders. And what good did it do? Of course, you who did Guadalcanal, Guam, Okinawa, or any of the other islands have also been wondering about that, if I understand you correctly."

"Right! The brass could have let the navy play around in the Pacific bathtub until the big bombs were used and put an end to everything," one corporal insisted.

A sergeant commented, "We were fighting a conventional war, and even many of the top brass didn't know about the atomic bombs. They were just theoretical weapons until they were exploded, and even then scientists were not sure they would work if dropped from a plane. B-17 and B-24 bombers were flying from Chinese and other bases, but the B-29 was thought to be the best plane for bombing Japan and some of the islands were better bases for that operation.

"Statistics show that 2,251 Superforts made emergency landings on Iwo Jima. It was highly unlikely they would have been able to return to Saipan or Guam. If Iwo Jima had not been available for landing, 24,761 airmen would have been lost at sea along with their aircraft. Both were desperately needed to deliver the war to the Japanese homeland. In addition, the airfields you took and helped re-build, provided fighter bases that were within range of Japan so the 29s had a fighter escort.

341

By military reckoning, Iwo was worth the cost. This would have been even more so if the war had not been terminated by the atomic bombs."

One angry private challenged, "Are you saying an airman's life is more valuable than a marine's?"

"Of course not, Eddie," one of the marines commented. "He's saying that in terms of numbers, the deaths of under five thousand marines and soldiers on Iwo saved the lives of five times that many fliers. And remember, those numbers would have increased dramatically if the big bombs hadn't been dropped. That's the way the military makes their calculations."

Danny continued, "Up until the big bombs were dropped, you knew that the Japs were not going to give up. You saw it on all the islands."

A marine interrupted, "Could you speak up, some of us in the back can't hear." Virtually every marine in the place had become involved.

"Those of you who participated in the Okinawa struggle also did more than your share. The Japanese listed their loss of military personnel at 120,000 killed and 42,000 civilians died. For the first time during the island campaigns, a significant number of prisoners, 10,755 of them, were taken when they surrendered.

"Our losses at Okinawa include 12,500 dead, and 35,500 wounded. The US Navy lost 36 ships sunk and 368 damaged. Add to that, 768 US aircraft were lost, all in that campaign.

"The air force's land-based planes and the navy's carrier-based planes were bombing and shooting up the mainland of Japan trying to soften it up for what was thought to be the inevitable invasion. We know the army would be deeply committed, but do you believe for one second that the marines would sit on the sideline and say that you'd already done your share?"

A murmur went through the barracks. "Right," one of the marines said. "Many of us have been notified that we will have thirty days' home leave and then are scheduled to return to active duty in the Pacific."

"The dropping of the two atomic bombs on Japan, and the subsequent surrender is now a fact in history. During your lifetime and thereafter, there will be many who will condemn the use of the atomic bombs as wanton revenge on a nation of people who were ready to surrender. Others may suggest that regular warfare was leading to Japan's surrender.

"You men, perhaps better than almost any others, understand one part of the Japanese war mentality that existed at that time. There were the military and political leaders who were determined to punish the Americans to the maximum extent for the inevitable defeat of the island empire of Japan. They would fight to the last man, woman, and child. They were prepared to subject their homeland to the total devastation that would result.

"There will be those who would assert that Japan was a beaten nation and had nothing left with which they could fight. In support of their argument, they would conveniently discount the fact that the homeland defense army consisted of a million men. They were well trained and equipped. They were ready to defend their homeland with fanatical devotion. They would have had many tactical advantages including familiarity with the terrain and support by their fellow citizens. Additionally, there was no known reason to expect any nonmilitary personnel to cooperate with the invading army.

"Although carrier-based fighters and land-based bombers and fighters of the US military flew missions over Japan almost unopposed, a homeland air defense still existed. These were being held in reserve to repel the impending invasion.

"The Japanese Army had in reserve twenty-five hundred combat aircraft. Of these, sixteen hundred were kamikazes. The navy had fourteen hundred suicide fighters and bombers awaiting action. In total, they had 5,130 combat aircraft ready to engage the enemy, us. Even relatively slow and flimsy trainer aircraft could carry bombs on suicide missions, and be effective against landing craft. Would you care to speculate on the costs in American lives if as few as 10 percent of the kamikaze aircraft reached their targets? Think in terms of primary targets being troop transports and supply ships, which are poorly equipped to defend themselves.

"Do you have any reason to believe the Japanese defense of their homeland would be any less fanatical, heroic, dedicated, or tenacious than it had been in defense of Iwo Jima, Okinawa, or any of the other Pacific island fortresses?

"Japanese and American strategists were already aware of how effective the kamikaze aircraft were, although the American public was poorly informed. Additionally, thousands of small fishing boats could be used on suicide missions against small invasion craft.

"It was reported that every informed military and political person in Japan knew that overwhelming defeat was inevitable. The all-out defense of the islands would be little more than a delaying action, but the cost in terms of human life and suffering would be incalculable.

"Private Japanese sources say that orders had been given to the commanders of all of their prisoner-of-war camps to summarily execute all prisoners when the first enemy soldiers set foot on the Japanese homeland. If it had been up to you to deploy the A-bombs or continue with conventional welfare for additional months, what would your decision have been?"

That was a rhetorical question that each man could think about, and they probably would discuss it with their own special groups of friends.

A sergeant summed up his own thoughts: "The Japs knew they couldn't win the war, but they wanted to make it so expensive for the Americans that we would back away from unconditional surrender. My guess is they would have gone after the larger troop transports first of all. Tankers would have been logical targets as well. Most of the larger warships were too well compartmentalized to be sunk by one kamikaze hit, but transports and supply ships were less well defended and one well-placed hit could sink them. You know we were packed in transports like sardines in a tin can. When you realize that a .50-caliber bullet can rip right through a freighter's hull and those of most troop transports, you can understand how really vulnerable such ships were."

A marine corporal added, "You can bet your ass that the shores of Japan would have been awash with American bodies and military transports would have been coffins for thousands of 'dog faces' who couldn't get out of the locked compartments when they went down."

"And those of us who did get ashore alive would face a Japanese Army of a million men, plus support from virtually every civilian."

A private reasoned, "I figure we'd be lucky to achieve a one-to-one casualty ratio during the first months of the invasion, and all of us would find that an unacceptable statistic."

"If every person living in Hiroshima and Nagasaki dies as a result of the two bombs, invading Japan and defeating their army on their own soil would claim many times more Japanese civilian and military lives than that," a corporal calculated. I don't know where the estimate came from, but my unit was told that 25 percent of the total population of Japan would be killed or severely injured in conventional warfare before their inevitable surrender."

A chorus of voices offered other numbers. "I heard a number closer to twelve million Japanese casualties."

A medical corpsman offered, "Make that number closer to fifteen million because the medical infrastructure would be unable to cope with even a small percentage of the injuries."

"In any war, the major concern has always been the number of casualties your own forces take," Danny suggested.

"You've got that right, Navy! And we were told to expect up to a million American casualties before Japan surrendered. If it were up for a vote, I'm betting that all Allied military would vote to end the war with the two big bombs."

"I hate what this war took from me,"—one leg was missing—"but killing additional millions of Japs won't bring it back. I figure most of us are sick of killing and mutilating each other. The war is over, and it is time to get back to civilian life, Japs and Americans alike."

Note

Immediate postwar statistics have been challenged in later years. US losses on Iwo Jima are listed in some sources at 6,821 dead, 19,217 wounded, and 2,648 cases of combat fatigue. In total numbers, US casualties exceeded those of the Japanese. However, the number of Japanese killed was more than three times greater than American deaths. This was a horrible toll for both nations and represents the total madness of mankind that resorts to war as a means of arbitrating differences.

44

Greg's Iwo Jima Story

Marines were being transferred in and out of the Parkside Hospital barracks on a daily basis. A few were being sent back to active duty, but most were sent to centers to be discharged.

It was during Danny's first week there that a new marine, Greg, moved into the bottom bunk of the double decker Danny was using. Greg was unusually quiet and seemed to be lost in his own haunted world.

Medical personnel did not staff the barracks. In fact, there were only a couple of personnel available to check documents of those coming and going, and to point out available bunks. There was no duty roster for patients, and they were pretty much at liberty to come or go as they chose. Passes to leave the hospital grounds were issued to prevent difficulties with shore patrol personnel.

A few days after Greg arrived, Danny emptied his sea bag and was sorting through his gear. Everything was laid out on his bunk including his throwing knives.

"*Where the hell did you get those?*" Greg exploded and his self-imposed silence ended. He developed a nearly crazed look in his eyes. "The medics said I was around the bend. They treated me as if I were psycho when I told them about a guy who used knives like those. They just about had me convinced that they were right. But there was a man on Iwo who had knives just like the ones you have right there. I know they are the same." Then Greg drifted off into a world of suppressed memories.

Danny interrupted Greg's struggles with himself. "These knives are real and up to ten thousand of them were supposed to have been taken to the Pacific Theater by special army personnel."

"You said army! That's what this captain said. At least he

said he was an army captain, but he had no identification and no uniform." Greg lapsed into silence as if he were trying to resolve the conflict between what he knew to be fact and what others had told him. "They said what I claimed to have seen was impossible."

"I'm exceptionally interested in the account of your experiences on Iwo. I've reason to believe you about seeing throwing knives such as these. Maybe it will help if you start from the beginning about the invasion. Don't worry about what others said or told you. Trust your own memory, that's what interests me."

"As far as I know, all of us marines were, first of all, combat riflemen," Greg said. "I was trained to operate a Caterpillar with a dozer blade, but I was still a rifleman. Even marine fighter pilots were supposed to be competent riflemen.

"There were thirty-four of us and our construction equipment aboard LSM 266; *LSM* indicates 'Landing Ship Medium.' That flat-bottomed bitch heaved and rolled with every swell and we wondered how the sailors could stand being aboard, let alone perform their duties.

"Most of us were dog sick and the landing seemed as if it would be a relief. We didn't want to die, but drowning at sea seemed the worst way to do it. We had been trained to fight on the land. If we were going to die, we at least wanted to have a chance at the enemy.

"Anyone who thought of this Pacific island as being a tropical rain forest hadn't seen Iwo. It was volcanic cinders and ashes. Existing vegetation was mostly scrubby stuff that provided almost no cover. Mount Suribachi was the highest point on the island, and it was really only a six-hundred-foot-high hillock. The Japanese had over twenty-one thousand men on that island, and they had made it into a honeycombed fortress. We were the second wave of the Fifth Marine Division to hit Red Beach, which was on the southeastern side of the island. The Japs concentrated firepower on ships bringing in men and material. The brass said only light resistance was offered to repel those who reached the beachhead. Maybe so, but there were lots of dead guys floating in the water, and more of them dead on the beach. The corpsmen were busy trying to care for the wounded. I've got to give it to the crew of 266. They stayed there in that big beached whale and took on wounded for transfer to hospital ships that were well away at sea. The crew manning their single forty-millimeter gun was in action taking a little shooting practice at the lookout points on Suribachi.

"Anyway, when the bow gates opened up and the ramp splashed down, I had my little Cat under way. The beach sloped upward and then the island proper began at the top of a ridge that was about eight feet high. That's where the Japs' weapons were aimed. Everything that showed above the top was met with a hail of bullets. The two of us dozer operators, who came from 266, went in side-by-side and cut a ramp through that ridge. The dozer blades made a pretty good shield against rifle and machine-gun fire from straight on. The two of us had armored cabs. We couldn't see so well through the metal slits in the armor, but that armor gave us welcomed additional protection.

"A poor bastard from a different LSM didn't have the armored cab on his Cat and he was shot through the head. Along about a mile and a half to two miles of that beachhead, thirty thousand of us went ashore on February 19, 1945.

"I spotted some foxholes where Jap machine guns were mounted. I lowered the dozer blade and buried the suckers where they were. God help the poor buggers, because I went back and forth over their area rolling them over and over and tearing them to pieces. My destination was Airfield Number 1, which was only half a mile inland. By nightfall, our Fifth Marine Division had reached the western side of the island, which included the southern end of that airfield. The Fourth Marine Division was knocking on the eastern side of the same airfield. The fact was that with a total of fifty-one thousand military personnel on the island, the place was crowded. Then the Third Marine Division landed with about fifteen thousand more men! But there were bullets enough for every person on the island ... them and us. Christian wisdom says it is better to give rather than receive. That sure was the case there.

"Anyway, I didn't know what was going on anywhere but in my own little area. Maybe I bulldozed three or four such nests before heavy fire came in from the side. My engine sputtered and died. The enemy gunfire had holed the Cat's diesel tank and I ran out of fuel. All I could do was to hunker down in the cab and hope someone 'friendly' would come up from the beach pretty soon. Some of the Japs started taking aim at the slits in the cab armor, and the occasional slug rattled around inside, but I was lucky until one of them tagged me in my shoulder.

"Finally night came and I hoped it would be safe to try to reach the beach, but I could hardly walk. A light tapping on the cab of my bulldozer was followed by an American-sounding voice that said, 'You did a good job with your dozer, but it's time for you to get out of there, so open up.' So I asked, how was I supposed to know he wasn't an English-speaking Jap?"

"'What do you want me to do, quote World Series or football scores with you? Or maybe it would suit you to hear me talk Louisiana swamp-a-billy with you. You make up your mind, but I have a lot of killing to do tonight, and then find a place to hole up until tomorrow night. I'm spending no more time here.'"

"I opened up and there stood this man who wasn't much bigger than most Japs, but he was more bulky and muscular than I thought Japs would be. He was wearing no uniform, carried a funny-looking rifle, and a whole bunch of knives. It seemed as if he knew where every gun emplacement was located, and they weren't far apart. He helped me along and we'd make noise as we approached a machine-gun emplacement from the land side. A Jap would come out of hiding and say something. The man used his strange-looking rifle and shot the guy in the neck, but there wasn't much more noise than a guy trying to blow a fly away from his cup of coffee.

"A second Jap came out to see what was wrong with the first guy, and the American threw one of those knives from about fifteen feet and killed him without a sound. He put a finger to his lips to indicate that there was one more of the enemy in that particular emplacement. Pretty soon I heard a Jap talking, and when he received no answer, it sounded as if the guy started cussing a blue streak, and he came storming out. He was skewered with a knife for his effort. Three of the enemy had died and a part of the defense network broken. Then the guy, who said he was an army captain, retrieved his knives and entered their nest.

"'Come on in and have some food and water,' he invited. 'You may not like their food very much, but I've been living off the Japanese supplies ever since I came on this stinking little island almost six months ago.'

"The next thing he did was dismantle the machine gun and damage it so it couldn't fire. Then he followed the phone cord to where it joined the main line, and cut it. We weren't there for more than five minutes before he motioned for me to go with him. We circled around to nine more emplacements and he did the same thing each time. Some were manned with two soldiers and some with three. He knew just how many would be there, and he took care of all of them the same way. One was killed by a shot that was nearly silent and all others were killed with his knives. Each time we entered one of the Japs' emplacements, he told me a little about himself. He said he was Captain Jacobs, also known as Dead Eye Jake, a former sideshow knife thrower, snake charmer, exhibition boxer, wrestler, and now a special forces operative on detached service from the United States Army."

Danny was so excited he could hardly contain himself. But Greg was unloading a burden of memories to someone who believed him, so he didn't interrupt.

"It seemed funny when I saw him take out a little knife that was no longer than four inches in length and finish his morning shave. He said he had been interrupted during the day by bombardments from the naval batteries and aircraft. He had to keep clean-shaven, including his head, if he hoped to pass for one of the few Japanese civilians who inhabited the island.

"On the way to the eleventh emplacement, he suddenly forced me down behind a small bit of scrub vegetation. I had sense enough to keep quiet. Japanese soldiers were on the move to infiltrate American lines. They knew this would be their last mission. They hoped to kill as many of the enemy as possible before they were killed themselves. Well, the captain did the killing first. The enemy usually traveled in pairs and Jake used his silent rifle to kill one and a throwing knife to kill the second. There usually wasn't time enough to reload and shoot again.

"One time there was a group of five of the enemy and he shook his head. 'Too many for us.' When they were about fifty feet away, he sent one of his silent bullets to claim one of them. They split apart and crawled away. A second turned to retreat

350

in our direction, and was about to enter one of the emplacements we had visited. He paused to look in our direction and a second quiet messenger delivered its tidings of death. The five were now three and they also turned to retreat toward us. The remainder ducked into the first emplacements they found. Prior victims of Jake silent warfare occupied it. My companion said that in this game it is foolish to become too greedy. He went on to say that my buddies would take care of the majority of the opposition. His job was to make it a little easier, and to terrorize the Japs. He emphasized over twenty-one thousand brave and skilled enemy soldiers were on the island, and all of them planned to die there. They knew the strategic nature of that island to the defense of Japan, and the only way for them to keep it was to make it too costly in lives for American forces to take it from them. They were also determined to punish the Americans for every success we had.

"I suggested to Jake that we might booby-trap emplacements we had 'visited,' but Jake reminded me that there was a fifty-fifty chance that the next occupants might be Americans and those were unacceptable odds.

"We went on to the eleventh emplacement and for the first time I proved to be of some use. The first man was shot as usual, but two others came out at the same time. He killed one of them with his throwing knife. I had my bayonet in hand and was close enough to kill the third man before he could shoot one of us. It was lucky that I had stumbled and lurched right into the Jap, because I might have been too late getting to him otherwise.

"Jake commented, 'I'm getting sloppy. After the first shot, I should temporarily abandon the rifle, and arm myself with a knife in each hand.'

"By this time, my shoulder wound was bothering me a lot and I sprained my knee when I stumbled. I wasn't much concerned with the blood on my bayonet and put it away without wiping if off. Captain Jacobs said that during the months he had been on the island awaiting the invasion, he had been playing mind games with the Japanese military's sense of security. His rifle was air-powered and he used the slugs from Japanese ammunition to do most of his killing. Since his rifle made almost no noise and absolutely no flash, he could pick off one of the

351

enemy without anyone knowing where the shot came from. He had killed several hundred Japanese at night even before the invasion.

"I asked about the rifle and he told me the concept was nothing new. The Austrians used such a weapon during the Napoleonic Wars, except theirs fired a round slug. It had a large bladder enclosed in the rifle stock and it was filled with air by a pump that was incorporated in the rifle. Jake's air rifle could shoot five bullets before being pumped. But each bullet had to be hand-fed into the chamber. As he said, it was slow compared with the Gerand, Springfield, Mauser, or similar rifles, but it was both deadly and silent, which was ideal for his needs. The effective range was in excess of a hundred yards.

"He told me he had watched the installation of some of the Japanese communications system and figured ways to disrupt it. I was the first American he had talked with since he made his own private invasion months before we landed. At first he torched their aviation fuel supply depot at one of the airfields, but he decided that he had done that too soon. They had plenty of time to replace the facilities and fuel. He thought it was more of a nuisance to them than anything else. It also put them on alert, which made future operations more difficult.

"I asked him how he was able to hide out and eat for such a long period of time without being caught. He told me that he was lucky. Then he explained that the hundreds of fortifications were all supplied with food and water pending the time the defense of the island was imminent. Only a few of the outposts were manned on a regular basis. Supplies were rotated on a schedule and the military presumed that soldiers were helping themselves to snacks when they didn't want to wait until regular mealtimes. In view of the nature of their assignment, it was the least the homeland could do for them. Besides, he never took everything from any single emplacement. The Japanese operated on a predictable schedule, so he was able to eat and sleep without being at any unusual risk.

"A favorite activity was to shoot a tire of a plane that had just taken off. When the pilot returned for a landing or tried to land at another field, he would almost always ground loop because of the flat tire. Since the pilot didn't anticipate any problem, the consequences were usually disastrous to both plane and pilot. Frequently the crash resulted in a fire that destroyed evidence of possible sabotage. I asked him how many planes he had accounted for. He said he couldn't be sure because many of them landed at other bases, but that he had shot at the tires of over a hundred planes. He presumed he missed some of the time, but that he was quite accurate with his air rifle. He watched thirty-four planes crash land on tires he had shot.

"Then he said it was time for him to continue his project, and that I should make my way back to the beach. He set me off with an enemy rifle and my own bloody bayonet. He warned me that if I couldn't walk all the way to the beach area, I should stop off at one of the shelters where we had killed the Japs and wait. He cautioned me to do a lot of long-distance talking before exposing myself to possible gunfire. Nervous and trigger-happy marines might shoot before thinking.

"The fact was, I continued to lose blood, and I didn't get back to the beach. I didn't even get into an enemy foxhole. I passed out on the edge of one of them. That was where a marine squad found me. When I regained consciousness, medics were working on me and a squad was proclaiming me the greatest war hero since Sergeant York during World War I. They had come across more than a dozen Japanese positions where a Japanese rifle slug and a bayonet (knife) wound had killed the occupants. Yes, I had the Japanese rifle Captain Jacobs had given me, and my bloody bayonet.

"I tried to tell them about Captain Jacobs, but they claimed that I had just lost touch with reality. Maybe I had bled too much and had become delirious. They said it was common for a person to imagine divine intervention or help. The most convincing argument from the Marine Corps point was that no army personnel had set foot on Iwo before the marines. They even checked with army brass and they had no records to support my claim. Besides, they had seen how I had used my bulldozer to wipe out some enemy emplacements, and the corps wanted a hero. I was selected, nominated, and ordained. I don't mind being classified as a hero, but I don't want credit for what Captain Jacobs did, but I couldn't get anyone to believe that Captain Jacobs even existed."

353

Danny had listened with anxiety to Greg's account. "Did you hear anything about Captain Jacobs later on?"

"No, but then I was loaded back on good old 266 and taken out to a hospital ship. They told me my war is over. The sailors on that ship said they had been in and out of the beach area several times. I'd lost track of time but it seemed to me that I had spent a lifetime there. Actually, it was closer to twenty four hours. Without Captain Jacobs, many more marines would have spent the last day of their life on Iwo."

"Did he tell you anything about his background, or about a special training program taking place in a jungle area of Brazil?"

"Hey Danny! You did know the captain, didn't you? I'd forgotten about that. He mentioned that he was one of the original group that talked about organizing special forces to work in areas where jungle warfare was going to take place. He said he recruited about a thousand guys who had grown up in swamp and bayou areas of the Deep South. They were to serve in teams consisting of two and three men to pester the enemy and help invading forces succeed.

"Then he laughed at himself for taking on Iwo where the only things familiar to his training were the enemy and the tools of his trade, the air gun and his throwing knives."

"Well, I know your story is true. Look at this little knife! It is a duplicate of the one I made for Captain Jacobs to use as a razor. And the throwing knives he used had a Japanese chop mark on them. He told me he would leave one of those behind in a victim to convince the Japanese that one of their own men was the killer. I made the original of those knives and did the steel tempering on all of them. But tell me, how was Captain Jacobs managing the strain of killing so many people?"

"He said he vomited the first dozen or so times he killed a soldier. So did I when I saw the blood on my bayonet and on me. He reminded me that there were as many as twenty-two thousand Japanese soldiers on the island. At its largest dimensions, Iwo is about a mile and a quarter across and just over five miles in length. It has a total of less than eight square miles. He assured me that being a prisoner of war was not an option for the Japanese. They fought and won, or they fought until they died.

"I guess you know that the Japanese had been on Iwo for

years and had set up an interlocking network of defensive field gun positions throughout those eight square miles. These gun locations were supported by a huge array of machine-gun nests and shelters for riflemen. A key to the defense system was an excellent communication network. The island was pockmarked by hundreds of natural caves, and man-made tunnels connected some of the larger caves. It required direct hits to neutralize such facilities. An elaborate underground communication system connected many field gun and machine-gun emplacements.

"The captain left me with one sound piece of advice: Never disrespect the Japanese as people or as an enemy. Their value systems are different from ours, and far more demanding in terms of sacrifice. They place honor and duty above all other considerations. Our priority places much greater emphasis on life. Even the life of the enemy should be preserved, if possible. We would like to defeat the enemy, but still spare his life. But on Iwo, that was not our choice. We had to kill him because he would not surrender. We considered that our care for wounded prisoners followed the best of humanitarian considerations. We prided ourselves on being humane and considerate captors. The Japanese viewed a prisoner of war as an embarrassment and even a disgrace to his family and country. That applied to prisoners they took and their own military men who were taken prisoners."

Greg sat quietly for several minutes. "You know, Danny, I use the common term *Jap* for Japanese. The term virtually ensures segregated and disrespectful relationships with the enemy. But for Captain Jacobs, and now for me, *Jap* is a term that embodies respect for a man whose dedication and loyalty to the principles of his society are beyond reproach. We regret that we were forced to kill Japs. But, again, we had no choice. And I hate them for what they did to my country, my comrades, and to me."

"Yes," Danny commented, with appreciation for what Greg expressed, "and there was also that other side of Japanese reality when they took thousands of Korean girl children who were even less than ten years old, and placed them in "comfort stations" as prostitutes for soldiers on leave. And there was the Rape of Nanking during which, if we are to believe well-researched documents, almost every female from five years of age to ninety-plus was repeatedly raped by Japanese soldiers. Some of it may have been done as an expression of pent-up need or lust, but more probably it was a demonstration of total power, domination, and disrespect for the Chinese, who have been their enemies for centuries."

Danny thought of his Watanabe family and treasured the loving care and nurturing they had given him. It was nearly impossible for him to relate brutality in any form, with his family. The *A Way* training and philosophy he learned from them emphasized resolution of problems before confrontation, and the use of the least amount of force necessary, if conflict could not be avoided. In each case, it was essential to convey respect to one's opponent, or the problem would fester and continue to be a source of future antagonism and probable conflict.

Danny realized that the mission his friend Dead Eye Jake had undertaken on Iwo Jima was very little different from that of twenty-one thousand, or more Japanese who were on that island and tens of thousands more Japanese who were stationed on dozens of other islands surrounding their homeland. They expected their own deaths, and each had a mission to extract as high a price as possible from the enemy of their country. In the case of the Japanese ... and Dead Eye Jake, the odds were overwhelmingly against all of them.

Greg and Danny spent hours talking about Captain Jacobs and the effect he had on both of their lives. Each asked the same question repeatedly, "Is there a chance he survived?"

They concluded that for almost anyone else, the answer would be no. Well, yes, if he would join the regular forces, but out there on his own, he was a target for both sides. And yet, he was Captain "Dead Eye Jake" Jacobs.

A gaunt marine sergeant had been listening to the conversation between Danny and Greg from its beginning. He had been nodding his head in agreement with what had been said. The shoulder patch on his uniform identified him as belonging to the First Marine Division. "Yeah, that has to be the same man, only I met him on Guadalcanal. He said he was a captain in a special forces unit detached from the army. He and three other men had been landed on that bitch of an island a couple months before we invaded it, and that was August 1942. Each man had set up his independent area of operation. As Jake said, 'If captured, we were unable to give the Japs any information about the others.' Anyway, that's where I met him."

Greg knew the sergeant by the name of Donaldson and encouraged him to tell what he knew about Jake. Sergeant Donaldson had been in the Parkside Hospital for several months and was finally making adjustments to the reality that his personal war was over. Hesitantly he said, "I promised Jake I wouldn't talk about him because it could put him in danger, but I suppose it's okay now."

"Sure, man, but start easy. You could tell us a little about yourself first and work into the story," Greg suggested. "What part of the States are you from?"

I grew up near Indio, California, and ended up on Guadalcanal. What a change in climate and terrain that was! All I knew before arriving in the South Pacific was a hot desert climate and basic flatlands. Guadalcanal sounded like a tropical paradise to me with all the trees and everything green and beautiful. What a joke that was, but it wasn't funny. Everything was radically different from anything I knew and I was totally disoriented ... lots of us were. Stinking hot and fetid conditions caused by oppressive humidity were everywhere. It wasn't the presence of crocodiles, poisonous snakes, and giant lizards that nearly drove us nuts, it was the tiny ones ... the mosquitoes and other insects. There was no way of escaping them. Malaria and dysentery plagued almost everyone, but not equally. The drugs worked for me, but others remained sick or at least debilitated. For many, the Japanese and the environment presented about an equal threat to our existence.

"Most of us were suffering from 'jungle rot,' which we used to describe what was happening to our feet and skin. Anyway, I was separated from my squad when Japanese soldiers engaged us. I sprained my left ankle and stumbled into a swampy quagmire and couldn't get out. The harder I tried, the more encased I became. I wasn't any more than waist-deep in the muck when my feet hit solid footing, but I couldn't pull my legs out of the sticky stuff.

"That's where I was when the Japs found me. They pointed and laughed. I couldn't understand their words, but the body

357

language was obvious. Hand and arm signals made it obvious that they figured a crocodile would be along soon. Others suggested snakes would have a good feast, and yet others made buzzing sounds and slapped as if trying to fend off the ever-present insects. One man aimed his rifle at me, but he was ordered not to shoot.

"Then a strange thing happened. One man simply dropped to the jungle floor for no apparent reason. No one saw or heard anything. A few seconds later, a second man dropped. From my low vantage point, I could see a red hole in the neck of each of the soldiers. Each had died without making a sound, and others were meeting a similar fate although the shouting and scrambling added to the chaotic circumstance. The officer must have ordered silence, because suddenly everything was quiet except for the usual jungle sounds. They formed a circle facing outward and each man's eyes desperately searched the jungle in front of him for a clue to the origin of the deadly missiles. Five of their companions lay dead at their feet. Tension built as each soldier awaited the arrival of death. Where the bullet hit him would indicate the direction from which it came and all other soldiers were prepared to open rapid fire in that direction.

"Nothing happened, but I could feel the tension building among the troops. In a subdued voice, the man in charge gave orders to the man near him. Obviously he didn't want anyone to overhear him. The message was passed from one man to the next until the information had gone full circle. Suddenly the area was filled with screams of 'Banzai,' and all the men bolted away from the circle. Half followed the officer and the other half followed the man opposite him. The officer made only one step before he dropped to the ground and the last man following his direction also died during his flight.

"I had no difficulty following the sounds as they fled into the jungle. It was as if every man was yelling the same thing."

"Do you remember what they were shouting sounded like?" Danny asked.

"I'll never forget it! I know the Japanese were dedicated and brave fighting men, but there was abject terror expressed in the sounds they were making ... it sounded like 'Yurei Koruso,' or

358

maybe the other way around. Anyway, the sounds of men fleeing the area faded, and my mind returned to my own predicament."

Danny mouthed the sounds. "It sounds to me as if what they were shouting would translate into 'phantom' or 'ghostly killer.'"

The sergeant resumed, "The smell of blood had obviously entered the water. A crocodile was making its way in my direction but there wasn't a thing I could do for myself. While thrashing around, I had lost my rifle, and my feet and lower legs were anchored in mud. The water was waist-deep. As the croc approached, I took my bayonet and contemplated driving it through my brain instead of going through the agony of having the animal rip and break me apart.

"From somewhere out there in the jungle a voice called out to me, 'It's too soon for such desperate measure.' Even so, the crocodile was making its way leisurely in my direction. A few moments later, I heard a huge splash and the croc's attention had been diverted. The giant reptile turned to the direction of the splash. From behind me I heard a chopping sound and soon a long section of bamboo had been extended to me.

"The voice I had heard earlier said, 'Use the long pole to extricate yourself. I'll scout out the area to make certain that the enemy has not circled around looking for me and to see what is happening to you.' Then he was gone, but I really hadn't seen him."

"I could hear some thrashing taking place in the direction the big splash had come from, and my sense of apprehension increased. Frantically, I tugged on the bamboo pole and found it was anchored to the shore. In what seemed an anxiety-filled eternity, I pulled one leg free and the other one was coming out as well. My instinct was to try to run to the shore, but I curtailed that and let my feet float out behind me as I used the bamboo as if it were a piece of rope. When I was safely out of the swamp bog, I looked over in the direction of the splashing and thrashing. Two crocodiles were parceling out one of the Japanese soldiers. It seemed obvious to me that Jake felt compelled to use the dead body of a Japanese soldier to buy me time to get me out of the crocodile's domain. The dead Japanese soldier provided the ancient reptiles the meal they had expected to make of me, and it gave me time to get myself out of the mess I was in.

"When Jake returned, he reported, 'I trailed the men who followed the officer and picked off the last in line, one by one, until none were left. There were fourteen men on the bank laughing at you and only four made it back to their headquarters. Now, give me a hand cleaning up this mess. I led a hunting party of five Japanese soldiers here a couple weeks ago. They suddenly found themselves in the same situation you were in. Downstream the water spreads over about half an acre and it is a major crocodile sanctuary. This crossing has proven to be a major trap for many jungle creatures that blunder into it. Hungry crocs come upstream when they hear the splashing and turmoil created by trapped animals. For your information, the bottom of this river is mostly solid except for this thirty-four-foot-wide section where there is a geological intrusion or collection of extremely sticky clay.'"

"What happened to the one Jap on the bank and those in the bog?" Greg asked.

"I don't know for sure, but I suspect they all got away. Luckily, my wound was painful, but not overly dangerous. I had to break off the operation and take the lieutenant back to our base where he was temporarily hospitalized and then shipped home."

"Where does your story go from there?" Danny insistently inquired.

"The lieutenant reported on the successes we had on the mission and also told about how he screwed up the last operation." Sergeant Davidson stopped as if he were finished.

"So what happened after that ... what did they do with you?" Greg asked.

"Good medical attention and some of the local herbal applications I learned from Jake, had me back in action three weeks later. One good thing the lieutenant did for me was to recommend that I be allowed to act as a solo jungle fighter."

"So?"

"So I did."

"So?"

"So I'm here and many of the enemy remained on Guadalcanal."

There was neither joy nor triumph registered on his face or in his voice. His body language was that of a man who had exhausted his lifetime supply of energy to do that type of work, or even to talk about it.

After a few minutes of silence Sergeant Davidson looked intently at Danny. "Thanks for providing Jake with the throwing knives. He gave me this one. Would you like it back?"

Following another pause, he looked at Greg. "I'm glad to know that Jake got off Guadalcanal okay and that he helped you survive Iwo ... but did he?"

Three pair of eyes searched the others, but there was no answer ... only hope.

Sergeant Davidson and Greg wandered away. They might be good for each other.

45

USS *South Dakota*, BB-57

It was a surprise to Danny to be assigned to the USS *South Dakota,* a battleship that had seen a great deal of heavy combat action in the Pacific. Once again, Danny felt he was an impostor among heroes. It was no comfort when a doctor aboard the ship informed him that he had been at far greater risk of dying from meningitis than if he had been aboard the ship since the first day it had been commissioned. However, there was an enormous gap between being in danger and doing something for your country. Most military personnel were sensitive to the distinction between being in the service during the war, and being in combat.

Somewhere along the line from boot camp to assignment, the records of Danny's language proficiency were lost. Two men from his boot camp company had been assigned to the Monterey Language School and they had no background in any language other than English. They had scored well on placement tests. That test was given to his first company the day he was hospitalized, and he had no subsequent opportunity to take it.

A prevailing attitude was that the only important thing was getting an honorable discharge. The war was over and getting out of the service was what mattered. "If you want a change in assignment, reenlist and ask for special schooling. Otherwise, don't bother us."

The ship and its personnel sailed from San Francisco. For Danny, it was an exciting and revealing journey. The sea was extremely rough; at least it seemed so for the new crew members. It was part of the initiation procedure to take the new men down into the powder magazine where the air was dominated by the odor of ether. That combined with the loss of a visual horizon, and the ship's motion encouraged an onset of seasickness. Great gulps of air taken directly under the air supply vent helped most of the newcomers to just keep from vomiting.

An abundance of fresh air was guaranteed with the next shipboard experience. Four of the new men, Danny included, were posted as lookouts in the crow's nest high up on the mast. It was a wonderful place to watch the ship as it plowed through the heavy seas.

The bow of the ship smashed into huge waves and disappeared along with turret one. The main deck, which was thirty-two feet above sea level when the ship was at anchor, was awash with waves from stem to stern. Then in a manner similar to a broaching whale, the bow of the thirty-five-thousand-ton battleship would rear upward, surface, seemingly, shake off the sea that covered it, and then attack the next wave, each of which seemed larger than the last. It was an awesome and exhilarating experience. All hands appeared to be pleased when the storm abated.

The ship's destination was Long Beach, reputedly a good liberty port. The ship's skipper was not a "busy work" devotee. The men and the ship had answered the call in time of battle. They could do much as they liked after providing for the necessities of operating aboard ship.

In the meantime, people in high places were trying to decide what to do with ships, which were no longer needed since the war was over. One thing the Pacific war demonstrated without a doubt was that the era of the battleship was over. Aircraft carriers and submarines held the keys to the future in naval warfare. The decision was made and Philadelphia was the next destination. The trip was to be made via the Panama Canal.

Before arriving in Panama, the ship's loudspeaker system sounded off, "Now hear this, now hear this. Ship's company will be granted leave for twenty-four hours in Panama City. When you are leaving the ship, each and every one of you will be issued a 'pro kit.' You are ordered to use the kit in the appropriate manner, and to report to the nearest pro station following its use for further attention. Shore patrol police can direct you to any one of dozens of these stations. You are to have your leave papers endorsed at the pro station with the time and date of your visit and treatment. If any of you return to the ship and are found later to be clapped up"—having contracted a venereal disease—"you will be given a general court-martial at which time you will receive

363

five years in the brig, a bad conduct discharge, and loss of all pay and benefits the government is offering. This is a direct order."

An officer was stationed at the gangway of the ship along with a master at arms. The latter slapped a kit containing condoms, an antiseptic ointment, soap, et cetera, into the hand of each departing sailor.

The two-day layover in Panama City provided recreational opportunities of many types, from tropical and historical sightseeing, to observing poverty levels not experienced even during the depths of the Depression. Most of the people appeared well fed, but their poverty must have been mostly in terms of cash flow. Young girls who looked to be twelve and thirteen were inundating virtually every serviceman with offers of, "fuckee, suckee ... five cents." There were other areas of the city where houses and people appeared to be very well off.

Danny was one of many who felt the challenge too intimidating. The approach from the very attractive young street girls, who had barely reached puberty, was too disrespectful and not at all romantic. It was also too risky. When young boys invited one and all to "fuck my sister," Danny found the prospects degrading. But many men paid the five cents, used the pro kit, went to the pro station, and then worried about the results of the next "short arm inspection."

Going to the head (toilet) aboard ship could occasionally be an adventure. The facility for division one, starboard side, was well forward, in the ship's bow. It consisted of one compartment with a stainless-steel trough perhaps twenty feet long, two feet wide, and about two feet deep. Seats were individual crescents, held in place by studs protruding upward from the fore and aft railings into the seats. These were removable for cleaning. A continuous torrent of water swept everything before it into a large-diameter scupper that took it to the unknown, but likely as raw sewage straight to the depth below. Its downward slope accelerated the force of water.

Navy dress blue trousers of that era had no pockets, but made up for that by having enough buttons to be an absolute nightmare for a person with arthritic hands or the "back house quick trots." Sailors carried their billfolds tucked into the waistband of their bell-bottoms, one flap under and the other half flapping freely, but under their middy, or jumper.

Lloyd returned from liberty and made a hasty beeline for the seat farthest forward. His actions were hurried and harried by the accumulated pressure of too much food, too much beer, and too long a time away from a head. Two explosions occurred almost simultaneously, one from each end of his alimentary canal. From his mouth came the exclamation, "Holy shit! My billfold." He had described the two items he had deposited in the trough. Every shipmate enthroned at the time did his best to slow the passage of the billfold down to the scupper by straining to make his deposit while Lloyd, hobbled by shorts and trousers around his ankles, hurried to catch his billfold before it disappeared through the scupper into the great void below. His success was almost complete. He must have sifted through the contributions of at least eight of his shipmates before his own deposit and billfold arrived. Success!

During particularly heavy seas, the torrent of water in the trough was reduced considerably but still a man had to take care that his "danglies" didn't come awash.

In Panama, a complement of marines boarded ship. They had been guarding "the big ditch" for up to four years. All were devoid of cold-weather clothing and bedding, and their arrival in Philly was going to be in January. As the ship plowed northward from the tropics into frigid temperatures, this became a bone-chilling experience for all personnel, but it was particularly trying for the marines. Blankets disappeared from navy bunks. An exploration of the ship's bilge storage area turned up a huge quantity of heavy woolen underwear with long legs and long sleeves. The word got around and hundreds of pairs were "requisitioned" by the desperately needy, before officers had the opportunity to secure the area. During the remainder of their stay aboard, marines, who weren't part of the ship's company, smelled of mothballs.

Upon arrival at Philadelphia, the ship tied up at Pier 4 and the process of putting the old girl "in mothballs" started. This involved utilizing the efforts of the ship's crew and an inundating swarm of civilian workers.

The Battleship *New York* arrived at Pier 4 after a two-day

swing from New York, and tied up to the port side of the *South Dakota.* The first individuals to leave the *New York,* under escort, were a couple of New York's finest street ladies. The story was that they had been arguing about their professional talents and ability to "service" men. In a conspiracy with some of the ship's personnel, it was decided that the arena for combat would be appropriately, in the lower handling room of turret one aboard the ship. All personnel were invited to participate. Repeat visits were allowed, but only if a shortage of volunteers developed. Official score keepers were appointed. There was a hundred-dollar wager between the two women, and each man who participated was asked to make a voluntary donation of one dollar to help defray the expenses of the women for their return trip to New York City.

The rules of the game were very simple. No man could be refused. Fast or slow, each lady was obliged to "unload" her client any way she and the client selected. A slow poke could not be dismissed as unserviceable. Once he entered her arena, she was not allowed to go to the next one until that man had "produced." At the end of the first twenty-four-hour period, a four-hour respite was taken. As is so often the case, some men were "touch and go" while others plowed the furrow both long and deep. By the time officers became officially aware of the situation, each woman had serviced over two hundred men, and the leader was ahead by only three men.

The stowaway duo had resolved nothing. One had taken an early lead, which appeared to be substantial, but the other contestant waged a mid-game rally and was closing rapidly. The competition was called a draw because of official intervention.

The officially escorted ejection from the Battleship *New York* ended at shipside. A resumption of activities took place at a similar location but on a different ship, not so much for the purposes of continuing the competition, but perhaps as a declaration that there was still life among the ruins. As one shipmate commented, "Having a go with either one of those gals has about as much appeal to me as trying to rape a five-gallon bucket filled with snot."

But it wasn't only ships, planes, tanks, and other military equipment that needed to be released from active duty. Wartime personnel with a couple of years of service time were quickly being separated from the navy. This included reserve officers. There was little need for line officers to remain in command of ships that were dead in the water and would likely never be put to sea again. The officers, men, and ships had done their time, completed their assigned tasks, and were essentially a liability rather than an asset. It was better to return nonprofessional personnel to civilian life. The ships had no peacetime function except as a possible deterrent to threats of future wars.

With each change of personnel officers, Danny would submit an inquiry and suggestion that he might serve the military interests more if he were utilized where Japanese, German, or Arabic language skills might be of value. It was evident that he would not be released very soon, because he did not have enough points for early discharge. And once again the reply was loud and clear, "If you want to change your status, reenlist for an additional four years and we will send you to Yokohama where you can talk as much Japanese as you want. Otherwise, you can stay here scraping paint and wire-brushing rust until your discharge number comes up." Four more years of military service did not appeal to Danny.

Off-loading the sixteen-inch projectiles from the ship was a navy job. The armor-piercing munitions weighed in at over twenty-six hundred pounds each and stood more than six feet in height. Each was snaked over a loading plate where a sling could be installed. This transporting device was attached to a chain hoist that lifted the massive unit, and it was subsequently lowered from the projectile ring through the armor deck and two decks below. From there, it was taken to the stern of the ship on another overhead rail system.

There was a special tube through which the projectile could be raised right out of the bowels of the ship by a dockside crane. The crane then placed it on a carrier or onto an ammunition barge next to the dock.

This roundabout pathway took the projectile below the ten-inch-thick armor plate of the turret's barbette and, eventually, up through the sixteen-inch-thick armor deck, which ran from stem to stern. The only other way of removing a ponderous unit was by loading it into one of the sixteen-inch guns and firing it.

The turret's chief petty officer rigged the sling to the chain hoist, but failed to screw the shackle pin fully home. It was suspended, with its butt down over the open deck hatch, ready for lowering two decks below. Two civilian workers were looking up from beneath this mammoth projectile. Danny yelled to them to get out of there. They had just started to move when the shackle pin bent, tore out a thread or two, and the massive load dropped straight down. The impact was so great that the butt of the projectile was imprinted in the steel deck plate. The foot or hook of the sling was broken off. To remove that part of the sling from the deck plate required nearly two hours of labor using a hammer and chisel.

This accident demonstrated the effectiveness of the safety design of the projectile's detonation mechanism. It had to be rotating or spinning around its longitudinal axis for the firing mechanism to line up and function.

Danny was the only person injured by this incident. The chain that was supporting the projectile snapped with the sudden release of all that weight and lashed out, hitting Danny on the right cheekbone. He was sent to sickbay for examination and treatment.

A chief petty officer aboard ship, with a sleeve full of gold hash marks, each representing four years of good conduct service, was awaiting discharge. Danny was in an adjacent compartment and overheard the ship's doctor and the chief in serious conversation. The delay in processing the chief's discharge involved his medical problem, a particularly resistant strain of syphilis. Standard treatments had not been effective.

The navy would not return the chief to civilian life until the disease was cured. Otherwise, his forty years of good conduct service and gold hash marks would suddenly turn to red. Reduced retirement benefits would result. Medical efforts to screen the chief from having his condition officially known were being challenged. This particular syphilis spirochete had been cultured in beakers and every individual drug that should have killed it failed to do so. They now were trying combinations of drugs but, so far, without success.

The chief left sickbay and the doctor was alone. The doctor was regular navy, not a civilian who was in for the duration.

He was dedicated to caring for the health, both physical and mental, of the men on his ship, and particularly those who had served before the emergency of World War II. The chief had done his time during WWI, through the intervening years, and now, the Second World War. The doctor was unwilling to give up on the chief. He, too, had his share of gold on his sleeves: four full stripes. His were not the stripes of a line officer, but those of a medical officer. He was as high as he could go in the navy in his specialty.

"Problem, sailor?" the doctor inquired.

"Just a little, sir," Danny replied and looked up at the captain.

"Well now, how did that happen?" he inquired as he prepared to clean and suture the injury. "You're lucky. An inch to the left and you would have lost your right eye. An inch or two closer to the chain could have resulted in a cracked skull. In any case, I want you here in sickbay for two days to make sure problems don't develop."

Later, the doctor stopped by to see Danny and the two of them were alone. Danny said, "I couldn't help overhearing your conversation with the CPO who has that resistant strain of syphilis. I couldn't see him, but I do understand a little about that particular problem. Would it be too presumptuous of me to ask a question and make a suggestion?"

"You are here and anything that might help the chief is welcome. I have time now. If you feel like it, we can go to my office where we will not be disturbed." The nameplate on his desk was inscribed DR. JAMES, CAPTAIN, USN. He nodded for Danny to take a chair. "Now, let's hear what you have to say."

"When I was in the sixth grade I was reading about a medical breakthrough in the treatment of syphilis that was in its final stages of evaluation. However, it had been abandoned because of the effectiveness of new forms of antibiotics that were just being developed."

"In what publication did you read about this, *Superman Comics?*"

"I believe it was in the *Journal of American Medicine,* but I can't be certain."

369

"You were reading things like that when you were in the sixth grade?"

"I read a lot, still do, and I seem to remember most of it. Don't ask me how a publication such as that showed up in our grade school library. There was only that one issue."

"Do you remember that treatment?"

"Yes, sir. Research had shown that the syphilis spirochete was very temperature-sensitive. It was greatly weakened at a temperature of approximately 101 degrees and started dying at 102. The initial research was an offshoot of studies in tropical medicine in which they found that people who had recurring malaria or yellow fever attacks almost never develop the secondary or final stages of syphilis. They were frequently infected and then mysteriously devoid of all symptoms, only to have symptoms show up again when they were reinfected. This 'yo-yo' cycle could go on for years, and death was almost always a result from fever, not from syphilis."

"Good God! I do remember reading something about that many years ago. And then they dropped all research." Suddenly the doctor was taking Danny seriously. "What else do you remember from the article?"

"If I remember correctly, it involved artificially raising the body temperature to 104 degrees Fahrenheit and maintaining it there for six hours. The trick was to keep the brain from becoming too hot. The potential for damage to brain tissue increased dramatically above 103 degrees. The mechanical equipment was rudimentary. They used a personal sweatbox such as those shown in the movies, where overweight men would sit in a chamber to sweat off a few pounds. The technique involved keeping a wet towel containing ice cubes around the patient's neck, and temperature monitoring."

"As of now, sailor, you are off all other details. You are transferred to sickbay." Then Dr. James wrote a note for Danny. "You will be released from our infirmary in two days. Give this transfer request to the petty officer in charge of the detail to which you were assigned. I want him to accompany you back here. It says so in the document."

Two days later the petty officer shrugged his shoulders,

grunted "Okay," to Danny, and shortly thereafter, he said to the doctor, "Yes sir! He's all yours."

The doctor handed Danny a manual to study. "You say you read a lot. This is the course of study for becoming a corpsman third class. Study it and let me know when you would like to take a test based on this book. We'll see if we can't get you officially qualified as well as promoted on the basis of my recommendation. I've hit a little snag in my plans for you to go to the Philadelphia Naval Hospital and to access their library files. In the meantime, go take a shower and report back to me in 'whites' along with needle and thread. You can stitch the corpsman badge on your sleeve and that will get all the work detail petty officers off your back."

About thirty minutes later Danny returned to the doctor as ordered.

"What I had in mind was for you to go to the naval hospital library and search for the article you mentioned, and follow through reading the publications of the next year or two. There may be subsequent information that could be interesting. My intention is to have you stay there for a week, or however long it takes for you to be satisfied that you have all the available information. The problem is that the library people there don't want to open files to untrained personnel. I can get the job done, but I'm going to have to pull some strings up the ladder, and I want to be careful to avoid stomping on anyone's toes. It may take a day or two."

"During those two days I can be studying the manual. With luck, I should be ready to pass the test by then," Danny said.

A mask of concern was reflected from the doctor's facial expressions. He cautioned, "Don't treat the test frivolously. By the way, how old are you?"

"I'm nineteen sir, and studying new subjects interests me. I have a good memory for things I've read and rapid reading is a skill I inherited from my grandmother. With a good medical dictionary, I should be able to come to grips with medical terminology. The problem, I suspect, will be lack of practical experience and just plain common sense that comes with that experience."

"You won't be put in a situation where that will be a problem. Naval medical personnel can be placed on special assignment, and remain under the command of a specific officer, for extended periods of time. My intention is to place you in the position to serve as a reader. This is not an officially recognized specialty, but you won't be doing bedpans, making beds, giving shots, handing out pills, or assisting nurses. I can keep you assigned to me until you are ready for discharge. If you can help us find a cure for the chief's problem, and believe me there are others like him, you will have earned your rating many times over."

Dr. James's consideration for his patients was in the best tradition of his profession, as well as the navy. He was not threatened by someone who was far younger, less educated, and without experience. He welcomed any source of information that could be helpful.

The manual for gaining a corpsman's rating contained diagrams and illustrations, which were expertly rendered. Danny marked specific areas, which were not clear to him because of his lack of background. Dr. James had instructed a corpsman first class to assist him when help was needed. This was not an unpleasant interruption for him, because the ship's personnel complement was greatly reduced, and there was little to keep him occupied.

The corpsman would demonstrate procedures that Danny didn't understand, so he would have something beyond just book knowledge. Danny didn't know it at the time, but Dr. James wanted assurance from the first-class petty officer that the young sailor could read, understand, and remember at a useful pace. The next day Danny heard the tail end of a conversation between the two. "Yes, he seems to remember just about everything and he reads at around two-thousand words a minute. It's as if he is just turning pages. I wish I could do that."

Danny found the bookwork interesting and he had no problems understanding procedures that were explained to him. Some of the practical skills would require more experience if he were going to be involved, but that seemed unlikely. The test was comprehensive and presented no problems. The doctor took Danny to a "two-and-a-half-striper" line officer who officially notified the appropriate authorities that effective immediately, he was now a third-class petty officer. The official ID card had been prepared. Then the line officer did a double take concerning

Danny's name. He asked in Japanese, "Are you the same Daniel who thinks he could be more valuable to the navy in a capacity that would utilize language capabilities?"

He introduced himself as Lieutenant Commander Williams. That began an exchange in Japanese. "Well, it is obvious that you converse in Japanese expertly, but do you read and write the language as well?"

"Yes, that was part of my early and continuing training."

Lieutenant Commander Williams handed Danny a document and instructed, "Would you please read through this and report to me if you can make heads or tails of it. It is a dispatch that was taken from an enemy plane that was intercepted on its flight from a prisoner-of-war camp the Japanese operated in northeastern China called Makdun. The navy apparently picked it up just after Hiroshima and before Nagasaki. This is just one of tons of documents that should be read and translated, filed or abandoned. It came to my desk today and I haven't had time to read it."

Danny studied the paper for some time. It seemed to be reasonably straightforward, but a little unbelievable. "Wow! I wonder if he really did it."

"Did what?" the officer asked.

"Maybe you'd better look through this, but I don't see any way I could have made a mistake in reading and understanding this. The commandant of the Mukden prison camp dispatched this letter to Tokyo high command saying that his family had all been in Hiroshima and that he was going to start the execution of *all* prisoners of war within two days if he did not receive direct orders to the contrary!"

"I don't know that happened. I just don't know. My guess is that this document got lost and forgotten. We were inundated with messages and the flood of paper associated with the surrender of Japan. This letter may be terribly important evidence in the coming war crime trials. I'll get back to you about this when I've talked with military intelligence in DC. You say the camp was called *Mukden* ... ? That doesn't sound Chinese to me."

"It must be the name the Japanese gave to it," Danny suggested. Lieutenant Commander Williams nodded his head. "We are over seven months too late to change whatever did happen.

On another topic, what do you plan to do after your discharge from the navy?"

"I'll attend university, but I don't know just where. I'm from Oregon and somewhere in the Pacific Northwest appeals to me. The only living relative I know is there, and I want to be within a day's bus ride from her. I also have a small business where she is and I feel a need to be able to go there to work on some weekends and during holidays. Based on what I've heard from some students, I'm leaning toward a small, liberal arts institution, but not a state-run university."

"I have a cousin who recently joined the staff at a college in Portland that he says has one of the most beautiful settings for study he has ever seen. It was a large private estate until a few years before the war when it was sold to the college at a giveaway price. He said the landscaping and maintenance were in the hands of Japanese gardeners until they were all interned at the beginning of the war. Anyway, that suggests that you might find some Japanese Americans in that area once the internment camps are closed, but we can talk about this some other time. Remember, if you don't like the medical arena, we can always have you transferred to my section, which is naval intelligence, provided we are able to clear you through security. I'd be derelict in my duty if I didn't suggest you think of enrolling in my university, even though it is about fifteen hundred miles from Oregon."

Vital opportunities were suddenly coming quickly. There was little time to consider the value and importance of each. Danny seemed to hear the wise counsel of Father Watanabe: "Think calmly, and do not rush. Soon you will know what to do."

"Just a minute, gentlemen," Dr. James said in English. "I have what I consider a medical personnel emergency that needs resolving in short order, and it involves Daniel. He is going to be away from the ship for some days doing essential research. You can have him later if you need him, but we'll be leaving for the navy's hospital in this fair city in about the length of time it takes to sew this third class rating insignia on the sleeve of his jumper."

Lieutenant Commander Williams nodded his head. "We are over seven months too late to change whatever did happen. Sailor, we can talk about this some other time."

374

46

Philadelphia Naval Hospital

Dr. James conferred with the head of the hospital who was also a full-fledged navy captain as well as a medical doctor. It turned out that both doctors had served with the chief petty officer who had drug-resistant syphilis. They agreed that the hospital's medical library would be open to Danny twenty-four hours a day with unlimited access.

Finding the original article proved to be relatively easy. Tracking other reference materials and subsequent information required more time. By the end of the second day, all apparent avenues of information had been explored. The two captains consulted with members of the original research team, two of whom were still active.

Seven cases of drug-resistant syphilis were identified in hospital records as participants 1 through 7. Their fever cabinet treatment was started immediately on a priority basis. In order to validate the effectiveness of the high temperature procedure, it was essential to have a comparison study. Seven other men who had syphilis would not receive normal drug therapy until they had been given the fever cabinet treatment. Out of the entire naval personnel in the USA, it did not take long to find the seven active cases of syphilis. If the treatment didn't work for them, they would be placed on a normal drug treatment regimen.

The seven resistant cases of syphilis were treated with artificial high-fever therapy as planned. Blood samples were taken at two-hour intervals for the first eight hours. After four hours of high temperature, no live spirochete could be detected. Blood samples were taken daily, then weekly. Results were 100 percent cures without the use of drugs. Controls utilized to keep brain damage in check involved a "cool collar" around the neck.

The chief petty officer from the ship retired with his good conduct gold hash marks. Dr. James asserted that good conduct really was not a factor of sexual activity or inactivity. It involved being ready, willing, and able to perform one's military duties under even the most difficult circumstances.

Dr. James and the hospital doctors kept Danny at the hospital library, searching through old journals for other obscure methods of treatment for common health problems. This continued for a week when a message came from the ship's executive officer recalling Danny.

The Mukden POW camp was readily identified as one in which some of the US survivors of the "Bataan Death March" had been incarcerated along with British, Australian, New Zealand, and Philippine personnel. About three thousand prisoners were liberated because of prompt action on the part of the Soviet Union. The service rendered by Soviet personnel was downplayed. Photos taken at the camp featured a handsome US Air Force officer. Actually, he arrived four days after all prisoners had been released. Chances were that he would have been liberating dead men, if the Soviets had not arrived before him.

Among the Soviet token liberating force was one woman, Tatyana. Her rank was about the same as a major in the US Army. She was the essential element in that Soviet presence. Although it was a force composed of less than two dozen military personnel, it carried the full weight and power of the massive Soviet army. She was the one person who spoke the three essential languages. She was fluent in Russian, Japanese, and English, as well as several other languages. Tatyana overheard the Japanese commander discussing plans for exterminating the prisoners. He had not realized that she understood every word he was saying.

Tatyana knew more than the language. She was fully aware of the procedures for diplomatic negotiations that would not cause the commandant to "lose face" or his sense of pride and dignity. They discussed the tragedy of Hiroshima to the Japanese nation, and the extremely stressful personal loss he must have been feeling. Using reason, logic, and tactful, yet forceful persuasion, she was able to deter him from his bloody path of vengeance.

News releases presented in the United States made no mention of the plan to slaughter all prisoners. They only mentioned, in passing, that a token Soviet presence was on hand to witness the liberation of Allied prisoners of war.

As fate would have it, the Soviet forces had arrived in Mukden the day before the executions were scheduled to begin. By accepting the commander's surrender, the responsibility for the prisoners was no longer a Japanese concern, and over three thousand prisoners of war survived.

Lieutenant Commander Williams had called Danny back to the ship to inform him about Mukden. He was a university professor with a wartime commission. Because of his expertise in the Japanese language and culture, he had been assigned to the *South Dakota* when it was the flagship for the Fifth Fleet. The "flag" was moved to a carrier, his transfer had been overlooked, and he spent the remainder of the war and post-surrender time with little to do.

The lieutenant commander and Danny were both underutilized as far as their language skills were concerned. It appeared as if each had two options regarding their careers. The first was to remain where they were until they were declared nonessential and discharged. The second option was to "re-up" for at least four more years, in which case they would likely be stationed in Japan as communications, cultural, and intelligence experts. In the officer's case, this would also include a promotion to full commander. His choice had been to return to civilian and campus life.

"Daniel, you now have some options that I can manage for you. Officially, I qualify for several aides, although in reality there is next to nothing to be done on this level. We are rapidly becoming a token military presence on what was once a proud fighting ship that is being retired by civilian workers. In any case, you can be transferred to my staff and be discharged when I am declared a surplus item. I expect that to come through within a month or two. I would recommend that, unless you want to pursue other options."

"Dr. James and the head of the Philadelphia Naval Hospital, Dr. Wayne, would like to have you continue researching documents dealing with common health problems that many of

377

our military medical personnel have not faced since being conscripted. Numerous medics have dealt with wartime trauma and professional problems involving young, essentially healthy men. This is not in keeping with what they will face when they reenter civilian practice. They will need to be rehabilitated so they will function efficiently in civilian life where they will deal with an older population and more female patients in a month, than they have seen during their military career. They think you could read a great deal of the literature on this field, and help them design a pre-discharge course of study.

"Another option is that I can have you declared surplus and order immediate discharge. Think about these choices and let me know your decision."

Danny remained partially obsessed with the fact that he had really done nothing for the welfare of his country, and the shadow of Ito dominated his thinking. If he remained with the ship's doctor and at the hospital, he might be able to help some of the men who had done the fighting. Danny's decision was to remain and read through publications, make notes, and research medical procedures and developments in the USA and overseas. He also started reading books dealing with medical history. He uncovered techniques, treatments, and herbal medical practices that had been part of standard practices from fifty to one hundred years earlier. Many had been abandoned with each succeeding generation's concepts of modern practice. He could bring them to light, but he was in no position to evaluate them.

However, it appeared to Danny that expediency was a genuine factor in the acceptance of many of the current drugs. Some of the older treatments fell out of favor because they might take a little more time. Others were not as convenient. The fact was that the country had become a nation of "pill happy" doctors and patients. In most cases the new medical practices were also more efficient, although there were always possible aftereffects.

He compiled a reference index of old and new approaches for treating a wide variety of diseases and conditions. These were duplicated and made available to the staff doctors.

Dr. Clark invited Danny to accompany him on his regular rounds visiting patients with all types of problems. One admiral had been temporarily decommissioned with a severe case of gout. He was accustomed to having his orders carried out, and was not patient with doctors who could not relieve the pain with all their modern medicines and knowledge. As circumstances would have it, Danny had been reading on the topic of gout in a medical volume dating in the early 1800s. It recommended that eating cherries, raw or preserved, would serve as a relief from the pain of gout, and, in some cases, be a preventive measure for this very painful and debilitating problem. The suggested minimum was to eat five cherries daily. In addition, fat-free milk was recommended.

A small dish containing ten canned cherries was delivered to the admiral's bed along with skimmed milk and other medications. Within an hour, the admiral was out of bed and using the head. This was the first time he had been up in a week. That evening, the admiral's doctor and Danny stopped in to see him. "At last you gave me a medicine that works. Why didn't you give it to me a week ago?"

"We didn't know about it last week. The corpsman here just discovered it, or I should say, rediscovered it, and called it to my attention."

"Well, come on, Dr. Clark, share the secret with me."

"Cherries and skim milk."

"Yes, I had them as a treat with my pills. I like cherries and milk, but what was the medication change?"

"Just cherries and milk!"

"Well, I'm ready to get out of here. I can take my cherries anywhere. But you say this corpsman, a third-class petty officer, found this out?"

"That's correct, Admiral, and it's not the only problem he's helped us with." Dr. Clark proceeded to tell about the syphilis treatment and cure.

"Well, what is he doing with only one stripe on his sleeve? It seems to me that he rates better than that. Don't you agree?"

"Yes sir, but two weeks ago he was a seaman first class. As you know, navy regulations specify a minimum period of time at each rating."

"That's correct, Doctor. However, admirals do have latitude and privileges that allow them to recognize major contributions and capabilities. When I get to my office, I'm going to bypass regulations. If the military can commission myriad civilians to become officers in ninety days or less, I sure as hell can pump a sailor up in rating. You are going to discharge me now, are you not?"

"Perhaps another twelve hours with us might be wise, if only to ensure the continuing success of the cherry treatment? Actually, we request your permission to keep you here for another twenty-four hours. We are totally new with this and can only hope your condition will remain stable."

"Yes, I suppose it is wise. Permission granted. But if I feel tomorrow the way I feel now, I'm leaving. Now tell me, how is my wife doing? Yesterday you told me she was in absolute agony from that damned outbreak of shingles."

"We will be seeing her in about fifteen minutes. Frankly speaking, there is precious little we know that will help. The patient simply has to endure until nature runs its course."

Danny's reading had included a description of shingles and a few photos, but nothing was suggested to relieve the pain, nor the ugly skin eruptions.

The next stop was to see the admiral's wife. The left side of her face and an area going down across her neck and right breast was a mass of weeping blisters that looked terribly painful and indeed, the poor woman was in agony.

"Please describe the pain you are suffering," Danny requested.

"It feels as if someone is burning my skin with fire and it won't let up. It's been like that for three days now and nothing helps except narcotics, and they can't safely let me have as much of that as I need for the pain."

Danny motioned the doctor to the side. "It may not be very good science or medicine, but I have a feeling I know something that could help her with her pain, and also keep those blisters from creating havoc with her skin. I'm sure it can't do any harm. It's raw egg white."

"Never heard of it, but as you say, it can't do any harm."

Five minutes later, a half carton of raw eggs and a bowl were at hand. Danny separated the white from the yolk of one egg, and had her apply the raw white, because she knew where the pain was the greatest. The moment the egg white touched her skin, the pain in that area nearly vanished. Her eyes were filled with tears of gratitude. "How can I thank you?" she sobbed. "Will the pain come back again?"

Danny replied, "Probably, but if it does, apply more raw egg white. Be careful not to use the yolk. You can apply it as often and as much as you want. I'd expect the skin to begin to draw and pull a little tight within the next fifteen to twenty minutes. When it does, don't panic; just give it another coat of egg white. After the third coating, it is likely that you won't need any more for several hours. That should give you an opportunity to relax and get some sleep, which you obviously need. Remember, this is not similar to a narcotic. You are encouraged to apply it the moment you feel even the slightest discomfort."

A slight noise at the door caused Danny and the doctor to turn around. It was the admiral. "You will be petty officer first class by this time tomorrow. If you come up with a couple more miracle cures, I'll personally put you up for lieutenant," the admiral said as he briskly walked over to his wife.

"You're walking!" she exclaimed, and they looked fondly at each other.

The doctor and Danny left the two of them talking comfortably with each other. They were relatively free from their individual pains, which had dominated their lives for several days.

"Daniel, was it really an intuitive inspiration about that egg white treatment, or did you have some sort of background information?"

"I read about shingles a few days ago and the appearance reminded me of sun-blistered skin. Since childhood, my family used raw egg white for sunburns, thermal burn, chemical burns, and abrasions. The egg white is a mild antiseptic and anesthetic. In addition, it provides a non-irritating second skin to seal out oxygen, moisture, and temperature changes. It insulates exposed nerve endings. So, actually seeing a case of shingles made it seem reasonable that egg white might provide relief from her pain.

"No one should expect it to cure the disease, since the viral infection really is left over from childhood chicken pox. That infection retreats along major nerve pathways to the brain stem, and hibernates there. Why it re-erupts perhaps fifty years later, and primarily among women, is a matter for conjecture. At least, that is the way recent medical literature explains it. But the use of raw egg white just looked to be a good risk since it works so well for other skin irritations and trauma. And it seemed to work in this case."

"I haven't seen the likes of your cherry and milk cure and now egg white treatment. We admit burn patients almost daily. We see each of the three types you described, as well as abrasions. We will set up an experimental clinic to use egg white treatment.

"We are going to have a staff meeting of most of our doctors tomorrow morning before rounds, and I'd like to have you there to present your two 'wonder drugs,' and also your information on burns and abrasions. Many of the staff will be skeptical. I would be, if I hadn't been there to see it myself. In fact, I still am wondering. However, by tomorrow, hospital scuttlebutt will have made most of the staff aware of the information regarding the two cases. There may be reluctance to accept the facts, for no other reason than the remedies are all too simplistic. Some challenges may seem to be a personal assault on you, and your lack of medical background. After all, the nurses and doctors have years of academic training, plus years of experience in the field. One thing you have going for you is their knowledge of the heat treatment cure for syphilis that you salvaged from obscurity."

They were walking along the hospital corridor when they heard a patient hiccupping. It was repeated again and again. Dr. Clark commented, "That has been going on for over three weeks, and nothing seems to help. Medical, psychic, psychiatric, folk medicine treatments seem not to work. Do you have any ideas?"

"Nothing original. Just something I read years ago in a book about Moroccan folklore. Does this man have diabetes?" The doctor shook his head. "Then we can try 'the sugar cure'."

They stopped at the ward nurses station and Dr. Clark asked one of the corpsmen to bring a bowl full of sugar and a tablespoon. They continued on the rounds passing through a ward devoted to men with various types of fractures. Progress seemed to be normal there. However, one patient had cast irritations of the soft tissue on the inside of his upper leg. The doctor looked at Danny, a crooked smile on his face, and questioned, "Egg white?"

"It couldn't hurt." The patient received a soup bowl containing raw egg white. The yolks had been removed. He applied it as needed and experienced immediate relief and comfort. Healing of the irritated skin was rapid.

At the nurse's station they picked up the bowl of sugar and a tablespoon. "Well," the doctor asked, "what's that for? I know it is for the chap with the hiccups, but how do you use it?"

They entered the room and Danny talked with the patient. "This is an old medication. You will find it quite sweet and pleasant. Take just a few grains to make sure your mouth and psyche won't reject them." Danny poured about a quarter of a teaspoonful in one of the little pill cups and emptied it into his own mouth. In a second cup he put a tablespoonful, and the patient tasted them with his tongue between hiccups.

"That tastes, hic, pretty, hic, good, hic."

"Okay, now get your mouth full of saliva. Don't swallow even when you hiccup."

After a few minutes, he said, "I'm, hic, full."

"Take this entire little cup full at once, hold it in your cheeks, and allow it to gradually mix with your saliva. Then start swallowing it very slowly as it becomes liquid. Concentrate on making it last at least three minutes, or more. Follow the sweep second hand on that wall clock."

The patient, following the instructions, slowly started swallowing the medication as it became liquid. He made it last four minutes. "Funny, it tastes just like sugar. I wish all medications tasted this good. Is that all there is to this treatment?"

"Just about. Repeat it a minute from now." They waited and his mouth continued to water because of the sweet "medication." Then he took the second little cupful. The seconds passed as he slowly swallowed his medication. Only one thing was missing ... the hiccup.

An amazed expression crossed the patient's face. Dr. Clark winked at him and said, "We will repeat the medication during morning rounds, if needed, but I'd guess you are cured for some time to come. We will check in with you tomorrow, but you can plan to leave then." They left another happy patient. The next morning the sailor took a final treatment with his sweet hiccup medicine, then left to return to his assignment.

"Where did you find that one?"

"I don't remember exactly where, but it was a standard treatment among one of the Berber tribes in Morocco. The difference was that they used sugar from a loaf instead of in granulated form. I read about it years ago."

The following day, Dr. Clark and Danny hurried to the morning medical conference. They had made the early check on the hiccup patient, because the doctor wanted to add that treatment to the list of strange cures he would present. The staff theater was filled with doctors and head nurses. Top brass personnel were seated front and center. Danny was led to the stage and seated.

All company present snapped to attention when a CPO called out, "Ten-shun! Flag on deck." The admiral strode forward from the right wing. From the waist up he was in full dress uniform. From the waist down he was still in hospital pajamas. There was nothing comical about his appearance. He was the admiral, but he was still a patient. To all present, his uniform, as he wore it, signified that he was in command, and yet, as a patient he was under the command of even the lowest hospital staff member. In matters dealing with the navy, he was the ranking officer. In the hospital, he was simply a patient.

The admiral said, "I know many of you. Throughout the United States, this hospital has a fine reputation for serving its patients. You, the staff, and those you represent are responsible for that. You have helped my wife and me from time to time, when we needed your assistance. We are grateful for your kind care and consideration.

"Those of you who attended me yesterday, know that I could not walk because this knee was as sore as a boil." He punctuated the statement with a resounding slap on it. "Now, I don't pretend I didn't feel that, but I'm comfortable enough with it to do it again." And he did.

"Anyone who did that to me yesterday would have been facing a court-martial. I know most cases of gout affect the big toe, but my guess is that what works on knee gout will work as well on toe gout. This sailor, who is wearing a third-class petty officer rating, did the research that has me comfortable, walking, and ready for hospital discharge in less than twelve hours."

The admiral proceeded to outline what had happened with his wife, the syphilis patients, the hiccup patient, and those who were experiencing irritations from fracture casts. He also pointed out that the egg white treatment for burns and abrasions was going to be thoroughly tested using scientific procedures. "All of us hope this corpsman will find additional innovative ways to make your patients' stay here shorter, and more pleasant. This should make your work with them easier and more rewarding. Now, let me introduce to you a third-class corpsman who, by order of the Department of the Navy, is now lieutenant junior grade, an officer with full privileges and responsibilities. He is assigned to this hospital to pursue his library and practical research until his hitch is up and he once again enters civilian life. He is answerable to your hospital chief of staff, Dr. James, and to me, *only*! Your full and complete cooperation is expected and appreciated. Thank you, ladies and gentlemen."

The admiral presented an officer's uniform to Danny. He was led off stage to a dressing room where he donned his new uniform. He returned to the stage to applause, which interrupted Dr. Clark's speech.

"So that is a quick outline of the research project dealing with skin trauma, burns of all types, and abrasions. Now let's hear a few words from our new j.g."

Danny's speech was simple and quick. "You are the doctors and nurses, the ones with the training, experience, and intuitive sensitivity to your patients' needs. I am a rapid reader with a good memory. You are busy doing the essential healing work. I hope my work will be helpful to you. If you have a problem, I may be able to find useful information among the literature you have not had time to study. I have the time to find data, you have the background needed to know what it means and how to use it."

One of the doctors asked, "What about the skin trauma research? How are you participating in that?"

"Let me field that question," Dr. Clark replied. "The skin trauma and egg white research is proceeding rapidly and with encouraging results. Our new officer is not actively involved. He is being kept informed about the results. I can tell you that it takes a narcotic painkiller to equal the relief provided by raw egg white. In skin trauma cases, particularly burns, pain relief is, as you well know, vitally important to survival. Raw eggs are available in almost every household for immediate use, and self-medication with raw egg whites is virtually risk-free. There is no need to touch the injury or rub it at all. Simply smear, or perhaps *slime* is a better word, the raw egg white directly on the injury. In most forms of skin trauma, this has performed better than other products or treatments, particularly as first aid. The use of egg white on burns is rooted in history on this and other continents.

"One should not use the term *opposition,* but rather say *non-support* to raw egg white may come from the pharmaceutical companies. For them, there is no money to be made from this product, and it is understandable that they would not devote time and money to verify its effectiveness. But I interrupted you, Daniel, please continue."

"Let me conclude by emphasizing my appreciation and respect for you, your training, experience, talents, skills, and devotion. It does not stretch the truth to say that the personnel at the San Diego Naval Hospital saved my life when I had spinal meningitis. The navy has granted me the luxury of time, a commodity that most of you have in short supply. You are busy with the constant demands of your work and patients. If there is any research reading you would like to have done, please let me know. Just leave your name and workstation or ward number in my mailbox. I'll come to talk with you at a time that suits your work schedule."

Danny went to his quarters at the hospital and found three work uniforms in the closet. It was time to change from the dress uniform into working clothes, because he and the doctor were going to do more rounds.

Weeks passed during which Danny spent most of his time reading and cataloging information that he felt might be of interest and help to the medical staff. He made occasional "rounds" with Dr. Clark. On one occasion, the doctor cautioned, "Daniel, this stop is going to be unpleasant. The man we are going to see was a civilian worker at one of the piers for the navy. A crane operator accidentally dropped a load of scrap metal. Warning shouts alerted most of the workers below. All the others got clear, but this man's scramble for his life was only partially successful. His legs were literally mangled by pieces of metal that crushed them." As they turned into a corridor, they were overpowered by the stench of rotting human flesh. "That odor is what I was talking about."

Involuntarily, they backed away and struggled to keep breathing. The doctor said, "Smell is one of the keenest senses. Research has suggested it takes less than one part per billion parts of air for us to detect it. As you know, we fall far short of many animals' sensitivities. We are fortunate that our sense of smell is rapidly exhausted and it's possible to make some accommodation. For the current dominant, gut-wrenching emanation, time and fatigue are only partially helpful."

Father Watanabe had taught Danny so many things about life, and one was how to establish a level of inner tranquillity. This made it possible to endure physical and psychic stress and unpleasantness.

They entered the room and Danny focused all his inner force and attention on the very large Negro man who lay in the bed. Danny did not know how the doctor was able to manage, but presumed he had a similar inner resource.

"Hey, man, you don't have to come in here. I know what it smells like. I can't get away from it, but you can. The men that bring me my food just hold their breath, drop the tray on the bedside table and run. I can't blame them. Some of the doctors who have to be here with me wear a gas mask. Sometimes I wish I had one myself."

Dr. James picked up the medical chart. "The medications that have been prescribed and administered are the best we have available. The problem is that tissue trauma is so extensive that it keeps dying, putrefying, and poisoning adjacent healthy tissue, and the patient's system. Temperatures ranging from 102 to 104 complicate the problem."

Danny looked at the chart and saw that the man's name was Carl Tipton. "How do you feel about your situation, Mr. Tipton? Do you think you are getting all the help they can give you?" Danny asked.

"Of course I am, the doctors are doing everything they can. They give me more pills and stick more needles in me than you

387

could imagine. Trouble is, I'm rotting away piece by piece. You don't have to be a medical genius to know that they are going to have to chop those rotting legs off me, and then what is there for a legless man to do to earn a living? I'm on my way out. They are just keeping me alive on pills and penicillin." Then he looked at the doctor. "Am I right, Doc? Is the chart right? Do you give me three more days and then you start whittling on my legs?"

The patient was in a room that had a screened outside window. It was wide open to let fresh air in and some of the stench out. Danny recognized the collection of blue bottle blowflies on the screen. They always accumulate where the smell of dead flesh promises a feast for their offspring maggots. These flies were desperately seeking entrance.

The buzzing reminded Danny of the time he, Ito, and Mr. Schmidt found the remains of a deer in the cow pasture. In his mind's eye he could see the fly maggots devouring the dead flesh.

"We'll be back in a minute," Danny said and motioned for the doctor to go out of the room with him. "Is what the patient said true?"

"Surgeons have already tried removing the dead tissue, but the problem is cutting away the rotten without damaging the living. Yes, all bets are that amputation will be the only lifesaving procedure."

"Then why don't we put it directly to the patient? Tell him outright what his situation is and that we'd like to utilize a technique from the past. All we have to do is open the screen and let those blowflies in. They will lay their eggs in the dead flesh and the maggots will eat away the dead tissue and not touch the living. It is a repugnant technique, but it has worked successfully for centuries. The archives list it as a standard technique."

"Good Lord, what an ugly procedure ... inviting maggots to dine ... or doctors to amputate. Okay, Daniel. You explain the options to the patient and let him make the decision."

They returned to the room and Danny asked, "Mr. Tipton, how long ago were you injured?"

"It's been ten days and nights of absolute hell, but you are welcomed to call me Carl."

"Thanks, Carl. Tell me, how do you see your future?"

"Like I told you, they are going to chop off my legs in three days—four at the most."

"And then?"

"Then I'm going to die, I'll see to that. I'm not going to go on living without my legs. No use talking about that. Other doctors have been here telling me about how people can get around and have a good life, but that's not for me."

Danny explained to Carl the old-time medical practice of using blowfly maggots to clean the dead flesh from a living body. After they had done their grisly task, the process of healing could proceed, and there would be a chance of saving his legs. He continued explaining how this was a technique that was extensively used for hundreds of years, particularly during wars when so many nasty spear, arrow, and sword wounds were common. Sometimes it was successful and sometimes it wasn't. It seemed sensible to the patient and the doctor that Carl's own chances would be better, because modern medicine could control some of the side effects that often followed the ancient treatment.

"Well, I'll be blowflied! That's just what my daddy did when old Rufus, our mule, got a big infection in his leg. I wanted to kill out all those maggots, and my daddy told me to leave them be, they were going to help old Rufus get well. And they did. Never thought for a minute they'd be put to work for me. What are we waiting for? Open the screen and let those flies do their job. You know what I've already put up with, and a few flies won't bother me one bit. In fact they are welcome to come in and have a feast."

Dr. Clark explained that this type of decision would require consultation with hospital medical staff members, staff at other hospitals, and final clearance from health administrators all the way up the chain of command.

"That sounds like two weeks of red tape, and by that time I'll be dead. You just move my bed over near the window so I can see out. Then make sure no one enters the room for a few hours. Also, would you mind moving that little table closer to the bed? I'd like to be able to put my book on it when I'm not reading. And if you have a cane handy, I could use it to exercise my arms." These requests were followed and the two men left.

The next stop was to see the admiral. He was just finishing dressing. "Gentlemen, it is good to see you, and it is a wonderful

389

day. Now, about your commission as a lieutenant junior grade, Daniel, the military has precedents that are to be followed. Standard procedures are outlined for commissioning an officer based on special attainments, capabilities, or military needs. Rather than do this unilaterally, I held a phone conference with the Navy Department in DC, and they wholeheartedly endorsed your commission. It would have been far more difficult to promote you to a rating or two higher as a corpsman, because rules and regulations specify tests to be passed and time to be spent at each level. In any case, your commission more nearly reflects the value you are to the service. Strangely enough, I was advised that a similar request had been submitted by a lieutenant commander from the battleship *South Dakota,* for you to be commissioned as a linguistic specialist with an assignment to naval intelligence. The commission he was suggesting was that at the level of full lieutenant. Would you know anything about that?"

"That would have been Lieutenant Commander Williams. His specialty is Japanese language and culture. I did just one bit of translating for him and we conversed for a time in Japanese. A four-year 'hitch' on my part would go along with the commission."

"Yes, that is what I understood. A background check indicates that you impressed your boot camp commander with your notable skills in hand-to-hand combat, knife throwing, and general physical capability. In your San Diego Naval Hospital records was an account about how you were effective in helping rehabilitate marine combat veterans who were having considerable difficulty reconciling their experiences before being discharged.

"As if the previously mentioned items were not enough, there are unconfirmed indications that you are fluent in reading, writing, and speaking Arabic.

"One officer with the navy had been with the State Department, and recognized your name as one of the makers of a particular brand of knife that had been presented to dignitaries from some of the Arab countries. He said 'State' had intended to exempt you from military service in order to keep the supply of knives available for diplomatic purposes. They thought this was imperative when they found out that the other two blade makers were dead. Dr. Clark, it appears we are in the presence of a rather unique individual. Why didn't you inform me?"

"What you just said is news to me, sir!"

"The thing I find most disturbing is that we had him down in the bowels of a battleship scraping and wire-brushing rust on a ship that is being put in the mothball fleet!"

"What you are saying is appreciated," Danny said. "But frankly, I'm concerned that I didn't do anything of significance for my country during the war. Whatever I can accomplish here helps me feel a little better about myself. It is an honor to be associated with those of you who have made such big contributions."

"Admiral, would you care to join us on our rounds?" Dr. Clark inquired. "We will be stopping to see a man whose legs have been rotting off. We hope an innovative program will reverse the only other option. Then we'll look in on your wife."

Dr. Clark updated the admiral on the case history regarding the accident involving Carl Tipton and his subsequent hospitalization.

The orderly reported to Dr. Clark that when he delivered Carl's food an hour before, he found the window was open and the screen broken out. Many big flies were buzzing around the room. The patient would not let anyone dress the wounds in his legs, but the stench of rotting flesh was not as bad as it had been. Then he demanded that no one was to enter his room for the following twenty-four hours.

The admiral asked, "How do you handle a situation such as that?"

"I think we will drop in on him now to reassure him that we are going to let the fly maggots complete their job for him. He need not worry on that account. After all, he looks at it as his last chance to live. Then we'll see if he will accept food and medications."

"Those maggots must be having a grand old time of it," Carl said after he had greeted his visitors. "Actually, I feel like something is tickling my legs where there used to be nothing but pain. Those little buggers are doing the job, and I'm going to live, if you let them continue."

"I still carry a little weight around here," the admiral said.

"I'll see to it that every procedure must be cleared through Dr. Clark." He smiled at the patient. A deep sigh of relief and smile of gratitude were his reward.

As they were leaving they heard a joyful conversation, "Come on, Mister Bluebottle Fly, ain't no one going to swat you. Just lay your eggs on my leg, there's food enough for all. You're going to live and so am I." The other side of the conversation was intermittent buzzing as more flies and maggots joined the feast.

The three went to visit the admiral's wife. She was out of bed, dressed, and ready to go home. As she said, "I have egg white at home, and don't need to have busy people here waiting on me." Those were her words, but the nonverbal communication between her and the admiral expressed more love and pleasure with the thoughts of being together than an hour of talking could. They left the hospital hand-in-hand.

One nurse was overheard saying, "Isn't it heartwarming to see someone of his rank still in love with his wife, and not afraid to show it!"

The following morning, the doctor and Danny went to see Carl, their special patient. They found the wounds were a seething mass of maggots. It was a revolting sight. Fly maggots were eating the man, but it was a welcome sight as well. Much of the putrefied flesh had been devoured. Jagged edges were meticulously clean and free from rotting flesh. Within another day, the maggots would probably have their job completed. Then the bright new muscle tissue would need time to regenerate as much as possible.

"There is one more part to the old treatment. Shall we go all the way with it or call it quits while we are ahead?" Danny asked.

"And what is that?" Dr. Clark wanted to know.

"It requires packing the wound with pure bee honey."

"Doesn't that beat all!" Carl exclaimed. "That's just what my daddy did for old Rufus, only you're missing one part of his treatment."

"And that is?"

"We always pissed on any cut or wound an animal got. Piss is supposed to be sterile and good for healing. I asked my daddy about putting alcohol on instead. He said to me, 'So how far from your neck do you reckon that mule could kick your head, if you heat up his hurt with that alcohol?' Well, we both pissed on old Rufus, and you know, he lived for a bunch of years."

The doctor smiled and nodded. "When the maggots are finished with their task, we'll flush the wounded area with a sterile saline solution and pick out the maggots. I'll order a half-gallon jug of pure honey before tomorrow's rounds, but I think we'll forgo the questionable practice of pissing on the wound."

"You aren't going chicken-hearted on me now, are you?" Carl smilingly inquired.

The doctor ordered observation and monitoring of the temperature of the patient at regular intervals. Within twelve hours the patient's temperature had fallen from 103 degrees to 99 and the odor of rotting human flesh had diminished. Most of the maggots had abandoned the site where they had been feasting, and were in search of food. They consumed only dead flesh and they had devoured all that was available. The exposed areas were coated with honey. It had been strained, heated to the boiling point, and then cooled.

Two days later, sure signs of healing were evident, and the scheduled surgery was canceled. Although not free from pain, the patient was optimistic about his future, and so was everyone else in the hospital. No one supposed for a minute that his legs would ever get back to normal, but his chances of walking again had zoomed upward from 0 percent to being highly probable. Confidence replaced despair among all concerned, particularly the patient. Everyone was aware that the change in attitude aided his recovery.

Standard medical miracles were evident on a daily basis. One amputee had lost one leg above the knee and the other at mid-calf. He had been fitted with artificial limbs and had undertaken extensive and expensive therapy, to the point that he was an excellent dancer even doing jitterbug, Latin, tangos, and sambas.

Another man was in his second year of continuing plastic surgery required for restructuring his face. Because of an explosion in the powder magazine aboard a ship, he was virtually featureless. His eyelids and lips presented problems that the doctors did not know how to attack. A fine brain remained within his head, and the sailor was aware of his status as an experimental specimen. Complicating the project was the fact that so much of his body had been burned, that there was insufficient healthy skin from which to form many of the needed grafts. Perhaps the greatest miracle resulted from the dedication of a supportive staff, which helped the man establish and maintain a sense of viability and hope for the future.

The hospital was undergoing the transition from treating war victims, to dealing with sickness and trauma that were the normal, and tragic consequences of peacetime activities. Certainly, the injuries sustained in automobile collisions were on a par with those caused by war. That work was never-ending.

About once a week Danny would receive a Japanese document to translate. Most of them were straightforward, but occasionally, there were references to situations that made those particular papers unclear. It might have been because it was out of context or was obscure.

"Danny," Lieutenant Commander Williams suggested, "I hope you will continue with your schooling when you leave the service. I intend to return to university teaching and I'm sure I will be able to place you in a program dealing with Japanese studies in my own institution or several others. Here is some printed material from the college where my uncle is a professor. He sent them to me and included his business card. As you can see, he wrote you an invitation to contact him personally if you go to Portland."

Danny thanked him for the information and the special consideration. The future was bright and offered a variety of challenges.

When Danny's turn to be discharged from the navy came, he was still reading medical material at the hospital library. Folk medicine from all over the world was collected there. He found the study fascinating.

Danny left the hospital feeling proud to have been associated with men and women of such high standards of professionalism and dedication. He had not been in combat. He was not a hero, but he had the feeling of having done something for combat veterans and his country.

It would be untrue to suggest that Danny thought of Ito every day he was in the service, but there were so many subtle reminders and memories. Every time he saw a Japanese American in army uniform, he asked about Ito. The responses were always the same. They were sympathetic, but they had no information.

He returned home after a little over one year in the service. This required another series of adjustments. Gran remained a constant source of stability and love. The increasing demand for DISKnives provided reassurances of financial security and viability in his choice of labor.

Note

In 2003, doctors in the Netherlands were using fly larvae to clean dead tissue from wounds to stave off probable amputation. They found the maggots not only ate the dead tissue, they secreted a substance that helped prevent infection. The study was reported by co-author Jaap van Diesel.

47

Discharged

It was in June 1946 that enormous personnel changes were taking place throughout the US military. *Discharge, separation, demobilization, liberation, mustering out:* All were terms used for what was taking place at a rapid pace. Millions of men and women formed a new category of Americans: the ex-GIs.

Dr. James was giving Lieutenant Commander Williams his final physical examination before being mustered out of the service. Only a skeleton crew was aboard the once proud fighting ship and both men were surplus to the needs of the navy. Dr. James carried on a running dialogue with his fellow officer. "Your blood pressure is 120 over 60, and pulse is sixty-six. That is remarkable for a man of your age and the pressures you've been subjected to these past four years. What's the key to your successful fitness program?"

"Regular exercise, low-fat diet, plenty of sleep, not smoking, and never getting drunk. A couple of other things could help. Keeping away from doctors who might tell you that you are sick and trying to sort out personnel problems before they become major confrontations."

"Do you have any regrets?"

"Yes, a few. My language expertise was underutilized. Flawed interpretations of Japanese intelligence reports accounted for the loss of at least two ships and numerous personnel. I could have helped our forces avoid those errors. This made me more sensitive to Danny's situation when he was scraping paint and wire-brushing rust, and off-loading munitions."

"Well, that worked out fortuitously for many of us. He ended up making major and multiple contributions in the hospital. Amazing that he overheard the conversation I had with the chief about the resistant strain of syphilis, and how one thing led to another. And speaking about Danny, what are his plans for the future? I know you talked with him about reenlisting and joining your staff as a language specialist in naval intelligence, but then you decided to go back to your university professorship. Where did that leave him?"

"That was not a factor. He had opted for discharge when his time came up so he could go to university. Besides, he has a going business making knives when he is discharged."

The doctor replied, "Then, by way of showing our appreciation, perhaps we can expedite his separation from the navy. As I understand it, his status is in limbo. Is he not still officially assigned to this ship and yet on assignment to the hospital? You know that was my doing."

Lieutenant Commander Williams excused himself. "That's my area of expertise. I'll look into that now, if you have completed the physical exam."

Twenty minutes later the commander was back with a smile on his face. "As of now, Danny has been declared "surplus" to the needs of this ship and is eligible for discharge. However, I checked with the navy and his status with the hospital is clouded. Perhaps you can inquire?"

"Shall *we* inquire?" the doctor asked. "I'd like you to have a full chest X-ray and some lab work done before you leave the navy. The hospital is a better place to do these things now and we can also consult with Dr. Wayne and Dr. Clark about Danny's status in their programs."

An hour later, the lab work had been completed and the officer had a clean bill of health.

"We are having a special farewell dinner for a number of our staff officers and doctors this evening. The hospital chefs are planning to outdo themselves, and we've always had outstanding meals in any case. We would be pleased to have both of you, Dr. James and Lieutenant Commander Williams, join us on this occasion. We jokingly call it an 'abandon ship party.' In reality, a number of us will officially announce that we are leaving the navy and/or retiring. This goes for the admiral and both Dr. Clark and myself."

"That is a timely celebration," Dr. James announced. "Thursday will be my last day on the *South Dakota* and in the navy. That has already been confirmed. One of the reasons we came to the hospital today was to confirm the status of Danny, the recently commissioned lieutenant j.g. We take a genuine interest in him because of his unique contribution to the welfare of one of our shipmates. You know, the chief who had syphilis."

"Yes, we know him well. Dr. Clark worked with him more than anyone else. The admiral is grateful to him on behalf of himself and his wife. The admiral asked Danny about his future plans with the navy and he said that he would be happy to serve as long as he could be helpful until his number came up for discharge, then he would like to resume his life as a civilian, a knife manufacturer, and a student. At the celebration this evening, the admiral will officially announce the names of those who are leaving the navy. Danny's name will be among those, but it will be a surprise to him. We will be pleased to include the two of you as well."

Lieutenant Commander Williams said, "That will be a significant reworking of personnel and responsibilities. How will you manage?"

"Extremely well, so far. In navy terms, we have been on an extended 'shakedown cruise' for the past three months. Transition trauma has been virtually nonexistent."

When it came time to bid everyone farewell, some tears were shed, handshakes were shared, penetrating looks of gratitude acknowledged, but in the end there was a dissolution of a team who had served well and valiantly. They had been assembled in the urgency of wartime, grown professionally, and then would reestablish themselves as civilians. Later, when they reminisced about their days in the navy, time and lack of contact would have taken their toll. Names would become less frequently remembered and perhaps forgotten. But the *impacts* so many people had on Danny's life would remain indelible.

Epilogue

Danny is aware that his adult life has just begun. Following *IM-PACTS*, a series of sequels build on his earlier experiences. Gran has been a staunch supporter, encouraging curiosity, a need to learn, and the desire to achieve. Her influence guides him as his story continues.

After losing his Japanese family, Danny seeks to reestablish this vital Japanese connection. In the first of numerous sequels, QUEST, college life and the future of *DISKnife* offer new directions. Dreams are fulfilled, but in unexpected and often startling ways.

There will be significant changes in his relationships, and in discoveries, as his life expands in additional sequels. He will encounter the diversity of other cultures, and find opportunities to contribute in various, unpredictable ways:

QUEST
MILES TO GO
BARAKA DAN IN MOROCCO
THE CYCLING TRIO
...and others.

About the Author

David Radmore was born, reared, and educated in Oregon. Later he lived, traveled and worked in other states and in foreign countries. This book is based on a lifetime of actual experiences and contacts that have been expanded through fiction. He is an avid storyteller and his diverse international background adds to the vivid reality of *Impacts*.

Mr. Radmore entered university after serving in the navy near the close of World War II. He interrupted his formal education at Lewis and Clark College in Portland, to work for two years with the Oregon State Police. Later, he took an additional two-year break to bicycle, explore, study, and work in Europe and Morocco before completing studies to receive his teaching credential and master of education degree.

He began his teaching at Franklin High School in Stockton, California, where, at age twenty-eight he met his wife of more than fifty years. Their fourteen-month honeymoon was spent bicycling, camping, and touring in Europe and Morocco and covered over fourteen thousand miles. The four winter months were spent in Tangier, where Mrs. Radmore did artworks, while David was writing, and had opportunities to make personal contacts with local residents of varied international backgrounds and interests. Additional travel included repeated trips throughout Western Europe by moped, motorcycle, and VW camper van.

David and his wife served two years as Peace Corps volunteers, teaching at the Women's Training Centre in Abeokuta, Nigeria. While teaching, he also traveled to Lagos, to work with numerous athletic coaches and the Nigerian Sports Council, training swimmers, and instructing track and field participants for the Olympics.

Mr. & Mrs. Radmore spent one sabbatical leave on an around-the-world trip with BMW motorcycles, while photographing, writing, and camping in Europe, North Africa, the Canary Islands, South and Southwest Africa, and Australia.

On four occasions in recent years, Mr. Radmore was invited to be a consultant on American culture and history at the American Center of the Linguistics University in Nizhny Novgorod, Russia, and to make presentations to students at other educational institutions, from grade two through high school.

Much of the author's writing reflects his belief that "People make their own happiness," and "If you can't *think* it through, you certainly can't *worry* it through." These concepts have been the foundation for his lifestyle and teaching. This provides an open, honest, and positive approach to his fiction.

He and his wife, Ruth Audrey (Turnbull) Radmore, have enjoyed numerous opportunities to stay in the homes of families overseas, and in turn, have hosted over 150 foreign guests from seventeen nations, for stays varying from four weeks to two and a half years. Some of these friends have made numerous return visits and have brought family members.

Throughout his life, there have always been alternatives, and his writings have been expanded by the underlying question, "What would happen *if*...?" This question has led to the many sequels to *Impacts,* and continues to make his own life an ongoing and varied adventure.